Eleanor Goymer spent many years working in UK publishing. Originally from London, Eleanor now lives and works in the US, where she is a publishing consultant and editor. When not reading or writing Eleanor likes to spend her time musing on how much the US is not like London.

instagram.com/eleanorgoymerwrites
facebook.com/eleanor.goymer.writer

T0357746

Also by Eleanor Goymer

The Fallback

THE PLOT TWIST

ELEANOR GOYMER

One More Chapter
a division of HarperCollins*Publishers* Ltd
1 London Bridge Street
London SE1 9GF
www.harpercollins.co.uk
HarperCollins*Publishers*
Macken House, 39/40 Mayor Street Upper,
Dublin 1, D01 C9W8

This paperback edition 2025
25 26 27 28 29 LBC 6 5 4 3 2
First published in Great Britain in ebook format
by HarperCollins*Publishers* 2025
Copyright © Eleanor Goymer 2025
Eleanor Goymer asserts the moral right to be identified
as the author of this work

A catalogue record of this book is available from the British Library
ISBN: 978-0-00-865659-1

This novel is entirely a work of fiction. The names, characters and incidents
portrayed in it are the work of the author's imagination. Any resemblance to
actual persons, living or dead, events or localities is entirely coincidental.

Printed and bound in the United States

For Nancy & Edie

Never be so polite you forget your power
~ Marjorie, Taylor Swift, Evermore

Prologue

'So, without further ado, will you all please join me in congratulating Allie Edwards on the publication of her seventh novel, *The Wishlist*.'

Verity Montagu-Forbes put her hands together in applause and stepped off the small stage which had been erected in the bookstore. She grinned at Allie, her star author, and then wrapped her arms around her in a hug. Verity whispered in her ear, 'This one is going to be your best seller so far, and I'm already excited about the next book.'

Allie breathed in Verity's words, she was excited, too. She was on a roll, six bestsellers in a row and it looked like this new one might smash them all out of the park. She took a deep breath, tucked a strand of her wavy hair behind her ear and listened to the applause, savouring the moment and trying to block out the whooping she could hear from the back of the bookstore which was almost certainly coming from her friends Tom and Jess, who somehow didn't know, or more likely didn't care that whooping at a book launch was frowned upon by the publishing elite.

Luckily, the publishing elite were not in attendance at Daunt's on Marylebone High Street on a rainy Tuesday evening in September, and so the whooping didn't matter. While Allie was a bestseller for Brinkman's, her publishing house, she was neither literary nor highbrow. And therefore her book launch party was attended by friends and family, her longstanding editor Verity, and the sales and marketing team at Brinkman's who were honestly indifferent as to Allie's genre of writing, but they did love her sales figures. And the free wine.

Allie walked the couple of steps up onto the stage, and turned to look out at the small crowd of people who had come to celebrate her. She waved at the sales manager who had been the person to call her and tell her that pre-orders of this, her seventh novel, were higher than the last two combined. And she grinned at Jess, her best friend, who she could see standing at the back, next to her husband Tom, clutching not one but two free glasses of wine. Allie felt a warm sensation inside her, something akin to happiness, which she decided to focus on, rather than focusing on the person who was missing, the person who should have been at the front of the crowd supporting her, her personal romantic hero, her very own leading man, her boyfriend Dominic. But she didn't want to think about Dominic, certainly not tonight, and often in recent weeks, hardly ever. She wanted to enjoy the moment of celebration which sometimes felt so far off when she was in the thick of writing; during those moments when she was failing to untangle a plot thread, or had forgotten the name of her latest main character, she couldn't believe she had got to where she was currently standing, which was a bookstore in London where a publishing house, *her* publishing house, was throwing a party to celebrate her seventh book. And then at other moments, like this one, when she caught the eye of her sister Martha in the audience and it looked like she might be on the verge of tears or saw Verity raising a glass of – albeit slightly warm – chardonnay to toast her, she absolutely bloody could believe it and she loved it.

'Thank you,' she said, at the same time pointing her finger warningly at Tom, who had now put his fingers to his mouth as if he was about to start wolf whistling at her. He lowered his hands and looked sheepish, which made her smile. Allie was not a natural public speaker, but she knew the drill. By now she could remember the people she needed to thank and the praise she needed to heap on her publishers and the booksellers present. And she also knew to keep it brief; despite what they might say, people were here for the free wine and canapés, not to hear her rabbiting on.

'Thank you,' she said again as the room went quiet, waiting for her to speak. 'If you'd told me eight years ago that I was about to sell a book to that wonderful woman over there...' She pointed at Verity, who smiled shyly. 'I wouldn't have believed you. I was twenty-five and earning rubbish money writing copy for an advertising agency. I'd always dreamed of writing romances, as my sister Martha will attest to, Martha, apologies for all those terrible love stories I made you sit and listen to.' Martha smiled indulgently and the tops of her ears went slightly pink. 'But I didn't know it was something I could really do, and also how many people and how much belief and support it takes to make it happen. And now I'm about to publish my seventh romance and I finally feel confident enough to answer the question "so what do you do?" with the answer, "I'm a romance writer."' There was a small smattering of applause and an audible 'YES' from the marketing assistant who Allie knew had aspirations of her own in this area. Allie grinned at her and made a mental note to seek her out later and ask her how her own writing was coming along. 'Firstly I want to thank Verity, who I just mentioned. Your editorial wisdom has made every one of my novels so much stronger than they would have been without you. I can't imagine having a different editor, so please don't ever leave me!' Verity smiled and blushed again, and everyone laughed at Allie's warm words.

'I want to thank my mum, who is in Spain and who told me that as she had been to every other one of my book launches, she knew exactly what to expect and that she was sure I would speak more confidently than I did at my first launch – so thanks Mum.'

More laughter rang out and Allie looked quickly at Martha, hoping that she had got the tone right and that it didn't sound too much like she was hating on their mum for not being there. Allie didn't mention their dad, she never did at these events. It was almost twenty years since he had died, and Allie still didn't trust herself to talk about him in front of a crowd, worrying that she would break down and not be able to continue, leaving her audience shuffling awkwardly and wondering if they were at a book launch or a grief group. Martha knew. Martha understood, she felt the same, Allie caught her eye and smiled, feeling grateful for the solidarity of sisterhood, however fleeting those moments were.

'Thank you to my sister Martha, for being my family here tonight and for reminding me that most people have proper jobs and don't just sit around in a cafe all day dreaming up adorable meet-cutes.'

'I never said that!' Martha protested and immediately looked panicked that she had drawn even more attention to herself.

Allie smiled, enjoying the reaction she was getting. 'I want to thank everyone at Brinkman's for getting me to this position, I know how hard you all work and I am well aware that I would not be here if it wasn't for all of you, so thank you!' Allie raised her glass to the back of the room where a cheer went up amongst the Brinkman's staff in attendance.

'Thank you to Daunt's as well for letting us use your space, and, of course, for selling my books. I think this is the fourth launch of mine we've had here, so I guess my mum has a point and I should probably think about doing something different for the next one.'

Allie shot a look at the bookstore manager who winced at her words. 'Simon, I'm kidding. I wouldn't want to hold a launch anywhere else. And I'll be back here next year if you'll have me,' she said confidently.

'Finally, I want to thank my boyfriend Dominic, who also can't be here tonight. Not because he's living it up in Spain, but because he is closing some deal and his boss has him working late.' Allie paused to let some boos for the mean boss ring out. 'People always ask me where I get my inspiration from, it's the million-dollar question for a writer. I like to maintain some mystery,' she gave a knowing smile to the crowd, 'so I'm not saying that Dominic *is* my inspiration, but I'm not saying he *isn't* either…' Tom let out the wolf whistle he had so obviously been dying to emit since the start of her speech. 'I mean, how can one write about romance when you don't know about romance? So, thank you to Dominic, and no thanks to his boss.'

There was laughter and cheers and Allie bit her lip waiting for both the cheers to subside, and her tiny pangs of guilt too. Because she was not being a hundred per cent honest, and if she caught Jess's eye she knew Jess would have an eyebrow raised at Allie's words and that her cover would be blown, everyone would see it written all over her face, just as clearly as her words on the page; so yes, she did draw inspiration from Dominic, but it wasn't inspired by his actions, but rather what she hoped he *would* do, what she had always imagined the love of her life to be like. But no one wanted to hear that, did they? Who would want to buy a book by a romance author who didn't have any romance in her life? Allie felt the familiar whorl of simmering disappointment pulsate inside her but she pushed it to the side, along with those suspicions as to why Dominic hadn't shown up for her, yet again. She pasted on her smile, thanked everyone once more for coming and urged those who had not yet bought the book to support Daunt's (and her) by buying a copy.

'Nice speech,' Verity said, moving swiftly to Allie's side as she walked off the stage and handed her a glass of wine. 'Definitely an improvement on book one.'

Allie rolled her eyes, making Verity grin. For her first book launch Brinkman's had invited Allie into their offices for a drinks reception. She wasn't at the stage of inviting booksellers or journalists yet and even her friends and family had to wait to meet her in the pub afterwards. Verity and the then publisher had congratulated Allie on the publication of her first novel and then offered her the microphone – which she had proceeded to splutter and stutter into until some kind soul in international sales had taken it from her hand and replaced it with a glass of wine.

'Are you ok?' Verity then asked, causing Allie to look at her sharply. 'I mean, I always feel for you when you talk about your mum and Martha and not your dad…'

Allie shook her head tightly and said, 'It's fine. One day maybe, maybe at the next book launch? But I didn't feel like mentioning him tonight.'

Verity nodded. 'Look, there's a new sales director I want to introduce you to.' Verity put her hand to Allie's arm and began to lead her towards the front of the store. 'But before I do, can I just ask about the next one?'

'Next what? Sales director? You lot get through them fast.'

Verity frowned away Allie's attempt at diversion. 'Your next book?'

Allie laughed and tried to shrug off Verity's hand. 'Verity, *The Wishlist* is only publishing tomorrow, can't we just enjoy that for tonight?'

Verity stopped by the table of handpicked-by-the-staff hardbacks and raised her eyebrows at Allie. 'Yes, it's just that you said you'd get me a plot outline this week and you haven't. And normally you're bursting to tell me the idea for your next book as soon as you've delivered the first draft of the current one.'

Allie picked up a copy of a book by an author she had never heard of and flipped it over to read the biog line. She then held it up to show Verity.

'Says here she was fifty-six when she published her first novel.' Allie pointed at the back flap. 'Which means I'm doing OK, don't you think?'

'Allie,' Verity said firmly in her clipped tones, 'you're doing marvellously. I just wanted to check that there wasn't anything wrong.'

'Wrong?' Allie snapped. 'What could be wrong?'

Verity sighed and took the book out of Allie's hand, laying it carefully back down on the pile and straightening the other copies. Verity had started out life as a bookseller, and it was still hard for her not to instinctively tidy and rearrange display tables when she walked into a bookshop.

'Come meet Jake Matthews.' She took Allie's elbow. 'And send me that outline, OK?'

Allie awkwardly agreed and made a mental note not to spend tomorrow how she had planned: hungover and in sweatpants. Instead, she'd actually open her laptop and pull up that draft outline she had started and check it was as good as she had thought it was when she typed it out at 1am high on margaritas and inspiration and a night out in Soho. She was sure it was, she knew what she was doing, she had the golden touch, didn't she? Verity had just told her that. Emboldened with excitement at writing again, she allowed herself to be taken to meet Jake Matthews, the new sales director.

Chapter One

Nine months later

Allie stared gloomily at her lavish surroundings and came to the conclusion that despite all the swank, this was almost certainly her idea of hell – a literary event when no one had ever described her writing as literary. A crowded party when all she wanted to do was be alone. A celebration for authors when she wasn't even sure she could describe herself as an author anymore. She did a quick mental calculation; it had been four months now since she had last written anything. And even the opening chapter she had started, four months and one day ago, was now confined to the trash folder on her laptop. How long could you go without writing and still call yourself an author? And if she was no longer an author, who was she and what was she doing here?

Allie gulped back the sense of doom she could feel rising inside her and tried to remember the breathing exercise that Jess had been boring on about during her previous, fevered love affair with yoga. Was it breathe in for two and out for two? Allie gave it a go, her breath speeding up as she did so, her eyes going wide as she realised that this technique definitely wasn't helping. She hiccupped slightly and stopped, cursing herself for being so dismissive of Jess's latest fad, wishing she had paid more attention, trying to elongate her breaths as she did so. She shouldn't be here, she should have turned down this invitation, she should have stayed home and tried to write, or at least not shown up at her publisher's party masquerading as a writer when she didn't even have a half-written book at home. But she'd had some foolish idea that tonight might inspire her, that being at a party with lots of other writers might just unblock her creativity and allow something – at this stage, *anything* – to pass from her fingers down through her barely used keyboard and out onto the glaringly blank page on her laptop.

God, that blank laptop screen. Allie was having nightmares about it. Sometimes, they seemed so real, so oppressively mundane, that she honestly didn't know if she was awake or asleep when they happened. More than once she had startled herself screaming, only to discover that she hadn't been asleep, just spaced out in front of the blank screen of doom, praying to the gods of words to grant her some. So far, her prayers had gone unanswered, which did nothing to change her opinion on organised religion in all its forms.

She felt her phone buzz in her pocket and picked it out.

WHY ARE YOU LOOKING AT YOUR PHONE?

Allie smiled – typical Jess.

> Because you messaged me?

> Stop checking it. Go back to the party.
> Mingle. TELL VERITY.

Allie's smile turned to a frown. The previous night she had disintegrated into a puddle of wailing self-doubt at Jess, panicking that she would never write a book again, terrified of seeing Verity and Verity discovering that her writing mojo had left the building months before and that Allie had essentially been lying all those times when she had told Verity that the manuscript was almost ready, just being tweaked.

'Why don't you just tell her?' Jess had asked in the kind of measured and reasonable tone that had Allie reaching for something to throw at her. 'What's the worst that can happen?'

'Oh I don't know Jess. Professional suicide? Financial ruin? My mum finds out?' Allie's eyes had gone wide in a comedic look of horror making Jess snort with laughter.

'Better or worse than Martha finding out?'

'Don't,' moaned Allie, 'I can't even bear to contemplate that.' Martha was Allie's younger sister but for the entirety of their relationship had consistently behaved like the more mature one. Right down to the fact that she was now married, which Allie definitely wasn't, and she had a job which had required many years at university (chemist,) which Allie didn't and, despite Martha's fondness for the written word, she had been permanently surprised that Allie had managed to make a living out of producing them.

'Seriously Allie, you do need to tell Verity. You can't be the first author suffering from writer's block?'

And, of course, Jess was right. It was a rite of passage for any author. Those sleepless nights trying to conjure up a new plot, googling past crushes to avoid working on edits, stress eating entire packets of Haribo and having to take a lie-down to sleep off the nausea. Although that last one, Allie would concede, was probably peculiar to her. And so what if she couldn't write another book? Plenty of authors retired, took sabbaticals, sometimes even permanent ones, or they pivoted to other professions. Allie gnawed her knuckles anxiously; retiring at not quite thirty-five probably wasn't viable, neither was taking a long-term sabbatical, so that left changing professions, which in turn left Allie … blank. Just as blank as her computer screen. She'd spent all her life writing, making up stories as a kid, making up copy for an advertising agency (which she hated) and finally, writing love stories for a living, which she had loved. But if she couldn't write anymore, what was left for her? It was too late to go back to college and retrain, she'd be the weird old woman sitting at the front of the lecture hall, actually on time and listening. And what would she study anyway? What did she actually care about other than words? And she was pretty prescriptive about which type of words as well, they had to be romantic ones, love letters, grand sweeping gestures of passion. All of which had been missing from her life for months.

Her phone buzzed again,

Allie?

What?

STEP AWAY FROM THE PHONE.

Well stop messaging me then.

I will, just checking you were actually at the party and not hiding in the toilets...Wait, you're not hiding in the toilets are you? Send me proof you're not or I'm calling you in 5... 4... 3...

Allie took a discreet snap of her surroundings and sent it to Jess.

Satisfied?

Very. Now go...

Going...

Allie...

Allie could detect the note of warning in Jess's text voice.

Putting it away now, mingling as I type...

She put her phone away, wondering if the 'find my' function had sufficient accuracy for Jess to be able to tell if she did indeed just go hide in the toilet. But all that would do would be to prolong the inevitable, she did need to see Verity, and she did need to tell her.

Warding off her panic at these thoughts, Allie swiped a glass of champagne from a passing member of waitstaff and with her other hand crammed a canapé into her mouth. If this was the last publishing event she would ever attend she was going to make sure she left it drunk and full. She turned, looking for the next tray...

'These ones have prawns in them.'

Allie felt a shiver snake up her spine. The voice was deep

and warm, with a gravitas about it that suggested it belonged to an adult, not to a teenager who might be working part-time at the party. She looked up straight into sparkly grey eyes that seemed to be expecting some kind of response from her. Which she couldn't deliver. Her mouth went dry and her brain scrambled, giving her the helpful message that this is what happens when you have gone too long without romance. It wasn't normal for a voice to have this effect, but then there were those eyes, and that hint of a smile, a dimpling to the side of a mouth, cheekbones that looked like they could slice through your heart. Allie gulped in what she knew to be a cartoonish manner, and tried to clear her throat. The eyes sparkled more, as if laughing at the effect they were having on her.

'Just thought I ought to warn you,' the ridiculously well defined shoulders shrugged, 'in case you're allergic.'

'Thanks,' she managed to croak, trying and failing to drag her eyes away. He either didn't seem to notice her very real struggle or was far too charming to comment on it. Instead, he flashed her a smile, which immediately made her fixate on his teeth. She smiled back, hoping that she didn't have any of the last canapé she had scoffed trapped between her own teeth.

'So, can I interest you?'

Allie flushed. 'Excuse me?' she stammered.

'In one of these?' He held out a tray of vol au vents towards her and Allie had to stop herself from willfully misunderstanding him and insisting that yes he definitely could interest her, very much so. Not in the vol au vents though, which looked too large and complicated to negotiate. But definitely in those beautiful eyes, and that smile. So far him and his cheekbones were the best thing about this party.

'So? Do you want one?' he asked. 'Because otherwise I

should go and see if those lot want to try them.' He nodded off towards the centre of the courtyard where a crowd of increasingly rowdy people were congregating around the cocktail bar.

'The last time I went over there they took the whole tray off me so this is your last chance.' Allie looked down, not at the tray, but at his tanned arms and at the tendrils of a tattoo she could see creeping up under the sleeve of his shirt, and at how the toned muscles made his white shirt sleeves strain. She swallowed and gave herself a stern shake, forcing herself to concentrate instead on the prawn vol au vents.

'Erm, OK thanks,' Allie said, taking one and wondering how the hell she was going to eat this thing without spilling half of it down her dress. Or having to do something as inelegant as trying to shove the whole thing in her mouth in one go. Why on earth did they serve these things at a party? If she ever got to organise a party again, she would make damn sure that only one-mouthful canapés were served. Nothing that needed two mouthfuls, or god forbid, two hands. Or even worse, cutlery.

'Let me know what you think,' he said as he stepped away from her. 'They're a new recipe.' He shot her another smile as he made his way off into the crowd.

Allie watched him go, hoping that he would come back although she wasn't sure what she could tell him about her thoughts that wouldn't have him running away in alarm. She shook her head a little. What was wrong with her? This was not normal behaviour, she needed to get a grip... on him...

She exhaled heavily and looked down at the vol au vent she was still clutching, feeling a sense of relief that the hot waiter wouldn't be there to bear witness to her attempt to eat it. Not that it would matter how she ate it. Yes he was hot, yes he was easily the best-looking guy at the party, but she shouldn't notice, much less care. This was a work event, she was a professional, here to network, not to pick up men. And anyway, she had Dominic, she remembered, almost as an afterthought.

Still, Allie allowed herself to watch him disappear into the crowd of people, his tray immediately picked clean by the seemingly starved partygoers. Allie contemplated the vol au vent and decided it would be much better off in the huge terracotta potted fern she was stood next to than in her mouth. She quickly shoved the whole thing under a leaf and then turned to brush her hands clean and looked back into the courtyard, hoping no one had spotted her. But no one had. In fact no one had paid her any attention at all, all evening, except for the cute waiter.

The central courtyard of the V&A Museum on a summer's evening was an incredibly beautiful place with the brick red building catching the setting sun, the fountains sparkling and the gorgeous glittery party attendees laughing as if none of them had persistent, painful writers block, it was the stuff of magazine spreads. Allie really was trying to appreciate it, but when the point of this party was to celebrate all the brilliant authors Brinkman's were publishing that year, and she had yet to produce a new title page, let alone a full manuscript, the gorgeous setting was beginning to set her teeth on edge. It was a tricky tightrope Allie was navigating, she needed to be seen at this party, but on the other hand, she really didn't want to be noticed. Especially not by Verity Montagu-Forbes, Allie's very brilliant, very ambitious editor.

Verity was the editor who had plucked Allie's first, unsolicited manuscript from the so-called slush pile and propelled her onto the bestseller lists. And for that Allie would remain forever grateful to her. Verity had been an incredibly supportive editor, always happy to talk through plot line challenges or agree to a short deadline extension. But recently Allie was getting the impression that Verity might have been losing her patience with Allie and she had her suspicions that a combination of Verity's ambition and her newly loved up status might be more than a little to blame.

Allie had first noticed something might be up when she kept getting Verity's out of office and began wondering just how many doctor's appointments one seemingly healthy, early-thirty-something woman could need before it became obvious that the doctor was a cover for something else – most likely job interviews. So far nothing had been confirmed but Allie was sure it wouldn't be long before Verity would be announcing her departure for a promotion several rungs up the career ladder at a rival publisher. And then Allie would be in the unfavorable position of having to ingratiate herself with a new editor at Brinkman's, one who hadn't acquired her and when Allie was four months behind on an already stretched deadline and still had nothing to share, even she realised she was not an attractive inheritance.

Allie knew it wasn't Verity's fault – she had her own career to think of. Plus, she had dropped enough hints that Allie ought not to leave it too long to send in her new manuscript, probably hoping to get Allie her delivery advance before she left. But Allie hadn't been able to write a single word, her seemingly endless source of romantic meet cutes had dried up just as Verity had got herself a new rich boyfriend. For all the years that Allie had known Verity, she had never known her to even date, and now, suddenly, she was practically getting married. And so, while Verity was in the throes of a whirlwind romance and just in the mood for another bestselling romantic comedy, Allie was left staring into her own personal Room 101 – a publishing party with no book to publish.

As if conjured from Allie's own fevered angst she heard Verity's tones ring out from the columned doorway of the museum.

'Allie! There you are.' Allie suddenly found herself engulfed in one of Verity's signature floaty floral dresses and partially asphyxiated by the scent of verbena.

'Hey Verity!' Allie did her best to put on her most upbeat, partyish tone and came off more first night out after suffering a severe bout of the norovirus, her voice sounding all scratchy and dry. Apparently, four glasses of champagne couldn't undo the croakiness caused by not speaking to anyone apart from a cute waiter for two hours.

'I'm SO pleased you made it,' gushed Verity. 'I was just telling Monica here,' Verity waved at the stern-looking woman on her left-hand side, 'how I just HAD to find my star author, and Monica decided to come with me!' Verity's eyes widened at Allie, just as a hostage's might while trying to deliver a secret message without their captor realising.

Allie was tempted to make a joke and pretend to look behind her to see exactly which star author Verity was referring to. She felt about as far from a star author as it was possible to feel right now and being called that made her feel uncomfortable and itchy. Allie tugged at the hem of her dress and wished she had gone for something more breathable; manmade fabrics and inauthentic social situations were not a good combination, and she was beginning to sweat.

'So tell me how the new bestseller is coming along?' demanded Verity. 'I am DYING to read it. I know your NEW new delivery date isn't that far off, but if you have a sneak peek I can see before then please send it.'

Verity's emphasis on the first 'new' didn't escape Allie. Allie knew exactly when her NEW new delivery date was – four weeks, three days and nineteen hours away. And if she could read the look correctly on Verity's face, Verity knew this too, and her desire to have a preview might have had something to do with the fact that this was the first novel where Allie hadn't yet shared anything with Verity, nothing at all. Not a brief outline, an elevator pitch, not even a mumbled, incoherent statement of intent. And this wasn't out of an abundance of secrecy, it was because there really was nothing at all to share.

The last year had been hard. Riding off the success of *The Wishlist*, Allie at first thought she just needed some time away from her laptop. But a few days had stretched into several weeks, and now here she was, almost a year later and with nothing to show for her sabbatical. This would be the first year in seven years that Allie wouldn't have a book to publish. And if things continued as they were, it was going to be a long time before she had anything she might comfortably be able to share with Verity. Allie had discovered that publishers didn't like it when an author decided they need some time off, there was always a hot new author ready to swoop in and steal those sales, but Allie had managed to persuade Verity, who in turn had persuaded Brinkman's, that she needed this time off, that she would recharge, stretch her synapses, think of other things. And she would emerge better than ever with her new book having come to her during this time off. So far, Allie was still sat waiting for it to arrive.

Allie smiled nervously at the stony-faced Monica, whose facial expression didn't appear to be capable of adjustment, and wondered if making conversation with her would be more or less painful than with Verity at that moment in time.

'Hi,' Allie said, 'I'm Allie, Allie Edwards.' She held her hand out to shake. Monica left Allie's hand hanging there just a beat too long, and then, just as Allie was wondering if she should withdraw it, Monica extended her own.

'Monica Billings, data analyst.' Monica gave Allie's hand one swift shake and then dropped it.

Verity laughed the laugh of someone painfully aware that a social situation was one comment away from disaster. 'Monica is an absolute whizz at telling us who is buying what, what's the best price point for maximum sales. All those clever things that actually make a book sell.'

Allie looked at Verity and raised her eyebrows. Verity saw the look on Allie's face and quickly clarified. 'After all the hard work of actually writing it, of course!' she followed up, laughing even more nervously.

Allie smiled. Monica did not.

'Anyway, Monica, do you mind if Allie and I leave you here? There's someone I have to introduce her to.'

Monica's face did something strange; there was a spasm and a constriction of muscles and finally Allie realised that this was possibly as close to a smile as Monica Billings could manage.

'Nice to meet you,' Allie said over her shoulder as Verity ushered her away.

'God,' Verity muttered, 'thank you so much for saving me from her. Honestly I don't know why I always get cornered by her at these things.'

'Erm, yeah, she seemed kind of hard work.'

'So painful,' Verity shook her head, 'you should try being stuck with her at a book launch, it's like all the joy is sucked out of the room.'

'Like a dementor,' Allie said.

'A what?'

Allie looked at Verity for a moment before deciding that she really didn't have the energy to introduce the wizarding world of Harry Potter to her editor at this advanced stage in their relationship.

'It doesn't matter.'

'Right, OK, well, here we are.'

Here appeared to be the furthest, darkest corner of the courtyard, one not yet touched by canapés and attractive waiters, Allie noticed sadly. She thought fondly of the prawn vol au vent she had cast carelessly into that poor unsuspecting pot plant. And then she thought of the waiter, his grey sparkly eyes. She cleared her throat, attempting to dislodge the strange stirrings of desire she felt within her. Odd that she hadn't experienced those for Dominic in a while.

'Hopefully, she won't find us here.'

Allie looked up at her editor and friend. Even without heels, Verity towered over her, her willowy frame encased in a dramatic ensemble of lime green and shocking pink chiffon. On anyone else, it would look frightful, but on Verity, it looked like something from last season's fashion shows. Actually, with her new rich boyfriend, Verity could probably afford *this* season's catwalk offerings. She could probably model the damn things on the catwalk and sell them just as well as she could hand-sell books.

'So.' Verity turned her head sharply away from the party and looked down at Allie. 'Tell me what's going on? Why haven't I read anything yet?'

Allie fidgeted with her now empty champagne flute and wondered whether to come clean to Verity right now. As Jess said, what was the worst that could happen? Images of financial destitution and professional shame flashed across

Allie's vision. The bailiffs at her flat, wrestling the keys away from her. Her arrival at her sister Martha's with nothing but a frayed rucksack on her shoulder. Strangely, the idea of turning up on Dominic's doorstep didn't seem to figure in her disaster planning. Allie mulled over her doomsday images briefly and then decided that Jess was wrong and that Brinkman's annual summer party was probably not the time or place to confess to Verity that her writer's block now seemed to be a permanent fixture in her life. She would email her first thing tomorrow instead…

'I'm just having a hard time pulling all the strands of the story together,' Allie mumbled.

'But you've got the outline? You've got some strands to pull together?' Without waiting for Allie to confirm this, Verity exhaled. 'Oh, thank goodness.' She smiled at Allie. 'For a moment there I thought you were going to tell me you hadn't written anything yet or, even worse, that you hadn't even got an outline for the book.'

'Ha ha,' Allie laughed weakly, 'that would be awful.' She steadied herself on a marble statue briefly before quickly removing her hand. Setting the alarms off at the V&A would just be the icing on the cake of this shitshow of a situation. Although, it might get the party shut down and Allie forcibly removed from social awkwardness, which could just be worth contemplating…

Verity grabbed Allie's free hand, stopping her just as she was about to make a move to topple the statue. Verity laughed along with Allie, failing to hear the thin wail of desperation in Allie's muted laugh. 'Ha! Yes, it would,' Verity exclaimed. 'Complete disaster. Just imagine!' Allie chose not to share that she had already done that, many, many times over. 'But listen,' Verity continued, her voice suddenly serious, 'if there's any way you feel you can share something with me now, or even just sooner than the deadline…?'

'Ok, sure.' Allie's face froze in a rictus grin of lies. 'Maybe I can get something to you later this week?' What was she thinking? Her brain scrambled to keep up with the promises her mouth was making. But as an inveterate people-pleaser, Allie couldn't help herself, and then there it was, the sweet hit of endorphins that flowed through Allie's body as Verity's face creased in a smile of relief and happiness.

'I'd love that!' exclaimed Verity, 'I can't wait to read whatever you're ready to share.' Verity put her arms out and enveloped Allie in a hug of gauzy gratitude.

Still clutching Allie by the shoulders, Verity stared deeply into her eyes. 'You know, all the years we have worked together and I still get excited when I know you're about to deliver me a manuscript.'

Allie felt her face flush and hoped that Verity would mistake the visible evidence of her lying shame for embarrassment. Verity released her. 'The thing I love about your writing Allie is that it's always inspired me.'

'Inspired you?'

'Yes, I mean through all of the terrible dates and heartbreak. Your novels have always inspired me to carry on believing in true love despite the odds.' Verity's eyes shone with excitement and perhaps a little too much champagne.

'Despite the odds,' echoed Allie weakly.

'And now,' Verity continued, 'now I know it was all worth it and you were right!'

'I was?'

'Yes! Now that I've met Richard, I know it was all worth it. And you were right all along, there is such a thing as *The One*!'

Ah, Richard, thought Allie. The elusive but often referenced

Richard. Allie hadn't yet met the man who had captured the heart of Verity, and still she felt like she knew him intimately. For the last six months every time Allie had spoken to Verity, Richard had been shoehorned into the conversation.

Unfortunately, given Allie's current situation, Verity's newfound status as a happily coupled woman made her even more enthusiastic about the world of romance publishing. As if every book about happy-ever-afters was a blueprint for her future with Richard.

'So erm, how is Richard?' asked Allie, hoping that Verity would regale her with whatever the latest act of romance Richard had carried out and prove a distraction from the case of the missing manuscript. Or even better, some inspiration for her book.

'Oh, he's amazing, Allie, I can't wait for you to meet him. Actually, speaking of which…'

Allie looked around her, wondering whether Richard was about to pop out from one of the porticos around the courtyard.

'I really need to introduce you to someone,' Verity continued. 'Or rather re-introduce you.'

'Oh?' Allie felt disappointed not to be surprised by Richard. 'Who?' she asked, trying to still sound interested.

'Jake Matthews.' A strangely flat tone had entered Verity's voice, completely at odds with the breathless excitement that she used when she had been speaking about Richard. Her eyes had also glazed over and Allie noticed with some consternation that Verity was now twisting her hands together in what looked alarmingly like a classic symptom of anxiety.

'Who's Jake Matthews?' Given Verity's reaction to speaking his name, Allie wasn't sure she actually wanted the answer to this but felt it was the polite thing to do when you were about to be introduced to the aforementioned.

Verity, who had been glancing over her shoulder into the courtyard behind, turned back and looked at Allie with surprise. 'Jake Matthews!' she exclaimed. 'I introduced you to him at your last book launch. Don't you remember?'

Allie shrugged. She wasn't sure if she did remember, she always found her book launches to be a bit of a whirlwind and she was introduced to lots of people that she could subsequently never remember the names of.

'He had just come over from Penguin, where he singlehandedly rearranged the sales and marketing teams and made them the most efficient in the business.' Allie noticed with interest that the breathy tone had made a reappearance in Verity's voice, which was quickly drowned out by a note of fear as she continued, 'And apparently had a hand in axing half of editorial at the same time.'

Verity stared at Allie, making her think uncomfortably of a rabbit in headlights.

'Right,' Allie said, unnerved by the fear that was coming in waves off Verity. 'Yes, I think I remember.'

'He's just been made publisher,' Verity said, her voice now sounding slightly strangled.

'OK,' Allie said warily, 'and I should meet him because…?'

Verity hustled Allie back into the throng of the party, her hand now like a grip of steel around Allie's elbow. Allie looked down at her arm and then back up at Verity.

'Verity,' Allie said firmly, 'why do I need to meet Jake Matthews?'

'Because,' Verity said as she steered them around the cocktail bar.

'Because what?' insisted Allie, watching the tray of mai tais sail off sadly into the distance and thinking that this might be it. This might be the moment she discovered that Verity *was* leaving her and that this Jake Matthews, the scourge of editorial, was going to be her new editor.

'Because he's important, and I think it would be good for you to meet him, OK?'

'OK. Erm, Verity, do you think we could get a drink before we go meet him?'

Verity sighed. 'Yes, of course, sorry Allie. I'm a bit on edge.' Verity stopped them in front of a white-shirted waiter who was carrying a tray of wine and water. Allie tried not to feel too sad that their sojourn to the far reaches of the party had obviously meant they missed the champagne window. And that the attractive waiter from earlier seemed to have vanished, too, leaving behind this disappointing, barely post-adolescent, unibrowed version.

'Here.' Verity handed Allie a glass of white wine.

'Anything you want to tell me?' asked Allie, suddenly emboldened.

'What? No,' insisted Verity. 'Just a lot going on at work at the moment,' she said mysteriously, 'and I do think it would be good for you to meet Jake. He *is* quite important, you know.'

'Understood.'

'So just try to be nice.'

'Wait, what?' Allie turned to stare at Verity.

'Remember that sales conference?'

Allie nodded.

'Yes, well, we don't want a repeat of that,' Verity said primly and continued to guide Allie through the party.

Allie couldn't remember whether it was between books three and four or books four and five that she had been invited to give a speech at the Brinkman's sales conference. Verity had persuaded her that it would be a 'really good thing' for her to do and so reluctantly Allie had agreed. The speech itself was fine, mainly because it was short, which everyone seemed really happy about. But afterwards the adrenaline had got to Allie, and that and the free bar went straight to her head. She had ended up telling the then sales director that he was a jumped-up asshole with no respect for women.

'He had it coming,' Allie mumbled.

'Yes, he did,' agreed Verity. 'And he retired soon afterwards. But it would have been better if it had come from someone else, rather than the author that we were asking him and his sales team to go out and sell.' Verity sighed. 'Just play nice, OK?'

Allie looked at Verity and thought about pointing out that her sales had gone through the roof after that sales director had retired, so it didn't look like his team had felt they owed him any loyalty. If anything, it looked more that they were rewarding Allie for ridding them of said jumped-up asshole. But she saw the look of determination on Verity's face and decided to calmly acquiesce.

She looked ahead to where Verity was leading and immediately remembered who Jake Matthews was and that she hadn't liked him the first time she had met him. Slim and tall with a sharply tailored electric-blue jacket, he exuded confidence and poise. His skin was alabaster white and his blonde hair, what was left of it, was slicked back, giving his face an even more angular look than it naturally had. He saw Verity coming and a look crossed his face. Allie couldn't tell whether it was irritation or anger, either way it definitely wasn't one of the warm cozy emotions that you would prefer someone to exhibit when you were about to speak to them at a social event. Everything, from his skin tone to his icy glare, gave Jake Matthews a look as if he wouldn't know warmth if it came up and enveloped him in a hug. He raised his eyebrows as Verity approached and turned from the person he had been talking to. This short man seemed to realise immediately he had been dismissed and he scurried off in the opposite direction. Probably in search of champagne, Allie thought sadly.

Verity stopped short in front of Jake and pulled Allie to her side.

'Jake,' she said, nodding her head in his direction but, Allie noted, not quite meeting his eye.

'Verity,' Jake replied and turned to Allie. 'You must be Allie Edwards, pleasure to meet you.' He smiled at Allie with a smile that got nowhere near reaching his eyes. Allie put out her hand to shake his and tried to ignore the air of misery Verity was exuding.

'Actually, we've met before.'

'We have?' If Jake had sounded any less interested in this fact, he could probably be declared medically dead.

'Yep,' Allie continued, looking at Verity who suddenly seemed very interested in retying the belt of her dress. 'My last book launch. You had just joined as sales director?'

'So I had.' He smiled that smile again. 'And, so, when are we publishing your next book, Allie?'

Allie and Verity exchanged panicked looks. 'Oh we agreed to give Allie a little time off before book eight, didn't we, Allie?'

Allie nodded enthusiastically in agreement with Verity.

'But she's about to deliver, aren't you Allie?'

Allie again nodded enthusiastically.

'Good,' said Jake. 'Because it's terrible when authors don't deliver on time isn't it, Verity? Or when they leave it too long between books.' He paused to allow the temperature of the party to sink even lower. 'I always think that's publishing suicide.'

'Right,' Allie cleared her throat. 'Well, it will be on Verity's desk shortly. I think it's going to be my best yet.' Internally, Allie rolled her eyes, why did she have to say that? Why couldn't she have just left it? But her enthusiasm seemed to reinvigorate Verity, who beamed between Allie and Jake.

There was a long awkward pause and then, because apparently she couldn't stop talking, Allie decided it was her job to break that silence.

'So this must be your first summer party then? It's quite an event, isn't it?'

Jake's eyes flitted to the centre of the courtyard where the cocktail bar now more closely resembled the last days of Rome than a civilised publishing party. 'Yes,' he agreed, 'it's quite the extravagance.' Jake used the term 'extravagance' like others might say 'depraved sex orgy'. All three of them stood and watched the drunken partygoers, Allie wondered who was going to have to break the silence next and prayed that her mouth wouldn't decide that it had to be her.

Thankfully, Jake was obviously done with this social chit chat. He turned to Allie and took her hand firmly. 'Allie, pleasure to see you again. I'm looking forward to our meeting.' And then he turned and was gone, obviously a follower of the mantra, *never apologise, never explain.*

Allie turned to Verity in confusion. 'Meeting?' she asked.

Verity blanched. 'Oh, yes, erm, Jake asked me to set something up. I'll do that. I'll send you some options soon.'

'But why do I need to meet with Jake?' Allie asked.

'Allie, I've got to go. I'm sorry but I've got another author I need to find before the end of the evening, and you know how long that could take.' Verity gestured to the crowds in front of them. 'It was lovely to see you, Allie, I'll email you.' And with that Verity too disappeared off into the party.

Allie sighed and looked down at her disappointing glass of slightly warm white wine. Realising that she wasn't going to get a better offer, she downed it in one and decided to go find the bathrooms. At least she had seen and been seen by Verity, even if she hadn't gone into full on confessional mode. Maybe she didn't need to email her in the morning, maybe she could explain when Allie went in for this meeting with Jake Matthews that curiously needed to happen.

Allie stared at her reflection in the mirror. Thankfully she seemed to have found the quiet bathrooms, the ones with no queue. Although wasn't it *too* eerily quiet for a bathroom at a party? Allie glanced around her. Perhaps people knew something she didn't? Perhaps this one wasn't even plumbed in? She tested the tap and was somewhat relieved to find running water. She went back to staring at her face. She pulled her auburn, wavy hair into a ponytail and turned in profile; this was the pose in the author photo that had been gracing the back cover of her books for the last four years. She tried recreating the smile but it fell flat and she dropped her ponytail in frustration. She'd lost that sparkle in her eyes – even if no one else had noticed, Allie had. She rolled her shoulders, easing out the burden of expectation: Verity's, her mother's, her fans, and weighing most heavily of all, her own. She thought about her dad. How proud she knew he would have been of her success. And what advice he might give her in her current predicament. She gnawed the inside of her mouth as she tried to recall his calm presence, his all-encompassing love for her, for Martha and for their mum. She blinked back the tears. With every year that went by it was harder and harder to recall his voice, harder to remember his words of wisdom. And yet, the one conversation she could conjure at the drop of a hat was the last one they had, of him telling Allie about when he met her mum, about the fireworks he felt and still felt, even right at the end when he was too weak to do much beyond lie in bed. And how he had wished that for Allie and for Martha, that they too would know a great love like their parents had. Martha had got it, she'd found it with Ruth, Allie could tell. Even their mum seemed happy in Spain with her new partner Nigel. But had Allie found it with Dominic? She contemplated this morosely and then turned her thoughts to the wild promises she had just made to Verity and Jake about her next book.

It wasn't that Allie couldn't write, of course she could. She'd written seven novels so far, all of them *Sunday Times* bestsellers, all of them the perfect formula of romance and laughter and happy-ever-afters. But what she hadn't admitted to anyone until right this moment, and even now it was only to her own reflection, was that she didn't want to write them anymore. She didn't want to write sparkly love stories, she didn't want to hint at passion and seduction, she didn't want to capture that moment when your breath caught, desire caused your mouth to go dry and the words to stop as the hero kissed your lips. Because she no longer believed a word of what she had written. What was the point in pretending when life wasn't full of romance and laughter and you had stopped believing in the happy-ever-afters? How could she create these stories when her own world felt dull and colourless? This realisation hit Allie like a freight train running at a hundred miles an hour; she was floored by her own cynicism, her words silenced by her loss of faith in the religion of romance.

Allie poked her tongue out at the mirror, frustrated by herself. She turned to go into one of the stalls. Even if she didn't actually need the bathroom she needed a moment of solitude, and she definitely needed to adjust the lining of her irritating dress, which was rucked up and uncomfortable. She made a note never to wear the dress again and to donate it to charity as soon as possible. She had just closed the door and turned the lock when she heard the door of the bathrooms opening and the sound of a giggling voice echo around the space. Quietly she set about readjusting herself and she was just about to flush and open the door, because how was the person out there to know that she hadn't actually used the toilet, and she didn't want them thinking her a monster, when she heard another voice, a male voice and she froze. Great, she thought to herself, that's all I need, stuck in a bathroom while a romantic tryst happens right outside my cubicle.

Allie stood for a moment listening, but whatever was happening outside the cubicle didn't sound like a hookup. There was the sound of rustling and whispering before the distinct sound of someone, the owner of the female voice, inhaling something and gasping with pleasure.

'Your turn,' she said, her voice sounding more nasal and congested than it had before. 'I brought extra, like you told me to.'

There was a long pause before Allie heard a voice she thought she recognised, saying in clipped tones, 'Not out here.'

The door of one of the cubicles along from her opened, then closed and was locked. Allie took the opportunity to fling her door open, and run, before she could find out who the voices belonged to and exactly how illegal the substances being inhaled were.

She stalked quickly down the corridor, glancing over her shoulder as she did so, hoping to put as much distance between herself and the bathroom as possible before either of the other party could work out that they hadn't been alone in the bathroom. In her rush, she took a left instead of a right turn and before she realised it, she was lost and probably about half a mile from the party, somewhere down a labyrinth of corridors. She stopped and looked around her, wondering if she could retrace her steps. Actually she didn't really want to get back to the party, but she did want to find the exit. And she really did want her coat back from the coat check, because this was London, and despite it being summer, it was coat weather by 10pm.

She pushed against a door she thought looked promising and tumbled outside onto the street. Before she could turn back, the door slammed behind her. She quickly scanned the side of the door where she was now standing and immediately noticed two things; firstly there was no handle on her side, and secondly the door looked amazingly solid for such an old building. Not such a promising door after all then.

'Dammit!' she shouted and kicked the door, then really wished she hadn't when the pain jarred through her leg. The strappy silver sandals she had chosen to wear for the party were not designed for kicking in heavy Victorian doors.

'It's locked,' came a morose voice from her left.

Allie swung round to see who was there and saw a man leaning against the wall smoking.

'So I gathered,' Allie said acerbically. 'Any idea how to get back in?'

The man shrugged. 'I believe this is the door they're using

for catering, so if you wait around long enough I'm sure someone will come through.'

Allie blew her cheeks out in frustration and leaned back against the wall, keeping a good distance from this strange man. Because after all, this might be a swanky publishing party but it was also a back alley in London. She contemplated asking him how long he had been waiting to be let back in and then decided against engaging a stranger in conversation for the exact same reasons – a back alley. London. Late at night.

He, it seemed, had no such qualms – the privilege of being male, Allie thought to herself, quickly sizing him up and wondering if she could take him on in a fight. If she used one of her sandals as a weapon then she might just have the edge.

'You were at the party?' he asked. His voice was deep with a hint of gravel in it, probably caused by the smoking Allie thought, looking again at the lit cigarette dangling from his fingers. As she looked more closely, she realised he was older than she had initially thought, definitely in his sixties – more plausible then, that she could beat him in a fight. And he seemed familiar, Allie felt sure she had seen him somewhere before.

'I was,' she confirmed. 'I was trying to find the coat check but it looks like I took a wrong turn,' she said, indicating their surroundings.

She was rewarded by a bark of laughter. 'Looks like you did. Personally, I never bother with them.'

'Parties or coat checks?'

He turned to face her and raised his eyebrow. 'It's a fair question, isn't it, seeing as we're both avoiding the party.'

'I wasn't avoiding it,' Allie smarted. And now, looking at him face on, Allie was sure she recognised him.

'I meant coat checks. Although I find nowadays parties are something I can take or leave as well.'

'Yes, well that's because you're a man. Try walking home in a dress and high heels and then see if you need a coat check.' Allie didn't mean to sound so caustic, she just really wanted to know how long she was going to be stuck outside, making small talk with a stranger.

The man shrugged and pushed himself up from his slouching position allowing the streetlamp to cast its light across his face.

'I know who you are!' Allie said, suddenly, and then was immediately embarrassed to have made it so obvious that she had been studying him. But he didn't seem the least bothered, as if he was used to this happening. He put his hand out towards her. 'Martin Clark,' he said, 'and you are?'

'Erm, Allie Edwards.' Allie wondered if he would notice how sweaty her palm had become during her race down the corridors and if she could get away with wiping it on her dress. She did a surreptitious wipe down, hoping that the darkness of the alleyway would hide the movement. He took her hand without seeming to notice anything amiss.

'I didn't realise Brinkman's published you.'

Martin Clark had been a huge crime writer in the 1990s. Every one of his books had topped the charts and Allie was sure that at least one of them had been made into a Hollywood movie. Something her dad had made her watch one long Sunday afternoon in her youth. And then, like so many writers, he had disappeared without a trace, and she couldn't recall him publishing anything recently. Allie shuddered at this fate. Martin made a noise that sounded halfway between a groan and a laugh. 'I'm not sure I can claim to be published by anyone anymore.'

Allie looked at him curiously, wondering just what the great Martin Clark was doing hiding out in the back alley behind a publishing party.

'You're not under contract with them?' she asked. 'I thought they were really picky about only inviting authors who are actually being published that year? I only just scraped in, by the way, in case you were wondering.'

Martin Clark didn't look like he was wondering anything of the sort. He looked down at the cigarette still smouldering in his hand and then lifted it to his lips, taking a long drag.

'Anyway,' Allie began, beginning to feel very awkward and wishing that someone, anyone, would open that door and rescue her from this conversation. She was just starting to think about trying to find her way back around to the front of the building and starting all over again when Martin suddenly spoke.

'Do you know how soul-destroying these parties are?'

Allie opened her mouth to respond, but Martin ploughed on.

'Having to make small talk, having to listen to speeches telling us how much we're all *valued*.' He said the word 'valued' as if it was something filthy. 'How important we all are. And all the while knowing that they're only interested in how soon you can deliver your next manuscript.'

'Actually,' began Allie, 'I do know.' She leaned her head back against the wall and stared up at the sky. 'It's been almost twelve months since my last book was published. I've missed three delivery deadlines, and I've now promised my editor I'll have something for her to read in the next few days. And do you know how many words I've actually written?'

Martin turned to look at her, his interest piqued by her confession.

'None,' she confirmed. 'Zero. Zilch. That's how many. And the worst thing is? I don't even think I can write anymore. At least certainly not the type of books I used to write.'

Martin's eyes began to sparkle, a ghost of a smile playing about his lips.

'Don't laugh,' she snapped at him. 'It's not funny.'

'Sorry.' He held his hands up in defense. 'I was only smiling because it's exactly the position I find myself in.'

'You too?' Allie looked at him in surprise. 'But you're Martin Clark, international bestseller.'

Martin fixed her with a glare. 'And when exactly did you last see my name on the bestseller lists?'

Allie looked down at her feet, not liking to admit that this was exactly the thought she had had not five minutes before. She shifted from one foot to the other, noticing that the toes in her left foot were now almost completely numb.

'A while ago,' she eventually admitted.

'Exactly.'

They stood in silence for a moment.

'So, tell me, Allie Edwards, what's your genre?'

'Romantic comedies,' she said as defiantly as she dared. 'I bet you've got a lot to say about that,' she said with a challenge.

'Don't stereotype,' he warned, waving his finger at her. 'There's probably quite a lot I could learn from your books.'

'I doubt it,' she huffed. 'Especially as I can't seem to write them anymore.'

He cocked his head in interest. 'Can I ask why not? Surely you're just the right age to be using your own romantic entanglements as inspiration.' He held his hands up. 'Or am I not allowed to say things like that these days?'

Allie raised her eyebrows at him, and even in the dim light of the alleyway he noticed.

'Sorry,' he said, 'this is exactly the reason my books are out of favour and why, I too, find it impossible to write.'

'Oh, OK. Right.' Allie didn't know what to say. She couldn't deny she was intrigued to meet Martin and to hear about his struggles, but at same time she wasn't really in the mood to offer champagne and sympathy to a rich, white man, who suddenly found his views and opinions a tad outdated. But the champagne from the party had obviously loosened his tongue.

'I'm a dinosaur, Allie. Apparently, I'm completely out of touch with what the readers want. Not able to write anything even vaguely inclusive or diverse.'

Allie grimaced. Given what she knew about novelists of his era, and everything he had said so far, he was probably right. She hoped she wasn't about to be asked to make him feel better about any previously questionable content he may have written.

'And that's just what my wife says about me.'

Allie couldn't help herself, she let out a big chuckle. Which she immediately tried to cover. Martin flapped his hand at her, giving her permission to laugh, which set him off too. And then Allie couldn't stop. She tried to remember the last time she had laughed so much and couldn't.

'Well, that's cheered me up,' she finally said when the laughter had subsided.

'Glad my disastrous career can be of assistance to somebody,' said Martin.

'So, if that's what your wife says, who by the way I like already, what does your editor think? Don't they have any good ideas on how to update your content?'

'I hate that word.'

'What, content?'

Martin nodded.

Allie grinned. 'Thought you would, that's why I used it.' She was beginning to enjoy baiting Martin.

Martin frowned at her. 'Very funny. My editor retired five years ago, and I haven't had a proper conversation with Brinkman's since his retirement party. And then suddenly, out of the blue, I get an email from a Jake Matthews who is apparently now very interested in the fact that Brinkman's still have a book under contract with me.'

Allie shuddered again, this time at the recollection of Jake's icy blue stare. She was fairly sure that if Jake got it in mind to get a manuscript out of an author he would achieve it more readily than getting blood from a stone.

'What about your agent?'

'Dead.'

'Dead?' spluttered, Allie looking aghast at Martin. 'I'm so sorry.'

'Don't be. It was a while ago, and it wasn't exactly a surprise. He was the type to take enjoying a lunch out to a whole new extreme.'

Allie nodded her head, picturing exactly what Martin was describing.

'Don't think me callous, but we weren't exactly close. I was useful to him when I made him some money, but he never seemed especially invested in my career or whether I was making wise professional decisions. My wife said I should have left him years ago, and then suddenly the decision was out of my hands. And as I haven't actually written a book since he died, there seemed no point in bothering the nice young man who apparently took over most of his authors at the agency. What about yours?' he asked.

'Maternity leave,' Allie said and then before Martin could respond she added, 'and yes, I understand that for most women, career wise, it's pretty much the same as what happened to your agent. And anyway, she seems to think I know what I'm doing and that she has higher priorities. Which I guess is understandable now that she's responsible for actually keeping another human being alive. Have you met Jake Matthews?' she asked, switching the subject quickly away from Mary Beth, because thinking about her agent just made her panic more real.

Martin nodded and took a drag on his cigarette, which made him double over and cough convulsively.

'You know those are bad for you?' Allie said sardonically.

'Thanks for the advice,' he shot back, not yet seeming able to straighten up. 'You know I haven't had one of these in fifteen years and then ten minutes after my first meeting with Jake Matthews and I find myself cadging one from the production director. Do you know him?' Allie shook her head. 'Great bloke,' Martin said, 'he's about the last of the old guard.'

Allie watched Martin as he slowly began to stand upright again. She almost made a rude remark about the publishing old guard but decided against it. She'd never met Martin before, or the production director he was referring to, and really she shouldn't bring her own prejudices to the party. Not that the publishing old guard had ever thought twice about bringing their own prejudices to the party, or the boardroom. Or indeed anywhere else they happened to be going.

'And let me guess,' Allie asked, 'you haven't written a single word of the novel you have under contract?'

Martin shook his head.

'So, what's your plan?' she asked.

'I've no idea. I've got a meeting with Jake Matthews coming

up, and at it I presume he's going to threaten me with having to return some of my advance, if I don't deliver a new manuscript.'

This was exactly what Alice had been fearing. In fact, she was so sure it would come to pass that she had already transferred the amount she would owe Brinkman's out of her savings account and back into her current account to make things easier.

'The only problem is, I don't have it anymore.'

'Oh.' Allie grimaced, surprised by the revelation and quite how confessional this moment was becoming. It might be awkward, but at least it was passing the time before she could get back into the party.

'Yes.' Martin continued, looking grim. 'Oh indeed. Turns out, having children is expensive. Take it from me. Think twice before you decide to have some.' There was a long pause while Allie thought about, and then decided against, telling Martin that she was fairly sure having children wasn't on her agenda anytime soon. She was beginning to imagine whether the topic of children would go down less well with her or with Dominic, when Martin continued. 'Although, to be fair, I do have one of each, a good one and a bad one I mean.'

Allie opened her mouth to ask Martin to say more on this topic, despite thinking quite how awful it would be for one of his children to overhear this and wonder which one they were, when at that moment, the door to the building swung open and both Allie and Martin lurched forward to grab it before it slammed shut again. Allie held the door open and stood to the side as she let a waiter walking backwards, carefully guiding a trolley of empty platters and glasses through. He came level with her and Allie watched his shoulders tense before her eyes ran down his arms, noticing the well-defined muscles and then recognising a tattoo she had seen earlier that evening. A tug in her lower belly immediately followed as he turned and fixed his grey eyes on her.

'Oh,' she stammered, 'it's you.'

He straightened up, his eyes meeting hers. 'It is,' he agreed. 'Hello again.' The way his cheek dimpled as he smiled floored her.

'Er, hi.' She smiled back thinking she could lose hours just staring at him and then remembering exactly where she was and how she might go about explaining her predicament without sounding like a complete idiot.

Before she could open her mouth, he said, 'Did you get locked out?'

She nodded. 'I was trying to find the coat check.'

'Happens all the time. Hang on to that door.' He finished pulling the trolley over the doorstep, pushing it away to the side of the building. She watched as he did so, wondering if that was the end of their conversation and desperately hoping it wasn't.

'Do you know where you're going?' he asked.

Allie shook her head and remembered to close her mouth, which seemed to gape open every time she looked at him. She didn't want to admit to being completely hopeless, and she thought that she *probably* could find her way back if she really had to, but she was also half hoping that he might offer to walk her back. And for once, luck and circumstance were on her side.

'I'll show you the way.'

Allie did a little internal cheer, managing to stop just short of punching the air, because really this was just a polite waiter showing her back to the coat check, and she needed to get a grip on herself. Which was hard when the waiter in question seemed to make her entire body resonate with a feeling she dared not give a name to. And if giving herself a stern lecture wasn't the equivalent of pouring a bucket of cold water over herself, then remembering that Martin was also standing behind her in the alleyway definitely was. Presumably he needed to get back in as well. Allie turned to look over her shoulder for Martin who had gone uncharacteristically quiet during her exchange with the hot waiter.

'Martin? This man...' She paused, realising she didn't know what to call the hot waiter. Waiter seemed unnecessarily distant, but hot waiter went in completely the opposite direction and she didn't want to be reprimanded by the organisers of the party for sexually harassing the staff.

'Will,' he said, straightening the trolley and yet again bunching the muscles of his arms as he did so, which Allie could have done without seeing if she was going to maintain any kind of professionalism about the whole situation. He put the brake on the trolley and walked back towards Allie, whose insides were doing something weird and tingly and had definitely not listened to the recent stern talking-to.

'Right, erm, Will,' she said, trying not to smile as she said his name. She cleared her throat and turned back to Martin. 'Will said he'd show us the way back. Are you coming?'

'I think I'll stay here a bit longer, see if I can leave it long enough that Jake Matthews has gone home,' Martin said morosely. He had resumed his position leaning against the building.

Actually, that sounded really appealing to Allie, too. The thought of having to make more painfully polite chit-chat with the ice man made her shudder. But more appealing was following Will down the corridors of the V&A without Martin crashing their one-on-one party. Even so, she did feel a tiny bit guilty about leaving Martin out there alone.

'Are you sure?' she asked, hoping that Martin really was sure and she wouldn't be kicking herself if he changed his mind.

'He's sure,' said Will, ushering Allie through the door and letting it close behind him. Allie decided not to dwell on quite how rude Will had just been to Martin, leaving him out there on his own, and instead chose to focus on the potential scenario that Will was equally keen on some alone time with her, because surely she couldn't be the only one feeling these vibes? They stood for a moment in the dimly lit corridor, Will looking down at her and Allie wanting to meet his gaze but worrying that if she did she'd never be able to look away.

'Shall we go?' he asked, and Allie nodded dumbly and followed as he led.

'So the party was that good, huh?' Will smiled at Allie and then pulled her gently to his side as another waiter came down the corridor towards them carrying trays. He nodded at Will as they passed each other.

'It was a mistake,' she said, trying hard to sound as if she was cross with him for teasing her and failing as the smile spread across her face. 'Obviously, I didn't mean to get locked out.'

He nodded and they were both silent for a moment. 'How was the vol au vent by the way?'

'The what?' Allie asked and then remembered. 'Oh right, yeah, the vol au vent. Don't tell your bosses, but I didn't eat it.'

'You didn't … why not?' Will sounded slightly shocked.

'Too big.'

'What?'

'It was too big,' she repeated. 'Too big for a party,' she

continued. 'How are you supposed to eat something like that with one hand? And one mouth,' she added, helpfully pointing at her mouth as if Will might not know which part of her body she was talking about.

Will didn't say anything at first, he just stopped and stared at Allie's mouth, making her wish he was kissing her, and that she hadn't just insulted his company's food. He turned to carry on, looking thoughtful as they walked along the tiled corridor. Allie was even more aware of the sound of her heels clacking on the floor in the aftermath of her confession.

'Sorry,' she said, feeling slightly bad that she had besmirched the vol au vents.

'Don't be.' He put a hand to the small of her back to guide her around a corner and she felt an electric jolt zip through her body. He took his hand away quickly as if he had felt it too. She looked sideways at him, just as he did at her. They both broke eye contact and smiled down at the ground.

'I'd just never thought about it like that,' he said, 'about the right size for vol au vents.'

Allie shrugged. 'Maybe you could give them some feedback?' she suggested.

'Maybe,' he agreed. 'So, you're published by Brinkman's then?'

'Yep. Well, sort of.' She paused. 'Actually, to tell the truth, I haven't written anything for ages. I think I'm having some kind of mid-life crisis to be honest. Promise you won't tell anyone?'

'Who would I tell?' he said, looking around them as if a publisher might be lurking nearby just in time for Will to spill her secrets to. 'And anyway aren't you a bit young to be having a mid-life crisis?'

Allie looked over at him again as they went round yet

another twist in the corridor. Honestly, she did need his guidance, she would never have found her way back on her own. She tried to work out how old he was. Probably about her age, maybe a little older, late thirties perhaps?

'Well, maybe not a mid-life crisis,' she finally agreed, 'just the kind of crisis where you question what you're doing, how you ended up doing it and how long you can keep doing it for before people discover you really have no idea what you're playing at.'

Will laughed. 'Got it. I can understand that feeling.' He pointed left and Allie obediently turned, wishing he would dispense with the pointing and go back to directing her with a hand to her waist because that made her feel all the internal feels.

'Hang on.' Allie stopped for a moment and picked her foot up swaying as she did so. Will caught her elbow, immediately steadying her. She looked up into his eyes and felt her stomach swoop, refusing to feel guilty for the shameless attempt to feel his hands on her body again. 'Sorry,' she said, 'I just need to adjust this.' She indicated the buckle on her silver sandals.

'No worries,' he said, keeping his hand on her arm, 'I've got you.'

Allie blushed and looked quickly down at her shoe. He had no idea how much she wished that were true. She rearranged the buckle, taking longer than she actually needed, just so he would keep his hand on her.

Finally, realising that he might start to think her a bit odd, she straightened up and he let go of her arm. She looked down in disappointment at the spot, rubbing it with her other hand, feeling the warmth that his skin had left on hers. She sighed and then reluctantly started walking down the seemingly endless corridor.

'So, do you work at a lot of these?' she asked.

He gave her a curious sidelong look as if he was thinking about what answer to give her. 'Some.' He shrugged. 'Just depends how busy we are.'

Allie felt a pang of guilt about her existential crisis over writing a book. At least she was earning, or *had* earned good money in her career so far. She wasn't on some kind of zero-hours contract, sat at home wondering whether today would be the day she got a call to work and would get paid.

'I guess that makes it stressful.'

He looked at her quizzically.

'I mean, not knowing whether they'll need you to work.'

Will seemed about to say something. He paused, and Allie wanted to ask him what it was, but suddenly they were back at the coat check, and Will had stopped walking. She looked at the cloakroom and then back up at him. He really did have the nicest eyes.

'Well, erm, thanks for showing me the way,' she said, desperate to prolong their conversation, hoping he might feel the same way.

'You didn't tell me your name,' Will said, staring down at her and standing just that smidge too close so that she knew, just knew, that he must be feeling something too. 'So I can look out for your books,' he explained.

Allie tried not to let her disappointment show. 'Allie Edwards,' she said, wondering exactly what she would do anyway if he did touch her, or ask for her number, or do any one of the things she felt desperate that he do to her right away. She suddenly remembered Dominic and felt horribly guilty to even be having these thoughts.

As if Will could read her mind, he stepped away from her. 'I should get going.'

'Yes, yes of course.' She nodded vigorously. 'I don't want to get you into trouble.'

Will cocked his head at her with that quizzical look on his face again.

'I mean, I don't expect your bosses would take too kindly if you're not there to help tidy up.'

Amusement played around his lips. 'Oh I don't know,' he said, 'I think this is all part of the service.'

Allie blushed and stared at his lips as they parted in a smile and made her wonder what it would feel like to press hers against them. She felt herself go even redder.

'OK,' Will finally said, breaking the tension, 'it was a pleasure to meet you, Allie, I hope I get to see you again.'

Allie watched him walk back the way he came. She had half a mind to chase after him and … what? Tell him that she thought him the most beautiful person at the party and confess that she'd like to kiss him? She could just imagine the look of absolute disapproval on the face of Jake Matthews if he caught them kissing in the corridor. Not to mention the fact she had A BOYFRIEND, she reminded herself once again. Instead, she sighed and started searching in her bag for her coat check token, all the while thinking about Will and his eyes and his lips, and the way her body responded when he touched her. She blushed furiously again as she handed over the token and waited for her coat to be retrieved.

Chapter Two

Allie put her key in the lock of the door to her flat, grateful that for the moment at least, she still had the means to pay for a taxi home. She did what she always did when she got home, which was to pat her front door, say hello to one of the most important things in her life and offer up a little gratitude that it was hers. This ground-floor flat had been in her life for the last five years, and for those five years it had been the only thing to have brought her constant pleasure. She never fell out with it, even when the plumbing went wrong. She never had to wait for it to call, second-guess what it was thinking, wonder if she was seeing it enough or too little. And she didn't have to worry that it wouldn't be there when she needed it. She shook off the thought of her beloved childhood home, and all the memories it contained, which her mum had sold, seemingly hours after Allie had left for university. Allie had paid the deposit for her flat with the advance from her second publishing deal and it had been the true love of her life ever since. On the ground floor of a converted Victorian villa, she had two beautiful bedrooms, one of which she used as her writing space, and a small but sunny private back garden. It was big enough that she could sit outside and enjoy the sunshine but small enough that she didn't actually ever have to worry about doing anything grown up, like gardening. And the garden had the added bonus of sporadic wifi connectivity; so, Allie could shut herself out there in good weather and write without the temptations of Google, Snapchat or just plain old online shopping.

Allie stepped through her front door and immediately bent to take her shoes off. She leaned against the pale grey wall of her hallway and rubbed one ankle and then the other, her mind wandering back to the corridor of the V&A and the way Will had held her as she adjusted her sandal. Much as she loved the scuffed walls of her flat, she couldn't deny that he was a step up in terms of places to lean against.

As she straightened up, she noticed that the light was on in her kitchen, Allie was sure she hadn't left it on. It had still been broad daylight when she'd left for the party. Pausing between wondering if she was going mad or was about to be attacked by an intruder, she grabbed the only weapon she had to hand with which to defend herself. Armed with one scrappy silver sandal and thinking that this was the second time this evening she had contemplated defending herself with a shoe, she burst into the kitchen brandishing it.

'Dom!' Allie exclaimed, lowering her sandal. She stood in the doorway, wondering if the normal reaction to discovering that your boyfriend had decided to surprise you was trying to attack them with footwear. She supposed that she should rush towards him, kiss him, be thrilled that he had come all the way over here and let himself into her flat, using the key that she really regretted ever giving him. She checked herself for any of those feelings and just registered irritation: about the key, about the surprise and about the fact that she wouldn't just be able to fall into her own bed, on her own, taking all the covers for herself.

'I wasn't expecting you.'

Dominic stood up from where he had been sitting on the two-seat snug sofa which faced the wood burner and Allie could immediately tell that this was not a booty call – something was up. Dominic had never been the sort of boyfriend who would think to surprise her after an evening apart. Nor had he ever been so into her that he would show up with one thing on his mind. Depressingly, Allie allowed herself to realise that she felt exactly the same way about him. Dominic was fine, their sex life was *fine*, but who wanted fine? Fine wasn't inspiring her to write. Fine wasn't going to be her hero. Allie was beginning to realise that *fine* was not going to dislodge her writers block, she needed to be swept off her feet.

But her feet remained firmly planted to the ground, as did Dominic's. Until he started shifting nervously from one foot to the other and then Allie knew what this was. She knew he was here to end it with her, and the overwhelming emotion she experienced wasn't sadness but annoyance that she hadn't got there first. A combination of inertia and just not caring enough had allowed her to drift along in this relationship until she suddenly discovered that there wasn't enough connection to really call it a relationship anymore. She looked over at Dominic, stood there in his suit, his banker striped shirt slightly crumpled, his tie loosened around his neck. He hadn't even taken his jacket off, so he was obviously planning a speedy exit.

As Allie stood and watched him, she wondered what she had ever really seen in him. What she had initially thought of as a solid torso would, she knew, soon run to fat. His face, which she had once thought of as boyishly handsome, now just looked shiny and red, and his blonde hair was receding fast. Give him a few more years and he'd probably more closely resemble Boris Johnson than the blonde, rugby-playing man she had met in a Richmond pub almost two years ago. She wondered if she had time before he ended things with her to break it to him that the whole thing had been an accident. She wasn't even meant to be in that pub; a broken-down train and delays on the line had propelled her towards a place that both served alcohol and had working toilets. And that was where he had been, several pints in and watching some completely incomprehensible – to Allie, at least – rugby match with his friends. The alcohol had made him bold enough to offer to buy her a drink, and the delays on the line had made her accept. And now here they were, two years later, with really nothing to show for it.

He had thought her sexy and quirky (his words, not hers) when they met. He'd never dated anyone who didn't have an office job, actually Allie thought he may not have ever dated anyone who didn't work in finance. But he was strangely proud of her 'alternative' choice of career, probably because she had been mainly solvent, self-sufficient and owned her own flat. It really said it all that this was what Dominic was looking for in his ideal woman. And Allie had been looking for her happy-ever-after and had been sufficiently disheartened by her earlier attempts at finding it, to consider that perhaps it was lurking in the mind and body of a city boy Durham grad.

Dominic ran one hand through his hair, causing that side of his hair to lie flat against his head while the other side stood up in a messy blonde thatch. Allie had to stifle a laugh. She wanted nothing more than this conversation to be over, for Dominic to leave and for her to be able to get into her bed on her own. If she laughed at him, she might have to tell him why and how she really felt about things and that would just prolong what was already a painfully awkward situation.

'Allie,' Dominic started, 'I, erm, I have something I need to say.'

Allie considered putting him out of his misery, telling him that she already knew, that she felt the same and could they please speed things up a little so that she could get into her pyjamas. But she was also curious to see just how Dominic might spin this, so instead she crossed her arms, regarded him coolly and allowed him to flounder a little longer.

'I feel like we've grown apart.'

Allie raised one eyebrow. He was going down that clichéd path.

'I feel like we both want different things.'

Her other eyebrow shot up and she had to stop herself from telling him that she was fairly sure they had wanted different things all along, but that somehow during the last two years she had lost herself sufficiently enough to consider that maybe she really did want summer outings to Henley, autumn weekends at Twickenham and a plan for 2.4 children and a loft conversion somewhere out past zone six.

'It's not you, it's me.'

Allie did a little cough and put her hand to her mouth to cover the expression on her face. Dominic shuffled awkwardly and Allie wondered if he'd find it easier if she cried.

'So erm, no hard feelings right?'

Allie exhaled heavily. 'Oh, Dom, really? That's the best you can do?'

Dominic shrugged and tried to meet her eye but failed. 'I'm not very good at this.'

'What? Breaking up with your sort-of girlfriend? Ending an

already dying relationship?' she questioned archly before feeling bad as the air seemed to go out of him.

'It's fine, OK?' she reassured him. 'I'm fine. Just, you know, disappointed, I guess?' Allie had been feeling disappointed in Dominic for the past two years but this was the first time she had allowed herself to voice it. 'Maybe you should just go,' she suggested, Dominic half opened his mouth as if about to say something else but she cut him off. 'Look I'm really tired, so maybe we can work out any practicalities another time?' As she said it she thought how few practicalities they really had to sort out, how depressingly un-entwined their existences were.

Dominic nodded slowly and gave Allie a small sad smile and for the first time she felt a pang of something. Not sadness, exactly, but nostalgia for the feeling of being attached to someone, having someone to talk to at the end of each day. His phone buzzed in his pocket.

'You need to get that?' she asked.

A slight flush rose in his cheeks. 'No, no, it's just my Uber.'

So, he wanted a quick getaway, too? Allie felt a little less bad for ushering him so speedily out of the door and she couldn't help but admire his immaculate timing and his attention to detail that meant his Uber arrived just as she was asking him to leave.

'Ok, well, bye then.' Dominic walked past Allie, briefly placing his hand on her shoulder as he did so. She couldn't help comparing the lack of electricity in his touch to that she had felt with Will earlier.

'Oh, Dom?' she said as he reached her front door. He turned and the look on his face told her he half expected her to beg him to stay. 'Can I have my key?' Dominic's face fell as he reached in his pocket. He held the key up and then put it in the little dish on the table by her front door. And then he walked through that door and was gone.

Allie stood for a moment and then a thought occurred to her about the immaculate timing of Dominic's departure and the expression that had crossed his face when he had received the arrival message from his Uber driver. She walked into her bedroom, which overlooked the road. Going to the window, she pushed apart the shutters and watched Dominic walk down the front path. On the street in front of her flat she saw a red sports car, which couldn't be his Uber, because Uber didn't send red sports cars. But it was the only car that she could see that had someone sat in the driver's seat. Allie shifted her position to get a better look, her interest now piqued, and sure enough Dominic walked towards the car and opened the door, illuminating the inside of the car. Allie watched for a few more seconds before turning away and throwing herself on her bed. She stared up at the ceiling thinking that it was unusual for an Uber driver to be female, and that if Allie was an Uber driver she'd probably wear something super comfortable like a sweatshirt and jogging bottoms to drive around in, because it couldn't be very practical to be wearing such a tight and low cut top for hours on end. And as Allie rolled herself up in her duvet and pulled one of her pillows over her head, she wondered how much extra you had to tip an Uber driver to be kissed on the lips like Dominic had just been.

The first thing Allie felt when she woke the next morning was relief, relief that Dominic had gone, relief that it was over. But as she stood and waited for her kettle to boil and watched the birds fight over some crumbs in her back garden, she began to feel anger that she hadn't had the guts to end things sooner. Allie poured the boiling water into her tiny one-person teapot, angrily sloshing the water over the work surface and wondering if she would ever have someone in her life who would make it necessary for her to get her bigger teapot out again; her anger only increased as she castigated herself for getting maudlin and over dramatic about teapots.

Taking her tea to the large farmhouse-style table, she sat on one of the benches and pulled her laptop towards her. Maybe this could be useful? She was actually feeling something for once, even if it was mild rage rather than burning ardour. Allie's hands hovered over her keyboard, waiting for inspiration to strike. She waited for some time, refusing to allow herself even a sip of her tea until she had at least written a sentence. But then her hands started to cramp and her tea started to get cold and, in frustration, she pushed her laptop away and picked her mug up, cradling it in her hands as she looked out the window.

Aimlessly, Allie picked her phone up and started scrolling. It was a complete energy, time and emotion suck and sometimes Allie wished she had the strength to be like one of those worthy writers who disengaged from their phone and social media when they wrote. But she wasn't and so here she was, scrolling through her feeds and making sure to like the latest picture of her literary agent's four-month-old munchkin. When Mary Beth had announced she was pregnant, Allie's first reaction had been to panic, but in hindsight it was probably a good thing that Mary Beth was on maternity leave and not constantly breathing down her neck and asking where her manuscript was. Allie wasn't sure if this was a chicken and egg situation though; had Mary Beth been breathing hard enough, perhaps Allie might have managed to produce something –

anything – by now. But Mary Beth was happily ensconced in nappy land and had better things to be dealing with than a neurotic, self-centered author and as she had signed off with a strong belief that Allie knew exactly what she was doing, and a brief introduction to the agency assistant who would help out should Allie need anything urgent, Allie now found herself freewheeling towards professional Armageddon.

Perhaps she ought to call Martha who would likely have some advice to give her on both Dominic and the writing situation, but then she decided that the kind of advice Martha would give would be good advice, and Allie didn't want good advice, she wanted someone to commiserate with her. And while Martha had many strong points, commiserating was not one of them.

Obviously, as her sister, Martha was an essential part of Allie's life. Who else could sympathise about their parents, recall ridiculous minutiae from their childhood, and still fight about an incident from twenty years earlier? And who else would Allie be able to speak to as her true, authentic self, and know that despite this, Martha would still always answer her calls? But despite all the positives, Martha didn't do wallowing, she didn't believe in sitting with uncomfortable feelings and analysing emotions. Martha believed in getting up and getting things done. Whereas Allie believed in long baths, mulling things over, and taking her time with decisions. Which was why Martha was a scientifically driven pharmacist working in clinical research and drug design and Allie was an English graduate who liked to play with words. Or not, as her current situation suggested. Allie looked accusingly at her laptop and leaned back as far as she dared on the kitchen table bench pondering once again her predicament as to what she was, if she wasn't a writer.

Allie's phone buzzed with a message from Jess, politely reminding her that they had arranged to meet in the pub that evening and could Allie please not be late this time because Jess really didn't want to have to make small talk with Tom's colleagues. Allie had met Jess their final year at university; Jess was a year older, studying languages and was returning from a gap year in Spain. She was tanned and healthy-looking, the way no one could ever manage naturally if they spent their summers solely in the UK. Jess only knew the other returning language students, and Allie had recently broken up with her university boyfriend and was determined to put him and his obnoxious group of friends behind her. Jess announced that this was the perfect moment to make lifelong friends, deeply suspicious as she was of people who met their BFFs during freshers week; because who made their best decisions when they were drunk and anxious and sleep deprived? It was the friends made in your final year that counted, she said. The ones made when you had a bit more of an idea of who you actually were, and were still hopeful for the future, the light not yet extinguished from your spirit by job interviews and corporate soul snatching.

Yes, Jess was what she needed tonight. Jess would give her some good advice and comfort. Fortified with that thought, Allie rallied and opened up her laptop again. She would talk to Jess. Tonight. But not before she had written 2,000 words.

Chapter Three

I t turned out it wasn't hitting her word count that got Allie out of the door that evening or even fear of Jess's wrath if she was late. In fact, Allie was early, really early. Early enough to be sat in a virtually empty pub while she waited for the 9-5ers to finish for the day. She nursed a glass of wine and tried to put from her mind the reason she was so early – that after four hours of staring at an empty word document Allie had fled her flat, escaping from the judgement of the blank white page of her computer screen.

And so Allie was guiltily daytime drinking in one of her and Jess's favourite haunts, an old-school pub in the heart of Soho, a tiny warren of dark-timbered rooms with the bar in the room at the front, overlooking the street. It was here that Allie had sat, thinking that inspiration might strike. Why not? It was atmospheric and cosy, it was quiet but there were enough customers to people-watch, perhaps this was what had been missing from her life? She didn't need romance, she needed a more inspiring workspace. And it wasn't as if she was asking for a fully fleshed-out plot, not even the bare bones of a synopsis, or even a title, all she needed was a tiny germ of an idea that she could sculpt and mould into something she could email to Verity without hanging her head in shame.

But the only thing that was filling Allie's head right now was Will, the hot waiter from the night before, and wondering what he was doing right now. Wondering if he had a catering job that evening and if so where it was. Wondering if their paths might ever cross again and hoping that they would. She thought also of Martin Clark, the crime novelist, and his depressing revelation that he too could no longer write. Allie really didn't want to be in his position in thirty years' time, washed up and irrelevant with one unwritable book still under contract. She wondered how he spent his evenings; did he also watch passers-by, looking for inspiration? Although his kind of inspiration would be quite different, she supposed; instead of wondering what romantic plans they had for the evening he would be wondering which one to kill off first.

Allie's eye was caught by a group of bankers who seemed to have veered off course and got lost on the seedy streets of Soho. Or perhaps this was where they intended to be all along, making their way to a strip club to expense their sordid activities on their corporate credit card. They were definitely bankers, Allie could tell from the way they dressed and the entitled manner in which they walked the street. It reminded her of Dominic's colleagues, and she took an angry swig from her glass.

That one, she thought to herself. *That one in the lead. With his pink shirt and expensive-looking loafers, he's the one I'd kill off first.* Allie was startled by this train of thought and looked around her, hoping that she hadn't actually said any of this out loud. But the pub was as quiet and sleepy as it had been before murderous thoughts had infiltrated her brain. Satisfied that she hadn't caught the attention of anyone in the pub, Allie turned back to her people-watching and wondered just how her murderer would do it. And who would be next on his list. By the time Jess walked in thirty-five minutes later Allie had worked out a central cast plus a few supporting characters along with the opening scene. She was beginning to wonder what Martin was making all that fuss about. Crime writing seemed to be easy.

'Hey you,' Jess greeted her, sliding into the bench alongside Allie and kissing both her cheeks. Jess's silky brown bob had, as was traditional, defied the weather. Allie did a brief pat of it and sighed as she tried to park her inevitable jealousy over just how it was possible that hair could look this good when it was ninety-eight per cent humidity outside and her own waves just turned to frizz. 'Don't touch the hair, bitch,' hissed Jess, making Allie laugh. 'I spent a small fortune on this at lunchtime and it will be ruined by the morning.'

'Seriously?' Allie narrowed her gaze and studied Jess's hair. 'It looks … exactly the same as it always looks.' Allie gulped. 'Amazing, that is,' she quickly added, noticing the savage look on Jess's face.

'Only you could get away with that.' Jess picked up Allie's wine glass and took a large sip, a tax for Allie's perceived slight. 'All the Gen Zs have been raving about this new blow dry bar.' Jess ran her hand through her bob. 'Thought I'd give it a go, try to keep up with the youth, y'know?' Allie smirked, Jess was constantly bitching and moaning about her co-workers but was secretly more happy and fulfilled in her job than a thirty-something corporate Londoner had any right to be. She had put her language degree to precisely no good use and ended up working at an advertising and design agency where, as far as Allie could make out, she spent her days terrifying and inspiring the junior staff, cadging freebies and getting promoted about every six months.

'So how was last night?' Jess asked on her return from the bar. She dumped most of the bottle of sauvignon she had been carrying into her own glass, before offering what was left to Allie.

'It was OK.' Allie scrunched her nose up hoping her response would be enough for Jess and knowing that, of course, it wouldn't be.

'What's OK mean?' Jess asked sharply, tipping her glass back and swallowing a frighteningly large amount of the contents in one go. 'Did you talk to Verity?'

'Yes.'

Jess gave her a pointed look. 'And did *talking* to her cover the topic of you not being able to write a new book?'

'Not exactly.'

'And not exactly means you covered the broad outline and Verity is on board and happy to help? Or you said nothing and dodged the topic entirely?'

'The latter,' Allie admitted in a small voice.

'Al!' admonished Jess. 'You said you were going to talk to her!'

'I was!' protested Allie, 'but then she made me meet this terrifying new publisher who I think wants to cancel my contract.'

'Riiight. And do you think not delivering a new book is going to make it more or less likely that he wants to cancel? Hmm?'

'More,' admitted Allie in the tone of a scolded child. 'But I do have to go in for a meeting sometime soon so I promise I'll talk to Verity then.'

'And is this promise more or less likely to be kept than the promise you made me that you'd talk to Verity last night?'

'Jess,' moaned Allie, 'you're making me feel bad.'

'Good. I'm only looking out for you. So how was the rest of the party?'

'Well, I met a hot waiter and a washed-up crime writer.'

'OK,' said Jess. 'Which one shall we start with then?'

Allie screwed up one eye and regarded her friend. 'Hot waiter?'

Jess raised her glass. 'Exactly what I was thinking.'

'But there's not much to say. I mean he was gorgeous and friendly but it's not like I'll ever see him again and, anyway, he's probably got a girlfriend.'

'Yep, and you have a boyfriend,' Jess reminded her.

'Oh yeah, about that...' Allie continued. 'Dominic dumped me last night.'

'What?' Jess's face creased in concern, her forehead wrinkling in exactly the sort of way that would make her ask Allie if she ought to get Botox. 'He dumped you?' Allie nodded. 'Last night?'

Allie nodded again. 'He was waiting for me when I got home from the party and yeah, he just ended it.'

'Oh, Al, I'm sorry. Are you OK?' Jess put her arm around Allie and squeezed her.

'Yeah, I'm fine.' Allie rubbed her face and quickly stopped, not wanting to end up with mascara and bronzer smeared everywhere. 'Honestly, Jess, I'm surprisingly fine,' Allie said. 'I mean it's not like I wouldn't have dumped him, too. I just hadn't got around to it yet.'

Jess narrowed her eyes. Allie knew how Jess felt about Dominic. But no matter any of that, she hoped Jess would understand it was never pleasant to be dumped, to find out you're surplus to requirements.

'Actually, what really sucked was when he left.'

'Why?'

'I went to look out the window and saw him getting into the car of his new girlfriend.'

'What?' Jess exploded.

'She drives a better car than I do, so maybe that's why he dumped me.'

'Allie,' Jess said sagely, 'you don't drive.'

'Exactly.'

'Surely he can't be that stupid. Maybe it was his Uber?'

Allie raised her eyebrow and looked at Jess. 'Tell me honestly if you've ever kissed an Uber driver on the lips as you got into the front seat of their car.'

Jess looked up at the ceiling and flushed slightly. 'Actually, there was this one time…'

Allie held up her hand to cut Jess off. She remembered and didn't need to be reminded of it, or of their long walk home after the Uber driver had subsequently refused to drive them and given Jess such a bad rating that for months she had had to use black cabs. 'Dominic was sober, you were not.'

'Well, he's an arsehole. I always said he was an arsehole.'

'No, you didn't,' Allie replied indignantly.

'Not to you maybe,' Jess bristled, 'I was trying to be supportive.'

Allie looked down at her drink. 'Is he though?' she pondered. 'An arsehole, I mean? Or is he just deeply disappointing?' She exhaled. 'I'm already looking back and wondering what I was thinking when we started dating. I just, I guess, I feel like I've lost my way a bit, do you know what I mean?' Jess nodded her head supportively. 'I feel like a romance writer ought to be better at picking boyfriends.' Jess stifled a giggle. 'No, it's OK, it's fine to laugh. It's stupid, isn't it?' Allie smiled wanly. 'But what if this is all connected? What if I can't write because I can't find my Mr Right? What if I'm doomed to a life of mediocre lovers and blank pages?'

Jess considered this. 'I think that's unlikely. I definitely think you deserve better than Dominic, and all the other ones. Hey, speaking of which, hot waiter from last night? Maybe some action with him will get you over Dominic and back into that writing groove?' She waggled her eyebrows suggestively, making Allie laugh. She much preferred Jess's take on the situation, than the 'told you so' she feared she would get from Martha.

'You're thinking about him, aren't you!' crowed Jess, seeing the smile on Allie's face.

'Maybe?' Allie gave her a sly sideways grin. 'I mean, he *was* really hot. But as I'll probably never see him again, there's no point in thinking about him. Unless... I can *use* him as inspiration for a new book.' A smirk played about her lips.

'Eww!' Jess protested. 'If you do, please tell me because I will NOT be reading that section.'

'Prude,' said Allie, swatting Jess's arm, safe in the knowledge that, of course, Jess would be reading whatever Allie wrote, because firstly she loved to dissect the sex scenes, and, secondly she was Allie's greatest and most vocal fan. Allie just needed to write a new book for her to fangirl over.

Jess leaned forward on the table, putting her chin in her hands. 'Couldn't you ask someone at Brinkman's about him?'

'Seriously?' Allie asked, incredulous. 'What part of how behind on deadline I am did you not understand? Do you really think anyone there wants to hear from me other than if I'm sending in my new book?'

Jess stretched back up from the table. 'They might if you fessed up. Told them you can't write but that you think a date with the hot waiter might get your creative juices flowing.' She gave Allie a wink.

'Jess!' protested Allie. 'Now who's being crude?'

Jess tipped her head back and laughed. The very act of seeing her bestie laugh so loudly made Allie do the same, a surge of love for her friend forcing out all her dark thoughts.

'You know, sometimes, when you make me laugh like this, I wonder why I ever bother with dating. I'd much rather be out with you, than on a second-rate date with a disappointing man.'

'Only sometimes?' Jess joked. She raised her glass. 'To my greatest love, to us!'

Allie's heart squeezed tightly and she felt the prick of tears in her eyes. 'Idiot,' she said, brushing her fingers under her eyes, wiping away the tears before her mascara ran. 'Don't let Tom hear you say that,' she said warningly.

'Oh he knows. I've always been completely upfront with him. You and Timothee Chalamet beat him every time.'

'Glad you have standards. Where do I rank against Timothee?' Allie asked.

'Don't push your luck, Edwards,' growled Jess. Allie laughed, she'd take that. It wasn't as if she expected to get upstaged by Chalamet anytime soon.

'Where is Tom anyway?' Allie asked, glancing at her watch.

'God knows. Working late. They've got a new artist they need to pitch to and apparently they're the next big thing.'

'Doesn't he say that every time?'

Jess nodded and sipped her wine. 'Yup. But there's no point telling him that. He truly believes it, until the next big thing comes along.' Jess turned to Allie and pulled a horror-stricken face. 'D'you reckon that's what he's doing with me? Waiting for a better, younger, less in need of Botox, version to come along?' She pulled her cheeks back and up and pushed her face up close to Allie.

'Don't be an idiot.' Allie pushed Jess away, laughing. 'Tom is far too scared of me to dump you,' she laughed.

'I think you're right. Maybe you're the only reason we're still together?'

'Oh shut up!' Allie protested.

There was a kernel of truth here. Jess and Tom had met through Allie, Allie and Tom having been next-door neighbours when they were growing up. They'd done all the usual stuff: play dates and sleepovers and getting locked in the shed by Tom's slightly psychotic older brother. Playing naked in the paddling pool before getting to the age where they quickly pretended that this had never happened and in fact they didn't actually know each other at all.

Allie had lost touch with Tom over the years. Around Christmas time she'd get an update from her mum who still exchanged Christmas cards with Tom's parents. But she didn't pay him much mind, still dealing with unresolved trauma from interactions with his older brother. And then, completely out of the blue, several years ago, Tom had turned up at one of her book signings. It was in a bookshop, just around the corner from his office. He had seen her name in the window and wondered if it was the same Allie Edwards with whom he used to skinny dip in the paddling pool, and so there he was, stood in front of her asking her to sign his book.

And what an amazing meet-cute that would have been if Allie had been even remotely attracted to Tom. But she wasn't. And the feeling was mutual. Which was fine because it turned out that when Allie introduced them to each other in a pub a few nights later, Tom and Jess couldn't keep their hands off each other. Allie had left them to it after the second drink, preferring to go home and watch Netflix, rather than the sex show that was unfolding in front of her eyes. And now here they were, six years later and married for the past three.

Allie had been both bridesmaid and best man at their wedding, which had confused Tom's terribly traditional parents, but as his brother couldn't set foot in the country at that time due to some legal mix-up, which Tom didn't want to go into and Allie was happy not to explore as it brought up memories of traumatic childhood incidents, there wasn't an obvious alternative to best man. And so Allie had stood in on the understanding that she have complete creative control over what she wore. It wasn't that she didn't trust Jess's taste, which was usually impeccable. But Allie knew what happened to women when they planned a wedding and quite often taste and perspective were thrown to the winds.

'Will he be here later?' Allie asked.

Jess shrugged. 'Not sure. Last night he didn't get home till after nine and I don't know about the night before because I was already asleep.'

Allie looked at her watch again and thought that the chances of her still standing in three hours' time were pretty slim if Jess was going to keep topping her glass up.

'So what's the goss with Verity then? Have you met Richard yet?' Jess didn't really know Verity, but Allie talked about her editor a lot and Jess had become strangely invested in this new relationship of hers.

'Nope, not yet. She's stopped suggesting it. Probably because I haven't sent her a book yet.'

'Ha! So she's mad at you then?'

'No.' Allie paused. 'It's not that exactly, although she'd

have every right to be mad. She seemed quite hyper last night to be honest. Desperate to read anything I could send her and terrified of her new boss.'

'Sounds like an excellent combination.' Jess grinned. 'Big question being, have you got *anything* at all you can send her?'

Allie shook her head. 'Nope, nada.'

'Not a rehash of an earlier idea? Not something you can find in the back of that distressingly tatty notebook you still use?'

Allie shook her head again. She paused and then said, her voice wobbling slightly, 'Jess, what if I can't write anymore?'

Jess looked surprised. 'Come on, of course you'll write again,' she said encouragingly, reaching out and rubbing Allie's arm. 'Remember with your second book where you didn't write anything for two whole months?'

'Yes, but then it all came pouring out and I wrote the whole first draft in a few weeks. And it's different, then I had the plot, I just didn't know how to write it. Now I have no plot and I haven't written anything in months.' Allie took a long swig of her wine.

Jess grimaced. 'OK, not good, I get it. So let's make a plan? I really think you should tell Verity. It's no good hiding from her and secretly panicking.' Jess had a worried expression on her face.

'I did promise that I would email her with my plot outline this week.'

Jess looked confused. 'I thought you said...'

'Exactly, no plot to send!' Allie spread her empty hands out in front of her. She groaned. 'I know, you're right. I will tell her. I'll do it at our meeting, face to face.' She looked at Jess for reassurance.

'That's good! Definitely talk to her, face to face. She's on your side, remember, we all are.' Jess looked pleased to have solved the crisis. 'Shall we get another one?' She waved the now empty bottle at Allie who grimaced slightly, feeling the sour wine settling hard in her stomach.

'Can we get some food first?'

'Do we have to?' Jess looked reluctantly round at the fast-filling pub. 'We have a table here, and seats?' She looked imploringly at Allie. 'Aren't those better than food?'

Allie rolled her eyes. 'And not having a hangover is better than having one. Especially when I need to write tomorrow.'

Jess pouted. 'But how will Tom know where to find us?'

'Jess' snapped Allie, 'we have these things called mobile phones.' She picked hers up off the table and waggled it in Jess's face. 'And anyway, you said yourself he probably won't make it. Come on, please?' Allie's voice took on a plaintive tone. 'I need to write tomorrow, I can't do that with a hangover.'

'It sounds like you can't write at all at the moment, hungover or not.'

'Hey! Not fair.' Allie was genuinely hurt and Jess, clearly realising she had probably overplayed her hand and admitting defeat, sighed and picked her coat up from the back of her chair, huffing and puffing as she did so.

'You'll thank me tomorrow,' Allie said smugly as they made their way to the door. Jess didn't look convinced as she glanced sadly back over her shoulder to see their table immediately swarmed by drinkers in desperate need of a seat.

Chapter Four

Allie sat nervously in the glass-roofed atrium of the Brinkman's building and tried not to bite her nails. She'd been here before, of course, but not without a book in her metaphorical back pocket. For several days Allie had been dutifully getting up at the crack of dawn, turning her phone off, disconnecting the wifi and trying to write.

It hadn't gone well. Yesterday, before breakfast, she had teased out minor plot lines from earlier novels, trying to work out if they could play out over a full-length novel. Before she allowed herself even a coffee she had mined the depths of her memories for terrible dates that could be the starting point for a meet cute. By 11am she had turned her wifi back on so she could google celebrity news to see if there was anything that might spark her imagination. And that had resulted in a tumble down the rabbit hole of the *Daily Mail* sidebar of shame. She was going for love hearts and breathless whisperings and instead she just kept coming back to the idea she had had in the pub the other night: that brief outline of a drunken corporate pub crawl that ended in murder. Thinking it better to have that than nothing and hoping that Verity might have a brilliant idea of how to flip this dark story into a rom-com, this was what she had brought and she grasped her notebook containing it to her chest as she sat and waited.

It was quiet in the atrium, all the doors leading off into the offices were closed and Allie was the only person waiting. Time was ticking slowly and Allie could hear the rumbling of her stomach, which seemed to echo off the walls; she was regretting being too nervous to consume anything more than a mug of tea that morning.

A door opened into the atrium, the sound from the offices beyond briefly filtering out into the open space before being cut off abruptly as the door swung shut. Allie looked up, and to her surprise, saw Martin Clark, the crime writer she had met at the party being shown out.

'Thanks for coming in, we'll be in touch,' the Brinkman's' employee was saying as Martin walked out. Allie couldn't catch Martin's response but from the tone it sounded about as upbeat as he had been the other night. She caught his eye and he did a double take. For a second Allie wondered whether to remind him they'd met or whether just to let him walk on out, back to his life or wherever he intended to head after his meeting. But the decision was taken out of her hands.

'Allie, right?'

Allie was taken aback, she didn't expect him to remember her. To him, the bestselling novelist, she was just someone he had met in a slightly strange circumstance at a party one night. But then she remembered that she, too, was a bestselling novelist, or at least had been, just like Martin Clark, and she silently told her imposter syndrome to go do one.

She stood up. 'Yes, hi!'

He nodded and put his hand out to shake hers. 'Futile to

say funny to see you, as we have already established that we're both published by or...' He cleared his throat. 'At least *were* published by Brinkman's.'

Allie bristled at his comment but chose to let it slide. 'How was your meeting?' she asked politely.

Martin ran his hand through his greying hair and looked back towards the door he had just come through. He then glanced over Allie's shoulder at the receptionist who was doing a brilliant impression of not listening in on their conversation. He took Allie's elbow, led her to the side and said in a quiet voice, 'It was with that Jake Matthews character. The one we spoke about?' Allie nodded, she didn't need reminding about him.

'I expect yours will be too,' he went on.

Allie looked confused. 'No, I don't think so, I'm meeting my editor, Verity, today.'

Martin looked at her, his eyes flashing under his greying bushy eyebrows. 'Well, don't say I didn't warn you.'

Allie frowned, recalling Jake's words at the party the other night. He had mentioned Verity setting up a meeting, hadn't he? But Verity hadn't mentioned that this meeting was with anyone else, and surely Verity wouldn't spring a Jake Matthews shaped surprise on her? A door swung open into the atrium and a girl in her early twenties said, 'Allie? Allie Edwards?'

A feeling descended on Allie, the sort of feeling one got before an unpleasant medical procedure, and her stomach churned. Allie turned. 'Yes?'

'I'm Tessa, Jake's assistant,' the girl said. 'Would you like to come through?'

Allie looked back at Martin in consternation. He gave her a

sympathetic look and said, 'I'll be over the road.' And pointed at a cafe across the street.

Allie didn't reply, allowing herself to be led down the corridors and into the lair of Jake Matthews, wishing that she was about to have that painful medical procedure instead. Tessa chattered away as they walked, asking Allie about her morning, if she had come far, whether she had enjoyed the summer party. At the mention of the party something clicked in Allie's brain, memories of being stuck in the bathroom listening to two other guests indulge in something potentially less than legal. Allie snuck a sideways look at Tessa. She hadn't seen either of the two people in the bathroom but she had heard both their voices, and she was becoming increasingly sure, as Tessa continued to talk, that the female voice belonged to none other than Tessa. Despite the situation, Allie smirked to herself. She probably wouldn't choose to share this with Verity who would disapprove of this kind of behaviour, but she would definitely be storing this information away for future reference.

'Here we are,' Tessa said. For a split second, lost in her thoughts of the bathroom incident, Allie looked down expecting to see Tessa offering her a line of coke, before realising that she was merely holding the door open to one of the meeting rooms.

'Thanks, erm, Tessa,' Allie said, smiling briefly at the girl and making her way into the room where Verity was waiting for her. Allie smiled in relief, her anxieties melting away. She knew it, there'd been some mistake, this was just a standard meeting with her editor, nothing to worry about. But Verity had a strange look on her face, a look that could have been indigestion but was more likely awkwardness and guilt and

Allie was sure she was mouthing something that looked an awful lot like 'sorry'.

'Allie,' came a voice from behind her. 'Thank you for joining us.'

Allie felt a shudder run down her spine. She looked at Verity and grimaced. Almost imperceptibly Verity shook her head. Allie turned and came face to face with Jake Matthews. He extended his hand towards her and unwillingly she took it, marvelling that his palm was as icy cold as his demeanour, which just about cancelled out the clamminess of her own hand.

'Jake,' she managed to say without shuddering. 'Pleasure to be here,' she forced out the lie.

'Sit, please.' Jake gesticulated to one of the chairs in the room and Allie had the distinct feeling that she was being instructed in just the way that Jake would instruct his dog, if he was human enough to even own a dog, which he almost certainly wasn't. Allie's eyes flickered to the left wondering if she should defy his instructions and pick her own chair in which to sit. It wasn't as if there weren't other chairs in the meeting room, she didn't *have* to sit in the one Jake told her to. He didn't own her. Except he did, and Allie knew it, and he knew it too. Reluctantly she sank into the chair Jake had offered her as he smiled his cold, cold smile. Jake sat opposite her and pulled his chair right up to the table, resting his hands carefully on the glass tabletop. Allie tilted her head, fascinated to see whether his palms would leave an imprint; she would put money on them not.

For a moment Verity hovered, looking unsure where she should sit until Jake wordlessly picked one hand up off the table and pointed at the chair next to him. Verity sat down on the edge of the seat, refusing to lift her eyes to meet Allie's.

'So, as I said, thank you for coming in.' Allie opened her mouth to respond but Jake continued. 'I'm sure you're aware that publishing has been facing a series of challenges over the past few years, it can't have escaped you that everyone's earnings have dropped in recent times.'

Verity looked up at this point and interjected. 'Actually Allie's sales have held up really well, better than other authors, in fact—'

Jake held his hand up, obviously not interested in Verity's assessment of the state of Allie's royalty statements. A flicker of irritation crossed his face. 'As I was saying, in light of these challenges we have had to make certain strategic decisions to streamline the business and make it a more efficient revenue stream for the shareholders.'

Allie stared at him blankly, wondering if he was really talking about books or if he had wandered in from the world of investment banking as this sounded frighteningly like the waffle she had sometimes had to listen to Dominic spout when she overheard him on the phone. She idly wondered what he was doing right now. She hadn't heard from him since he'd left and at some point she should probably contact him and ask him if she could collect her belongings from his flat. She was just trying to remember what she had actually left there – a toothbrush definitely, her old hairdryer, probably some underwear? Did she really need any of those things back? In actual fact, she probably never had to speak to Dominic again and she didn't know whether to feel cheered or depressed by this fact.

'Allie?' Jake's stern tones interrupted her thoughts.

'Yes?' Allie sat up straighter, feeling like she had just been caught daydreaming in school.

'I was explaining about what needs to happen with your new book after Verity hands over the reins.'

'Yes, exactly. Wait, what?' Allie's jaw dropped, and her horrorstruck face went from Jake to Verity. The realization of what Jake had just said was sinking in. Deep down, Allie knew that this day would come, it wasn't as if she had expected Verity to stay at Brinkman's forever, although she had harboured a hope. But she really hadn't expected it to be when she was still under contract and with no book to deliver. Or that she would be left in this nightmare scenario with a snake-like Jake Matthews in charge of her creative future. 'You're leaving?' she stammered, her eyes fixing on Verity.

'Well...' Verity's face was a picture of distress, her eyes watery with tears, her lip wobbling. Allie wanted nothing more than to leap over the table and hug her beloved editor, but she had a very real fear that Jake Matthews might stab her if she did.

Jake interrupted. 'Happily, Verity has found a new role and while we are sad to see her go it does of course make things easier with the streamlining process.'

'You're leaving Brinkman's?' Allie stuttered again. 'You're leaving *me*?' Even though Allie had suspected this was on the cards she couldn't help the feeling of abandonment and tears pricked the back of her eyes.

Verity's face crumpled. 'I'm so sorry, Allie,' she whispered.

'Well, now that this is all out in the open, we can discuss delivery of your new book.'

Allie turned to look at Jake, who was blithely unaware of the emotional trauma that was unravelling right under his nose.

'Now,' Jake began, 'I understand you're quite behind with delivery.'

Allie glared at him. 'Actually, it was agreed that I would take some time off because, as I'm sure you know, I've been writing a book a year for seven years.'

Jake didn't look as if he really cared what Allie had been doing or not doing for the past seven minutes, let alone years. 'We have an agreed date, don't we?'

'Yes.' Allie nodded mutinously.

'Good. Well, that's fine then, I will expect it on or before that date.'

Allie felt like she had just been issued with a homework deadline by the teacher consistently voted 'most hated', rather than treated as an equitable adult in a work meeting.

Jake stood up and despite the shocking news that she was still digesting, Allie couldn't help checking the glass tabletop in front of him for handprints. Nope, definitely no handprints, probably not warm-blooded enough to produce any, Allie thought darkly.

'I think you've met my assistant Tessa.' As if on cue the door to the meeting room opened and there stood Tessa, Stepford Wives smile fixed to her face. 'She'll see you out.'

Before Allie could register what was happening, Tessa was ushering her out of the door.

'Wait,' Allie called over her shoulder, 'can I have a quick word with Verity?'

'I'm afraid Verity has another meeting to get to,' Tessa said smoothly, closing the meeting door with one hand and using the other to ever so gently, yet insistently, push Allie out towards the atrium.

'Please do send your manuscript to me,' she told Allie, putting a business card in one of Allie's hands, while she propelled her towards the revolving doors at the front of the building. 'Well, have a lovely rest of your day,' Tessa said as she gave Allie a little shove, which sent her through the revolving doors and out into the street. It felt like a practised move.

For a minute, Allie stood blinking in the sunlight wondering whether what had just happened had, in fact, been a hallucination. She reached into her bag, fumbled around for her phone, pulled it out and scrolled down for Verity's number. She hit dial and put the phone to her ear. There was a long silence before the computer-generated voice told her that this number was no longer in use. Allie slowly took the phone away from her ear and stared down at the screen. Had they taken Verity's phone away from her already? Allie remembered the cold eyes of Jake Matthews and decided that they almost certainly had.

Allie looked back into the atrium of Brinkman's and considered marching back in there, demanding to talk to Verity, not taking no for an answer. And then she heard Jake's voice echo round her head and her stomach turned to water. If she had a killer manuscript to deliver then she might have the guts to go rescue Verity and tell Jake he could go stuff himself. But the only thing she had was the outline of her serial killer novel, and she thought that put her on distinctly shaky ground with regard to any bargaining. Allie's thoughts turned to her *killer* manuscript and she found herself thinking of elaborate ways in which Jake Matthews might meet a grisly end. She looked up and saw the cafe over the road, remembered Martin Clark's invitation and stalked angrily across the road to hear how his meeting with Jake had gone down.

'Wasn't sure you'd take me up on the offer,' Martin said, half rising out of his chair. Allie merely nodded, not trusting herself to say anything yet.

Chapter Five

Allie hadn't intended to go and meet Martin after her meeting and she certainly hadn't intended to stay in the cafe for as long as she had. But it turned out that Martin was surprisingly good company, especially in the aftermath of the devastating news about Verity's departure. Periodically Allie would stare at her phone hoping that Verity would call her and when her phone remained blank she felt a horrible mix of sadness and nausea.

And Martin seemed to get it because whenever he noticed Allie looking miserably at her phone he would launch into another publishing anecdote, which was helping to take her mind off the predicament she found herself in. He had just finished telling her about the time he had witnessed a fist fight break out between a Booker prize winning novelist and a disgraced ex-politician, Allie was beginning to suspect that his stories might not be a hundred percent true, when her phone rang. Allie's hand shot out to pick it up.

'Is it her?' Martin asked, sitting forward in his seat, fully invested.

Allie appreciated his enthusiasm but shook her head. 'No, it's a friend. Another author actually. I bet she's calling to remind me it's her book launch tonight.' Allie let out a big sigh and put her phone back down. 'I promised I'd go but to be honest I'd rather be anywhere but around publishing people right now.'

'Thanks.' Martin grimaced as he sat back and crossed his arms.

'Sorry, I didn't mean…'

'It's fine, I was joking. I understand.' Martin watched her keenly across the table. 'Do you want my opinion?'

Allie shrugged, out of any other options. 'Sure.'

'I think you should go tonight.' Allie started shaking her head but Martin pressed ahead. 'Look, it's always good to keep in with your contacts. And you never know where inspiration might strike. Could be tonight.'

Allie raised her eyebrow, wondering exactly how long it had been since Martin had been invited to a launch party. It was no longer excessive drinking, fights between authors and dangerous liaisons in the cloakroom. Although she thought back to her inappropriate thoughts about Will, the waiter, outside the cloakroom at the V&A and how hard she had been wishing for any kind of liaison. She flushed slightly at the memory.

Martin noticed the look on her face and smiled. 'OK, well, what else are you going to do if you don't go this evening?'

'Write a novel?' Allie parried.

'Fair point. And remind me how the new one is coming along?'

Allie frowned. 'Alright, point taken, I'll go to the party.' Martin looked rather smug. 'Anyway, if you're so full of advice on what I should be doing now, tell me what your plan is?'

Allie didn't intend to sound quite so belligerent but she managed it anyway. 'Sorry,' she apologised. 'But seriously, what are you planning to do?'

'Offer to buy you another cup of tea in the hope I can put off staring at a blank piece of paper for a little longer?'

Allie laughed. 'Sounds familiar. I'll get these ones.' She went to the counter to order more drinks and by the time she came back Martin looked like he was having a bad break-up conversation with his phone.

'You OK?' she asked tentatively, sliding his requested cup of Earl Grey across the table to him. Really, she felt that Martin ought to be nursing a single malt whisky in an old pub in the city, not sitting across from her in a bright, modern cafe with a view of the Tate Modern. But this was where she had found him, and Earl Grey was what he had requested. He raised his shadowed eyes to look at her then slammed his phone down on the table. Allie winced and hoped he wasn't going to have to add 'get phone fixed' to his list of things to do.

'My daughter, causing problems again.' He sighed and ran his hands through his grizzled hair. It was mainly grey now and his face was much more lined than the author photo Allie remembered seeing years back. Still, she could see that he had once been a handsome man. Probably still was if you were in the market for a (significantly) older man. Allie's thoughts flicked briefly to her friend Louise who didn't think a man worth dating unless he was at least two decades older than her. Which was sort of fine now that she was in her thirties but had been incredibly creepy when they were teenagers.

Allie smiled in what she hoped was a supportive manner. 'You told me you had kids the other night, warned me never to have any!'

'Did I?' Martin sounded bemused. 'Yes, I probably did. But

don't let me put you off. My son is no bother at all, owns his own business, far more successful than I am.'

Allie wrinkled her nose. 'Don't worry, chances of me becoming a mother anytime soon are slim to none.' Martin raised an eyebrow quizzically. 'I got dumped recently,' she confessed, 'actually, right after I met you at the party and that waiter showed me out.'

Martin looked puzzled. 'That waiter? Oh right, yes.' He looked as if he was going to say something else and then paused. 'You got dumped that night?' He sounded genuinely upset by this news.

Allie nodded and smiled sadly.

'Well, I am sorry to hear that. I guess that's not a storyline which is going to feature in your new book?'

Allie laughed. 'No, although I had been worried that someone might discover what a disappointment my love life was and out me as a romance writer who knows nothing about love. Dominic, my boyfriend… my ex-boyfriend,' she corrected herself, 'was not exactly leading man material.'

'Right. And the reason you stayed with him was?'

'Inertia mainly.' Allie paused and picked her mug up. 'To be honest, I don't know,' she continued. 'God, why am I telling you this?'

'Because I'm here and I asked?' Martin shrugged and Allie found herself warming to him, wanting to tell him about Dominic and about her writing. Because he didn't really know her and he came to her situation with no prior knowledge, no expectations for how she ought to behave or knowledge of what she had done in the past. She didn't owe him anything, after this cup of tea she might never see him again, and there was something very freeing in that knowledge.

'I guess I was attracted to him at the start. I mean, why else does anyone ever date someone. Actually,' she paused, 'forget I said that, there are SO many reasons people date other than mutual attraction.' Martin smiled wryly. 'But it also seemed like the sort of thing I ought to be doing in my thirties,' she continued, 'you know, get boyfriend? Settle down? How old were you when you met your wife?'

'We met at university. Been together ever since.'

'Exactly!' replied Allie enthusiastically. 'That's what people are supposed to do, isn't it? And if you're in your thirties and writing romance novels and don't have a boyfriend yourself your readers are going to think you're weird, aren't they?'

Martin shrugged. 'Not being a woman in my thirties and not being so au fait with the genre, I'm not sure I'm the right person to ask. Couldn't you write a novel about the struggle of finding real love?' His face suddenly lit up and he looked incredibly thrilled at his own suggestion, which meant that Allie really didn't have the heart to tell him that this was exactly what most romances were about, but that they also needed to have a happy ever after and that's where she was failing. She had no problem writing about the trials and tribulations of hunting for love, although she was struggling to put a jocular, light-hearted spin on the storylines – it was getting her characters to their happy ever after that was proving so elusive.

'Actually, I think Dominic might have inspired me to start writing a completely different genre. The other night, I was sitting in a pub in Soho, waiting to meet a friend and killing time by people-watching. A group of bankers walked past and before I knew it I had concocted half a plot about a serial revenge killer, out to pick off the corrupt bankers one by one.'

Martin smiled and said, 'That actually sounds rather intriguing, do you have more?'

'Well, I thought it could start with a pub crawl that gets gradually more and more debauched and over the course of the evening the bankers get picked off one by one. And the killer could be some crusader, out to bring down the corrupt banking system and expose fraud and general bad behaviour.' Allie waited, thinking that she may have actually lost her mind. She was sitting here sharing some half-baked idea about a serial killer with a writer who had made his name writing some of the bloodiest crime books of the 1990s.

'It's clever,' Martin eventually said. 'Nobody likes bankers, which gets you around the thorny subject of killing off popular characters. The only problem is you then have a sympathetic killer and publishers sometimes baulk at condoning murder.'

Allie shrugged. 'What about *Killing Eve*? No one felt sorry for all the bastards Villanelle killed.'

Martin looked thoughtful. 'Point taken.'

'So, what do you think my chances are of persuading Jake "Iceman" Matthews that I should change genres now?'

Martin grimaced, visibly pained at the idea of having to engage with Jake Matthews on any level.

'Tell you what,' she grinned suddenly, 'if I can't persuade him that I should be allowed to switch genres, you can take my banking serial killer and run with it. But you'll need to swap it for some romantic plot lines that I can work with instead.'

Martin looked horrified. 'I really don't think...' he stammered.

'Oh, come on,' she teased, 'you're happily married. Two kids. That's the goal in all these rom coms, isn't it? You must have secrets you can share on how to reach a happy-ever-after.' She ignored the look on Martin's face, which was screaming that he would rather be talking about anything other than his secrets for a happy marriage. But Allie was suddenly inspired, energised by Martin's praise for her plot and keen to get some nuggets in return. 'Come on, tell me about your wife,' she asked, intrigued by who Martin Clark might be married to. She had the feeling that being the wife of a hard-boiled thriller writer might be quite hard work, what with the writer's block, plot twists and heavy drinking to contend with.

'Angie?' Martin said, his face visibly softening as he said her name. 'She's amazing. She's the reason I ever had any success with my writing.' And there it was, Allie thought, the supportive wife dutifully standing behind the creative maestro.

'She's the smartest woman I know.' He looked down at the table and then out of the window. 'Brilliant mind. Funny as hell, warm, kind. She forged her own career, solid, dependable, well-paid roles so that I could sit at home and work out how to murder people.' He laughed suddenly at the shocked look on Allie's face. 'Come on,' he teased, 'I can normally only get away with telling that joke to people who don't know what I do for a living!'

Allie smiled tentatively, still thrown by the curveball revelation about Martin's wife, who sounded anything but the stay-at-home stalwart Allie had been expecting. 'But yes, Angie,' Martin continued, 'she's brilliant, hugely successful in her field, an expert, esteemed professor of epidemiology. But really she has the heart and voice of a jazz singer. And that's what she should have been, if I had been the one to go out and get a sensible job.' He looked down at his hands and Allie was momentarily terrified he might start crying. And if he did then this was not the pick-me-up cup of tea she had been hoping for when she had crashed into the cafe reeling over Jake Matthews' betrayal.

Allie wasn't sure what to say. 'She sounds great.'

'Not what you were expecting?' Martin looked up at her with a wry expression on his face.

'No, not really,' she confessed. 'Do you think she minds? That she gave up her dream so that you could pursue yours?'

'I don't think so, no. I think it was actually my dream, I don't think she had any real interest in becoming a jazz singer, although she loves to sing any chance she gets.' Martin got a wistful faraway look in his eyes. 'She's the pragmatist and I'm the one who always has my head in the clouds. And she blames me for our daughter being the same way. Actually, that's not fair, she doesn't blame me for that. She blames me for mollycoddling our daughter and pandering to her, and I can completely accept the blame for that.'

'Oh.' Allie was wondering if she was too far into this conversation to pretend she had a prior important engagement but also rather intrigued to know what revelations Martin was going to make next. This was far more interesting than a literary punch-up from decades back, although she still worried that Martin might start crying.

'So, what's up with your daughter then?' she asked, deciding that it was worth the threat of tears to hear exactly what went down in the marriage and home life of the great Martin Clark.

Martin pulled a face. 'Don't get me wrong, Angie adores both our kids but she's always thought I was soft on our daughter and it's true, as I did most of the childcare when the kids were little, I probably spoiled her more than I should. Gave into her demands when I should have stood up to her. Which was manageable when she was a little girl, but now she's a grown woman and doesn't seem to know how to stand on her own two feet.' Martin looked out the cafe window. 'Despite being incredibly smart, just like her mother, she's never held down a job for any length of time and is completely reliant on handouts from us.' He stopped and sighed. 'OK, full disclosure, she's reliant on handouts from me, which Angie doesn't know about.'

Allie's eyebrows shot up into her hairline.

'Yes. So, you can see why it's important I get this book written. I can't pay back the advance because my daughter has already spent it and Angie has absolutely no idea.' He looked up and caught Allie's eye, flushing at his confession.

Allie cringed for him. She could just imagine how dreadful that conversation would be. It was all terribly car crash, and Allie found herself inextricably drawn to the drama.

'So, what are you going to do?' she asked, starting to feel that Martin was actually in far more of a bind than she was. At least she hadn't given her advance away and didn't have to confess to doing so. She guiltily took some solace from this fact.

'Well, I know what I *should* do. Come clean to Angie and stop bailing out our daughter.'

'And will you?'

Martin stared back out the window looking morosely at the rain that had started to fall. He sighed deeply. 'Yes, I think I will this time. It's gone on too long and Angie deserves to know, before everyone else does.'

'How do you think she'll take it?' Allie asked.

'Badly,' he deadpanned and looked at Allie. 'Wouldn't you?'

'I guess so. Do you think you'll be able to fix it?'

Martin's shoulders slumped. 'God I really hope so. I can't imagine life without Angie. She's been my everything since the first moment I saw her. She's the only person I ever really want to talk to and I still find her endlessly fascinating even after all these years. And god she's beautiful, so beautiful. She has such presence and grace, the world is just a better place when she's around.'

Allie could feel her eyes well up with tears as Martin spoke. The way he spoke about his wife was so moving, maybe she needed to try and bottle these feelings, get them down on paper later on. See if they could actually inspire her to write.

'Wow,' she said after a pause. 'I mean, she sounds amazing Martin, she really does. I hope you can fix things.'

Martin smiled wanly across the table at Allie and they both sat in silence for a moment.

'Have you told her this?' Allie asked. 'The stuff you just told me, about how she's your everything, about how much you adore her?'

Martin waved his hand. 'No!' Seeing the look on Allie's face, he added, 'She'd just think I was being soppy.'

'Aren't you?'

'Well, yes,' Martin admitted, shuffling in his seat a little. 'But it's not like you actually *say* these things when you've been married as long as we have.'

'And how long is that?'

Martin looked up at the ceiling, obviously doing a mental calculation. 'Thirty-seven years, no, hang on, it must be thirty-eight. Our son is thirty-seven and he was born the year after we got married.' Allie made a mental note of the look that came over Martin's face and decided that if her future husband had that expression on his face when recalling their thirty-eight-year marriage, then she would be winning. Hell, if someone half-smiled after a second date right now she'd take that as an achievement.

She sat forward and put her hands on the table. 'I'm going to level with you, Martin.' Martin looked nervous. 'Firstly, I think you should always know exactly how many years you have been married,' she said slightly prissily. 'I don't know why men seem to find that so hard.' Martin had the sense to look a little ashamed. 'And secondly, this is exactly why you should tell her this! You shouldn't lose the romance just because you've been married for years. If the romance has gone, Martin, you need to get it back,' Allie exclaimed, 'before you lose her forever!'

Martin shifted back in his chair and looked alarmed, which was fair enough because Allie was fighting the urge to lean over the table, grab him by the lapels of his tweed (of course tweed!) jacket and shake him until he ran out of the cafe, all the way home and arrived on his doorstep, soaked through with rain and sweat, got down on one knee, declared his eternal love for the amazing Angie and begged to be allowed to renew his vows.

Instead, Allie took a deep breath and downed the last dregs of her tea, all the while staring across the table at Martin, daring him to defy her orders. Martin meanwhile looked as if he was starting to regret taking pity on this strange romance writer and inviting her for a cup of tea.

'Is this like the plot of one of your novels?' he asked tentatively.

Allie put her head on one side and considered it. 'It could be. Although I'd want you to win her back with grand romantic gestures, put the spark back in your marriage and fix the problem with your daughter too. Think that's possible?'

'Anything is possible within the pages of a book!' Martin said, smiling wryly at Allie who snapped, 'Martin, I am trying to fix your marriage!'

'I'm not sure I asked you to,' he snapped back grumpily.

'Sounds to me like you're trying to use my marriage as inspiration for your next book.'

They glared at each other across the table. An uncomfortable silence hung in the air before they both started speaking at once.

'Actually,' Allie began.

'I've had an idea,' Martin said.

They looked at each other, a smile creeping across both of their faces.

'Are you thinking what I'm thinking?' Martin asked.

'Yes!' exclaimed Allie. 'One hundred per cent! We should absolutely definitely have Jake Matthews kidnapped, lock him up somewhere and take over Brinkman's ourselves.'

'Oh.' Martin looked both shocked and crestfallen at the same time. Allie laughed. 'Sorry, I couldn't resist.'

Martin bristled. 'You're actually pretty funny, Allie Edwards,' he said grudgingly. 'I can see why your books are so successful.'

'And how would you know that?' It was Allie's turn to look shocked. 'You looked me up?'

'Of course. Isn't that what the internet was designed for?' Martin rolled his eyes. 'Thought you young people knew all about that.'

'Ha bloody ha,' Allie retorted and then paused. 'But going back to your idea...' She felt a delicious smile taking over her face.

Martin started smiling too. 'We could switch plots.'

'How would it work?' she asked.

'Well,' he began, 'you've already given me the outline of a plot – serial killer with a penchant for cleaning up the financial industry. And I'm guessing you've got more in your head than you told me?'

Allie nodded, not yet wanting to admit that she had mapped a lot of it out and that the demise of the bankers was especially grisly and gruesome, in particular the one who, in her head, would look like Dominic in the Netflix series.

Martin grinned. 'Thought you might. And *you've* given me some input on where I might be going wrong with Angie.' He gave Allie a look as if to say that some of her input wasn't altogether welcome. He sighed. 'What if I start thinking about some "grand romantic gestures" I could make?' – he said this as if describing some unspeakably unpleasant act – 'and then you see if there's a story there you can weave from?'

Allie could feel her creativity sparking back into life. Maybe this wasn't a totally crazy idea. Maybe she just needed a writing partner? She looked across the table at Martin; on paper, and if she had full control over her situation, she wouldn't have picked veteran thriller writer, Martin Clark. But maybe it could work? Their differences could only make each other stronger. Or some other life-affirming nonsense she might have heard on any one of the therapy podcasts she was always listening to.

'Have you ever had a writing partner before?' she asked.

'No, but then I've never been this far behind on a deadline before. Or in so much potential trouble with my wife.' He looked over at Allie. 'So I'm in if you are?'

Allie paused. She should really think about this. Maybe discuss it with Jess before she committed to anything. At least run it past Verity … and then she remembered that Verity was no longer a part of her writing life. Taking a deep breath and throwing caution, and any kind of previous good sense to the wind, she said, 'OK,' with far more conviction than she actually felt.

Martin's face lit up. 'You'll do it?'

'No, *we* will do it' Allie emphasised. 'I'm not just handing you my brilliant serial killer plot, I need something in return. You have to win Angie back, relight that fire, remember?'

'That sounded like something straight out of one of your books.'

'You *read* one of my books?' Allie felt her face flush. 'Wow, Martin,' she gushed. 'I mean googling me is one thing. But actually parting with cold hard cash to read one of my books? Now I'm flattered.'

'Don't get too full of yourself,' he frowned. 'I got it from the library.'

'Of course you did.' Allie couldn't stop herself from smiling.

'So now you've prised my shameful secret from me...'

'Not shameful, Martin. I will not have that. Be a proud reader of romance. My books will provide you with excellent research material,' Allie quipped.

'Alright,' he growled, 'moving on. How about we meet back here once a week? You can share some thoughts on my plot. I can give you some anecdotes from my life for yours. And then we give each other writing prompts to go away and work with before the next week? What's wrong?' he asked, seeing the look on Allie's face.

'Could we agree *not* to meet here?' Allie gesticulated to the office block over the road. 'I would rather not run the risk of seeing Jake Matthews each and every week unless I really have to.'

'Good point,' agreed Martin. 'And, actually, maybe we should make it a different place each week? We take it in turns to pick. Somewhere we think might be useful for one of us in terms of writing? Somewhere inspirational?'

'Great idea,' Allie said enthusiastically. 'We can scout out locations for your grand romantic gestures!'

'Steady on,' grumbled Martin. 'I was thinking more a bunch of roses and maybe a new scarf from John Lewis.'

Allie rolled her eyes. 'Roses and scarves are neither going to save your marriage nor me from the clutches of Jake Matthews. Bigger, Martin, you need to think bigger!'

Allie's phone sprung into life and she grabbed it from the table, still hoping it might be Verity telling her it was all a big joke, or that Jake had made a mistake and that Verity was still going to be Allie's editor at Brinkman's. Or even better that Jake had met with a nasty accident and that...

'Shit,' she declared, seeing the alert. Martin raised an eyebrow. 'My sister,' Allie explained, 'I'm supposed to be meeting her and if I don't get going I'll be late. Martha doesn't *do* late.'

'Are you going to tell her what's happened?'

Allie thought for a moment. 'I think I'll explain about Verity leaving,' she paused, 'but I don't think I'll tell her about *us*.'

Martin raised his eyebrow.

'Ugh, Jesus, Martin. You know what I mean.'

'I do,' he said, laughing. 'It's OK, I've never managed to do the sleazy older man thing, or wanted to, I should clarify.'

'Good,' Allie said decisively, 'because it's wrong and disgusting and simply plays into the power dynamics of the patriarchy.'

'Oh that's a good line,' Martin declared, obviously impressed. 'Can you make sure I can use that in my plot? I'm imagining a DI who has clawed her way up the rungs of the Met, despite the inherent and systemic sexist attitudes. And who is now determined to crack the case that none of her cisgender, white, male, overweight, insert many other stereotypes, colleagues have managed to.'

Allie clapped her hands in delight, 'Martin this is excellent, see how far you've come in just one session?'

'Alright, no need to patronise me.'

Allie laughed. 'Sorry, but seriously, you've already come up with a lead character, that's amazing!'

Martin gave in and grinned. 'This could be fun, don't you think?'

Allie nodded. 'And I hope you don't take it the wrong way, about me not telling people about this? I would just rather keep it to myself for the moment. Between my sister and my friends they have A LOT of opinions, and I don't think I need to hear them right now.'

'A lot of opinions?' Martin looked wryly at her. 'Sounds as if you have much in common.'

Allie narrowed her eyes in response.

'Agreed,' he said, 'we keep this to ourselves for the time being.'

Chapter Six

Allie was glad she had decided not to divulge to Martha the writing plan she had concocted with Martin. Martha was even more full of opinions than usual. She had been outraged on Allie's behalf about Jake and the goings on at Brinkman's (which was good) but had scoffed at Allie's wailings about Verity (which was not the supportive attitude Allie had been looking for).

'What do you mean you can't contact her?' Martha had demanded. 'So what if they've taken her phone?' Martha rolled her eyes in frustration, which was a look that always came to Allie's mind when she thought of Martha. 'This is the digital age,' she continued, 'for goodness' sake, Allie, of course you can contact her if you put your mind to it.'

That was Martha's answer to everything in life, it was all achievable if you put your mind to it. Thank god Allie's writing career had been successful, putting aside this latest, recent hiccup, because Allie couldn't imagine the disparaging remarks she would have had to endure if her writing gig had involved sitting around all day at home *and* making no money.

And from Martha's perspective, it was true, she had worked hard, got an excellent job doing something unfathomable to Allie at a pharmaceutical company. Had met her partner Ruth through friends and they were now deeply, madly in love and absolutely devoted to each other. So whenever Allie was feeling especially bad about not having lived up to her father's ambitions for her, she felt glad that at least one of his daughters had. And maybe Martha did have a point. Maybe if Allie had put her mind to things more, she wouldn't find herself both single and cynical, with a terrifying lack of job prospects on the horizon.

'Do you ever wonder what Dad would think of our lives now?'

Martha looked sharply at Allie, but her eyes immediately softened. 'Yeah, course. All the time. You?'

Allie nodded but didn't say anything. Martha switched to concerned sister mode 'Allie? Are you OK? I mean apart from the work stuff and the Dominic stuff?'

Allie shrugged. 'I can't help worrying that I can never live up to his expectations.' Martha looked at her curiously. 'Why would you think that Allie, he would be so proud of your writing, you know that!'

'I actually meant more my disastrous love life,' Allie said in a small voice. 'And my inability to pick the right man.'

Martha looked like she was considering saying something and then thought better of it. 'Oh Al, don't be silly. He would just want you to be happy.'

'But I'm not, am I? You are. You've got Ruth, he would have loved her. And Mum had Dad, and we all know how happy they were. And she seems happy with Nigel now, doesn't she?'

It was Martha's turn to shrug. Nigel had been on the scene for the last ten years and to be fair to him, he was the best kind of pseudo stepdad. He never overstepped the mark, never pretended to be their dad, was always respectful at moments where one of them might be thinking of their dad. He made their mum happy, which was all they could ask for, and he owned a villa in Spain, which meant that they didn't have to worry about their mother's vitamin D levels.

'But he's not Dad,' Allie confirmed.

'No, course he's not. But, yeah he's OK, and yeah, Mum seems happy. Why are you so worried you're letting Dad down?'

'Oh, it's nothing.' Allie shook herself. She had never told Martha about her last conversation with their dad, never divulged his hope for their happiness and perhaps it was best not to rehash the past right now. 'Just feeling a bit sensitive at the moment, that's all.'

After her lunch with Martha, and inbetween making some notes for Martin, Allie conceded that of course Martha was right, she *was* being ridiculous thinking that she couldn't track Verity down. She quickly sent her a DM on Instagram, like any normal person would have done hours ago. Allie felt a little embarrassed not to have done it before, but in her defence, she thought, she had been blindsided by life and wasn't thinking straight.

Later that evening, in need of some fresh air, Allie stepped outside the bookshop in Dulwich, and checked her phone for the billionth time. Verity still had yet to reply, but perhaps she didn't use social media in the way Allie did; to distract her from work and to pretend she was conducting useful research.

She sighed and looked back in the bookshop windows, it

was a lovely shop, full of handpicked staff favourites and special editions, all bespoke curated, but as predicted it had taken her two train changes and a bus to get to. Still, the author in question had been good to Allie when she had been starting out as a writer. So it was the least Allie could do to show up, buy a copy of the book that she probably wouldn't get around to reading for months and praise the author on her latest success. She looked back down at her phone trying to decide whether she really needed to go back into the shop again, or whether she had networked enough.

'Hello.'

Allie looked up from Google Maps straight into some familiar dreamy grey eyes.

'Hi,' she said, startled. 'Will, right?'

He smiled, his eyes creasing, a hint of dimple flashing in one of his cheeks. 'Allie Edwards.' The way he said her name, not as a question but as a statement of fact, made her stomach drop. She immediately began fantasising about him saying her name in a much more intimate setting.

'You remembered!' Allie couldn't help exclaiming despite realising how pathetic this might make her sound.

'Hard to forget meeting a bestselling author, especially when I saved her from a dark alley.'

Allie laughed.

'Don't mock,' Will said, deadpan. 'I felt like the hero in one of your books.'

For the second time in a day Allie felt genuine amazement that someone had read one of her books, before reminding herself that he didn't necessarily mean that he'd actually *read* one of her books, just that he understood the standard tropes of the romance genre.

'Are you here to save me again?' she asked, realising with a delicious thrill that maybe she was actually flirting with this man.

'Do you need saving?'

Allie felt her cheeks turn red and nodded in what she hoped wasn't too eager a manner. 'I could do with an excuse not to go back into the party.'

'Then I'd love to be your excuse,' Will replied, 'come with me?'

The way the invitation was issued made Allie exhale deeply. 'Yes,' she replied, embarrassingly breathily.

He led her round a corner to the back entrance of the bookshop and held the door open, ushering her inside and then leading her back into a small kitchen area. The penny dropped.

'Oh, of course, you're working tonight. Sorry, I shouldn't interrupt.' Allie began to back out of the doorway, mortified at believing that Will had been flirting with her. He caught her hand, stopping her. 'It's OK. I'd like the distraction. Stay with me while I plate these up?' He gestured to some boxes of food laid out on the surface behind him. 'It won't take me long.'

Allie looked down at her hand held by his and then up into his eyes, feeling a wave of heat sweep through her body.

'Erm, OK, sure.' She allowed herself to be pulled back in.

'Not many places to sit, sorry, but I won't tell health and safety if you want to sit up here?'

Allie contemplated the brushed steel surface he was pointing at and before she could think through any complications she hopped up onto it and crossed her legs, realising this brought her almost eye level with Will. He smiled at her and rolled his sleeves up, giving her another tantalising glimpse of that tattoo. She cleared her throat, embarrassed by the way she was quite clearly ogling him and tried to think only pure thoughts as she watched him deftly unboxing the food and laying it out on the platters.

'Hungry crowd tonight, this is the second round. My colleague dropped off the first round earlier.'

'Leaving you in charge tonight?'

He turned and looked at her, his eyebrow raised in amusement. 'Yes, I'm in charge *tonight*.'

Flummoxed by his inflection, she said nothing.

'Here, try one of these.' Will leaned over, holding what looked like a tiny goat's cheese tart. She took it from him, their fingers brushing, and he watched as she ate it, not taking his eyes off her lips.

'What do you think?'

Allie didn't know how to respond. Was it appropriate to say that the tart was almost as delicious as the man who had handed it to her? It was all she could manage to say 'mmm, good,' without spraying crumbs everywhere.

Will bit back a smile as if well aware what was on her mind. 'Do you want to try this?' he said and for a split-second Allie was hoping he was pointing at himself. Rather disappointingly, it looked like he was offering a small puff of pastry. He walked over to her, so close now that her knees touched the fabric of his shirt, and she looked up at him, wondering if he felt that spark running through him every time they touched.

Knowing that she was staring, she quickly took the food, managing this time to rather more eloquently ask afterwards, 'What was in that one?'

'It's choux pastry, filled with crab meat. Actually I probably should have checked first that you're not allergic.'

Allie clutched at her throat.

'Oh god, you *are* allergic!'

'I'm joking!' Allie laughed, grabbing his arm as she did so. 'Sorry, that was mean. The look on your face though.'

Will's face relaxed, and he placed a hand on his toned chest, causing Allie to once again look at the way his shirt stretched over it. 'Thank god, because I have to confess my knight in shining armour routine doesn't stretch to handling anaphylactic shock.' He went back to his food prep and then looked back at her over his shoulder. 'I'm glad I didn't poison you, wouldn't say much about my cooking.'

'Wait, you *made* them?' Allie looked at him in amazement. 'I thought…'

'You thought I just handed them out?' His eyes twinkled with amusement. 'Nope. Multi-talented. Just not adept at handling allergic reactions.'

'Wow, well, I'm impressed. Must make you a valuable employee.'

Will looked back at her again, his expression of amusement still fixed in place. 'Do you want to go for a drink?' he said suddenly.

'I thought you were working?'

'This won't take me long. I just need to take these inside and set them up on a table. Five minutes, max, then I'm all yours.'

Allie's mind went to all sorts of wild scenarios where Will really was all hers. None of them were appropriate for family-friendly viewing. And was this particular scenario a date? Was he asking her out? She looked at his back as he plated the food up, wondering if she could deduce what he was thinking from the way his muscles tensed under the pale blue shirt he was wearing.

'Don't they need you to hand food out tonight?' She

pointed at the trays of food that Will was now loading onto a trolley.

He looked over at her, his mouth twitching at a joke she wasn't sure she quite got. 'No, *they* don't need me to hand them out tonight. It's a table buffet. I just need to put the platters out on a table at the back and then come and pick them up in a few hours' time.' He looked at his watch. 'So if you still need rescuing, I'm free to do so.'

Allie still wasn't quite sure what to make of this cute waiter, with his hidden talents for cookery, and whether he actually was flirting with her. 'OK,' she said slowly. 'As long as you won't get into trouble.'

Will looked amused again. 'Stay there,' he said, 'I'll be five minutes.'

Allie kicked her legs up and down as she sat on the work surface wondering if Will would actually reappear, or if he'd simply walk out the front and leave her in here, and how long she should wait before accepting that it was all an elaborate hoax and there was no way a guy as cute as Will was into her. She had just pulled out her phone and was writing a message to Jess when he reappeared. Allie looked up and quickly stuffed her phone into her bag before Will could see exactly how she had been describing him.

'So,' he said, 'I have time to kill. Want to join me?'

Allie looked up at him and broke into laughter. 'Wow, you know how to make a girl feel special!'

Will grinned back. 'You'll be doing me a favour.'

'And how could I refuse an invitation like that?'

Will put his hand out to take hers. 'Come on.'

'So let me get this straight, your first book went to number one?' Allie nodded. 'Your second book did too?' Allie nodded again. 'And your third book has been optioned for a film?'

'But not actually made into one yet!' she protested. While she was enjoying lapping up the adulation from a cute guy, she was also trying hard to keep things in perspective. Which was hard when his leg was pressed up against hers under the table and she could feel the heat of his body which, contrary to the laws of physics, was making her shiver.

Will waved his hand, dismissing her statement. 'And yet you have nothing better to do than sit in a pub in Dulwich with me?'

'Don't flatter yourself, I was at a book launch remember? I'm doing *you* a favour.'

'How could I forget.' Will held a hand to his chest and pulled a stricken face.

Allie laughed.

'Seriously though,' Will said, edging even closer to her, 'I think it's pretty amazing.' He held her gaze and Allie felt herself flushing under it.

'Thanks,' she replied, flustered. 'But what about you? How long have you worked in...' She paused, wondering how to describe his occupation. Was it OK to say catering? Would he be offended if she called him a waiter? 'Erm, events,' she settled on.

Will picked up his drink, his body language suddenly screaming discomfort. 'I've been with this company for a few years now.'

'Oh wow.' Allie couldn't hide her surprise, part of her had presumed Will would have been doing this as a stopgap, or perhaps as a filler between, she didn't know, acting jobs or something. She kicked herself at her inner snobbery. It wasn't as if her career had been one of graduate fast-track schemes and actually, mostly it was just luck that she hadn't had to pick up part-time jobs over the years.

'So, you like the company then?' She quickly tried to cover her pause, but Will had obviously noticed, though if he was offended, he didn't seem to show it.

'Yeah,' he gave her an inscrutable look, 'I feel rather attached to them.' He stretched out on his chair, his leg pressing against Allie's again, her stomach now in free fall. 'I believe in what they stand for – organic where possible, healthy event food which doesn't scrimp on flavour.' He laughed. 'I've really drunk the Kool-Aid, haven't I?' Allie tried to focus on what he was saying instead of just staring at his teeth, which were beautifully straight, and white, and yet, amazingly didn't look fake. 'But it's good to get customer feedback on the menu. By the way,' he caught Allie's eye, 'we won't be serving those vol au vents again.'

Allie blushed. 'You told them what I said?' She felt completely mortified and Will laughed at her stricken expression.

'It went straight into the ear of the person who needed to know.'

'Oh god,' Allie panicked, 'sorry. Honestly, don't listen to me. I'm sure they were delicious, I just find it impossible to do party talk and eat enormous canapés at the same time.'

'It's a perfectly valid point. Smaller vol au vents next time.' He raised his beer towards her glass of wine while looking at her fixedly in the eyes.

Allie gulped and tried to look away before she blushed an even brighter shade of red. She could lose herself in those eyes of his, not to mention the sensation of those pin prickles of desire that crept across her skin every time he looked at her.

When was the last time she had experienced this? Had she *ever* experienced it?

'Anyway,' she flustered, putting her glass back down and finally breaking eye contact. 'It's not like I'll be organising any book parties for a while so you really shouldn't worry about my opinion.'

Will raised an eyebrow at her and Allie felt her stomach dip. She'd much rather sit here and swoon over Will than recall today's events, but he was obviously waiting for an explanation. She sighed. 'I found out today that my editor is leaving.'

'I'm sorry. She's been your editor for a while?'

'Yep, since my first book,' Allie said, 'dragged me out of the slush pile.'

'That's got to be hard. Editors and writers have pretty close relationships.'

'That sounds like you know something about publishing,' she risked giving him a nudge with her elbow and was amazed to discover that when you really fancied someone, even touching them with your elbow did funny things to your insides.

Will shrugged. 'I go to a lot of book launches, for work,' he clarified. 'I hear a lot, that's all.' He seemed keen to dismiss this line of questioning. 'So, who will your new editor be? Do you know yet?'

'Nope.' She shrugged. 'But, in the meantime, I have to deal with Jake Matthews, who is a snake of the highest order.'

Will smiled. 'I didn't realise snakes had a ranking order.'

'Er, yeah.' Allie frowned. 'You'd really put a python up against a grass snake?'

'Well, technically I think a grass snake is a type of worm.'

Allie laughed. 'You're funny.' She swiped at him with her hand, which he caught in his.

'Good,' he said, not letting it go, 'because I like your face when I make you smile.'

Allie felt the breath catch in her throat. Will was suddenly closer than he had been before. The distance between them was shrinking every second. 'And I like hearing you laugh,' he continued. He spoke into her ear, his breath against her cheek making her shiver again. She looked up into his grey eyes, which seemed more serious now. She turned imperceptibly towards him, he noticed, shifting his body to mirror hers. His hand went to her face, brushed a strand of her hair softly from her eyes and ran his fingers across her cheekbone. Allie shivered at his touch. He paused, catching her eye, waiting for her to make the next move. It didn't take her long.

And as her lips touched Will's, she sighed and knew that she was ruined. This was the spark she had been writing about for so many years that had, up till this point, been missing from her life. And that now, she could never go back to mediocre men, Will had ruined every future kiss with any other man. Not that she was complaining. If this was her last ever kiss, it was worth every second of its deliciousness. Will's lips were warm and dry, his touch like an electric charge across her skin. And even as they kissed, in her mind, she could see the words on the page as she would describe it all later.

Chapter Seven

'You smell of sex.'

'I'm sorry, what?' Allie muttered sideways through gritted teeth. If Jess's intention was to distract Allie, then it was working. She wobbled dangerously and then collapsed on her mat out of her ardha chandrasana, just as the yoga teacher instructed the class to come slowly to a sukhasana, whatever the hell that was. Allie checked her neighbours and carefully crossed her knees, trying to pretend Jess hadn't said what she had just said.

'I said, you smell of—'

'I heard you the first time,' Allie growled.

'Ladies…' the yoga instructor murmured, reminding them to focus on their breathing and shut out the outside world.

Allie surreptitiously tried to smell herself, pretending that nose in armpit was a well-known yoga stretch. Pulling a face, she shifted her mat as far away from Jess as she was able to in the overcrowded yoga studio.

'I told you, we didn't have sex,' Allie murmured in protest.

'Yeah but you want to,' Jess said out of the corner of her mouth, 'you're giving off all the pheromones.'

Allie opened her mouth to protest again but caught the eye of the instructor who looked as if she was about to completely lose her ohm with the pair of them. Allie couldn't help herself, she started to giggle. Jess looked over and saw Allie's shaking shoulders and then she started too.

'Did you get this for free? The class I mean?' whispered Allie. Jess was always blagging freebies through her work. And if this class had been one of those then Allie felt less bad about making Jess leave early.

Jess swivelled on her yoga mat to turn and look at her. 'Yes. Shall we get out of here?'

'Definitely.' Allie was already quietly rolling her mat up and grabbing her towel and water bottle.

'Sorry, sorry' they muttered as they clambered over the prone bodies now trying to relax in shavasana. The instructor shot them a filthy look as they finally got to the door and closed it behind them.

'I don't think we can go back there,' said Allie, still giggling.

'You'd want to?'

'Nah, bit too trendy for me. I prefer my yoga in a community hall, with old ladies letting go and farting.'

Jess rolled her eyes. 'Come on, let's go get breakfast.'

Jess led the way to a cafe she said she knew and Allie hoped it wouldn't be in the same vein as her morning so far; she wanted bacon and eggs, not quinoa and green tea. Ten minutes later, she ended up settling happily for black coffee and smashed avocado and hoping that the toast would contain as much gluten as possible. She stretched her legs out in front of her as she waited for it to arrive.

'So, tell me everything,' Jess demanded, scraping her chair across the floor and making Allie wince.

'I've told you everything,' protested Allie.

'No, you haven't.' Jess gave Allie a hard stare. 'You messaged me yesterday to tell me you'd got with hot waiter guy but this morning told me you hadn't smashed. That is not enough detail Allie, look at you!' exclaimed Jess.

'What?'

'Your face, it's got this kind of sexy goofy expression on it. God, I hope that's not the kind of face you pull around hot waiter guy, because I can tell you now, it does nothing for you.'

'Will,' said Allie, 'he's called Will.'

'OK, sorry, *Will* then. Do not pull that face around *Will* next time you want to bang him.'

'Thanks for the advice, *Jess*,' Allie said, pulling the cup of coffee which had just been put on the table towards her, and feeling more than a little sorry for the girl serving who looked mortified by Jess's statement.

'So, tell me all about *Will*.'

'Do you have to use that inflection every time you say his name?'

'Sorry, I'm just enjoying seeing the effect it has on you. Wow, now I'm imagining what you must look like when *he* says *your* name.' Jess took a large swig of her drink and pulled a face in disgust.

'What *is* that?' asked Allie, pointing at the glass of sludge that Jess seemed to be drinking.

'A cleansing juice.'

'Looks disgusting.'

'It is.'

'So why are you drinking it?' asked Allie, barely managing

to keep the tone of irritation in her voice below extreme vexation.

'Detox.'

Allie rolled her eyes. She well knew that Jess would be drinking and vaping again that evening so why she bothered with the pretense of a detox was beyond Allie.

As if reading her thoughts, Jess said, 'Baby steps. I figure if I'm good during the day then I can get away with being naughty at night.' She grinned wickedly at Allie. 'But that,' she said, pointing at her glass, 'is truly disgusting. And no amount of excess can make it worthwhile.' She pushed the glass away from her and fixed Allie with a look. 'Seriously though. Tell me what happened, I haven't seen you looking this dreamy-eyed over a boy since…' She paused, looking thoughtful. 'Actually, I'm not sure I've *ever* seen you look this dreamy-eyed.'

Allie smiled a little shyly. Jess was right, she didn't recall ever falling this fast or this hard for a guy.

'I really like him,' she admitted.

Jess grinned at her. 'I can tell. And Al? I'm so pleased. You deserve it. Has he called you yet?'

Allie shook her head and Jess looked momentarily downcast.

'But he's messaged.' Allie's lips twitched in amusement as she saw Jess's face completely transform.

'Yay!' Jess exclaimed. 'Al that's great.'

'Yep. I woke up to a message saying what a great night he'd had and checking I had got home OK. And then he messaged to ask if I was free next Thursday night.'

Jess clapped her hands together in glee, looking more like an overexcited toddler at Christmas than a thirty-something professional woman in workout gear. 'Tell me you said yes!'

'Of course I did!' exclaimed Allie. 'Honestly, Jess, he does funny stuff to my insides every time I think about him. I'd cancel on you if it meant getting to see him again.'

Jess pretended to frown. 'Er, I thought we had an agreement, friends come first—'

'When?' Allie interrupted, genuinely surprised. She put her coffee cup back down. 'Did you put me first when you cancelled our night out at the cinema so you could meet that skanky boy you kept hooking up with in our final year?'

'Oh my god!' Jess practically shouted. 'You're never going to let me forget that are you?'

'Nope.'

'You didn't even want to go to the cinema. In fact, I remember you saying that if you were made to sit through another *Pirates of the Caribbean* film, you would personally hunt down Jack Sparrow and condemn him to Davy Jones's locker yourself.'

'Did I?' Allie felt pleased with herself. 'Sounds rather eloquent, very much like something I *would* say.' She raised her eyebrows. 'Anyway, it's irrelevant. I'm not cancelling on anyone to see Will. I had no plans other than to try and get some writing done.'

Jess grimaced. 'Dare I ask how that's going?'

Allie smiled up at the waitress as she put the food down in front of her, grateful that Jess wasn't shouting something smutty at that precise moment.

'Actually, I think I've had a bit of a breakthrough.'

'You have? Allie, that's great. Another thing to celebrate.' Jess pulled her plate towards her and started attacking the bacon and eggs on there with gusto. 'See?' she said, with a mouth full of food. If Jess wasn't so gorgeous it really would be a revolting spectacle watching her eat. 'It's all coming together, sex and your career!'

'I told you,' Allie said forcefully, 'I haven't slept with him.'

'Yeah, but you will. And soon.' Jess grinned at Allie, ketchup smearing her mouth a little.

'How's the detox coming along?' Allie asked, raising an eyebrow.

'Sod off,' Jess mumbled through another mouthful of bacon. 'And don't change the subject,' she continued, waving a piece of toast threateningly at Allie. Allie picked up her own cutlery and regarded her plate. She'd told Martin that she didn't want anyone to know about their arrangement. But now that she was sitting here with Jess, she wondered whether it wouldn't be such a bad thing to run it past her? Was it really a good idea? She didn't know Martin, only by reputation. And it could end up being a colossal waste of time. Or even worse, Allie could end up writing Martin's book for him and getting nothing in return. But on that thought, Allie paused. Yes, she didn't really know Martin, but her gut feeling told her that he was one of the good guys. And she was intrigued to find out more about him. Especially if it meant she might get to meet the amazing Angie, although Allie couldn't yet envisage the circumstances under which that might actually happen; she found it hard to imagine Martin leading with the introductions, 'Hey Ange, I want you to meet Allie, she helped save our marriage.'

Allie felt another flicker of excitement in her stomach at her plans. Because, actually, while she was excited to see if working with Martin might help both of them write, she was also excited to see if everything she had learned on paper about love and romance could be put to practical use in the real world. If her experience writing romance might just help save Martin's marriage. And maybe things with Will would spark some real-life romance in her own life.

'Earth to Allie! Stop drooling over *Will* and tell me about the book.'

'Alright. But stop calling him *Will*. His name is Will.'

Jess bit her lip in amusement and pretended to pull a serious face. 'Will it is.'

Allie made a split-second decision as she swallowed a large mouthful of toast. 'I've got myself a writing mentor.'

Jess looked confused. 'A writing mentor? How does that work and where did you find her?'

Allie found it interesting that Jess would assume her mentor to be a woman. Some definite bias that presumed only women wrote romance, and that they wrote it solely for other women. She decided not to correct Jess. Best to keep things as vague as possible until she really knew how things might pan out. Until then, she could amuse herself by imagining the look on Jess's face when she unveiled her mentor as a straight, middle-class man approaching retirement age.

'I met them at a publishing party. We kind of clicked,' Allie explained. 'They're going through something similar and we agreed to meet up regularly. Help each other out, encourage each other and set targets. You know,' Allie shrugged, 'that sort of stuff.'

'Cool,' said Jess. 'But do you think you'll have enough done to meet your deadline?' Allie had told Jess all about Jake's new, set in quick-dry concrete, deadline. Right before she had told Jess in excruciating detail every last painful piece of torture she planned to exact on Jake if she ever got the chance.

'Ugh, honestly? Allie looked pained. 'I'm not sure. I hope I can get enough down to buy me some time for a second draft. And anyway,' her expression switched from pained to coy, 'maybe Will might help inspire me?'

'Aw yuck. I am definitely not reading this new one.' Jess

pretended to vomit and then had to assure the waitress who had just come to collect their plates that there was absolutely nothing wrong with the food. 'It was bad enough last time when I kept wondering if you thought about Dominic when you wrote your sex scenes.'

'Jess!' protested Allie. This was a perennial source of anxiety for Allie. Would people think it was autobiographical? Would they think that she was writing about her own fetishes? What would her *mother* think? It was this kind of thing that would wake Allie in a cold sweat at night. And something she didn't want her best friend questioning her about over breakfast.

Jess didn't seem to think it was an issue and smiled sweetly back at Allie, drinking the cappuccino she had ordered to make up for the undrinkable cleansing juice.

'Do you know, I find it a bit depressing to realise how little I miss Dominic and how easy it was for him just to walk out.'

Jess looked serious for a moment. 'Yeah, I get it. I mean it's good that you weren't so invested but at the same time, makes you wonder what it was all for.'

Jess had hit the nail on the head and in the process made Allie tear up. Because this was exactly how she had been feeling for months, maybe even for years. Every time she had written a new book she had wondered what she was missing out on and why she could never get the happy-ever-after that she wrote so lovingly for each of her characters. She wondered where she had gone wrong and again, what her dad would say if he could see her now, settling for mediocre men.

'Oh Al, I'm sorry. I didn't mean to make you cry!' Jess looked mortified and reached across the table to grab Allie's hand, almost making the revolting juice fly across the cafe.

Allie righted it just in time, only to be rewarded with a

smear of green slime on her wrist. She wiped the rancid mess on a napkin and shook her head at Jess. 'It's fine, I'm fine!' she insisted.

Jess gave her a look that Allie hadn't seen in a while. It was the 'I know you're pretending to be brave, but I also know there's more to this' look.

'Ugh, OK. I'm fine about splitting up with Dominic – see, I even said splitting up and not "being dumped".' Allie gave Jess a meaningful stare but was not rewarded with the praise she was seeking.

There was a moment of silence, and then Allie broke, 'OK, alright. I don't care about Dominic, but I do care about what this says about me and about my relationships with men.' Allie was now properly on the verge of weeping, her voice had gone all wobbly and was getting higher in pitch with every word she spoke. She fumbled in her rucksack for tissues but came up with only a sweaty headband and a damp yoga towel. Briefly she considered using one of these to mop her tears before realising that Jess was holding out a packet of tissues towards her. Of course she was, you didn't perfect 'the look' without thinking ahead of the consequences of using that look on unsuspecting individuals.

'You know,' Jess said, pulling a tissue free and giving it to Allie, who had been grappling with the packet and was in danger of just shredding the lot. 'It's totally normal to be upset about a relationship ending, even if you're glad that it has.'

'But that's just it!' wailed Allie. 'I'm not even sure it was a relationship!' She held the tissue to her nose, which had started leaking just as much as her eyes. 'How can you call it a relationship when there's nothing to sort out after it ends? We had literally *nothing* to disentangle.' Allie took a deep breath and tried to calm her ragged breathing.

'Hey, hey, it's OK.' Jess grabbed her arm awkwardly across the table and tried to comfort her.

'Yeah, I know, it's fine. Really. I'm fine,' Allie insisted again. 'It's just a bit depressing. Two years and nothing to show for it. And I keep wondering why I bothered staying with him.'

'Apathy? Inertia? Al,' Jess said encouragingly, 'we've all let a relationship drag on when it should have been marked do not resuscitate. It is what it is.'

'But what if it means I suck at relationships?' Jess gave Allie a 'please, listen to yourself' look. But Allie was on a roll. 'What if not only do I suck at relationships but that's the reason I can no longer write books about them? Look, I really like Will, he's seriously hot, but I don't think it's a good idea right now just to launch myself into another relationship.'

'What?' Jess exploded. 'How did we get from maybe I suck at relationships to maybe I should ghost the first guy who's given me the feels in years?'

Allie shrugged. She wasn't sure herself, but somewhere, deep down inside her she feared that all the situation with Will would lead to was disappointment and eventual apathy, because that's all she knew.

Jess frowned at her. 'Firstly, this thing with Will, maybe it doesn't have to be a relationship, maybe it could just be fun. And secondly, just enjoy it, Allie.'

'I don't think I should.'

'Why not?'

'Because, because … because things are really messed up right now and I don't think I should be dragging someone else into that mess.'

'OK.' Jess was now using the voice she used when dealing with children and irrational clients. 'You need to get a grip, it's not a mess. You got dumped.' Jess waved away Allie's protest at her choice of language. 'And...' She paused for effect. 'You have already met someone who makes you feel like ... like...' She searched for the right words.

'OK, this isn't working,' Jess said eventually.

'This?' asked Allie.

'Yes this,' Jess waved her arms around, 'yoga, cleansing juices, avocado on toast. You need something to knock some sense into you, make you realise you're great, you're a catch! You're allowed to have fun, flirt, kiss hot men! You're a bestselling author, Allie! Who yes, I concede, might be having some trouble writing her next book, but as I understand it that's not uncommon when you've been churning out books for years.'

'We prefer you don't use the term "churn" when describing the writing process,' seethed Allie.

'Shut up,' snapped Jess. 'Allie. You're great. You had a shit and uneventful time with disappointing Dominic. Did I ever tell you that this is what Tom and I always called him? No? Well, now you know. But that's over. And now you've met a new guy who is making your pants ping and he's got the serious hots for you too. Enjoy it. And yes, maybe it will help you write, maybe it won't. But just enjoy it for god's sake, because you deserve it.'

Allie gaped at Jess's outburst and wondered whether to be offended by Tom and Jess's nickname for Dominic. 'Does anyone really say "got the hots" anymore?' she eventually asked.

Jess rolled her eyes and grabbed Allie's hand, pulling her up from the table and pointing at her yoga bag, indicating Allie should pick it up. 'Where are we going?' asked Allie.

'For cocktails.' Jess sounded like she meant business.

Allie glanced at her watch. She dithered momentarily,

wondering if Jess would actually take no for an answer before deciding that 10am really wasn't too early for cocktails, especially when you'd been dumped by an ex and kissed by an insanely attractive man all in short succession. And this was Soho, if they couldn't find somewhere here to serve them cocktails at this hour, then this was not the Soho Allie knew and loved.

Chapter Eight

By the time Allie got home she was definitely feeling better about the world. It might have had something to do with the three mimosa margaritas she had downed in the dimly lit cocktail bar Jess had dragged her to, the place where Jess had to persuade the barman that his bar *was* open and that he *was* indeed happy to serve them. And from out of said bar, both women had come stumbling out into the daylight like two half-blind moles with coordination issues.

Or it might have been the increasingly flirty messages she had been exchanging with Will, who had innocuously messaged to ask if she was happy to meet him in Richmond on Thursday evening and was now the recipient of Allie's drunken friskiness. Even as she typed her replies Allie felt she might come to regret the tone of some of them when she had sobered up a little. Especially as she was really no clearer on how she should be handling this situationship. She liked him, he had an exceptionally pleasing effect on her body, but she'd just come out of a disastrous relationship and she'd lived long enough to know that the rebound thing was real. Nor was she sure she wanted to introduce a new man to the person she became when she was trying to write. It wasn't a side of her personality she was especially proud of. But surely some half-drunken messages wouldn't hurt? And she was just agreeing to meet him on a Thursday night, it was hardly a declaration of serious intent.

She found herself, still in her yoga gear, sat in front of her laptop after many hours had passed and she was still writing. It had been such a long time since she had done this that her wrists were beginning to ache from an activity they were no longer used to. By the time she called it a day, the sun was beginning to set, she had gone into and come out the other side of a minor hangover and had got down some more of her plot outline for Martin. And not only that, but there was something new; it was only the very beginning, barely just a shadow of an idea, but it was there on her computer screen, the ghost of a romance inspired by her conversations with Martin, and spiced up by her feelings for Will.

Allie stretched back from her laptop and grinned to herself. Maybe Jess was right. Maybe, just maybe, Will could be everything she had been waiting for and more. Or at least, he could be something that was right for her just now. And hell yes, she did deserve it. No more disappointing Dominics in her life. Allie closed her laptop, got up from her chair and, sniffing herself, decided she really did need to take a shower before doing anything else.

She stood waiting for the shower to warm, and as if summoned from the ghostly halls of bad boyfriends past, her phone sprung to life with a message from Dominic. Her good vibes disappearing faster than the sale rack at Liberty, Allie swore and swiped her screen off lock. What did he want? And why did he have to put in an appearance just as she was feeling better about things? Allie considered ignoring the message, but she never had been able to handle sitting patiently with her impulses so she clicked the message open and read it, frown lines appearing on her forehead as she did so. Apparently he was 'sorry' things had ended the way they had and 'sorry' for his abrupt departure; images of red sports cars flashed through Allie's brain as she read this. And he wondered 'if it would be OK' for them to meet up sometime, arrange to swap belongings. Allie thought back to the paltry possessions she had left at Dominic's and once again decided that she really could do without them in her life, in much the same way as she could do without him.

Sighing, she wished she hadn't read it. But she could at least make him wait for a response and leave him on read while she took a shower. Standing under the warm water, thinking of messages left unread, Allie suddenly thought again of Verity and of the fact that she still hadn't surfaced. It was very strange. Alarming images ran through Allie's mind of Verity under the lock and key of Jake Matthews. She got out of the shower and stood, watching her face disappear in the misted mirror, wondering if Jake should be the killer in her thriller or one of the victims and which she would find most satisfying. Then she shook her head, towelled herself vigorously and told herself to stop being such an idiot.

'And you've really heard nothing back from her since?'

Allie shook her head and sidestepped a patch of thistles. 'Are you sure you're OK walking in those shoes?' This was not the first time Will had expressed his concern for her footwear. 'I should have suggested you wear trainers, I'm sorry.' He grabbed Allie's hand and led her round the puddle in the path.

Momentarily Allie forgot to reassure him, so surprised she was, yet again, by the effect of his touch on the rest of her body. She was just enjoying the tingling sensation running down her spine when the blister on her left foot interrupted her thoughts. 'It's fine, it's lovely to walk,' she said in what she hoped was an encouraging tone. Honestly? She wanted a comfortable chair to sink into, though really she would be fine with anywhere she could sit and take her sandals off and never have to look at them again, but she didn't think that would be the response Will was looking for.

And their surroundings *were* beautiful, Richmond Park in the early evening sunshine. The grass and the leaves still brilliantly green. The light was catching the skyline of the City and yet again Allie wondered why she rarely ventured out to Richmond, it wasn't exactly far. And then the stabbing sensation in her foot reminded her why. She was a city girl, and this was a different world, and while it was all rather lovely, there were no cabs nearby to save her from her blisters.

When Allie had started writing she had entertained romantic daydreams of where she might write, finding cosy cafes in which to people watch, gaining inspiration from her surroundings, scribbling down some early drafts. Sitting in London parks with a notebook, drawing character studies. Long walks along the Thames as she hashed out tricky plot lines. The reality was a little different. Initially, she wrote notes on her phone as she commuted to and from her office. She got up early, stayed up late, writing and writing. And then later when she was successful enough and confident enough to believe that this might actually be a viable career choice, she had quit her office job and quickly realised that cafes were noisy. There was always someone sat in the chair you wanted to sit in. Or coffee smeared on the table you wanted to use. Parks were full of children screaming, ant bites and grass stains. And, as the current situation showed, she couldn't be trusted to choose the correct footwear for long walks anywhere.

'Sorry,' she said, reaching a tipping point. 'Actually, this isn't working for me,' she admitted. Allie spotted a tree trunk and went over and sat down. Will followed and stood, looking down at her with concern. Once again, Allie found herself marvelling over just how *tall* he was, and how he looked ridiculously handsome from this angle. Although Allie had yet to find an angle from which he didn't look ridiculously handsome. He was rocking the sexy lumberjack look, very appropriate for their current surroundings, wearing a checked shirt, slim fit, with the sleeves rolled up and Allie couldn't help but wonder if some ex-girlfriend had once told him how nice his arms were, and that now, subconsciously, he always rolled his sleeves up. The glimpse of that tattoo was tantalising and made her want to explore the whole picture.

'Allie?'

'Sorry, what?' She looked back up at him, determined not to fixate on his arms again and lose her mind entirely.

'Are you OK?'

'Yeah, yeah I'm fine. Just these shoes…' She gestured at her sandals, which were now looking more as if they had lived through three days at Glastonbury than been on a brief jaunt across Richmond Park.

Will sighed. 'God, I'm sorry. I should have asked you if you wanted to walk, not just presumed.' He looked down at her, his stupidly handsome face creased in a frown of concern for the wellbeing of her toes.

'You did ask me,' reassured Allie. 'And I said I wanted to. I didn't want you to think less of me if I said I had a blister, and now...' She pointed forlornly to her feet again.

'You have a blister?' Will's face was a perfect etching of distress.

'Honestly, it's fine. I get a blister every time I wear these.'

Will scratched his head. 'This might be a stupid question but why do you wear them then?'

Allie pulled a face at him as if he had asked her the most moronic question possible. 'Because they're cute and they look good with this dress?' She looked down at the polka dot sundress she had picked out especially for their walk. 'Oh and because they cost a stupid amount of money and so I refuse to accept that they're uncomfortable and will go on wearing them until my feet are cut to ribbons.'

Will laughed at that and went to sit down on the tree stump next to her. 'There's a shorter way back to my car. I was going for romantic, but we can just cut straight down the road and we'll be there in less than five minutes.'

Allie fixed him with a stare. 'You mean you've put me through this—' she gestured to her blisters '—when there was a short cut?'

'Hey!' he protested. 'I said I was going for the romantic option.'

Allie bit her lip and looked up at him. She should tell him now, she should confess everything; that this wasn't a good idea, that her track record proved she wasn't good girlfriend material at the best of times, and, putting aside this 'date', she was definitely not in the best of times. But instead, she said, in a small voice, 'I liked it.'

'Even with the blisters?'

'Even with the blisters.'

The look on Will's face told her everything, that she was already in too deep, and he was too. She took a breath, committing this feeling to memory so that she could pour it out into her laptop later.

'Where did you go?' he asked.

'Sorry?'

'You were miles away. What were you thinking?'

'Nothing,' she replied hastily, deciding that although it might be flattering, she didn't want him getting the idea she was purely using him for research purposes. His grey eyes crinkled at the corners as he smiled; he really was the best research project Allie had ever worked on.

'Come on,' he said, evidently realising she wasn't about to elaborate. 'We'd better get going. I made us reservations.'

Allie frowned slightly. 'I thought your friend ran this pub?'

'He does. But that doesn't mean it's easy to get a table there.' Will looked at his watch. 'And if we're late, he won't do me a favour the next time I want to take a beautiful woman there.'

Allie swatted his hand playfully away. 'Allie,' he said slightly gruffly as he successfully grabbed her hand this time and pulled her to her feet. 'This might be too early to say, but I'm going to say it anyway. I'm not planning on inviting any other beautiful women out for dinner.'

'What about average-looking ones?' she quipped.

Will's face did something which made her stomach dip and her heart start to pound. Dating etiquette could go to hell, there was nothing sexier than a man being straightforward and honest about what he wanted.

Chapter Nine

'That's it, I absolutely cannot stop seeing him.'

'Yay! I'm glad you've seen sense, what persuaded you?'

Allie had caught Jess during her lunch break to let her in on a startling revelation; that a date with a hot man led to increased productivity the next day. It was the morning after the night before and Allie had woken up, in her own bed, alone, but still with the sensation of Will's lips on hers, the scent of him lingering in her hair. She'd got up, and before the kettle had even boiled had opened her laptop, pulled up her new document and started typing.

'I need him in order to write.'

'Okaaay.' Jess sounded unconvinced. 'I mean, I guess I don't really care why, just glad you're enjoying yourself ... finally.'

'I know how to enjoy myself,' Allie said tartly.

'Hmm. Do you? It's not like you were enjoying yourself with Dominic, was it?'

'Hey!' protested Allie, 'I'm not with him anymore,

although, incidentally he does want to meet to swap belongings.'

'Just make sure swapping belongings doesn't segue into swapping something more intimate,' Jess said warningly.

'Not going to happen, and anyway, he doesn't really have anything of mine I'm desperate to get back, so it's not urgent.'

'Apart from your self-esteem.'

'Jess!'

'Sorry. But anyway, I'm glad you've decided to continue seeing Will. But maybe just enjoy yourself Allie, don't see this as a means to an end.'

'I'm not!'

'You are. You're not letting yourself enjoy this just because. You think you have to justify it because you believe that seeing him inspires you. And incidentally? You're a damn good writer and you don't need a man to make you that.'

'Yeah yeah,' Allie said somewhat sulkily, 'I thought you'd be happy that I'd decided to go with the flow and see Will.'

'I am. Of course, I am. But just make sure you *are* going with the flow, and not doing this because of some half-baked idea that you need him in order to deliver your next novel.'

'Right, well, thanks for the advice,' Allie said in a tone that suggested she was in no way thankful to receive anything Jess had just said. 'I've got to go meet my mentor now.'

'Ooh fancy! And Allie? I *am* pleased for you, you deserve this...'

Allie thanked Jess and ended the call. She quickly cast her eye over everything she had written that morning and then slid her laptop into her bag and headed out the door.

The Tube was filled with school kids out on an outing, jostling each other with their rucksacks and running their teachers ragged by the sounds of it. Allie shuffled down in her seat, hid behind her book and hoped they would all depart at South Kensington for the museums. She sighed in relief when they did, and prayed for the safety of their teachers. She spent the rest of her journey re-reading the notes she had made for Martin, worrying they weren't half as good as her euphoric typing earlier had led her to believe, but realising that it was too late to do much about it now.

John Lewis was its usual respectable self and Allie had absolutely no trouble finding a quiet, clean table on which she laid out her laptop and allowed herself some downtime daydreaming about Will before Martin showed up.

'Hello.' Martin did a double take, obviously noticing the dreamy expression on her face and not quite knowing whether he was allowed to comment on it. 'You look...'

'Happy?' she suggested.

'Yes, that's it.' He smiled gratefully at the lifeline she had thrown him, and sat down in the chair opposite her. Martin had chosen their first meeting place, and although you couldn't really go wrong with the John Lewis cafe, it hardly screamed 'grand romantic gesture', making Allie realise she was probably going to have to point this out to Martin if this was top of the list of places he planned to take his wife. Still, Allie was in charge of where to meet next so for now she'd suck up the middle England comfort of John Lewis and pump Martin for information on what had made him choose this place over everywhere else in the whole of London town.

She waited for him to settle himself, which seemed to take some time. Finally, he pulled out a notebook and pen.

Allie frowned. 'Didn't you bring your laptop?'

'No,' harrumphed Martin who went back to searching through his bag for something. He looked up, sensing the note of disapproval in her voice. 'What?'

'I thought you might have brought it, that's all. I mean, we're here to write, aren't we?'

'I mainly use longhand at this stage in my writing. And then I type each chapter up when I finish it.' Martin sounded defensive.

She smiled at him in what she hoped was a reassuring manner, a smile that said – *no judgement from me on your archaic habits*. Martin went back to patting down the many pockets in his, yes tweed again, jacket before settling on the one just inside the left-hand side. Triumphantly he pulled out a pair of glasses and put them on. 'Right, better, OK.'

'Did you want to get something?' Allie asked, gesticulating at the extensively stocked cafe counter.

He frowned at her from behind his spectacles. 'How about we make a start, and then I'll go get us something when we need a break?'

This sounded reasonable. Business-like. To the point. Exactly as Allie had hoped. Their relationship as writing mentors was entirely professional. No need for Martin to know the real reason she was dreamily smiling to herself when he arrived. No need for him to know anything about her private life at all. It was completely irrelevant to their writing that Allie kept having to suppress a ridiculous smile. That her thoughts kept wandering back to Will. Memories of his lips, his arms, his...

'Allie?' Martin sounded concerned. 'Are you OK?' He peered at her, his face creasing in frown lines.

'Sorry, right.' Allie tried to focus, to peel her mind away from the hotness that was Will, to wipe the goofy grin off her face every time she thought about... It was tough, but necessary. She needed to concentrate if she was ever going to get this next book written.

'Why don't I start?' she suggested. 'I've been thinking about your book and I've made some notes. Do you want to take a look at this...' She swiveled her laptop round so that Martin could see the screen and nervously held her breath. He peered at it, his eyes squinting slightly. He began patting his pockets again. There was a long pause before he produced a second pair of glasses, carefully took the first pair off, and put the new pair on. 'There, right, now I can read it.'

Allie did a massive internal sigh. It wasn't Martin's fault that he was older and had bad eyesight, and she shouldn't hold it against him, because before long it would be her carrying around several pairs of glasses, not knowing which pocket she kept which pair in. Although hopefully she wouldn't be wearing tweed. She made a mental note to add 'wearing tweed' to the regularly updated list of reasons which gave her and Jess permission to shoot each other.

'What is this?' Martin asked, taking his glasses off and looking up at Allie. For a moment Allie was thrown off balance by his eyes, she hadn't noticed before how intense they were when they were focused on something. Especially when that something was herself. And there was something familiar in them, almost as if Allie had looked into these eyes before. Except not quite these eyes. There was something... but Allie couldn't quite put her finger on what it was.

'It's a chapter breakdown of your next book,' she said, tearing her eyes away from his and looking back at her laptop. 'Well, at least it's the first ten chapters. I haven't quite worked out how and when the detective finds the second body. It's a work in progress.' She shrugged and turned the laptop back towards her.

'It's amazing Allie, I'm impressed.' Martin was cleaning one of his pairs of glasses, Allie couldn't tell which. 'Are you sure you've never written crime or thrillers before?'

'Far as I know,' laughed Allie. 'I don't think Waterstones would shelve any of my novels anywhere other than the romance section.'

Martin smiled at her, his eyes disappearing underneath his overly shaggy eyebrows. Allie couldn't help staring and wondering if they had always been this shaggy, and if not, how quickly growth like that creeps up on you and what Angie thought of them. And at what point in a marriage it became acceptable to request that the other party start trimming their facial hair. Her hand went unthinkingly to her own face, feeling for random stray hairs.

'Are you sure you don't want to use this yourself?' Martin asked with concern. 'It's really good, you know.'

Allie thought for a moment. It could be fun to write something different, publish it under a different name. But she knew where her heart lay and it wasn't at the bottom of a shallow unmarked grave, it was in the pink-tinged section of romance, or at least it would be, once she had managed to revive it. 'No, it's the start of an outline that's all. Just a collection of initial thoughts. If I ran with it I'd probably end up with the detective falling in love with the killer and that would be sick and wrong.'

'But not without precedence,' mused Martin.

'Yeah, but my romances don't tend to involve murder.' Allie bit her lip, thinking back to how much she had actually felt like murdering Dominic over the past couple of years and deciding not to share that thought with Martin. 'I was intrigued to see what I came up with but I don't think it's quite my style. And anyway, we had a deal.'

Martin looked a little awkward and made a move to stand. 'Shall I get us tea?'

Allie regarded him. She was almost entirely convinced that this cup of tea would come with a side order of 'I'm sorry, the dog ate my homework', but, despite having had a surfeit of tea already that day, she agreed and watched Martin amble slowly over to the counter.

She took a deep breath and once again contemplated whether this agreement with Martin was really going to be worth it or whether she should just call the whole thing off. What was she actually going to get out of this? She had just handed over a partial synopsis to Martin and all she had got in return was the promise of a cup of (admittedly high-quality, well-steeped) John Lewis tea. This didn't look like a fair trade by any metric. Maybe she shouldn't have been so quick to show Martin what she had written. Maybe she should have asked him what he had done for her book first. She looked back to her right, watching Martin as he stood in line. He wasn't a bad man, she knew that, she was sure if she told him she was calling the whole thing off he wouldn't even consider using her plot. He had integrity, she knew that. But if she did call it off, where did it leave her in terms of her own book? Things seemed to be going great with Will, and she was starting to write again, and not just murder outlines... but what if things with Will ended? What if her passion for him stopped translating into passion on the page? No, she decided, she'd stay the course a little longer. See what Martin came up with, because she had a deadline to meet and very few other options available to her.

She sighed, looking away from Martin and over to her left

where a mother was busily berating her two children for eating their sandwiches with their fingers. Allie rolled her eyes, feeling sorry for the kids. They were dressed as if they were actually *in* the John Lewis ad, not just sat in the cafe – starched shirts and dresses that looked uncomfortable for grown-ups to wear, let alone kids. Allie held back a laugh and watched with interest as the mother unfolded actual linen napkins and tucked them over the laps of her progeny. The children didn't look startled or concerned, as if this kind of event happened to them every day.

'Are you seeing this?' Martin put a mug of tea in front of her and gesticulated with his elbow to the events that Allie was observing.

'Uh-huh,' said Allie, unable to drag her eyes away from the two exquisitely dressed tweens, now expertly eating sandwiches with their cutlery. 'As far as I can make out, they're called Marmaduke and Artemis,' she hissed under her breath.

Martin rolled his eyes and sat down heavily. 'Are you sure they're not cats?'

He said this rather more loudly than Allie would have liked. 'Shhh!' She winced.

'We used to bring our two here when they were little.' Allie's gaze flitted quickly away from their neighboring table and back at Martin.

'Aha! So that's why you chose this place.'

Martin nodded.

'I was wondering.'

'You don't approve?'

'No, it's not that,' Allie paused 'It's just … don't take this the wrong way, but it hardly screams romance.'

'You don't think so?' Martin deadpanned, raising an eyebrow. 'Oh fine, no, maybe it's not romantic to everyone but it reminds me of Angie and that's romantic enough for me,' he said gruffly.

Allie felt her heart constrict and decided to cut him some slack. Maybe this was the chance to get him to talk more about Angie, get him to express some emotion. She snuck a look at him, wondering when she could safely start questioning him, but in the end she didn't need to do a thing, Martin started without needing a prompt.

'Angie loved bringing the kids here at Christmas. We'd go see the Christmas lights, maybe a show. Bring them here for high tea afterwards.' He raised his voice. 'Never made them use cutlery to eat sandwiches though.' He shot their neighbour a withering look.

Allie waited for him to continue, but he fell silent, looking around the busy cafe, a wistful and slightly sad expression now on his face.

'So,' she nudged gently. 'How are things going with Angie?'

Martin looked down at the floor which was suddenly extremely interesting to him. 'Have you talked to her yet?' Allie pressed. 'About your book? About things with your daughter?'

'Not exactly.' Martin raised his eyes to meet Allie's and had the grace to look sheepish. 'But I did buy her flowers.'

'Well, that's a start, I suppose.' Allie was not impressed and replied in an icy tone that suggested that if this was the start then they might as well skip the rest of the winning-the-wife back part and move straight on to a decree nisi.

'I used to do it all the time, buy her flowers, I mean.' Martin was starting to sound like a man who had just been served those divorce papers, and despite her irritation Allie's heart went out to him. It was so obvious that he adored

Angie, but that he had completely forgotten how to show her that.

'So why did you stop?'

Martin shrugged. 'I guess it just didn't seem necessary after a while. She made some comment about it being an extravagance and I took her at her word.'

'And you never bought her flowers again?' Allie was aghast. 'Never?'

'Well, I mean I'm sure I did…' Martin tailed off indicating that actually he was pretty sure that he didn't.

'Wow, I mean, Martin, it's nice you *listened* to your wife. But I'm guessing she didn't mean *never buy me flowers again*. What did she say when you gave her the flowers the other day?'

'She said they were lovely and then went out to her pottery class. She's learning how to use a wheel at the moment. Very tricky, apparently.'

Allie had absolutely zero interest in pottery wheels and whether they were tricky or not, although she did file that hobby of Angie's, just in case she could use it at a later date in her quest to help Martin win Angie back. But right at this moment, she was more concerned that neither of them would ever get to that stage. How did two married people in love get to the point where flowers were no longer bought, kind words no longer exchanged? It made her wonder whether she hadn't got the whole thing right in the first place and that romance was dead and there was no such thing as happy-ever-afters.

She was just about to pack her things up, tell Martin he could stuff their plan and that she was keeping her serial killer for herself when an image of Jake Matthew's cold, dead eyes flashed into her mind and she realised she was screwed. And not in the desirable, sexy way, but in the totally well and truly fucked, having to hand back the advance, losing her job and her house kind of way. She had to keep going, this was going to be a challenge, sure, but she had known that the first time she had locked eyes on Martin's tweed elbow patched jacket. No, she needed to see this through. And not just for her, Angie deserved better.

Allie took a deep breath, deciding now was the moment to level with him. If she was going to do this, he needed to pull his weight or it would end in disaster, for all of them, and especially for Allie's writing career. 'Look Martin, I don't want to cast judgement.' He raised his eyebrows at her. 'Yes alright, I don't want to, but I'm going to do it anyway. I've written you an outline, I've put some real effort into this. And so far you've bought your wife flowers and arranged to meet me in the cafe you used to take your children to. You should bring *her* here. You should tell *her* that you miss her, remind her of the good memories, of Christmas when your kids were little, all those warm fuzzy things!'

'I'm working on it!' protested Martin.

'Well, work a bit harder, OK?' Allie demanded. 'Because in case you had forgotten, we're both on a book deadline, and I, for one, need some stronger inspiration.'

They stared at each other in a somewhat hostile manner. 'I'm taking her out to dinner later this week,' Martin eventually said.

'Good, and it had better be somewhere special.' Allie sulkily played with a teaspoon and once again wondered why on earth she had agreed to do this.

'It's our son's restaurant.'

'Nice. I didn't realise he ran a restaurant.'

'Well, his business partner mainly runs that side of things. He's more involved in the... Oh my word, what is she making them wear?'

Allie looked to the side and saw West London Mummy shovelling her children into matching velvet overcoats, buttoning them up aggressively as the children stared into the middle distance and pulled on white gloves.

'It's boiling in here. They'll expire!' He looked aghast at Allie. 'Surely that's child abuse?'

Allie pulled a face. 'At the very least, we're looking at years of therapy. After which one of them will undoubtedly turn into a goth, rejecting everything their mother ever forced them to wear.'

Martin laughed, causing the mother in question to turn and look at him, tutting loudly at the interruption his outburst had caused in attending to her children's attire. His face loosened up, the tension in the atmosphere from their previous tetchy exchange vanishing. Allie grinned at him, preferring to have this version of Martin, and not the morose defensive version from earlier.

'You know, no matter what you do with your kids, no matter how much you give them, spend time with them, there will *always* be something they blame you for.'

Allie nodded vigorously. 'I still hold it against my mum that she never bought me a Sylvanian Family caravan.'

'I don't even know what that is.'

'What?' Allie looked horrified. 'Your daughter never had Sylvanians? No wonder she hates you.'

'She doesn't hate me,' Martin explained patiently, 'she just ... gets frustrated when I refuse to give her things.'

'Like Sylvanians.' Allie was finding it hard to give up this topic. 'How old is she?'

'Thirty.'

'What do you remember her begging you for at Christmas?'

Martin scrunched up his face. 'To be honest the same stuff that she still does: clothes, shoes, money.'

Allie felt her eye twitch. What eight-year-old put clothes and shoes above cute fluffy woodland animals?

'Gigi was always…'

'Gigi?'

'Gigi, my daughter. It's what everyone calls her.'

Allie waited, wondering what horrors Martin might be about to reveal about Gigi next, but he didn't. 'Let's not get onto Gigi. It's a complicated subject and as we have established, the source of one of the major tensions in my marriage.'

'Sounds like a good reason to discuss her,' Allie said, experiencing an unusual degree of interest in someone who she was quite sure she would loathe. 'I mean, if she's a source of conflict, maybe you need to resolve that before you can move forward with Angie?'

Martin ran a hand down his face. 'We've been trying to fix the problem that is Gigi for years. To be honest, I think it's high time I accepted what Angie has been saying about her for a long while, she needs to get on with her life and stop expecting us to mend her mistakes.'

'So, you should tell Angie that,' Allie said insistently, 'tell her you've realised she was right. We all like to be told we're right!'

Martin smiled wanly. 'Yes, I've noticed that. The trouble is, if we start discussing Gigi, and all that entails, I will have to come clean about the money I've given her.' Martin rubbed his face again.

Allie pulled a face. 'I feel like we need to be in an establishment that serves alcohol to deal with this.'

'Yes, that sounds like the story of parenting Gigi. They do those little bottles of wine here?' Martin looked hopeful.

'I was thinking we needed something stronger.'

They sat in silence for a moment.

'I've got an idea.' Martin paused for a second. 'I actually don't know why I didn't suggest we meet there.' Allie could feel her mouth twitch into a smile, sensing the note of excitement that had crept into Martin's voice. 'How long have you got?' he asked.

'Honestly?' said Allie, 'I have nothing else on for the rest of the day, other than to go home and probably not write. I'm in your hands, especially if they're going to lead me to something I can use in my book.'

Fifteen minutes later, Allie found herself gawping at the beautiful central courtyard of the Wallace Collection.

'I can't believe you've never been here before.' Martin was staring at her as if she had sprouted an extra head. 'How long have you lived in London?'

'Long enough to know far more rooftop bars than I bet you've ever been in.'

'I doubt it. Remember, I was going to publishing parties when you were still in nappies. Back in the days when they had the budget to spend on them.'

'Fair point, best I've ever had is warm wine in a bookshop. Oh, apart from the summer party of course.'

'Of course. Good food at the last one, wasn't it?' Martin gave her a curious look and Allie wondered whether he had noticed the vibe between her and Will during their brief conversation in the alley behind the museum.

'It was OK,' she said noncommittally. 'But this?' She pointed to her gin julep, which she was dangerously close to finishing already. 'This is just delicious.'

'I'm glad you like it.' Martin looked pleased with himself. 'But I still can't believe you've never been here before, you heathen.'

Allie grinned at him. Strangely she didn't mind being insulted by Martin, it was a whole lot better than him being buttoned up and morose. He'd relaxed, his whole being seemed completely different to the miserable, tense creature he had arrived as that afternoon. And she liked the transformation, she even liked the way he was teasing her. It was a strange sort of friendship they had begun to create.

'OK,' she leaned back in her chair, reluctantly putting her drink down, 'tell me what this place makes you think of?' To Allie it made her think of Brideshead, of dances and cocktail parties, the likes of which she would never be invited to.

'Meeting Angie here, before we had kids? She would sneak off for an extra long lunch break, and I wasn't yet published, so I'd be at home trying to write. I'd find her in one of the galleries, staring at one of her favourite paintings. And then we'd spend a glorious hour together, giggling at the nudes, making up stories about the painters, feeling superior to everyone else in only the way that the young and in love can. You know that point when you still believe that no one else has ever felt this way before, that it will last forever and that you're the luckiest couple in the world to have found each other? It was all the inspiration I needed to go home and then write something amazingly grisly for the afternoon.' He grinned at Allie. 'Hang on, what are you doing?'

Allie's eyes had misted over at Martin's words and she had

leaned forward and grabbed her laptop from out of her bag. 'Do you mind? I thought I'd take some notes.'

Martin looked confused, thrown off his stride. 'I guess not. Are you actually going to use some of this?'

'I'm not sure yet. But honestly, Martin, it's amazing listening to you talk about Angie. I love the history you share, the memories.'

Martin smiled and looked around the courtyard. To Allie he immediately looked as if he had been transported back three decades and was sat waiting for Angie to appear, to inspire and delight him.

'You should bring her here, you know.'

'I know I should.' He took his glasses off and put them down on the table. 'It's hard though. When you haven't done something like that in so long. I worry she'll think I'm being soppy.' He looked away from Allie, down at his hands, 'I worry that she'll say no.' He paused and then looked up. 'I worry about what she'll say when I tell her about the money.'

Allie puffed her cheeks out and exhaled. 'Ugh. I feel for you, Martin. At least I don't have anyone else to worry about in this whole mess. But you know it will be worse if you don't tell her? She's going to find out eventually.'

'Not if we get these books written!'

Allie fixed him with a stare. 'Martin, stuff like this *always* comes out. You have to tell her. It's best she hears from you and not from Gigi or anyone else. Hang on, does anyone else know?' Martin shook his head. 'Not your son?'

'Liam? No. I mean, he knows Gigi is a problem, and I suspect he realises that me and Angie aren't getting along as well as we used to. But he's busy. Running his business. Living his life.'

'Does he have a family? Is he married?' Allie asked.

'No, he's been single for a while. Had a couple of bad experiences, I think. Not that he told us much about it, but he seems to have closed himself off from meeting someone. Which is something else for me and Angie to worry about.'

Allie bristled. 'You know, it might sound crazy to you, Martin, but people can be happily single. Perfectly fulfilled. Happy on their own.'

'Who are you trying to persuade?' Martin asked dryly. 'You or me?'

Allie harrumphed. 'I'm just *saying* that maybe he's concentrating on running his business at the moment, making that a success.' She tried not to dwell on the fact that the disaster zone that was her personal life was not resulting in a stellar professional outlook right now. 'Maybe he's OK being single. I mean I am,' she said somewhat defensively.

'Are you?' Martin queried.

'Yes!' protested Allie, 'I'm definitely better off without my ex.'

'No, that's not what I meant. I meant *are* you single.'

Allie peered at Martin. 'Weird and somewhat personal question, Martin.'

Martin rolled his eyes and pointed at her laptop. 'I couldn't help noticing the other document you had up on there just now. Looks like you've started writing again... Looked like it might be personal too...'

Allie flushed a bright crimson remembering some of the notes she had been hastily scribbling that morning and berated herself for not minimising the page before she had let Martin look at her laptop. 'It's just, just some notes I've been writing, not personal no...' she floundered. 'I mean, well, look, there is this guy I like. But it's nothing really ... just, well ... it's kind of inspiring.'

Martin bit back a smile.

'What?!' she protested.

'Nothing, nothing. It's nice, that's all. And great that you've met someone who's inspiring you to write again. I'd hate to think you were totally reliant on my outdated version of romance for your book.'

'You don't think it's bad?'

'Bad? Why would it be bad?'

'I just thought, maybe I'm using him. To inspire me?'

Martin looked at her curiously. 'Are you single? Is he single? Are you both consenting adults? Then it's fine.'

Allie felt surprisingly reassured by Martin's pragmatic approach. He was right, she and Will were both consenting adults. She liked him, she thought he liked her. She needed to stop overthinking things, enjoy it and get some words written.

'Anyway, I won't embarrass you any more. Sounds like Liam might have started seeing someone as well. Yesterday I asked him if he wanted to meet for a pint and he said he was busy. I got the impression he was meeting a girl. Sorry,' Martin stopped himself, 'a young lady.'

Allie stifled a giggle. She could just imagine Martin describing his son's girlfriend as a 'lovely young lady'. And she wondered what the young lady would make of Martin, of his tweed jackets and lost glasses. If it were her she would be in awe of such an amazing writer, even if he was at the end of his career. But she knew that not everyone was as fascinated by writers as she was. She sighed, thinking how lucky this girl was and that she might not even realise it.

'Well I'm pleased for him if he has met someone. Maybe that will give you and Angie one less thing to worry about. But on that note, we need to work out what you're going to spend the next few days doing about your marriage, how you're going to fix it and if you're going to give me enough material to write my next book.'

'Alright. So what should I do?'

'You said you're taking her to your son's restaurant?' Martin nodded. 'Is that special enough?' Allie squinted at him. 'You're not getting this for free?'

'No, not at all!' Martin protested. 'Honestly. Liam is barely involved in the restaurant side.' Allie continued to give Martin a hard stare. 'Cross my heart,' he said, which made Allie laugh.

'OK,' she replied still chuckling. 'But make sure there's champagne.'

'Angie doesn't like champagne.'

'Martin!' snapped Allie. 'You know what I mean. Make sure it's special.' Martin nodded meekly. 'And then report back to me, OK? I'll think of somewhere fabulous and inspirational for our next meeting.'

'I'm not sure whether you're using this young man you're seeing, but sometimes I feel like you're just using me,' Martin said, back to his morose self.

Allie clicked her fingers and pointed at her laptop. 'I am. And you're using me. Get used to it. I'm emailing this over to you now so stop whinging.'

Chapter Ten

A llie considered letting the call go to voicemail. She wasn't in the habit of picking up to strangers and this number had called twice already that morning, not leaving a message either time. She was on her way to meet Martha for lunch, who had demanded an increase in their scheduled meet-ups, which Allie was convinced was Martha's way of keeping an eye on her and making sure she wasn't doing anything stupid. Which for Martha would cover pretty much most of Allie's daily existence. And so, lacking anything better to do on the bus journey, she finally picked up her phone.

'Hello?'

There was a long pause on the end of the line. 'Hello?' Allie tried again.

'Allie, it's Verity,' came the whispered response.

'Verity!' Allie almost dropped her phone in excitement. She had been impatiently waiting for Verity to reply to her messages and now felt irritated with herself that she hadn't picked up her phone earlier when this number had rung.

'Shh!' Verity hissed.

Allie looked over her shoulder. She didn't know about Verity's location but the 306 bus was empty, so she wasn't going to be disturbing anyone with her phone call.

'Verity, I've been trying to get in touch with you!' she exclaimed.

'I know, but shh. Here's the thing. I'm not supposed to speak to you.'

Allie felt puzzled. 'You're not?'

'No. Jake made it abundantly clear that I was not to contact any of my authors, that it would be a violation of my NDA and that he wouldn't hesitate to seek legal redress if I did.'

'Wait! Hang on, he made you sign an NDA?'

'Yes, just before I left the building.'

'Verity... Sorry,' Allie apologised for using her name when she heard the intake of breath from the other end of the phone. Of course Verity couldn't see her but she cupped her hand around her phone, attempting privacy of some sort. 'Erm, I'm pretty sure he's not allowed to make you sign one of those. And that if he did it's not actually enforceable.'

'I don't know,' Verity sounded miserable, 'he was pretty persuasive.'

'He's such a shit,' Allie said definitively.

'Agreed. But he did. And I did sign it and now I really really shouldn't be talking to you. Allie, you have to stop contacting me!' Verity pleaded.

'Wait, what? No!' Allie protested. 'I'm not going to stop contacting you. I don't care what that awful Jake Matthews says. I need you! I can't publish a book without you!'

There was a long pause on the other end of the line. Allie was about to ask if Verity was still there and then remembered that she shouldn't be using her name.

'How's the book coming along?' Verity eventually asked.

'Erm, it's coming…'

There was a long sigh. 'I see.'

'Look, I really do need to talk to you about my book. Can we meet?'

'No!' Verity exploded. 'Allie, I can't! Imagine if someone sees us?'

Allie took a deep breath, it was obvious that Verity was not thinking straight. It was hardly likely that Jake was having her followed, although probably only because Brinkman's didn't have the necessary budget to facilitate twenty-four-hour surveillance of one of their former staff members. Briefly Allie wondered under what budget line such an outlay would be placed. But she did understand Verity's nervousness about being spotted in public together.

'What about if you came to mine?'

'I don't know, Allie,' moaned Verity.

'Ver… Sorry! Look, he's not having you followed, is he?' There was a long pause. 'Have you noticed anyone suspicious? Cars parked outside your flat? People in trench coats? Binoculars?' Allie stifled a giggle.

'Ha bloody ha. I don't think you're taking this seriously.'

'No, I am! I promise I am. And I understand not wanting to meet up. But I don't think Jake will ever know if you come round to my flat.'

Allie held her breath. She almost started talking again, but she took another breath, waiting for Verity to feel comfortable.

'OK,' Verity exhaled. 'When?'

'I'm on my way out to meet my sister but I'll be back by 3pm?' Allie gave Verity the address and then hung up. She looked quickly over her shoulder to check that the bus was still empty; Verity's nervousness was infectious.

As she opened the front door to her flat later that afternoon Allie half expected Verity to be in disguise and was a little disappointed when she wasn't. Allie made a point of bundling her into the flat and then checking both sides of the street before she slammed and locked the door behind her. Allie put her back to the door and pretended to wipe her face in relief with her sleeve. 'Phew,' she gasped.

'Very funny,' Verity said, her mouth a thin line as she handed her coat over to Allie.

'Sorry, childish I know.' Allie was trying not to snigger as she hung Verity's coat for her. 'Come through.'

For all the years they had known each other, Verity had never once been to Allie's flat. They always met at Brinkman's. Or smart restaurants in town. Suddenly, Allie felt self-conscious of her little flat, which was perfect in her mind but seemed rather pedestrian now that Verity, with her seemingly impeccable taste and generations of pedigree, was stood in it. Still, Verity had made it quite clear that they couldn't meet in public and Allie was fairly confident that Jake Matthews wouldn't have any interest in staking out her home. She led the way down to the kitchen at the back of the flat. 'Tea? Coffee? Something stronger?' she offered. Now that she could get a good look at Verity in the light streaming through the patio doors, she noticed that she didn't look good; she was thinner and more drawn than she had been the last time Allie had seen her. And probably in need of that stronger drink. Verity paused. It was obvious she too felt she needed something alcoholic but was being too polite to ask for it.

'How about I open a bottle of wine?' Allie suggested and Verity smiled at her gratefully. Allie led her to one of the chairs at the kitchen table, pushed her gently and Verity sank down, looking decidedly shaky.

'I know you think I'm overreacting,' Verity said, unwinding one of her floaty scarves and then winding it back up again, 'but honestly, I did have to check over my shoulder several times on my way over here.'

Taking two glasses from the cupboard, Allie poured them both a large glass and put one down in front of Verity. 'There, have a gulp of that. You look like you need it.'

'Thank you.' Allie watched in amazement as the usually demure Verity practically downed the glass of wine in one go.

'You want another one?' she asked.

Verity shook her head. 'Maybe later. Drinking isn't really helping me at the moment.' She glanced down at her now almost empty glass and looked as if she was ready to fill it with tears. 'I either get sobby and maudlin or angry and filled with rage at Jake and bloody Brinkman's.'

Allie was fascinated to see Verity filled with rage, she had only ever known her composed and professional. Fleetingly, she thought it might be quite fun to witness and wondered if Verity's rage could be weaponized to take down Jake Matthews before she remembered that her friend and editor was sat in front of her almost in tears and that this was the time to be moved to compassion.

'Jake said you'd found a new job though?' Allie asked optimistically, she decided that confronting Verity for abandoning her wasn't appropriate right now.

Verity's face twisted and she laughed hollowly. 'Yeah, that's what that shit would like you to believe.'

Allie grimaced, both at hearing Verity swear, which was beyond surprising, and also the duplicity of Jake. 'But he made it sound like you'd left of your own accord?' Allie asked, trying not to sound combative.

'Hardly. I wasn't given a choice in the matter. Told it was cost cutting. Made to sign an NDA. My electronics were confiscated and then I was marched out of the building. I left out of the back door about thirty seconds after you were taken through the front.'

Allie stared at Verity in horror. This was truly terrible. It was all very well her and Martin making up amusing ways of doing away with Jake Matthews but the truth was that he really was a monster.

'But what about all those doctor's appointments?' Allie floundered for an alternative explanation.

'What?'

'I sort of presumed you were out for job interviews, because, you know, you seem pretty healthy to be having so many doctor's appointments...' Allie was beginning to regret this line of questioning and her voice tailed off accordingly.

'There's more than one type of doctor, Allie.' Verity sighed. Allie said nothing, trying to piece together what it was Verity was getting at. 'Therapy?' Verity eventually offered. 'I've been having therapy to deal with the stress of working for Jake. But hey, the good news is that now we've moved on to discussing my trauma surrounding losing my job.'

'Oh Verity, I'm so sorry.' Allie reached across and squeezed Verity's hand. 'Is there anything I can do?'

'Do?' Verity laughed hollowly. 'There's nothing any of us can do.'

'But surely—'

'Allie, don't you think I've thought about this?' Verity's beautiful lip curled in frustration and anger. 'Don't you think

I've analysed every possible alternative scenario? There's nothing I can do but suck it up and look for a new job.'

'But…'

Verity glared at her ferociously and Allie held her tongue. They broke away and both stared at the table for a while in contemplative silence.

'And I need to find one fast, because I have rent to pay.'

Allie didn't know how to put this politely. She had always presumed that with a surname like Montagu-Forbes, Verity didn't have to think about money. And from everything she knew about the industry, it was almost essential to come from money in order to survive in it.

'Erm, couldn't you ask your parents?' she offered.

Verity laughed hollowly. 'Ha! Yeah right. Like they have cash to spare.'

'What does Richard think?' Allie decided now was not the moment to ask any further questions about Verity's parents' cash reserves. But given how loved up Verity had been the last time Allie had seen her it would be just the icing on the cake of unravelling disasters for her to have split up with Richard.

Verity sighed. 'He thinks the same as you,' she looked at Allie mulishly, 'that I should fight it.'

'I never said that…' Allie began to protest.

'No, but you think I should.' Verity dared Allie to challenge her assertion. 'And I wish I could.' Verity's tone shifted suddenly, from stubbornly resistant to pleading. Allie felt her heartstrings tug and decided that although she sometimes found Verity frightening, she preferred that to this diminished version. 'God, I do wish I could. I want to take down Jake Matthews and get my job back as much as you and Richard want me to. But I can't, can I?'

Allie was grateful that Verity barely paused before

continuing. She wasn't sure what she would have said if Verity had left that last statement hanging in the air – *Yes you can? Yes you should? Why on earth can't you?*

'What you and Richard don't seem to realise is that everyone in the industry thinks Jake Matthews is a shit. But nobody *does* anything about it. And so how can I? He's protected. It's a conspiracy of silence. And if I do say something he'll retaliate. He'll sue me over this stupid NDA, or make sure I never work in publishing again. Or both!' Verity threw her hands up in frustration.

'Can he do that?' Allie asked dubiously. Jake Matthews did indeed seem like an insidious creep but the way Verity was describing him made him sound like he controlled the industry like a mafia cartel.

'Yes, he can do that,' spat Verity. 'Publishing boys' club. One word from him and all his "mates" at the other companies will close ranks, I'll never work for a reputable company again!' she wailed.

Allie wrinkled her nose. She really wasn't sure that in this day and age companies could work like that but given the state Verity was in she didn't think it would be constructive or supportive to challenge her. And really what did she know? Maybe Jake really was pulling the strings behind the scenes. It wasn't like the precedent was lacking.

Ignoring Verity's previous comments about alcohol, Allie stood and went to the fridge, returning with the bottle of wine. Not a word of protest passed Verity's lips as Allie refilled both their glasses. Allie sat watching Verity. She was so far from the serene goddess that Allie had always known her as, the saviour of Allie's writing dream, the one who had plucked her from nowhere and who had had the vision for her very first book. And it had been Verity who had *always* championed

Allie's books, plugging away at the sales team so that they tried harder, getting her book covers just right, and guiding Allie, seemingly effortlessly, from one success to the next. And now look at her. Allie hated to see how ground down she had become by Jake's actions, how hollow and sad she seemed. Allie's heart went out to her, to both of them, sat as they were, an editor with no job and an author with no book. She owed it to Verity to try and fix this.

'I do wish there was something we could do,' Verity said eventually. 'Some way of taking him down.' Simultaneously they reached for their glasses and took a sip of wine, both enjoying separate fantasies of destroying Jake Matthews.

'Hey, I'll tell you something funny though. That assistant of his – Tess? Teresa?'

'Tessa,' confirmed Verity gloomily.

'Tessa, that's right. I'm sure I heard her in the bathroom at the summer party doing coke.'

Verity sat bolt upright in her chair. 'You did?' she asked in a strained voice.

'Er, well yeah. I mean I thought it was her voice. I didn't see her or anything. And I mean, I only spoke to her once, when I came in the other week...' Allie's voice trailed off. There was a peculiar look on Verity's face and Allie really didn't know what to make of it.

'You said you heard her voice?'

'Yeees,' Allie confirmed nervously.

'In the bathroom?'

'That's right...'

'She was talking to someone else in there? In the bathroom, I mean?'

'Erm, yes?' Allie really wasn't sure where Verity was going with this.

'So there was someone else in the bathroom doing coke with her?'

'Well, like I said,' Allie floundered, 'I didn't *see* any of this. I was in one of the cubicles. But the girl, Tessa, at least I think it might have been Tessa…' Allie felt less and less sure of this the more interest that Verity took. 'Anyway, whoever the girl was, it sounded like she'd been asked to bring the coke by the other person.'

'Male or female?'

'I'm sorry?'

'Male or female?' Verity's voice was icy cold. 'Was the other person male or female?'

'Male. Definitely. Verity, where are you going with this?'

Verity sat back in her seat and swirled her wine around in her glass. 'Just thinking.'

There was a long pause. Allie wondered if she should be offering more wine, some snacks, maybe Verity's blood sugar had plummeted and that was why she was being so antsy about a snippet of gossip that Allie had innocently thought would amuse her.

'Any interest in sharing with me what you're thinking?' Allie asked eventually.

Verity leaned back in her chair, far enough that Allie considered warning her to be careful. Her kitchen chairs weren't the most robust and Allie feared Verity was about to plunge backwards and she really didn't have the time for a long wait in A&E.

'Well, there are loads of rumours flying round about Jake. One being how he got to where he is now. Another being just what dirt he holds on people to allow him to get away with behaving in the way he does. But the one I'm thinking of, is the rumour about his monumental drug habit.'

Allie's eyes went wide at Verity's words. 'You don't think…?'

Verity nodded slowly and shifted in her seat, inching herself forward. Allie could sense the excitement and tension building in Verity. 'Allie, think very carefully. The voice you heard in the bathroom with Tessa. Could it have been Jake's voice?'

Allie cast her mind back to the night of the party. To the bathroom where she had gone to escape from the party. She remembered hearing the voices and initially thinking that she was about to interrupt an illicit tryst before quickly realising that she was overhearing something quite different. She hesitated. 'I'm not sure … maybe? Yes? I think it could have been him?'

She looked up and saw Verity staring at her. 'But even if it was, what good will it do us?'

Verity suddenly looked deflated. 'I'm not sure,' she admitted. 'I guess I just had a crazy idea that if we could expose Jake's drug habit then maybe I could get my job back, be your editor again.'

'Er yeah, about that,' Allie said awkwardly. 'I'm not sure this is the right moment to confess this outright but as it stands, right at this moment,' Allie flailed around trying to find the right words, 'I don't actually have a book for you to edit.'

Verity gave her a strong look of disappointment. 'I had guessed that.' Allie hung her head in shame, mortified that Verity had known all along. 'And we're going to fix that,' she said briskly, 'just like we are going to fix Jake Matthews.' A smile started playing around Verity's lips. 'I'm beginning to get an idea…'

Allie took a deep breath, this was more like it, she was

starting to see the old Verity in front of her, the *real* Verity. And god, how she had missed her.

'OK, so, Jake first, what's your plan?' Allie asked.

'Tessa must be what, twenty-two? Twenty-three?' Verity mused. 'Definitely no more than twenty-five right? And she's Jake's assistant?' Allie nodded again. She trusted Verity to know this kind of thing. 'Which makes what he is doing wrong on many different levels, right?' Verity continued.

'IF he is,' Allie countered, nervous that Verity was going to go off on a wild goose chase based purely on hearsay from Allie.

Verity flapped her hand at Allie in a dismissive gesture. 'Not only is he doing drugs at a work party, but he's doing them with his assistant and, if what you're saying is correct, he got Tessa, *his assistant*, to get those drugs for him!'

'We can't prove any of this!' Allie protested.

'No, we can't. But I could ask Tessa about it.' Verity's eyes sparkled.

'Hang on,' Allie asked in confusion, 'I thought you'd signed an NDA?'

'Yes and?'

'So, you can't very well march up to Tessa and ask her if she's been doing coke with her boss and if it was him that asked her to get him that coke.'

'Actually,' Verity grinned, 'the NDA was quite specific. You see I can't speak to you,' she pointed at Allie, 'or any other authors, but it makes no mention of other employees.'

'Right,' Allie folded her arms across her chest, 'so you're just going to come straight out with it and ask Tessa whether Jake Matthews is using her as a drugs mule?'

Verity's face fell. 'God, you're right. I can't, can I?' She wrung her hands nervously, immediately making Allie feel terrible that she had banished confident, poised Verity and brought back cowed, broken Verity.

'But maybe *I* could?' Allie's words surprised even herself. What on earth was she signing herself up to?

'What?' Verity's head snapped back up.

'Well, I need to be in touch with Tessa about my book. I guess I could see if I could befriend her, get her to confide in me?' Allie really couldn't believe what she was saying now. She was in a deep enough mess without attempting to uncover an underground publishing drugs ring. But saying these words and making these promises was worth it to see the eager look on Verity's face.

'You'd do that?' Verity cried.

'Well, I'm not making any promises,' Allie faltered, 'but yes, I guess I could see if I can.'

Verity stood up and flung her arms around Allie.

Allie fought for air and then when she got her breath again she laughed. 'OK!' she protested, pushing Verity off a little bit. 'I said I'll try. First I need to write something for her to read.'

'Yes, about that.' Verity sat back down in her chair immediately business like. 'I can't believe you were lying to me about your next book.'

'I wasn't lying!' Allie quailed under Verity's look. 'I was just protecting you from some distressing information.'

Verity raised her eyebrow.

'Ugh, OK. I admit it. I lost my mojo. Couldn't write for ages. Had a long dark night of the soul moment and started wondering if I should turn to crime.'

Verity's eyebrows shot higher.

'I meant for my writing!' explained Allie, but Verity's eyebrows remained stubbornly aloft.

'You want to write a crime novel?' Verity asked in surprise.

'No, not really. Well maybe. I mean, I considered it briefly.' Allie stood, deciding that now really was the time to distract Verity with salty snacks. If she was being honest, the wine had completely gone to her head. She had already promised to help try to bring down Jake Matthews by befriending and abusing any trust she managed to gain with Tessa. She needed to eat something and fast, before her mouth made any more promises that her weak will and cowardice couldn't fulfill. She rummaged through the cupboards, disappearing from Verity's view as she did so.

'Here.' She reappeared again, clutching Doritos, Pringles and salted pistachios. Allie pulled some bowls out of another cupboard and dumped snacks out into them, carrying them over to the kitchen table where Verity was sitting. She was heartened to see Verity take a large handful of Pringles and eat them decidedly less than daintily.

'Carry on,' Verity said through a mouthful of crumbs.

Allie stalled, trying to remember what she had been saying before the interruption of the snack stop. 'Oh right, yes, crime novels. Well, I came up with an idea about murdering bankers, you know, a serial killer with a grudge against the immorality of the banking industry, decides to pick them off one by one in a grisly way, as recompense for the sins of their business.'

Verity sniffed. 'Not a bad premise,' she said.

'Thanks.' Allie felt rather proud of herself. 'Inspired by Dominic.'

'What?' Verity said in alarm.

'Oh, yeah, I didn't get round to telling you, what with your firing and then disappearance and all the rest. Dominic dumped me. The night of the summer party in fact. Left here,' Allie gesticulated in the direction of the front door, 'in the car of his new girlfriend. I mean, I presumed that's who she was.'

Allie looked up to realise Verity's eyes had filled with tears again. 'Oh, no, it's fine really!' she said quickly. 'I didn't like him all that much anyway. I've got a feeling he was the reason I couldn't write. Lack of romance you see...'

Verity didn't look any less close to crying so Allie tried a different tack. 'Honestly, it's fine. I've already been on another date AND...' She paused for dramatic effect. 'I've started writing again. I mean, it's not much, and I could really, really use your help if I'm honest.'

'Crime?' Verity asked. 'I mean, is it the crime novel you've been working on?'

'Oh no,' Allie said hastily. 'Don't worry. I've parked that idea.'

Verity looked relieved to hear this.

'I've given it to Martin.'

A look of utter confusion passed over Verity's face. 'Who?'

'Martin Clark, the author?'

'OK, I have a few questions.' Verity placed her immaculately manicured hands down on the table. 'Firstly, Martin Clark? The famous crime writer?' Allie nodded. 'The one who wrote *In Darkness*? *Total Eclipse*?' Allie nodded again. 'Secondly, how do you know him?'

'Met him at the summer party,' confirmed Allie.

'Right, OK. So thirdly, WHY does he have your plot idea?' Allie opened her mouth to respond but Verity held up a finger to silence her. 'And finally, I don't want to forget that we need to cover who you've been on a date with.' A look crossed her face and her mouth dropped open. 'Oh god... Not Martin Clark?'

'Eugh, no!' shouted Allie. 'He's old enough to be my father.' Verity gave Allie a funny look, which Allie couldn't get a read on. 'But I mean he's still very handsome,' she continued, cheekily enjoying the look of horror that was spreading across Verity's face. 'If I were older,' she eventually clarified, 'or he was younger,' she mused.

Verity pushed her now empty again wine glass towards Allie, indicating that if this was the direction that their conversation was going to take she was going to need more wine.

'I'm not dating Martin.' Allie laughed, deciding that despite her and Martin's agreement, she owed it to Verity to explain. She poured another generous glass for Verity. 'But he *is* helping me with my writing. Or at least he's supposed to. But so far, it's mainly been me helping him.'

It took two more glasses of wine before Allie had adequately explained the arrangement that she and Martin had reached and before Verity was suitably assured that Allie wasn't about to run off with a man almost twice her age. By the time she left Allie's flat, Verity still looked dubious but seemed to be more accepting of Allie's life choices. Especially when they were backed up by promises that Allie would actually *be* writing again, and that between them they would track down Tessa and somehow persuade her to do the dirty on Jake.

Chapter Eleven

Allie was enjoying her new morning routine. She had got so used to waking up with a feeling of dread that at first she didn't recognise the new sensation. She had forgotten what it was like to have butterflies, the good kind. Not the kind that made you wonder if you were about to be sick, but the kind that fizzed inside you, sending a delicious thrill of anticipation for the day ahead. Allie would wake, say hi to her new internal butterfly pals, stretch out luxuriously and see how long she could resist before she checked her phone. So far, she had managed forty-eight seconds, but she was hopeful that by the weekend she might get to a minute.

She'd roll onto her stomach and check her messages and every morning so far there would be one from Will. Sometimes it would be something funny that had happened at whatever event he happened to be working at the previous evening. Sometimes it would be something ridiculous his sister had done (she seemed to be a constant source of bemusement and often irritation to Will, and Allie liked to match his stories with ones about Martha). Quite often it would simply be the last message of the conversation they had been having the evening before, and these were the mornings that Allie would wake with no need to roll over to check her phone, because she was still clutching it in her hand.

She grinned as she saw a picture of tiny, yet perfectly formed canapés, which he had sent with the question – 'are these the right size for you?' She liked him teasing her, she liked the familiarity it suggested. She liked knowing he was thinking of her, because she sure as hell was thinking of him; sometimes too much. It was great she was feeling so inspired by him to write, but sometimes she drifted off and time ran away from her as she lost herself in a daydream about Will. She couldn't imagine ever getting bored of him or his funny messages or ever not wanting to hear from him as soon as she woke. But even as she thought this, a new realization of what this cosy familiarity might lead to washed over her and a cold leaden feeling began to travel up from her previously warm and fuzzy toes. It reached and then smothered the butterflies before she allowed herself to acknowledge it. Because what Allie knew, from life, from her previous experiences, was that this too would pass. Sure she might still be happy to hear from Will, she might even catch fleeting memories of what it had been like when they had been in this honeymoon stage, but that's what this was; the honeymoon stage, the getting to know each other stage. When everything about the other person was endlessly fascinating, when you felt like the only two people in the world who had ever found a soulmate like each other, and when boring mundane stuff hadn't yet entered the picture. But it would end, and Allie knew it would. Every single boyfriend she'd ever had ended up that way; even Martin and Angie, who seemed to have adored each other in the early days, had now completely lost their way.

And when that happened what would happen to her writing? Where would her creativity spark from?

And so, Allie lay in her bed, no longer feeling the butterflies and instead trying to work out how to get them back and more importantly how to make them stay.

As she made herself a cup of tea she pondered, as she ate her toast she plotted and by the time Jess rang her to check she was still alive because she hadn't heard from her in almost twenty-four hours she thought she'd cracked it.

'I've figured it out.'

'Good, great, glad to hear it. What is "it" by the way?'

'Oh, sorry. I've been trying to work out how I keep writing.'

'Does it involve putting pen to paper?'

'Ha bloody ha.'

'Sorry, fingers to keyboard?'

'No seriously, Jess, listen. OK, so everyone knows that the honeymoon stage of a relationship is the best stage, right?'

'Weeeeelll maybe…'

'Maybe? What do you mean maybe?'

'I'm not convinced.'

Allie paused, startled off course by Jess's statement. 'You're not?'

'No. I mean yes it's great in lots of ways. But it's also exhausting and terrifying. And yes exciting and sexy too. But sometimes I just want to put my big pants on and curl up on the sofa. And you can't really do that while you're still trying to impress someone, can you?'

Allie contemplated this. 'I guess not. But don't you ever look back and think about how exciting it was when you first got together with Tom? How every date was a big deal?' Allie was thinking back to all those nights when she'd had to counsel Jess over what to wear, endless fit checks, panicked photos back and forth, pre-drinks in bars and the promise to come rescue her if it went wrong. Which it hadn't. And the ring on Jess's left hand was proof of that.

'Oh of course,' agreed Jess, 'it's definitely fun.' This gave Allie a bit of the confidence she'd had knocked out of her theory back. 'But then it's nice to look back on those moments and see how far we've come. And how much more I love him now.'

'You do?'

There was a silence. 'Allie, was that meant to sound like a question?' Jess didn't sound impressed.

'No, no. I meant you *do*. It was a statement. I mean of course you love him more now, right?' Allie hoped she had done enough digging. 'But I just, I guess I'm wondering how do you hang on to that excitement?'

'Well, you don't. But you get the excitement in different ways. Sorry, why are we discussing this in the first place?'

'Oh, right. Yes, well, I think I've worked out where I've been going wrong all these years.'

'By dating Dominic?'

'Thanks, Jess.'

'Sorry.'

'So, every relationship I've ever had has started off with the butterflies, right? And then they disappear, and at that stage I either move on or don't.'

'And we're back to Dominic, aren't we?'

'Can you please stop interrupting me and bringing up Dominic?' Allie pleaded. 'But yes, agreed, Dominic was a low point. Instead of moving on, I stayed, and it ended with me not being able to write, right?!' Allie said.

'Right!' Jess agreed enthusiastically.

'So, what I need to do, in order to keep writing, is keep those butterflies going with Will!'

'Yay!' Jess sounded confused more than excited. 'And how do we do that?'

'By keeping him at arm's length, not getting too attached. No getting comfy and familiar!'

There was another long pause. Allie's triumphant feelings at having cracked the formula for having her cake and eating it – i.e. smashing hot guy AND fulfilling publishing contractual requirements – were beginning to feel a little shaky.

'Al?' Jess said dubiously. 'I'm not sure that's going to work.'

'Why not?' Allie was on the defensive now. She liked those triumphant feelings and she wasn't going to give them up without a fight.

'Because you like him, right? So you're going to get closer. It's just the way love works.'

Allie spluttered, 'Love? Jess, c'mon. I'm after lust here.'

'Yeah, I know you are. But that's my point. Lust only lasts so long. So either you get closer and it turns into something else, or the lust fades and gets replaced by nothing and that's when you call it quits.'

'*Exactly!* I just need to keep him in the lust zone while I get this book written. And then—'

'Then what? Allie, I don't see this ending well for you. I don't think you can hope you'll find someone to lust after every time you need to write a book.'

'Why not?'

'Because...' Jess sighed. 'What happened to happy-ever-after? Maybe *that's* what you should be looking for.'

'I don't believe in happy-ever-afters anymore,' Allie said mulishly.

'OK, Allie, whatever. But, you want my opinion? You

should *start* believing again. Maybe *that's* why you can't write? Maybe Will *is* the one? Maybe you should give him a chance and see what happens rather than holding him at arm's length? Maybe those butterflies you're chasing will one day transform into something lovely and permanent.'

Allie thought about Jess's advice. She thought about the kid she had been with her head in those romance novels, who would rather have died than admit during her angry teenage phase that what she really wanted, more than anything else in the world, was to find her happy-ever-after and run off with him into the sunset and catch those butterflies together. And she wondered when it was that she had lost that dream, when she had become so cynical. She cradled her phone between her neck and her ear as she scrabbled in the bottom of her wardrobe for her trainers.

'Al?' Jess asked. 'What are you doing?'

'Looking for some shoes.'

'Right. Are you OK?' Jess sounded concerned.

'Yeah, just, you know, lots to think about.'

'OK, I'm sorry if I upset you. I just hate to think about you not grabbing this opportunity and not making the most of things with Will. I know this sounds sappy, but you light up when you talk about him. I can see it in your face and hear it in your voice. Don't miss out just because you think it will help your writing.'

Allie said nothing, putting the phone down on the floor as she pulled on the trainers she had found. 'I'll think about it,' she finally said as she stood and went to grab her keys.

'Where are you off to?' Jess asked.

'Just out. Walking. Clear my head, you know?'

'Erm, OK sure.' Jess did not sound sure, in fact she sounded more convinced that Allie's impending ramble was a sign that she was completely losing it. 'Look, call me anytime, OK? And just don't do anything rash.'

'I promise I won't,' Allie said, ending the call.

As Allie headed out her front door she felt justifiably sure that she hadn't made a promise to Jess that she couldn't keep, as one person's definition of rash was another person's sensible course of action. But that didn't stop her from ruminating all the way down the road, past the Tube station, past Earl's Court and right through Brompton Cemetery. She realised about five minutes in that she had forgotten her earbuds but she knew if she went back for them then she would find an excuse to take her trainers off, sit back down on the sofa and stew over her situation at home. So she kept going and she thought about what Jess had said, and she played out a scenario where she threw herself full into a romance with Will, where instead of tantalising text messages, they discussed mini breaks and potentially moving in and before she could stop herself they were lying side by side in bed with their reading glasses on and failing to give each other a goodnight kiss. She really couldn't bear it.

So she did a U-turn and headed back out of the cemetery, past the playground, which seemed more attractive to the emo youth rather than the intended target market of pre-schoolers, past the bus stop, out onto the main road and straight into the Starbucks there. She stood in line assessing just how much caffeine her body could take right now before ordering a double shot flat white and sticking two fingers up at those who would tell her she had already had more than enough.

She was nose-deep scrolling on her phone waiting for her coffee when she took a step to her left to avoid a pushchair and stepped straight into...

'Will!' she exclaimed. She shoved her phone into her pocket

and hastily smoothed down her hair, which had gone more than a little wild during her walk. 'What are you doing here?'

'Oh, I just like to hang out in Starbucks.' His face split into a grin as he saw the look of confusion that washed over Allie's face. 'Same as you? Getting coffee?' he clarified.

'Very funny,' she rolled her eyes, 'I meant why here, why *this* Starbucks?'

'I had a meeting nearby.'

Allie fought a brief internal battle as she recalled her earlier decision. She was fascinated by anything and everything to do with Will, but was showing too much interest in his life getting too close? If she asked too many questions, would she be filing a joint tax return before she knew it? Unable to completely contain her curiosity, she squeaked out a 'How did it go?'

He shrugged. 'It was fine. I'm keen to work with this company, but the ball is in their court now. I just wait to hear.'

'I'm sorry.' Allie pulled a sympathetic face. 'That must be tough.'

Will shrugged again. 'Not really. I'm quite relaxed about it. I think our values are aligned, but if they don't think so then that says a lot and probably best if it doesn't work out.'

Allie considered his relaxed attitude towards work and tried to be impressed that he could keep things so cool, but really she didn't think she could get on board with such a laissez faire attitude towards earning money and it made her all the more determined not to destroy the only employment she could envisage herself ever having. And then she realised that Will's response had been very offhand. He hadn't sounded like he wanted to tell her more about his meeting and in fact, come to think of it, he'd told her very little about his life overall.

She glanced sideways at him, assessing the situation. Could

he possibly be doing exactly what she was trying to do? Keeping things cool and casual? Keeping her at arm's length? She remembered his comment in Richmond Park, that he wasn't seeing anyone else, wasn't planning to. But that didn't necessarily mean that he was expecting anything serious with Allie, did it? Maybe he was just a serial no-strings monogamist who had a hard time keeping tabs on one relationship let alone many, so preferred to keep things streamlined in that department.

'Is that yours?' Will interrupted her confusing thoughts and pointed towards a cup which had just been placed on the to-go shelf and was emblazoned in sharpie with ALLEY. Allie looked at Will who grinned at her. 'I like the way you spell it,' he said and gave her a wink which made her stomach flutter. 'Do you have time to join me? Were you heading somewhere?'

'No. I mean yes,' Allie stuttered. Will had that effect on her ability to string normal sentences together. She took a breath and tried to ignore the amused look on his face. 'No, I'm not heading anywhere, I was just out for a walk. And yes, I do have time to join you.'

'Good.' Will picked up both their drinks and ushered Allie to a sofa in the corner of the cafe. It was one of those huge old brown leather sofas which had seen better days and presumably this was why it had been relegated to the corner of a Starbucks. She sank down next to Will and felt herself crush up against him, the lack of stuffing in the sofa further confirming the fact it was past best.

'Sorry, sorry.' She attempted to sit upright, which only resulted in her floundering all the more and sinking ever deeper into the sofa.

'Don't apologise, I like you throwing yourself at me.'

'I wasn't throwing myself...' Allie spluttered. She

170

apologised again as she disentangled her limbs and inched closer to the front of the sofa, trying to plant her feet on solid ground again. Will had his hand on her lower back and she desperately tried to ignore the tingly sensation this was giving her. She took a deep breath; *keep this flirty and fun*, she reminded herself. *Keep things casual. Don't. Get. Comfortable.* She looked back at Will who had obviously picked up on the signal and moved his hand.

'So, how's the writing going?' he asked.

'Actually pretty good.' Allie stared into Will's eyes and mentally ran through how she would describe them in detail later. She ran her eyes over his thick, dark hair, which she had already described the feeling of running her hands through. She hadn't quite captured the way his skin dimpled on his right cheek when he smiled... God, he was hot. She cleared her throat and tried to clear her mind of all the impure thoughts that were now racing around it. 'I shouldn't tempt fate, but maybe I'm through my writer's block?' Of course, he didn't need to know that he might well be the reason for that.

'Allie, that's great!' Will's voice was soft and warm, and most importantly genuine. 'Do you ever let anyone read it while you're still writing?'

'Sometimes.' Allie drank some coffee. 'Sometimes I share stuff with Verity.' She paused, her voice catching in her throat. 'But obviously I can't do that at the moment.'

'I'm sorry, that must be hard.' Allie turned to look at Will. His grey eyes were soft with concern; she felt desire pool, low down in her stomach, and bit back the urge to kiss him. 'You know,' he said hesitantly, 'I'd be happy to read something if you wanted me to? I mean, I'm not an expert but I do like reading. And my dad was a writer. So if it would help you...'

'No!' exclaimed Allie. She thought back to the words

written on her computer, the story that was starting to take shape. How some of it was inspired by her feelings and desire for Will. If Will read it and recognised it for what it was… Her face went red at the thought.

Will, reading her flush for something else, leapt in with an apology. 'Sorry, stupid idea. I didn't mean to presume.'

'No, it's not that, it's just…' Allie struggled to think how she could possibly explain any of this to Will without him feeling in some way that she was using him. 'I just don't feel confident sharing anything with anybody at the moment.' She gave him a weak smile.

'Understood.' Will smiled back but there was an awkwardness hanging in the air between them now.

'I didn't know your dad was a writer?'

Will seemed to tense at the question and once again Allie wondered whether he really didn't want her getting close.

'Used to be,' Will said firmly. 'Hasn't written anything for ages. And definitely not in your genre so I'm not sure why I mentioned it.' He flashed her a tight smile.

Allie wanted to ask all the questions. But she got the sense his dad's career, or lack of, was an uncomfortable and off-limits topic. She sipped her coffee, frantically trying to think of something light and breezy to say. 'So,' she eventually began, 'what else do you like to do in your spare time, other than reading?' She cringed as she spoke, this was nothing like the easy carefree flirtatious banter she had been aiming for, more like uncomfortable filler, a follow-up interview question.

'I love cooking, obviously, but I don't think that counts as a hobby.'

'Why not?'

'Well, because of my job?' Will looked at Allie as if she had not only missed the point but was totally unaware that a point was there to be noticed. 'Erm...' Will frowned. 'I like films?' he eventually offered. 'Actually, there's a retrospective on Japanese arthouse cinema at the BFI, do you fancy going to see something?' He sounded hopeful and turned his grey eyes on her with the full force of their allure.

Allie was momentarily floored by the pull of his gaze. She cleared her throat and imperceptibly shook her head to clear her mind. Was going to the cinema on her list of approved activities? Did it scream comfortable boyfriend/girlfriend dynamic? Or would the dimly lit backseats of the BFI be the perfect place for some tantalizingly placed hands, some passionate kisses before the lights came up at the end? She paused, not only considering whether this aligned with her aims but also whether she really could stomach an arthouse retrospective when her grasp on cinematic culture rarely strayed past romantic comedies. She looked up at the ceiling as she made her decision. 'Sure, I'd love to,' she said. Low lit, steamy passion would be a good way to pass the time if the retrospective ended up being as unappealing as it sounded.

Will put his hand on her back again and leaned in to whisper, 'I'll bring the sweets, and I promise if it's too boring we'll make a run for it. You just say the word, I'm in your hands.' If the allure of sweets was not enough to make Allie shiver with desire, the kiss that Will then placed just below her ear did exactly the trick. And, as if by magic, the chemistry between them was back.

Chapter Twelve

Everything pointed to the fact that Allie was nailing this. She was writing again, Martin was regularly messaging her with anecdotes about his attempts to reignite the romance in his marriage; albeit these were long-winded emails rather than the brief imagination-inspiring voice notes Allie was hoping for. But she wasn't going to complain. She'd arranged another date with Will, and Tessa had agreed to meet with her so that Allie could hand over a flash drive with her new draft on it. The twenty-something Tessa was completely bemused by this request but had seemingly decided to humour Allie in her ancient ways, completely unaware that Allie had an ulterior motive in getting her to meet face to face. And even Martha had invited Allie round for Sunday lunch with her and Ruth, apparently purely because she wanted to see Allie, not because she needed to lecture her about something or felt Allie to be incapable of feeding herself. Still, Allie decided she'd do a brief overview of her financial situation ahead of Sunday, just so she couldn't be blindsided about pension contributions and mortgage rates.

So, it was completely understandable that this blissful state couldn't last. And when Allie answered her phone to a panicked-sounding Martin, she quickly realised that those brief halcyon days were definitely behind her.

'Disaster!' boomed Martin down the phone.

'Oh, hello Martin, nice to hear from you. I'm fine, thanks for asking, yourself?'

'Yes yes, very funny,' barked Martin. 'Allie, I need your help.'

Reluctantly, Allie asked, 'Why? What's happened?'

'Angie knows.'

This was the news that Allie had both been dreading and also, if she was being honest, hoping might happen one day. Because secrets could never be good in a marriage, and from everything Martin had told her about Angie, she sounded pretty awesome, and therefore deserved not to be lied to by her husband of thirty-eight years.

'Oh,' she replied, in what even she would admit was a useless summing up of all the emotions that this hammer blow of a reveal should conjure.

'This is a disaster. What do I do?'

'Well,' she played for time, 'is it really a disaster?' She could hear Martin spluttering on the end of the line. 'I mean,' she continued quickly, 'we discussed this, she was going to find out sometime. And if everything you've been telling me is true, you two are getting on much better at the moment?' Allie restrained herself from inserting a comment praising herself for this state of affairs. 'Maybe this was the best time for her to find out,' Allie said with more certainty than she actually felt.

'Oh god. Maybe? I don't know. But what should I do now?'

Allie racked her brain and wondered whether she ought to have had more serious training in marriage counselling before embarking on this kind of writing relationship. 'How did you leave things with her?'

'I didn't. I mean…' Martin floundered. 'Well, I was out and had my phone turned off. When I turned it on I had a message from Angie.'

'Okaaay. So what did you say when you called her back?'

'I haven't.'

'What do you mean you haven't?' Allie asked incredulously. 'Martin,' she was now severely pissed off, 'do you mean to tell me that you rang *me* rather than your *wife*??'

'Yes.' Martin replied, sounding more like a meek twelve-year-old boy, than the aging bestselling novelist that he was. Or used to be.

'Martin!' Allie exploded. 'This is not OK. Get off the phone with me and call her back right now.'

'But what should I say?' Martin wheedled.

'I don't know! Maybe tell her you're sorry. That you shouldn't have given Gigi the money in the first place. That you should have told her from the start. But that you've realised the error of your ways, you won't do it again, and that you're writing another bestseller?'

'You're good,' Martin said. 'Any chance you could do this for me?'

'You had better be joking,' Allie snapped.

'I am, don't worry. But you're better at this than me.'

'This being?'

'You know, relationships, reading people, understanding emotions.'

'Oh, stop being so pathetic. You're a grown man Martin.'

There was a long silence. 'Martin?' Allie asked. 'What's that sound in the background?' Allie had heard something she thought she recognised. 'Martin, where are you?' There was another long pause and then Allie groaned, 'Martin, please don't tell me you came to see me rather than calling your wife back?'

'How did you know?' Martin asked meekly.

'I recognise the man who stands outside the Tube shouting,' Allie huffed and then sighed. 'Alright, I'll text you my address. Come over, we can discuss this but then you must promise to call Angie.'

'I promise,' Martin acquiesced.

Allie put the phone down and while she tapped out her address she cursed her previous self for ever mentioning her closest tube station.

'You do know how wrong this feels?' Allie asked when she answered the door a few minutes later. Martin was standing on her doorstep with two cups of takeaway tea in his hands looking sheepish. He offered one to her and she snatched it from him with an, 'I have better tea here.' And then she immediately felt bad for being so churlish. Yes, Martin should have called Angie back, rather than turning up on Allie's doorstep, but it was rather sweet that he thought Allie such an expert on romance and love that he should instinctively seek her advice first.

'Honestly?' he said, taking off his coat and hanging it on the back of one of the kitchen chairs as Allie had refused to take it from him in the hallway. 'I was in your neck of the woods already; I had lunch with my son. And when I got Angie's message I was only a few minutes from your Tube stop.'

He sat down at the table which Allie glared at him across. 'I know it was the wrong thing to do,' he admitted, 'and I will call Angie, of course. But I wouldn't mind having a cup of tea with you before I do so. I guess I feel we're mates now?'

Allie couldn't help but feel flattered, and it was true, the time they had spent together in the last few weeks had been enjoyable as well as being useful. Allie had really started to look forward to seeing Martin and found his outlook on life so refreshingly different from hers. But she was still annoyed that he was at her kitchen table unloading his disaster upon her when everything in her world had been going so well. And she really wanted to get back to writing; she was on a roll with a romance inspired by Martin's lifelong devotion to Angie and spiced up by the way Will made her feel. She glanced at her watch surreptitiously.

'I didn't realise your son lived round here,' Allie said grudgingly. She presumed that Martin, like all affluent writers who had made it big in the eighties and nineties, lived in north London. Allie took a sip of her tea and wished again that Martin hadn't bothered and she could have made something more drinkable.

'He works in Hammersmith, that's where his office is located.'

'Right. You said he had his own company.'

'Yes.' Martin took a sip of his tea and pulled a face that suggested he agreed with Allie's hot take on the beverage.

'Running a restaurant, right?' Allie asked when it became clear that Martin was not about to elaborate.

'Well, actually, that's his business partner's side of things. He runs the catering arm. Does a lot of functions. Anyway, sorry, this is totally irrelevant, you're right. I need to talk to Angie, I'm going to do it right now.' He started to pull his phone out of his pocket.

'Martin, no!' Allie practically shouted. 'Good grief, not here! Not in front of me.'

Martin blinked at her. 'Oh right, yes, sorry.'

He looked panicked, absolutely out of his depth and she felt terrible for the mess he found himself in. He so obviously adored Angie and wanted to make things right. Yes he'd made a stupid mistake and he should have confessed a long time before, but Allie really hoped that Angie would understand that although misguided, his heart was in the right place.

She sighed and regarded this man who had suddenly inserted himself into such an important position in her writing life, who singlehandedly might end up saving her from Jake Matthews, and then she had a thought. 'Oh hey, I heard from Verity.'

'You did?'

'Uh-huh. She's pretty messed up by this whole thing but she seems to think we can come up with a plan to bring Jake down.'

Martin raised one of his eyebrows questioningly. 'How?'

'Tessa. His assistant. She's supposed to be working on my book and Verity thinks she might have dirt she can spill on Jake.'

'Don't they all have dirt on that man?'

'Yes, but this is weaponized, career-ending dirt.' And so Allie told Martin everything that she and Verity had found out and Verity's plan to end Jake Matthews once and for all, and Martin's eyebrows got higher and higher as she went on.

'Impressive,' he said eventually. 'Do you think Verity could work out my mess too?'

'I thought *I* was helping,' Allie replied primly.

'Sorry, yes you are, and you have, and I should go,' he said, standing up. 'I'm really not sure what I was thinking coming here. I can only apologise.' And buttoned-up Martin was suddenly back, all business-like and tweed.

'No need.' She waved her hand at his apology as they walked back to her front door. 'I'm glad you felt you could come and talk to me.'

'Thank you,' Martin said somewhat gruffly. 'I do value your advice,' he continued stiffly. 'You know, you're a damn good writer, Allie, and you should have more faith in your ability. Keep me updated with this plan of yours for Mr Matthews?' With that and a wave of his hand, he was off, leaving Allie stood in her doorway, feeling emotional and watching him go through a film of tears.

She shook her head. 'What on earth is going to happen next?'

Chapter Thirteen

Allie didn't have long to wait to find out. That evening Martin rang her again and despite thinking it would probably be best to let it ring through to voicemail, her lack of self-control meant she couldn't. Evidently, Martin had confessed everything to Angie, including the writing relationship that he and Allie had devised. Allie considered having a go at him, reminding him that they had agreed to keep this a secret before she remembered that Martin had done one of the bravest things he could and that now wasn't the time to be bringing up minor promises with which to beat him. And anyway, she'd already told Verity, so really she didn't have a leg to stand on.

Martin told Allie that Angie had been furious at first, both with him and with Gigi, but had now calmed down and was actually keen to meet her.

'Me?' exclaimed Allie in consternation. 'Why?'

'Because, as I have now discovered, she's read your books and is a fan and is trying to pretend not to be impressed by the fact I know you.'

Allie preened herself a little at Martin's words.

'And also, it might stop her thinking we're having some kind of affair. So, will you come?' he asked.

'Come where?'

'To our house, for dinner. Tomorrow night?'

And that was how Allie found herself on the doorstep of a beautiful white Regency villa the following evening, feeling foolish that she had presumed Martin lived in Hampstead, just because he was a rich, white literary male, but not quite as foolish as she felt agreeing to this dinner in the first place. And anyway, she thought to herself, this might just as well be Hampstead, given she was a stone's throw from the heath that gave Blackheath its name, and that the house in front of her would probably set her back a few million. She took a deep breath, begged her imposter syndrome to take the night off and rang the doorbell.

The door swung slowly open giving Allie the chance to catch a glimpse of stunning black and white tiling and stairs sweeping off into the many other floors of the mansion.

'You must be Allie.' Angie was suddenly smiling at her as Allie tried not to gape. Angie was certifiably gorgeous, tall and curvy with dark luscious hair, which she had swept back from her face into a low chignon. Her skin glowed with a luminosity that came not just from what Allie would presume was an expensive skincare regime, but also from a genetic gift which left Allie feeling short-changed for herself and the rest of the average-looking sisterhood. She wore a dark blue, silk soft jumpsuit that clung to her in all the right places and Allie wondered just what alchemy was at work which led a mother of two in her sixties to look this good. And then behind her was Martin, bobbing around, looking just as uncomfortable as Allie felt.

'Hi!' Allie said and gave them both a little wave.

'Come in.' Angie swept the door wide open and went to hug Allie as she made her way across the threshold. Panicked by the sudden intimacy, Allie went stiff as a board before finally, gingerly succumbing to Angie's embrace. And just as suddenly it was over and Allie was left wanting to inhale more of whatever the fragrance was that Angie was wearing.

'Here,' she said, thrusting the bottle of wine she had picked up on the way at Angie, 'this is for you.'

'You shouldn't have,' said Angie magnanimously and managing to sound as if she was truly touched by Allie's gift. 'But thank you. Martin, take Allie's coat.'

'Hi, Martin,' Allie said, shrugging herself out of her coat and handing it to him.

'Thank you for coming,' he whispered. 'I owe you one.'

Allie raised her eyebrow at him as Angie gestured for Allie to follow her deeper into their enormous abode. 'You do,' she confirmed. 'You can pay me back in more ideas for my book, OK?'

Martin nodded and looked relieved to have got off the hook this lightly, before leading her into what was probably referred to as the drawing room in a house like this. It was high ceilinged with lamps placed at strategic points around the room, bathing the space in a warm golden light. Large windows at the back were covered with curtains that had yet to be drawn against the encroaching evening, and through them, Allie could see a sizable walled garden with tall trees at the back and a sweet little patio area just beneath the house itself. It reminded her of something out of *Notting Hill*, just in a different postcode.

'Allie, what can we get you to drink? White wine? Red? A gin and tonic?' Angie was stood framed in the doorway which looked like it led to the kitchen, if all the gleaming white marble behind her was anything to go by.

'Erm, what are you having?' Allie asked.

'Shall we start with a G&T?' Angie waited for Allie to nod before turning to Martin and saying, 'Be a dear and make them?'

As Martin left the room to follow his instructions, Angie led Allie to one of the sofas that framed the giant fireplace. 'Sit,' she said, pulling Allie down to sit beside her. 'I've been dying to meet you, ever since Martin's confession.'

'Yes, about that…' Allie began, 'I don't want you to think—'

Angie waved her hand, dismissing Allie's concerns. 'That I would be concerned that my husband was getting writing advice from one of my favourite authors?! Allie, it's a dream!'

Allie giggled slightly, she knew from the very first conversation she'd had with Martin about Angie that she would like her and now that she was sitting on Angie's sofa, in Angie's beautiful house, under Angie's gorgeous brown eyes, she was completely smitten. This woman was like catnip to Allie's senses.

'Well, that's lovely of you to say, but I feel quite awkward about the whole thing. I mean, I'm not sure how I would feel if I found out my husband had been keeping secrets from me and that some random writer knew all about it.'

'Are you married?' Angie leapt in to ask.

'Er, no I'm not. I meant, hypothetically speaking.'

'Well, I don't mind. I'm actually relieved that Martin has found someone to talk to. It's been obvious for a long time that something wasn't sitting right with him. And I wasn't over the moon when I discovered what it was … although I probably should have guessed it had something to do with Gigi. God I love that girl but she is ALWAYS at the heart of all our troubles. Do you have children?'

'Er no...' Allie was beginning to worry that her lack of partner and kids would mean Angie would feel she had very little of interest to add to this conversation, but before she could feel any more awkward Martin reappeared with a silver tray of drinks and put one down, carefully on a coaster, on the coffee table in front of her.

'Angie darling, don't quiz Allie about her personal life. It's hardly polite, she's only just arrived.'

'See?' Angie turned triumphantly to Allie. 'Martin would never previously have considered whether it was polite or not to ask personal questions. If he was interested he would ask, if he wasn't he wouldn't bother. You've really had an effect on him, Allie.' As Angie beamed at her, Allie caught Martin's eye roll and bit back a snigger.

'OK, enough with the personal questions about you, Allie. Tell me whether you think my husband can actually write this new book?'

Allie looked between Angie and Martin: Angie's eager face beaming at her and Martin looking really quite uncomfortable behind. She fixed Martin with a look she hoped conveyed the belief she had developed in him and said, 'Absolutely. In fact, I think it could turn out to be his best yet.'

Martin sank down into the sofa opposite and smiled gratefully over at her. 'You're kind to say that, but we both know that the outcome for most of this rests upon the mercurial mood of our friend Jake Matthews.'

Allie grimaced and looked at Angie, who in turn was looking in concern between her husband and Allie. 'Allie, what do you make of this Jake character? Is he as bad as Martin makes out?'

'Honestly? I am dreading sending my new book in. I don't think it matters whether I, or anyone else, think it's any good. I'm sure Jake will make me feel about two inches tall when he reads it.' She exhaled heavily and picked up her drink in which Martin appeared to have forgotten the correct ratio of gin to tonic. Despite the fiery taste she was grateful for the immediate hit of alcohol to her system. Talking about Jake Matthews was just the worst and Allie needed a drink to take the edge off the whole thing.

'Well whatever Jake Matthews thinks, personally I cannot wait to read your new book. I've loved all of them.'

Allie blushed a deep crimson colour. Of course, she was used to fans praising her books, but this wasn't just any random romance fan, Angie was smart, sophisticated, intelligent. Allie was about to go on before she checked herself and realised she was doing all of her fans, in fact, every fan of romance, a disservice. They were ALL smart, sophisticated and intelligent, and their choice of reading material just proved that, she told her inner patriarch sternly. But she would put money on the fact that not many of her fans held PhDs in an obscure branch of science, could sing jazz AND looked that good in silk jumpsuits. It was that combination that set Angie apart from mere mortals.

'Thanks, that's really kind of you to say.' Allie tried to will the blush from her cheeks. 'Did Martin tell you that I met up with my editor the other day? My ex-editor,' Allie corrected herself.

'He told me some of it.' Angie looked at Allie with a worried expression. 'I'm so pleased you got to talk to her, I have to say, I wish Martin could talk to his old editor but he's long gone now and actually it was always a bit hit and miss how helpful he would be. But this plan you've got. Do you think it's wise? I have to say, I'm worried about you getting caught up in all of this. If Jake is as unpleasant as you and Martin suggest then I'm concerned for you.'

Allie looked into Angie's eyes. She didn't really know her, and yet the worry etched across Angie's face was real; Allie felt a rush of emotion for this kind woman who had invited her into her home, showed her compassion, praised her books. She wasn't sure that her own mother would have listened for long enough to grasp the issues at stake or to show such genuine concern for Allie's well-being. Her voice got choked up as she tried to explain.

'I know. I'm worried too to be honest. I'm already on the wrong side of Jake and if this doesn't work and he gets wind of the plan or that I'm involved then it's going to go very, very badly wrong for all of us. But I also can't just sit back and do nothing. This man might be ruining my career but he's also ruining a lot of other people's too. And he's doing it from a position of power and privilege with absolutely no recourse. I can't let him do that.' She looked over at Martin who was nodding too and then back at Angie who was no longer looking at her with concern but with something that looked quite a lot like admiration.

'I love Verity, my editor,' Allie explained. 'She's the reason I have this job, she has always believed in me, always done everything in her power to make my books successful. I can't stand to see what Jake has done to her, and I won't stand by and not do something if there is anything I can do to help. And Tessa, his assistant? I don't know her at all, and perhaps she's an awful person and deserves to have Jake as her boss. But perhaps she's just a young misguided kid who doesn't realise she is being used, and doesn't know she has the power and the right to stand up to Jake. And if I can help but I don't, I don't think I will ever forgive myself.'

Before she knew what was happening, Allie found herself engulfed in Angie's arms and Angie was saying over her shoulder to Martin, 'I KNEW I would like her in person.' She held Allie away from her and looked her in the eyes. 'You're very brave. And if there is anything Martin or I can do to help you must let us know. Isn't that right, Martin?'

But Martin wasn't there, Martin seemed to have disappeared off into the kitchen. Angie looked scathingly at Allie. 'Powerful women showing emotion makes him nervous. Always has done. That's why Gigi has always been able to walk all over him.'

'Is that her?' Allie pointed to one of the photos on the mantelpiece. It was a black and white head shot and Gigi was undeniably beautiful, like a younger Angie but with a likeness to someone else that Allie couldn't immediately think of…

'Yes. That's one of her headshots taken for her portfolio. It's a couple of years old now, back when she wanted to be an actor.'

'She doesn't anymore?'

Angie laughed hollowly. 'Oh goodness no. I think she was through that phase before the photos were even developed. That,' she pointed to the photograph, 'is quite possibly the most expensive piece of artwork in the entire house.' She smiled at Allie, 'Oh don't mind me. I'm used to Gigi and her ways. One day, she'll learn, and maybe that day will come sooner now that her dad is going to stop bailing her out.'

Allie stood and walked over to the grand piano in the corner. 'Martin told me you sang. Do you play too?' She ran her hand over the smooth polished wood of the piano, feeling the coolness to her touch.

'Occasionally, but Martin is the real piano player in the family, isn't that right, darling?'

Allie spun round in surprise at this revelation that Martin's talents stretched beyond the literary and into the musical realm. 'You are?'

Martin was standing with his arm around Angie staring adoringly at his wife. He shrugged slightly at Allie as she asked him, 'Would you play something now?'

'Only if Angie agrees to sing.'

'Oh Martin, no, it's too early for that. We haven't even finished our first drinks yet.' Allie could hear what Angie was saying but the tone in which she was saying it screamed, 'Please ask me again, and then I'll say yes.'

'Please?' Allie asked plaintively, enjoying the way Martin and Angie were gazing at each other, pretty much oblivious to her existence right now.

'Oh OK, if you insist.' And before Allie could say anything more Angie was round the other side of the piano, flicking through the music on the stand and beckoning Martin to come and sit. 'This one?' she said, pointing to the page.

'Whichever one you want, my darling.' If Allie hadn't been so invested in this relationship she might have thrown up there and then, what with the amount of PDA flying about the room. But she was a hundred per cent here for this and stared as Martin settled himself in, running his hands up and down the keys as a warm-up.

Allie was not a jazz afficionado. In fact, she didn't know much about any type of music, which made the time she decided to write a romance featuring a musician as her lead a questionable choice and something which led to months of frankly unnecessary research when she could have just switched professions easily enough. Something that Jess had unhelpfully pointed out on the night of the book launch.

But tonight, Allie would officially declare herself in love with jazz. Angie's voice alone would have convinced her, it was rich and low, with a resonant quality which echoed around the room and seemed to strike Allie right in her heart. And then there was the way Angie's hand rested ever so lightly on Martin's shoulder, tensing at the high notes and relaxing as the song made its way through the sentimental crescendo. Martin obviously knew the piece off by heart, he didn't need the music in front of him, he didn't even need to be looking down at what his fingers were doing, all he needed to do was to look up at Angie, which he did often. And the two of them would smile at each other, a secret, private smile which Allie could just tell held the multitude of their memories and their life together. She sighed deeply, and wondered if Will played the piano, or sang. And then remembered that she did neither and so it wasn't likely that she would find herself reenacting a similar scene and anyway, musical duets did not fit into her arm's length strategy she reminded herself sternly. She broke into enthusiastic applause as the song came to an end.

'That was amazing!' she gushed, walking over to the piano. Angie and Martin smiled at each other and then at her.

'It's our party trick.' Angie said.

'We've been playing that piece for years,' Martin confirmed.

'I keep telling Martin we should find new music but he won't have it. Doesn't like change...' Angie rolled her eyes at Allie who glanced quickly over at Martin to discover that he too was rolling his eyes at Allie. And just like that the spell was broken. These two were adorable, thought Allie, but also perfectly normal and flawed, just like every other couple in the world.

'Is that your son?' she said as she peered at some of the photo frames facing outward from the piano. The boy had dark hair, beautiful eyes and Allie could see the resemblance both to Angie and to Martin as well. She wondered what he looked like now, he was a good-looking child who had hopefully fulfilled his potential and grown into a good-looking adult.

'Yes, but those ones are ancient. The kids look so young in them. There are more recent ones this side.' Angie pointed to the frames which faced towards the keys of the piano, ones that Allie couldn't yet see. 'Here he is, this one was taken just last year at my niece's wedding...' Angie turned the photo around just as Martin said, 'Actually, you've met him...'

Allie stared at the photo, not fully understanding what she was seeing. She was well versed in the tropes of an out-of-body experience, but while she couldn't put her finger on whether her own individual brand of dissociative state was to feel as if she was underwater, or floating over her own body, what she did know, was that neither her body nor her brain were doing what they ought to be doing. Martin's voice had gone all strange and slow and echoey, and while she recognised that what Martin was telling her was important, her ears didn't want to hear it, her eyes wanted to pretend they hadn't seen it and her brain sure as hell didn't want to deal with the implications. Which all resulted in the feeling that her body wanted to be somewhere very far away and very quickly.

'Are you OK?' Whether Martin had truly seen the real state she was in was debatable but he had definitely noticed something was up. 'Allie? You've gone very pale.'

'Here, come and sit down.' And now Angie was taking her by the arm and steering her back towards the sofa, which she should never have left the safety of. Allie looked up blearily but could still see the offending photo turned towards her.

'Martin,' Angie was now all authority, 'go get some snacks. Maybe she needs something to eat. Allie, dear, when was the last time you ate?'

Allie shook her head, she honestly couldn't remember. And why was eating so important anyway when her world was spinning upside down and back to front?

Martin was hesitating in the doorway. 'Now, Martin,' snapped Angie, completely destroying Allie's brief image of them as the perfect couple.

Martin was obviously familiar with the tone of Angie's voice because he was back incredibly quickly, carrying a bowl of something and a glass of water, both of which he put down on the table in front of Allie.

'Here, drink some of this.' Angie placed the glass of water in her hands and then eyed the contents of the bowl before shooting Martin a questioning look. He shrugged and picked it up to offer it to Allie, and the fact that it contained a mixture of Hula Hoops and Twiglets went some way in making Allie feel a little better about the mess of a situation she was just beginning to uncover.

'What did you say your son was called?' she stammered, putting the glass down and sloshing half its contents over the side.

'William. We call him Liam, but his friends all call him Will.'

Still Allie clutched on to the hope that she was mistaken. That there was more than one Will who looked identical to the one she had kissed, the one who made her heart beat faster, the one who made her catch her breath when she saw him, laugh loud when he teased her, fall hard when she should have been keeping him at arm's length. Because the idea that her Will, the one who was going to save her writing career along with a lovely side order of some, as yet to be delivered, smashing, was the same Will who was posed in the family photographs up and down the piano was unconscionable. It didn't compute, it couldn't compute, she wouldn't let it.

'And you said I've met him?' Her voice sounded thin and wavery, asking a question she wasn't sure she would like the answer to, while all the time running through the conversations she had had with Will, her Will, about his job.

'Yes, he did the catering for the summer party, you know where we met at the V&A, or more accurately, outside the V&A!' Martin chortled to himself while Allie felt like throwing up. 'He was the one who showed you the way back in?'

'But, but,' Allie gabbled, 'you said he owned the company? The man I met was a waiter, wasn't he?'

Martin frowned at Angie and then they both smiled indulgently at the memory of their darling boy and his japes, how amusing it was to get writers all confused as to his job and his parentage when showing them the way back into a party.

'No, no Liam likes to be involved at all stages. He isn't always as hands on at the actual events, but if they're short-staffed, or he feels like it, he'll help with handing out canapés, setting up and clearing up. That kind of thing.' Martin paused and Allie felt the cold wash of dread run over her. She was going to have to tell him, wasn't she? And she wasn't sure whether she meant Martin or Will. Both eventually would need to know, wouldn't they? But which one first, and how should she break this piece of libido-quenching news? And why hadn't *her* Will told her that he owned the company? Why had he left her thinking that he was waitstaff? And if he hadn't let her in on this pretty damned important part of his life, what else was he keeping from her? *Was* he keeping her at arm's length, just as she was supposed to be doing with him?

'Actually, I keep meaning to ask Liam whether it was at that party he met his new lady friend.' This was directed at Angie. Allie shuddered when she realised that the 'lady friend' Martin was referring to, was, in fact, her.

'Oh do you think so?' Angie mused.

'Well he hasn't said as such, but I think he might have met her there. Bet he was glad he decided to help out that night! Finally, his workaholic tendencies might have paid off!' Angie and Martin chortled contentedly and for a brief moment Allie felt like punching both of them and probably would have done so if it had meant that the nightmare she now found herself in would end, and she would wake up in her own bed and laugh at the ridiculousness of her own sub-conscious coming up with stupid ideas about Will, her Will, being the son of Martin and Angie. But no amount of physical violence would turn this real-life situation into a dream, and so she sat on her hands instead.

'Well, we'll be pleased to meet her, won't we?' Angie said to Martin who nodded enthusiastically. 'He's always so *secretive* about his love life.' This last was directed confidentially towards Allie who was hoping that this secretive nature might continue long enough for her to figure her way out of this mess.

'Anyway, how are you feeling now you've got some Twiglets inside you?' Martin asked as Allie stress stuffed half the bowl into her mouth in one go. 'Do you think we should eat dinner?'

'Yes, good idea,' Angie said, standing up. 'I'm sure that's why you felt faint, dear. Low blood sugar. You need to be careful. Now you don't have any food allergies, do you? I know Martin said he checked but you never know with him. Liam called in earlier on today and dropped off some new dishes he's trialling for his business, we thought we could have those. I know he'd be grateful for some unbiased feedback, sometimes I think he doesn't really trust me and his dad to be objective.' She laughed brightly.

Allie really wasn't sure how unbiased she could truly be given the circumstances. Nor was she sure how much of anything other than Twiglets she would be able to consume given the nausea which kept rising in her throat. But she allowed herself to be led through to the dining room, and seated in a chair while she fought the urge to run screaming from the house.

When Allie looked back on the rest of the evening, which she tried not to do, she really couldn't recall how she had got through it. She had little recollection of the food, only partial recall of the conversation and absolutely no idea how she had made it back to her own flat. Later, the only thing she could truly, hand on her heart, swear had really happened, was her release of the howl of foreboding which had been building up inside her, ever since Angie had turned that photo to face her, and which she just about managed to muffle with her hand as she slammed her front door behind her.

Chapter Fourteen

'Are you sure you're OK?' Will's face was the picture of concern. It wasn't the first time he had asked and it wasn't the first time Allie had replied to him with a complete barefaced lie.

'Yes, yes, absolutely fine!' She tried to grin up at him in what she hoped was a reassuring manner but probably made her look like she was battling severe wind. She quickly looked down and carried on walking along the river, towards the cinema, where Will was about to make her sit through some arthouse film, which she was sure she wouldn't like *or* understand. *And* they probably didn't even allow popcorn. *And* he still hadn't come clean to her about the business and had, in fact, been busy telling her all about a party he catered for the other night from the POV of a waiter.

'I don't mean to keep asking, it's just...' Allie waited for how Will might describe her current febrile mood. 'It's just you keep looking at your phone...you flinch when I touch you...you're as jumpy as a stressed out rabbit.' In the end he went for, 'You don't quite seem yourself,' and reached out and took her hand and Allie did her utmost best not to flinch this time.

'Sorry, just thinking about work.' Which wasn't a complete lie. She *was* thinking about work, more precisely about the fact she had just discovered that Will's dad was the man she was working with and that Will's mum was amazing, and that Allie might be a little bit in love with her, and that Will's mum had just found out that Will's dad had lent Will's sister money, that he may or may not need to pay back to his publisher, depending on how his and Allie's writing plan played out. And that Will possibly didn't know about *any* of this, and he certainly didn't know about the connection between his father and Allie because if he did he wouldn't be looking at her in the way he was doing, which made her want to jump him. And all of it was horribly unfair because how was she to know that these people used *two* names, one for family and one for friends, which was just asking for exactly the kind of mix-up that had happened. Allie decided to keep these precise details of her thoughts about work to herself.

'How's the writing going now?' Will asked, seemingly genuinely interested, as well he might be, given that his dad was a *famous novelist* and he probably knew more about the writing process than he had previously been letting on. Allie pushed that intrusive thought to the part of her brain reserved for late night spiraling.

'Erm, OK?' she squeaked. 'You must know something about writing though, you said your dad was a writer?' She winced as she asked the question, and wondered whether he would take the out she was giving him and come clean.

Will laughed. 'Ha! No. *I've* never written anything.'

But you lived in the same household as a novelist for your entire childhood, she felt like shouting. She held her tongue, because shouting at Will was hardly fair. They had been on a handful of dates, nowhere near the stage of finding out what the parents do for a living. That was surely several dates down the line, a stage which they might now never reach if Allie didn't fess up about the whole situation.

'How's your day been?' Allie asked, putting off the inevitable uncomfortable reveal, which would have to happen at some point.

'Not the best,' Will confessed. 'Had lunch with my dad today.' Allie's stomach dropped but her ears pricked up, hoping she might get a nugget of intelligence about Will's relationship with his dad, which could help defend her character when Will finally discovered Allie knew Martin already.

'You two don't get on?' she asked hopefully, wondering whether it would be better if they did or better if they didn't.

'Oh no, nothing like that. We get on great. Always have done.'

'So…?' prompted Allie.

Will took a deep sigh, letting Allie's hand drop from his and shoving his hands into his pockets. If ever there was the body language for 'I really don't feel comfortable having this discussion,' this was it. It was probably exactly what Will would look like after he had got over the confusion and betrayal stage when he found out about Allie's arrangement with Martin. Once again, Allie parked that thought to add to her list for late-night panicking.

'I spoke to my mum after and she told me a few things. And now I'm wondering why my dad didn't tell me any of these things himself. And whether I should get involved.' He paused. 'To be honest, I'm wondering if I can pretend I don't know because I'd rather not. Oh and I need to decide exactly how mad I am at my sister about the whole thing.'

'Oh.' Of course Allie knew what he was talking about, but she wasn't supposed to and her brain was desperately trying to think of what she could ask or say that wouldn't give this away but that also couldn't be held against her in the future when it came out that she DID know what he was talking about. After what seemed like an exceptionally long time, she decided that 'oh' was actually all she could manage.

'Do you get on with your parents?' he asked, in an admirable form of deflection.

'Yes. Well, with my mum. She spends most of her time in Spain now with Nigel,'

'Nigel?'

'Her husband. So I don't get to see that much of her, and that's probably why we get on so well.'

'And your dad?'

Allie took a deep breath; she hated having to tell people this. What was worse than people feeling sorry for you, was when people really didn't know what to say at all and so ended up saying something idiotic and panicking, and then *she* would end up having to make them feel better. 'He's dead. Died when I was a teenager. Cancer.'

And then, because Will wasn't *other people*, he simply took her hand and said, 'I'm sorry' and sounded like he genuinely meant it.

'Yeah, me too. He was kind of awesome and I still miss him, and I still spend a lot of time and energy wondering what he would think of my life choices.'

Will laughed, a gentle, kind laugh. 'Not having ever met him, I'm not going to pretend I can make you feel better about that.'

Allie looked sideways at him, appreciative of his kindness. 'Thanks. You know, people never know what to say when I tell them, so that's about the best reaction I've ever had.'

'Can I tell you that I'm feeling good about your life choices right now?'

Allie grinned at this honest and funny response.

'And sorry,' Will said, squeezing her hand. 'I shouldn't be boring you with stuff about my family.'

'No, it's fine,' Allie protested, and then, before she could stop herself, 'I'm happy to listen if you want to talk?' Because she was. Even if the end result was bad for her, she found Will completely fascinating. And there was part of her that felt maybe it would be better if she knew exactly what Will knew about Martin's situation.

Will stopped walking and pulled Allie round to face him. He wrapped one arm around her waist, pulling her towards him. And then he lifted a hand to cup her chin and looked her in the eye. 'Thank you,' he said before he kissed her hard, pushing all thoughts of impending doom from her mind.

'That wasn't talking.' She bit her lip and smiled.

'It wasn't?' he asked innocently. 'Sorry, I can stop if you want me to?'

'Please,' she whispered, 'don't.'

'So you didn't tell him?'

'No,' Allie snapped. 'I didn't tell him. We were at the cinema, it was one of those arthouse places. You know, the kind that frown on popcorn and chit-chat during the screening. I didn't have a chance.'

There was a silence from the other end of the line which

only made Allie even more aware that her excuse was pathetic. Of course, she could have told Will, of course she *ought* to have told Will. She'd had plenty of opportunities to do it, like immediately after she had realised who he was and who his father was. Or even when he was busily confessing to her his feelings about his father's behaviour. Over the dinner they'd eaten after the movie would have been a good opportunity. There was no ban on talking during dinner. To be honest, a text informing him of exactly who she was to his father and how much she knew about his parents' marriage would have been preferable to what she had actually done. Which was precisely nothing. And which was why she found herself panic-calling Jess, asking for her advice.

Jess eventually broke the silence. 'I can't believe you didn't tell me your writing partner was Martin Clark.'

'That's it?' Allie queried. 'That's all you've got to say on the matter? And how the hell was I to know you would even know who Martin Clark is?'

'Al, everyone knows who Martin Clark is. Tom?' There was a muffled noise. 'Do you know who Martin Clark is?' Allie heard Tom confirm that yes, he too knew who Martin Clark was.

'Jess? Am I on speakerphone?'

'What? Yes. I'm driving. Say hi, Tom.'

'Hi Allie,' Tom said, somewhat wearily. 'You OK?'

'Not really,' Allie said grumpily, 'but you'll have heard all about it already. Jess? Can you tell me next time you put me on speakerphone? What if I'd told you something I didn't want Tom to hear?'

'Like what?' Jess sounded genuinely perplexed that there might be something that Allie didn't want Tom to hear.

'Oh, never mind. So, what do you think I should do?'

'Do?' Jess asked. 'I think you should tell him. And I think you should tell Martin. Allie, you know this can't end well.'

'But what if he doesn't want to see me again?' wailed Allie. 'I really like him! And I'm writing again. I can't afford to jeopardise that.' Allie thought of all those lovely words that had poured out of her onto her laptop over the last few days. A combination of the anecdotes Martin had been feeding her and the romance vibes with Will. Right up till she discovered who he was, and now she just felt awkward about seeing him, desperate though she was to do so. 'And anyway,' she continued defensively, 'I think he's doing exactly the same with me!'

'Meaning?'

'Keeping me at arm's length. Honestly Jess, if he thought this was going anywhere why hasn't he told me that it's his catering business? Why hasn't he told me his dad is a novelist too?'

'I thought he did tell you his dad was a writer?'

'Well, yeah, but he did it in such a way that I then couldn't ask him about it. He's pretty closed off at times.'

'Have you tried asking him why?'

'No!' exploded Allie. 'It's becoming quite hard to ask him about anything right now, what with all the things I know about him but am not supposed to know about him.'

'Which brings us straight back to the point, that you *should* tell him,' Jess said emphatically.

There was a silence before Allie shot back, 'Yeah, well anyway, he's going away for a couple of weeks, some work thing in York, but as he's good at keeping his cards close to his chest,' she said pointedly, 'he hasn't told me much about it. So I won't have the opportunity to tell him before he's back.' Allie could hear Jess's eye roll down the phone. 'I don't want to do it over the phone,' she insisted, before Jess could call her out on this nonsensical excuse. 'Better to do it face to face, right?'

'Better to have done it as soon as you found out, I'd have thought.' Jess replied drily. She sighed. 'You're not going to tell him, are you?'

'No.' Allie sounded more confident than she felt. 'Not until he's back. Anyway, speaking of writing—' they weren't, but it was an exceptionally handy moment to end the call '—I have to go, I've got a meeting with Jake Matthews' assistant right now.'

'OK.' Jess sounded sceptical. 'But Al? I want it put on the record that I think it is a really *really* bad idea not to tell Will. And I'm going to struggle not to say I told you so if you refuse to listen to me. OK?'

'Fine,' snapped Allie. 'Where are you going anyway?'

'Oh, just out for a drive.'

'In the middle of the day? Don't you two have jobs to do?'

'Gotta go, losing my signal...' Allie heard the distinctive tone of Jess putting her phone down. She sighed. She knew Jess was right, of course she was right. There was no way that this was going to end well once Will found out who Allie was, *and* that Allie had known about the connection and not told him. But there was a small part of her that hoped he might understand and that she might get a little more of her novel written before the whole thing fell apart. She wasn't sure which she was more invested in, Will or her novel, and she was feeling really rather riled that the universe seemed insistent that she choose one or the other. Stuffing down all of these feelings, she took a deep breath and pushed through the revolving doors of Brinkman's and hoped that Tessa hadn't booked the same meeting room as the one in which Jake had delivered his devastating news, as she wasn't sure she could cope with the flashbacks.

Allie was taking the mission to unseat Jake, free Tessa from his tyranny and get Verity her job back incredibly seriously and had been consistently buttering Tessa up over Messenger for several days. Tessa had seemed confused at first by Allie's questions but now seemed really rather pleased to be counted as someone who might have a valuable opinion on one of the books that Brinkman's was publishing. Which Allie thought showed how very little autonomy Jake had given her so far, and proved an interesting chink which Allie might be able to exploit – all in the name of freeing Tessa from the evil influence of Jake, of course. In actual fact, during their many messages Allie had begun to feel something akin to fondness for Tessa, not to mention very sorry for the working conditions under which she operated. Even in the brief time they had been corresponding, Tessa had managed to let slip several incidents which would not go down well in front of a workplace tribunal. Allie was making a mental note of all of these and hoping that with a little persistence and some charm, she might just be able to get Tessa to deliver the fatal blow which would bring Jake's reign of terror to an end. Or, at the very least, get him to behave in a more acceptable manner and get Verity her job back.

Luckily for Allie's post-traumatic stress, Tessa had arranged for them to meet in a different meeting room. A smaller one, she noted, one with no outside windows. Someone as lowly as Tessa probably wasn't allowed to book one blessed with access to daylight. But Allie didn't mind as the very nature of the conversation she planned to have with Tessa would work best in a small, confined space.

'Thanks for seeing me,' Allie said warmly as she followed

Tessa into the room. 'I know I could have just left it at emailing you the first part of my draft, but to be honest, I really wanted to pick your brains on what you think.'

'Of course,' she said smoothly. 'I've loved what I've read so far,' she went on gushingly.

'You have?' Allie tried to keep the note of surprise from her voice. But the truth was, she *was* surprised. Allie had been floundering in the realm of writer's block for so long that she no longer trusted her gut on her own writing. But Tessa seemed fairly genuine, or as genuine as Allie thought her capable of being. Despite feeling some sympathy with Tessa's situation, Allie couldn't hand on heart say she truly had faith in her judgement.

'I mean, I think there are things we can iron out and work on during the editorial process.'

'Yeah, about that,' Allie said quickly, keen not to get Tessa started on the very real issues and plot holes in the story she had written so far. 'Do you know yet who Jake plans to have edit it? I mean, I am presuming he won't have the time to do it himself.' She chuckled knowingly, trying to pull Tessa into camaraderie.

'Jake doesn't edit.'

Of course he doesn't, thought Allie. He wouldn't know a good editor if they came up and slapped him in the face, and she would put money on there being a long line of editors willing to test this theory. She wasn't absolutely certain that Jake would truly understand what a physical book was. He probably thought it was something used for decoration in tea rooms and National Trust properties. Jake probably only read on screens, and never a book, possibly long-form essays if they especially piqued his interest in climbing the corporate ladder and obliterating all who stood in his way. But actually, his main source of information was probably the *Financial Times* and Reddit forums. Which said it all really.

'Of course,' she said smoothly, keeping all these dark thoughts from Tessa. 'So, any clue who it might be?'

Tessa blushed, looked down at her hands and then fiddled nervously with her sleeves, Allie watched her in fascination, wondering if the *real* Tessa was about to make an appearance. 'Well, erm, I was kind of hoping... I mean I haven't actually asked Jake yet ... and he hasn't mentioned it ... and I'm sure he has someone very experienced in mind...'

Allie wondered how long to let Tessa flounder before she threw her a lifeline and in the end, she couldn't stand to watch for very long. 'Do *you* want to edit it?' she asked gently.

Tessa looked up in surprise. 'Oh! I mean, I would LOVE to. Would you want me to?'

Allie thought for a minute. Really she wanted Verity back. But probably the only way that was going to happen was if they got rid of Jake. And to get rid of Jake she needed to get Tessa to divulge everything she knew. And a really, really good way of getting her to do that was to spend more time with her, which she could easily do, if Tessa was to edit her book. She gritted her teeth, hoping that Tessa's editorial skills were up to the task.

'I think you would do a brilliant job.'

Tessa looked like she might cry. 'Thank you!' Maybe Tessa was a good kid after all, maybe she had just been under the influence of Jake for too long. And maybe she didn't have a huge amount of experience, but perhaps Allie would be doing the right thing by allowing her to demonstrate what she was capable of. And it might go some way in assuaging Allie's guilt over the fact she knew that really she was using Tessa for her own ends.

Tessa barely paused for breath before she launched into all her thoughts so far about Allie's book. And they weren't all bad, she made some half-decent points about the plot and the character dynamics, which Allie thought she might actually take on board. 'But what I really love about it are the two central characters. It's actually pretty nice to think that even old people might fall in love.'

Allie winced at her choice of words and wondered exactly what Martin, and for that matter Angie, would think to be described as such because, as had become increasingly and uncomfortably apparent to Allie, while she wasn't using their story verbatim, it was a hundred per cent the central hook of her story. And although they were definitely only holding names and she planned to change them, so far this draft's central characters were called Martin and Angie.

'I think,' Allie said carefully, 'I think it might be best to pitch it as second-chance romance, reigniting the spark so to speak – rather than romance for old people.'

'Oh yes, yes of course,' Tessa agreed enthusiastically. 'But I do just love them both. I mean Martin is so grumpy and blind and Angie just so slay that at first you wonder how on earth they ever ended up getting together. But then as the story unfolds you see how they used to be, and how they lost their way. I really hope they will find it again, please tell me it has a happy-ever-after!'

Allie laughed at the pleading note in Tessa's voice and couldn't fail to be touched by how much Tessa seemed to have taken Martin and Angie to heart. And how well Allie must have drawn them for Tessa to describe them so precisely. Perhaps Tessa had previously undiscovered depths and capacity for feeling, and maybe all she really needed was a little time away from Jake.

'Don't worry,' Allie said soothingly. 'They get their happy-ever-after. I mean, that's what we all want don't we?'

Tessa practically sighed with relief.

'So, what's the next step?' Allie asked. 'Do you ask Jake about editing? Do you think he'd be open to the idea?'

At the very mention of Jake's name, Tessa seemed to do a 180-rotation. Her face closed up, her hands clenched, her body went all stiff and boardlike. Really, it was quite the fascinating anthropological study if it hadn't been so downright disturbing.

'Are you ok?' Allie asked. 'You seem a little, erm, nervous about talking to Jake?'

There was a long pause and Allie wondered if she had pressed too hard too fast, but just as she was about to give up all hope and just ask Tessa to email her with any updates, Tessa let out a slightly strangled noise. 'He's not that easy to talk to,' she said and then cast a terrified look at the door, as if Jake might materialise there at any moment.

You don't say, Allie thought to herself, but managed instead to verbalise, 'Oh wow, it must be kind of tough to have an unapproachable boss.'

Tessa seemed to visibly deflate, as if one sympathetic comment from Allie had released all the fight from her. 'It really is,' she squeaked.

Allie pulled what she hoped was a sympathetic expression but stopped short of reaching over and taking Tessa's hand, because this was still a business meeting, despite the nefarious therapy set up that Allie had engineered to get Tessa to talk.

'I'm so sorry,' Allie said soothingly, 'how long have you worked for him?'

'Eighteen months,' Tessa said miserably, making it sound like a life sentence.

'That's a long time.'

'It really is. And do you know what? I don't actually think he's said one nice thing to me in all that time. Unless you count good morning, and to be honest, with the tone he uses, I don't think he actually means it.'

'Do you have colleagues you can talk to?'

'God no!' Tessa looked horrified. 'I mean, I'm sure they all think the same but we're all too scared of him to say anything.'

'Why?' asked Allie, genuinely interested in how one person could invoke such a powerful wave of fear and misery that a reasonably large coterie of people all refused to speak up and challenge him. And there was a small part of her that was impressed Jake could have this effect. Imagine what could be achieved if his power could be harnessed for the good? And then she remembered it was Jake Matthews that she was thinking of, whose powers were beyond the reach of goodness.

'Well, this is just me. I don't know about anyone else. But I feel that if I get on the wrong side of Jake, he'll fire me, and I'll never work in the industry again.'

Allie thought how closely Tessa's words echoed those of Verity who still feared the same thing, despite not even being employed by Brinkman's anymore.

'That seems, erm, a bit paranoid? Surely you could just look for another job?'

'I can't!' Tessa gasped. 'I mean … what if … he might…'

Allie held her breath and prayed that this would be the confession she was after. Tessa would tell her all about Jake's hold over her, the fact he used her to get his drugs, and presumably then threatened her with all sorts of legal and personal ramifications if she was to ever tell anyone. And once she had confessed it all, Allie could deal with the fallout; she would need to carefully handle a tearful Tessa, lots of reassurance and comfort, and then just at the right moment, when she had built Tessa back up, given her the confidence she so needed, she would go for the kill and persuade Tessa to blow the whistle on Jake, and bring his reign of terror to an end. Or something along those lines. The finer points definitely needed some work.

What actually happened was Tessa's phone began to ring, interrupting whatever she may or may not have been about to divulge to Allie. She saw the name on the screen and vigorously wiped her teary eyes, taking a deep breath and visibly steeling herself before she answered.

'Jake,' she said so smoothly that you would never have imagined that literally thirty seconds before she was a shaking mess, about to confess all sorts of misdemeanours to Allie. 'Absolutely,' she confirmed. 'I'm just finishing up. I'll be with you in five.'

Tessa stood, picking up her notebook and phone. 'Thanks for coming, Allie, I'll email you with Jake's decision soon. And keep up the writing.'

Allie watched Tessa, alarmed at how quickly and convincingly she had managed to switch characters, and left the meeting wondering which one was the real Tessa.

Chapter Fifteen

Allie was missing Will and not just because she had reached a sticky point in her manuscript and was hoping a date with him might just unstick her. She actually really missed him. Like one might miss a boyfriend, not that Allie would know because she had never truly missed Dominic when he wasn't around. Of course, when they first started dating, she was pleased when she saw him, enjoyed spending time with him. But she didn't crave him in the alarming way she was beginning to crave Will. Or maybe she was really craving those words on the page that Will's presence seemed to encourage because since he had been gone she had managed to write only a handful of words, and if she was being honest, most of these were filler.

She knew he was only away for a couple of weeks. It was something to do with work but she hadn't pressed him for details. Ever since she had found out who he really was, she had avoided asking him anything about his catering and restaurant company, terrified that she might accidentally splurge out her true identity, or reveal she knew *his* true identity. Or in any case something incriminating which would make him think twice about the motivations of this girl he was seeing.

Not that they had discussed exactly what they were to each other. Were they dating? Was this casual? Will had suggested that he wasn't seeing anyone else, and she certainly wasn't, but they'd never defined this, never had the exclusivity conversation, let alone the boyfriend/girlfriend one. Allie hadn't had either of these with Dominic, they had just sort of drifted into a relationship, which was probably where they had gone wrong. If Allie had had to meaningfully commit to Dominic, perhaps they wouldn't have lasted beyond the first month. Allie sighed – thinking of Dominic always seemed to make her do that. And she remembered that she still hadn't replied to his message asking if they could meet up. Yet another item for her list of things to feel slightly guilty about.

Allie leaned back in her chair and fiddled with her phone. She took it off do not disturb in the hope that Will might have messaged but he hadn't. Neither had Jess, which was annoying because Allie was hoping Jess might have changed her mind and decided that Allie was one hundred per cent right in not telling Will about who she was and that she knew Martin. Not just *knew* Martin, but was working *with* Martin, helping him with his manuscript and in exchange mining the depths of Martin's marriage with Angie for inspiration for her novel. She cringed at the thought. Emboldened by Tessa's words she was beginning to sense that what she had written so far was good, but she couldn't help but wonder if it was really worth it. And what Will would say when he found out and whether she wanted to risk losing him just so she didn't have to lose face (and cash) in front of Jake Matthews.

Ugh. Jake Matthews. Tessa had been remarkably quiet since

their last meeting. Allie had been hoping that something might have shifted and she would wake up one morning to a long, heartfelt voice note from Tessa confessing all the evils that Jake had committed. But so far, all Allie had got was a curt email thanking her for coming in and asking when Tessa could expect the next part of her manuscript. And Allie couldn't give her an answer, at least not a truthful one. So she had avoided responding , which was becoming a theme in her life.

Going back to her messages, she pulled the latest one up from Martin. It had been two days since he had last messaged her, and she still hadn't replied. He'd asked when she wanted to meet that week, and as Allie hadn't yet written anything worthwhile since the last time they saw each other she hadn't felt like replying.

Her phone sprang into life with a new message from Martin.

> Are you ignoring me?

Allie grimaced. She didn't want to be honest, because that would involve telling Martin exactly what was going on. But she could go for a version of the truth.

> Yes.

> Oh. Should I be worried?

> No, it's my problem not yours.

And then she followed up with the confession.

> I haven't been able to write anything the last few days.

Allie sat and watched the three blue dots appear and disappear. She waited for Martin's response, rocking her chair back and forth as she did so. She sat forward, nudged her phone again. The dots were still there. She picked up her tea from earlier on and took a sip. It was cold and fairly disgusting. She thought about putting the kettle back on. Still nothing from Martin; the dots were appearing and disappearing as before, so he must be writing half a novel in response. She hoped it might be something she could steal inspiration from for her own. She took a swig from her water bottle to wash out the taste of the tea and stared out into her garden. A robin on the table stared back at her judgementally. She looked away, knowing that it was not a logical response to believe the bird was shaming her for her lack of creativity and drive. Again, she picked up her phone, watching the dots appear and disappear. And then nothing; they disappeared and didn't come back. Allie let out a stifled scream. Bloody Martin.

When she was supposed to be writing and couldn't, Allie liked to pretend she found solace in walking, as it seemed like the kind of thing an author would do. She'd stick in her earbuds, put whatever was trending on Spotify, or a podcast she liked listening to, and walk. It normally didn't last long, she'd run out of steam three roads over or she'd suddenly have an urgent thought that she felt compelled to hurry home and commit to paper before it disappeared entirely. She stared morosely out of the window where the rain was now falling steadily and decided she couldn't face a walk in this weather. So she did the other thing that often worked, or at least gave her a break from the feelings of inadequacy; she went into her bedroom, lay down on her bed and took a nap.

When Allie woke she initially couldn't work out whether she'd been asleep for a few minutes or a few hours. She groaned and rolled over on the bed to reach her phone, which was chirping away and had woken her. She looked at the time and was pleased to see that it was only mid afternoon, so she still had time in which to turn things around and not end the day feeling she had achieved nothing.

Martin's name was flashing on her phone and she remembered that she had been waiting for his response to her earlier cry for help.

'Allie?' he asked as soon as she answered the call.

'Yes?' She couldn't muster more enthusiasm than this and she wasn't quite ready to forgive him for not replying sooner.

'Are you OK? I got your message and I was typing out a reply, but our therapist told me I needed to turn my phone off and be more present if we were ever going to make any progress, or words to that effect.'

'You're in therapy?' Allie tried and failed to hide the note of utter surprise in her voice. She couldn't imagine Martin willingly signing up for therapy.

'Angie insisted,' he replied, somewhat bleakly.

Of course, she did. That made much more sense now.

'She said that if I was serious about saving our marriage then it was going to take more than an extended trip down memory lane and that I was going to have to put in the hard work and agree to go to therapy with her so that we could discuss the intimate details of our lives with a complete stranger. Again, I paraphrase.'

'Not a fan of therapy then?' Allie was smiling already. Martin was infuriating at times, opinionated, obstinate and completely stuck in the past. But he also had an uncanny knack of making Allie laugh, just when she was least expecting to.

Martin harrumphed. 'I mean I'm sure it's all very well, but I just don't know what talking to a stranger is going to do to help.'

'Like with me?'

'What do you mean?' he asked sharply.

'Just that I'm a stranger, you've been telling me your life story and don't you think it's been helping a little bit?'

'With my writing! This is completely different.'

Allie wasn't sure that it was, but decided that Martin was obviously in one of his moods and perhaps now wasn't the time to tell him he was wrong. She could park this with all of the other things she planned to tell people at the right time. Like telling Martin that she was seeing his son, and really hoped to be 'seeing' a whole lot more of him. Allie went all hot and shivery; half fantasizing about Will, and half terrified of not having confessed to either Will or Martin. She cleared her throat to dislodge the feelings of awkwardness and guilt that seemed to be uncomfortably lodged there.

'Anyway, well done for going,' she said in what she hoped wouldn't come across as a patronising tone. 'I think it's great you're agreeing to do this with Angie.'

There was silence from Martin which suggested that Allie had failed to strike the right note and he was quietly seething at her words. Eventually he spoke.

'So, what's going on with you?'

Allie considered this and decided that if she was going to tell either Martin or Will about the other one, she should probably tell Will first, so now wasn't the time for complete honesty.

'I'm stuck again, can't write. I've barely written a word since we last met.'

'Oh.'

Allie waited, hoping that Martin might have more to offer than this.

'So, the dating thing isn't going so well then?'

Back in the before, when Allie didn't know that the hot waiter she had started developing a thing for was Martin's son, it hadn't seemed such a big deal to tell Martin that she was seeing someone. Martin had been rather excited by the news and so she had tried to downplay this with the result that Martin had come away with the impression that Allie was merely using the nameless man in question to get her rocks off and as literary inspiration for her writing. In hindsight, Allie recognised that it was less than ideal that Martin had this opinion of the man Allie was seeing because the man Allie was seeing was Martin's son. And, although she had no first-hand experience, she presumed that most fathers wouldn't take kindly to their sons being used in such a way. Especially as Martin had now indicated on more than one occasion that he believed his son (Will/Liam) to be seeing someone, and that his son (Liam/Will) seemed really rather keen on this mystery person, (Allie.) Sometimes, Allie was pleased to actually be so invested in this scenario that she could (kind of) keep up with what was going on and who was what to whom, because she wasn't sure she could manage to keep tabs on the subterfuge if she was merely a bystander. But mostly she just wished that Martin and Will could miraculously become unrelated so that she didn't have to expend so much emotional bandwidth thinking about the whole mess.

'It's fine.'

'Doesn't sound it.'

'He's away at the moment,' Allie said through gritted teeth and then immediately regretted giving Martin even this tiny insight into things with Will.

'Ah … not getting your inspiration right now?'

Allie rolled her eyes, not that Martin would appreciate this. 'Martin, that sounds lascivious.'

'Ah,' repeated Martin, the intonation in his voice changing completely. 'Sorry, that wasn't what I intended.'

'It's fine, just … let's not discuss my love life, OK? I'm not sure it's helping.'

There was a long silence.

'Hmm.' Martin sounded thoughtful. 'What are you doing right now?'

'Right now?' Allie sounded startled. 'Honestly? I've just woken up from a nap.'

She could hear Martin chuckling on the end of the line. 'That's what I do too when I can't write.'

'Really? Well, that makes me feel better. I mean I sometimes go walking, but it was raining, and I thought getting wet would just compound my misery.'

'It's cleared up now though, hasn't it?'

Allie peered through her shutters and agreed that yes, it had, and that it looked like it was turning out to be a nice evening after all. Bloody typical.

'How long does it take you to get to St James's Park?'

'Why?' Allie was immediately suspicious, she never liked to answer a question unless she knew where it was leading.

'Half an hour?'

'More like an hour,' she agreed grudgingly.

'Meet me on the corner of Horse Guards and Birdcage Walk in an hour.'

'Why?' she asked again.

'We're going walking,' Martin said and put the phone down leaving Allie sitting on her bed, staring at her phone and wondering, not for the first time, whether this was all worth it. But she had nothing else to do and nowhere else to be and if she stayed in her flat she would probably drive herself crazy staring at her computer. And anyway, maybe she could message Jess and see if she was out in town tonight and arrange to meet her for a drink after meeting Martin. She quickly tapped out a message to Jess and went to get her things together and to see just how crazy her hair looked after she had slept on it for half the afternoon.

Chapter Sixteen

'There you are.' Martin was already waiting for her on the corner of St James's Park, where Horse Guards Parade met Birdcage Walk. Allie loved this part of London, she loved the old buildings, the sense of history, she hated the tourists though, they always seemed to be teeming about. But this evening was an exception, the earlier rain had put paid to sightseeing.

'Here I am,' Allie concurred. 'So, what now?'

'We walk. We walk, we talk, and we carry on until you know where to go next with your book.'

Allie was familiar with this drill. She had done it many, many times over the years. Sometimes with a friend by her side, sometimes on her own. But she had got out of the habit, her recent writing drought proving too strong for her to believe she could walk her way out of it. Still, it was nice to hear that it was something Martin relied on as well.

'OK, so where to?'

'Let's start in the park. We'll go round the lake and see where we are when we've done that.'

They made their way into the park, taking one of the pathways that would, sooner or later, lead them to the lake.

'Do you walk with Angie?' Allie asked. Martin raised an eyebrow quizzically at her. 'I meant when you're writing?' she clarified. 'When you're stuck. Or when you got stuck in the past.' She thought jealously of Martin's manuscript, which seemed to be speeding towards the finish line at an impressive rate, while hers limped tortuously at the back of the pack.

'Sometimes, although not that often. There was always something else to do. Something else dragging our attention away from each other. Normally I'd walk on my own, or with one of my friends. Sometimes my son would come, when he was younger. He's too busy with his own life now, of course.'

Allie felt a pang at the mention of Will. Martin had often mentioned his children in the past, before Allie was aware of who Will was, and she had enjoyed listening to Martin talk about them. But now it gave her the ick, and made her heart beat too fast thinking about all the lies. Not *lies*, she corrected her internal monologue, merely an omission of the full facts. That clarification made her feel *so* much better.

She could see the lake ahead of them now and was enjoying watching the water catch the end-of-the-day sun through the trees up ahead. Neither of them spoke as they came closer to the water's edge, and then both of them stopped to take in the view. Here, it was busier, tourists and Londoners alike gathered under the ancient London plane trees, feeding the ducks under the willows. Allie leaned against the metal railing, which stopped people from getting any closer to the water. She took a sideways glance at Martin who was gripping the railing and looked lost in thought.

'Memories?' she asked, suddenly realising that perhaps this was why Martin had suggested the park.

'Hmm,' he neither agreed nor disagreed. He loosened his grip on the railing and turned around, now leaning his back against it. Allie looked up at him.

'What does that mean?' She wasn't willing to let this opportunity get away, not just because she suspected she might be about to strike the jackpot with anecdotes she could weave into her novel but also because Martin looked like he wanted to get something off his chest – she was nothing if not altruistic.

'Angie used to work right over there.' He pointed off in the general direction of 'outside the park'. Allie honestly couldn't say if it was north, south, east or west and she wasn't even going to hazard a guess.

'She did?'

'She did. She worked at a research institute for years before taking the job at Imperial.'

'Wow.' That stream of words didn't make much sense to Allie, although they sounded impressive.

Martin smiled ruefully. 'She loved working there, but the money was terrible. Ironic, really, that taking a job in academia was so much more lucrative. And they offered her tenure, so there was that security, too.'

Allie nodded wisely, wishing she had paid more attention to Martha when she talked about sciencey stuff like this. She presumed tenure was a good thing from the way Martin said it, although to her it sounded like it could be a low level and specific type of torture.

'I wasn't exactly in a position to offer any kind of financial security, so it made sense for her to take it. And she never complained, she does love being at Imperial.'

'It was so nice to meet her the other night.'

'Hmm? Oh yes. She loved you. I don't think I had realised that not only had she read *all* of your books, but she owns every one too. You know she thought about getting her copies out so you could sign them but then she got embarrassed and decided not to.'

Allie blushed at this, the very idea that Angie, with all her poise and class would be too embarrassed to ask Allie to sign her books. The very idea that Angie would *have* all her books, had read them all *and* wanted Allie to sign them. It would have given Allie a warm glow had it not been for the fact that Allie wanted desperately (and secretly) to bang her son, which poured a quenching torrent of cold water on those feelings.

'That's so sweet of her. I'd be happy to.' Allie risked adding, 'Next time,' in the hope that she might get to meet Angie again. 'I'm so pleased you two are talking again and working things out.' She glanced over at Martin whose shoulders had slumped at her words. 'What is it? You don't seem so thrilled?'

Martin said nothing.

'Oh…' The penny dropped for Allie. 'You haven't spoken to Gigi about the money yet have you?'

Martin groaned, which was pretty much what Allie felt like doing (both in a good and a bad way) when she thought of his children, or more specifically, one of his children. Martin's groan however, was definitely a bad groan.

'She's away at the moment, on some kind of retreat.' Allie rolled her eyes and was amused to catch the tail end of Martin's eye roll too. 'We've agreed to talk to her about it when she gets back. Not that she'll still have the money, of course. But Angie says, and she's right, I know she's right, that that isn't the point and that we need to finally lay some ground rules down with Gigi. Of course, Liam's furious about the whole thing.'

It took a moment for Allie to recall that he was talking about Will, that this was Martin's nickname for him. It was beyond jarring.

'He is?' she finally managed to croak.

'Yes. I think he's always known that we… I,' Martin corrected himself, 'have bailed Gigi out. But I don't think he realised the extent of it. And he's really cross with me for not telling him, and especially for not being honest with his mother.'

There was a long pause during which they both watched a group of tourists attempt, unsuccessfully, to get close enough to one of the pelicans so that they could pose with it in a photograph. The pelican in question was having none of it, and seemed to be mocking them. Letting them get just close enough that they thought they were in with a chance and then inelegantly waddling away as they tried to frame the shot.

'He used to love the pelicans.'

Allie was jolted away from the comedic scene. 'Who?'

'Liam. I used to bring him and Gigi here at lunchtimes in the summer, when they were off school and Angie was working over there.' Martin pointed outside the park again. 'Liam was obsessed with the birds. Always more interested in feeding them his sandwiches than in eating them himself. Which was probably due to my terrible attempts at sandwich-making. And probably why he ended up getting so interested in making his own food at such a young age. Desperate to escape my cooking,' Martin laughed.

Allie was fascinated by this insight into the life and times of young Will. She knew no matter how many questions she asked him herself, she would probably never have unearthed this tiny tableau of his childhood. And she was deeply aware that Martin probably wouldn't be sharing half of this with her if he knew that Will and Allie were seeing each other. *Were* being the operative word here. Will might not feel like seeing her again once he knew that she had used false pretenses in order to prise these priceless nuggets of his childhood out of Martin.

Allie coughed to cover her shame. And then, once she started, she couldn't stop.

'Are you OK?' Martin asked in consternation as Allie bent double, going redder and redder in the face. She put a hand up to tell him that really she was fine and that actually this was a wonderful way to get him to stop talking about his children. He got the first part, but the latter was lost in translation, which was probably for the best.

'Shall we go on?' she eventually managed to ask after having taken a long drink from her water bottle.

'You're sure you're OK?'

'Allergic to pelicans,' she said as they made their way back onto the path.

Despite the awkwardness of her near choking experience by the lake, and Martin's insistence on repeatedly bringing 'Liam' into the conversation, it had been good to catch up with Martin. He understood what she was going through, he'd been there before, and he knew what had worked for him in the past. Also, she'd got some really good material to work on and if she could only park her thoughts about Will for the time being she might even get something down before her next meet-up with Martin. Which he had insisted on scheduling for before the end of the week.

'Keep up the pressure,' he had said as he extracted a promise from Allie to meet him sometime on Friday. And she had agreed, because really she had no other alternative.

Allie had left Martin at the north-west corner of St James's Park. She wouldn't have called it that, she'd have identified it as being somewhere near Buckingham Palace, where the tourists congregated for real, and therefore somewhere she really didn't want to be. Martin had ambled off in the direction of Victoria and Allie had checked her phone, hoping for a message from Jess. She should have gone straight home to write, get the ideas down before she forgot them. But first, she really wanted a drink and a debrief with Jess, who unfortunately hadn't responded. Taking matters into her own hands, Allie called her. Jess picked up on the second ring.

'Hey!' Allie said. 'How's things?'

'Hey, not bad. Where are you?' Jess could obviously hear the sounds of the excited tourists chattering in the background.

'Buckingham Palace.'

'Right. Why?' Jess asked incredulously.

'I went walking with Martin, we ended up here.'

There was a pause. 'Did you tell him? About Will?'

'No.' Allie didn't even try to prevaricate.

'Allie!'

'Alright,' Allie was irritated, 'I didn't call you so you could judge me. I called to see if you were out tonight.'

'No, not tonight. Having a quiet one.'

'Uff, when do you ever have a quiet one?'

'I do! Just not very often.'

'Does it have to be tonight?' Allie whined. 'I want to talk to you!'

'We are talking.'

'Not on the phone! Face to face. Preferably over a drink.'

Allie could hear Jess sigh. 'Not tonight, Allie, OK? I'm home, I'm not coming back out. If you want to talk we can talk now.'

Allie was silent. 'What about later on in the week?'

'I'm free Friday?'

'OK!' Allie latched on deliriously. 'Friday's good! I'm meeting Martin for a catch-up but can be free whenever you get off work.'

'Allie?' Jess asked in a dangerous tone. 'You are planning on telling him on Friday, aren't you?'

'Well, yes, I mean, no, I mean, maybe? I think I should tell Will first, don't you think?' Allie's voice was pleading. She was desperate for Jess to agree, desperate to be let off the hook for just a few more days before her world came tumbling apart.

Jess exhaled. 'Maybe you're right.'

Allie experienced what she could only describe as absolute delight to have had her decision verified, only for a caveat to be firmly put in place.

'But that just means you should tell Will *before* Friday. Then you can tell Martin afterwards.'

'But he's away,' wheedled Allie. 'And as I said before, I think I should do it face to face.'

'Ideally, yes. But we don't find ourselves in ideal circumstances, do we? So now I think you need to make the best of a bad situation.'

Allie scowled. Jess was not playing ball. Maybe it was better that she wasn't free this evening. It was easier to ignore her when they weren't opposite each other, only separated by a bottle of chilled sauvignon.

'OK, whatever. I'll tell him.'

'Good. I'll message you about Friday.'

Allie put the phone down and stomped off in the direction of Green Park Tube station, trying not to feel too guilty about the fact she had just lied to her best friend. She would tell Will, of course she would. She just hadn't been completely clear with Jess about *when* exactly she planned to do this, because she wasn't really sure herself.

Chapter Seventeen

Verity picked up her phone for what felt to Allie like the millionth time and then slammed it face down on the table between them.

'She isn't coming,' she said defiantly.

'Relax Verity, she's not even late yet.' Allie checked her watch and tried to pretend to feel as relaxed as she was urging Verity to be. In reality, Allie was pretty jumpy herself.

It had taken levels of subterfuge previously unknown to Allie, to set this meeting up and she still couldn't quite believe that Verity was out with her in public – although she *was* wearing a big coat and sunglasses, even though they were sat inside, and even though London had not seen the sun in days.

Verity had suggested the location in an email sent from her mother's best friend's email address, saying that Peckham Library was the last place that Jake would think to look for a meeting dedicated to his removal from power. She had casually mentioned that Jake had probably never even heard of it and Allie still wasn't clear on whether she meant Peckham or a library, before settling on the fact it was extremely likely that Jake hadn't heard of either. Allie had to convey the time and place to their third member and was told by Verity that she must never, ever, mention her name in any follow-up communication confirming the meeting. Needless to say, all of this had obviously rubbed off on Allie who kept nervously looking over her shoulder and then pretending she wasn't, which was giving her a crick in her neck and a headache to boot. She rubbed her right shoulder and tried to ignore her rising sense of panic that really she ought to be at home, writing, not getting all caught up in publishing subterfuge, however much she would enjoy having a hand in the downfall of Jake Matthews.

And her mood and muscle spasms weren't helped by the fact that she was currently perched on a fake log, which was designed to support people half her height and probably a third of her weight. And yet here she was because if the big coat, dark glasses, south-east London location and a large building full of books wasn't enough to throw Jake Matthews off the scent, Verity had to go and pick the children's section as the least likely place in which to meet. Storytime had just ended, and several parents had given Verity strange looks on their way out, and Allie was beginning to worry that if Jake Matthews didn't find them, then security might be the ones to bust up their meeting with reports of strange women looking shifty in the kids' section.

Verity was just about to start on again about what a waste of time this was all turning out to be when quite out of nowhere, a shadow slunk onto the seat (log) next to Allie and tried to shrink into the wall behind. The shadow pulled their scarf tighter around their throat and issued a muffled 'Hello.'

All of the puffed-up panic left Verity immediately and she deflated with relief. 'Tessa,' she gushed, 'how are you?'

'Thinking I shouldn't be fraternising with the enemy,' Tessa said testily from behind her scarf.

Allie shot Verity a warning look, knowing full well that Verity was about to launch into an impassioned defence of their actions, a high-octane speech about how they weren't the enemy, that the enemy was hiding in plain sight in the Brinkman's offices and that they were only here to help Tessa. Allie could just tell that anything like this would startle Tessa into fleeing the scene. Instead, she engaged her best comforting tone and said, 'I know. It must have taken a lot of courage to come here. Thank you.'

Tessa looked over at her through narrowed eyes. 'So what exactly do you want from me?'

Verity opened her mouth and Allie shot her yet another warning look. Evidently, this new emboldened Verity was determined to get her speech in however inappropriate it was to the situation.

'Tessa,' Allie began in what she hoped was a measured and reassuring tone, 'I'm going to be honest. We do want something from you. But we also think that if you can help us, it will help you too.'

Tessa allowed her scarf to slip slightly and fixed a flinty stare on Allie. 'At least you're being honest.'

'Look, I want to get Verity her job back. And you told me yourself what a monster Jake is to work for, so you must see that if we work together, we can all benefit?'

Allie held her breath and silently urged Verity to hold her tongue. Tessa obviously needed some time and space to think about what they were asking.

'I don't know,' Tessa eventually replied sullenly. 'Seems like I've got a whole lot more to lose than either of you.'

Verity opened her mouth again to protest but her voice came out as a squeak due to the pressure Allie was exerting on her foot.

'Yes, I can totally see that. But you've also got a lot to gain, too. Think about what it would be like to not work for Jake. To have a different boss...' Allie resisted the urge to wax lyrical about how wonderful and normal it would be not to have a boss who controlled through fear, who blackmailed his employees and got them to risk themselves by supplying him with wraps of cocaine in the toilets at work events. She really had to restrain herself in order not to scream at the absurdity of how wrong this all was in Tessa's pinched face.

'He *is* awful,' Tessa eventually said.

'I know,' Allie replied soothingly.

'And we *are* all scared of him.'

'I can't imagine how that must feel.'

'He tricked me into getting him coke at the summer party, and now whenever he wants any he reminds me that he could have me fired for supplying drugs, or even arrested if he was feeling especially vindictive.' Tessa's eyes started welling up and Allie resisted the urge to look at Verity, who she knew was just desperate to shout out that she had been right, and that it had been Jake and Tessa who Allie had overheard in the bathroom at the V&A.

'And there are people he is even worse to...'

Allie and Verity shared a nervous glance because what he had done to Tessa seemed pretty awful to them and they didn't dare to imagine what she might be about to share with them next.

'Do you want to tell us?' Allie delicately asked.

Tessa hunched her shoulders. 'Apparently there's a girl in marketing that he had a fling with, he treated her really badly, and when he got wind that she might go to HR he cornered her and told her he had incriminating photographs of her that might just find their way onto social media if she pursued it.'

Allie and Verity's jaws hit the ground. 'What?' blurted Verity as she wrestled her dislocated jaw back into its rightful position. 'Who?'

'I'm not going to tell you that,' Tessa said in outrage. 'It's bad enough it's happened. I'm not going to spread her name around.'

'No, no of course not. Sorry. I'm just so shocked.' Verity had gone a very strange colour. Allie put her face in her hands, considering the awfulness of what Tessa had just told them. It shouldn't come as a surprise, she knew what kind of a man Jake Matthews was, but deep down, she had been hoping that, for the sake of humanity, Verity had been exaggerating his depravity. Unfortunately, it looked like she had been underestimating it. Allie rubbed her eye sockets and exhaled heavily.

'Tessa, I know I said I'd be honest with you. And I was being honest. Both of us have a vested interest in Jake Matthews getting his comeuppance but... Look, it's more than that. I can deal with not having Verity edit my books, and I'm speaking for Verity here, but I'm also confident she can deal with not getting her job back because she's awesome and any other publisher would be lucky to have her. But after what you've told us, I don't think I can deal with knowing that Jake Matthews is out there, riding roughshod over the #MeToo movement and ruining young women's lives. I can't live with myself if I don't do something about this. And I know I'm asking a lot, and I wouldn't do it if I could think of any other way, and if there is another way then please, please tell me and I will do it instead, because I would do anything not to be putting you in this position but … if you decide to go ahead and go public with this, please know that I am right behind you and I know a lot of other women will be too.'

'And I'll be right next to you,' Verity said in a voice thick with emotion. She went to grab Tessa's hand, but Tessa jerked it away, evidently not ready for the touchy-feely vibes Allie and Verity were giving off. The three women sunk into silence and Allie tried hard to resist the urge to re-alphabetise the picture books that had been carelessly cast aside following story time, so desperate to do something with her hands that didn't involve punching the wall and alarming everyone.

Eventually, after sharing several looks with Verity, Allie conceded that they weren't going to get any more out of Tessa today and that they should take it as a win that she had even showed up. 'Look I think we've both said enough, and I think you've got a lot to think about. Neither of us want to put any more pressure on you than we already have. So, Verity? Shall we leave Tessa in peace?'

Verity nodded and she and Allie stood up to leave. 'Thank you for listening,' Allie said and squeezed Tessa's tense shoulder as she passed.

'Wow. That was heavy,' Verity said as they walked slowly towards the exit. She had already made it clear that they needed to leave at staged intervals so as not to be seen outside the building together.

'It really was,' agreed Allie.

'Do you think she'll go for it?'

'I don't know. It's a lot to ask. And I'm now worried about what might happen to her if she does decide to go public. He's a shit, we know that, but I worry that he'll manage to outshit himself and do something to completely surprise us.'

Verity nodded.

'Well let's hope that if Tessa does come forward, other women do too,' Verity said. 'He can be a shit, but he can't shit all over everyone, can he?'

'God, I hope not.' Allie shuddered at the thought.

Chapter Eighteen

Whether it was Allie's walk with Martin, or the fear that Tessa might not come through and Allie might end up having to meet Jake Matthew's deadline was unclear, but by Friday Allie had written three new chapters and was feeling as good about life as she could while still dwelling on her conversation with Tessa and Verity. She was managing to distract herself from the pervasive misogyny of the world with writing. She hadn't worked this hard since the time she'd written a new book in the space of a month, and she was enjoying it. Martin sent her regular little messages of encouragement, all of which sounded like they could have been lifted straight out of the mouth of General Kitchener. Jess had been in touch with plans for that evening and Allie was beginning to think things were looking up again. She had even contemplated sending the new draft to Verity, just to get her opinion, but Verity had visibly blanched at the suggestion and whispered the words 'NDA' at her and rapidly changed the subject. Allie sent over some silent positive vibes of fortitude and bravery to Tessa, in the hope that they might help her decide whether to out Jake Matthews or not.

Will had been in touch just the right amount, sending sweet messages along with some delightfully suggestive ones. Even if neither of them were truly being honest with each other, she *knew* he was definitely keen to see her when he got back.

Allie had surprised herself by saying, 'I wish you were here,' when they'd spoken the other day on the phone and then immediately held her breath, grimacing, holding the phone away from her ear, waiting for Will to get cold feet and swiftly end both the phone call and whatever type of relationship they were currently in.

'I do too,' Will said straight back. 'I've really missed you.'

Allie bit her lip and smiled. Her stomach swooped, which was a nice feeling, and her palms went sweaty, which was a less pleasant sensation to endure. But this wasn't the plan. Telling Will she missed him was not 'keeping him at arm's length.' It was not playing it cool, getting her writing done and then figuring out if he might still like her after he discovered she had been essentially lying to him. But it would *also* be lying to say she hadn't missed him. She had missed the way he made her laugh, the way he held her hand, the way his hand tightened around her waist as he pulled her close to kiss her, and god dammit, if she wasn't falling for him hard. Her already overactive mind was literally screaming at her to stop, to pull back, to remember her deadline, to focus on her career. But instead, she asked in a small voice, 'When do you get back?'

'In a day or two? I really want to get back to London and see you…'

He had left the suggestion hanging in the air and Allie in

suspense as to all the things he might have in mind for his return. She had gone back to her laptop frustrated yet inspired and, courtesy of these thoughts, written a steamy chapter for her new book. She told herself she was back on track, back to getting what she needed from Will and pretended she wasn't getting in too deep.

———

So, it was in just such a confused mood that Allie found herself sitting in a hip rooftop bar near London Bridge waiting for Martin. The location had flummoxed her. Much as she was invested in the love story of Martin and Angie, she wasn't blind to its limitations, and lack of hipness was certainly one of them. She couldn't imagine this being somewhere Martin was scoping out to take Angie on their next married couple date night.

'This is very nice,' she said, once Martin had picked his way through the city suits towards her.

'You like it?'

'I do! Good choice.' Martin blushed a little under her praise. 'Somewhere you're thinking of taking Angie?'

'Brought her here the other night actually.' Martin failed to conceal the note of pride in his voice at this revelation.

'Good for you!' Allie reached across the table and gave Martin a friendly punch on the arm, causing him to spill his beer.

'Sorry!' Allie handed him a napkin so he could mop up his beer. 'So, did she like it?'

'She did. We'd been to see a play at The Chocolate Factory and Liam had suggested this place.' Martin smiled. 'I think he's thinking of bringing his new lady friend here, he wanted an in-depth report on the ambience of the place.' He started laughing. 'Sorry, I just find it peculiar he would trust us with checking the location, it seems like a big responsibility because he seems to really like this friend.'

Once again Allie wished she had come clean sooner, and then she and Martin could be sitting here having a perfectly normal conversation about writing without all of this subtext and subterfuge roiling away under the surface and giving her heartburn. She rubbed the top of her ribcage.

'By the way, I hope you don't mind but I told him I'd be here. He's been away but he said if he was back in time he'd call in and have a beer with me. I'm still trying to make it up to him for not being honest about everything. I hope that's OK?'

Allie's eyes widened in panic. Will was coming here? To meet Martin? His dad? With absolutely no knowledge that Allie would be here, not even realising that Allie knew his dad? This was not OK. This was very far from OK.

'He's … he's … coming here?' she spluttered.

'Maybe.' Martin shrugged. 'As I said, he's been away but he said he'd be back tonight, just not sure what time.'

'Does he know you're meeting *me* here?' Allie's mouth had gone incredibly dry, which was an interesting and new side effect of utter panic.

'Well he doesn't know it's *you*,' Martin said, in slight bemusement at Allie's line of questioning. 'I mean, he knows I'm meeting a writer friend here, but I didn't tell him your name. Should I have done?' He raised a bushy eyebrow at Allie.

'No! I mean, no, no, of course not. I mean, he wouldn't even recognise my name, so what would be the point?! Ha ha! Completely stupid, of course!' Which was a charge that Allie felt could be levelled at her right now. 'So he's coming here, when?'

'I don't know!' Martin frowned at her. 'Are you OK? You seem extremely bothered about the fact Liam might be coming here. I know we discussed not telling anyone about helping each other out. But it's only Liam, I didn't think it would matter.'

'Matter? Oh no! Of course it doesn't matter.' Allie took a large gulp of her wine and tried to look at her watch to gauge the time, wondering if she could finish up her meeting with Martin and hot foot it out of there before Will showed up, and manage all of this without seeming like a total lunatic to Martin, who was already looking at her as if he might have suspicions about that.

'So tell me how writing has been this week?'

'Great! Fantastic,' babbled Allie. 'Almost done.'

'You are? Well, that's amazing, Allie, congratulations. Wish I could say the same for me.'

Allie grimaced – this wasn't working. Even if she could persuade Martin that she had almost finished her manuscript (she hadn't) then he was still going to want to talk about his, and that could take a while, in fact, it could take right up until the moment Will walked up the steps, out on to the rooftop bar and destroyed Allie's happy ever after forever.

'Yes, I'm really rather stuck on the third murder. What do you think about it happening on the trading floor of the bank? I was thinking about having a wall of those monitors collapse on top of Harry. Or do you think it would be better if there were balconies overlooking the trading floor and he plunged to his death, crashing into the bank of monitors as he went? I mean, I'd have to rewrite that description I have in chapter two, because I don't mention any balconies, but I could easily put them in. But then I also have to think how Chastity planned all of this. I mean, if he's to plunge to his death, then surely she has to push him, and do you think she could? She's supposed to be quite petite so I'm not sure about the logistics of her pushing a six-foot man over a balcony. Maybe it's better that she has rigged the monitors to collapse on top of him.' Martin paused for breath mid-muse. 'What do you think?'

What did Allie think? Allie had a lot of things on her mind at that precise moment, none of which involved the intricacies of how Martin might kill off his third victim. She was scanning the entrance of the bar for Will, trying to work out how long a train journey from York would take and the subsequent Tube journey to London Bridge. Would he go home first? That would give her a little longer to wrap things up with Martin and then get the hell out of there. And that was the main focus of all her thoughts. She knew that it ought to be how she should handle it when Will found out she knew Martin, but instead she was single-mindedly concentrating on how to make a speedy exit and prevent him from finding out this unwelcome fact tonight. Martin was aware of none of this, still pondering the logistics of a balcony plunge vs a monitor collapse. Either of which Allie would have been grateful for as a distraction right about now.

'Allie?' he asked again.

'Hmm? Oh yes, right. No, I think that definitely works.'

He frowned. 'But which one? The balcony shove or the monitor collapse?'

'Definitely the balcony shove, I love what you did there,' Allie said with far more conviction than she felt.

Martin's frown intensified causing his eyebrows to completely meet in the middle and, not for the first time, Allie could see the family resemblance between him and Will. Not that she had seen much of Will frowning, but there was something that the intense frown did to the shape of Martin's eyes that made him resemble his son, or presumably, the other way around.

'You think it's plausible Chastity would be able to push a six-foot man over a balcony? I was trying to work out momentum, where she would need to push him, how low the balcony would need to be so that a stumble and a shove could send him plummeting to his death. I presume these places have health and safety rules that require a minimum height for a balcony railing.'

Allie allowed herself a small smile at the wormhole Martin was evidently travelling down. It was something very familiar to her – not the murder and the balcony shove, but the logistics of making a plot plausible. And she thought of all the weird google searches she had done over the years to work out things like whether a five-foot-four woman would need to stand on tiptoes to kiss a nearly six-foot man. Just how long it takes the Eurostar to get through the tunnel on its way to Paris and whether that's long enough for an entire relationship to unravel and come back full circle so that by the time the train shoots out into the French countryside the two romantic leads are kissing passionately in the luggage compartment.

'I think it's OK to allow a certain amount of suspension of disbelief in novels, don't you?'

Martin didn't look convinced so she tried a different tack. 'OK, maybe you're right, maybe it's too much to expect her to be able to pull that off. How about you have her rig up the monitors to collapse for *this* murder and save the balcony shove for later?'

Martin's features visibly lightened. 'Good idea, but you

don't think it's too repetitive to have two murders happen on the trading floor?'

Allie contemplated this. 'Well, how about Chastity commits the first murder, and then she manages to torment Archie—' the VP at the bank and the worst offender of the lot '—enough that he is provoked into the final act, and it's actually *him* who pushes the chairman to his death from the balcony, just as the police swoop in. So they see Archie commit the final murder and, as Chastity has planted enough incriminating evidence, they pin *all* the murders on him?'

Martin gave a low whistle. 'That's good,' he said admiringly. 'Are you sure you don't want to try your hand at writing crime? You could save this for your debut crime novel?'

Allie shrugged. 'I appreciate the gesture, maybe at some point, but I did double check, and my contract is quite specific – my next novel for Brinkman's needs to be a romance. And while I'm sure some editors would see the benefit of an author writing in two genres, I am sure Jake will use this as some way to further ruin my career.'

'I despise him,' Martin said bleakly and took a sip of his beer.

'Yup. Me too. Sounds like most of publishing does.'

'Got any further on your plan to ruin him?'

If Allie hadn't been so nervous about the outcome of her recent meeting with Tessa she would have more deeply appreciated the way Martin so casually asked this; as if it was perfectly normal for the two of them to be discussing taking down their nemesis. And maybe it was for Martin because while Allie was usually trying to engineer meet-cutes, Martin was conspiring to commit murder. She wondered just how much to tell Martin that wouldn't impinge on Tessa's privacy.

'I met with Tessa the other day,' she confessed.

Martin's ever-expressive eyebrows shot up. 'And?'

'And ... it's complicated. It's a lot to ask of her.'

Martin shook his head. 'Maybe he doesn't treat her as badly as we think he does?'

'Martin,' she said sternly, 'I thought we'd done the work on you being an ally? Her *boss* is using her to get drugs, threatening her with professional death if she exposes him, and generally playing in to the systemic corporate patriarchy by proving that men always hold all the power.'

To his credit, Martin looked suitably ashamed.

'This is not about being a feminist,' lectured Allie, as if reading Martin's mind, 'it's about recognising the structural issues in place which prevent women from holding any kind of power in the workplace.' Martin nodded, as though keen to ensure that Allie realised he was fully behind her and totally invested in smashing the patriarchal structures that enslaved both men and women.

'Also, Jake is a complete ass. Everything she told me just confirms that. She definitely knows it, how could she not?'

'Well let's hope she either comes to her senses or we both manage to deliver our manuscripts. Either would be OK with me right now.' Martin broke off, his face suddenly creasing into a broad grin as he stood up from the table. Allie had become so engrossed in discussing Martin's plot and outlining her righteous indignation at the behaviour of Jake Matthews, that she had completely forgotten her pressing need to finish up this drink and make herself scarce before there was any danger of Will arriving on the scene. Her stomach dropped as Martin exclaimed, 'Liam! Good to see you,' and she realised she was too late.

Allie kept her gaze firmly focused on the table in front of

her so she was only half aware of Martin grabbing Will by the shoulder and pulling him into the awkward hug, double pat release, that was widely recognised as the symbol of male-on-male affection. If Will had made his entrance from behind her then there was obviously another way in and out of the bar. Slowly, she began to push her chair back from the table, keeping her head down. She hoped she might be able to get far enough away in this position that she could then do a crouching turn and make a run for it before Will could get a good look at her and realise who she was. Her chair scraped loudly on the floor and Allie cursed the idiot who had decided to install trendy metal chairs in this bar. Not only were they uncomfortable, but they got too hot, and when they got too hot, they burned the back of your thighs, *and* you got stuck to them. Which made getting up out of them a less than graceful move; it was hard to maintain an air of dignity when you were welded to a chair.

'Allie?' With her head down and her hair hanging over her face she realised her cover was blown, and now she was two feet from the table in the awkward position of looking like she was about to make an escape. Also, there was still the chair situation to work through, Allie wished she hadn't chosen a bare leg and short skirt combo that evening.

'Will!' She slowly turned and grinned up at him, hoping a full-wattage smile would divert him from the awkwardness of the whole situation. 'Erm, lovely to see you!'

Lovely to see you? Was that the best she could come up with? For goodness' sake, who said 'lovely to see you' to a person who you had basically seen naked? Allie felt herself begin to blush, her colour only deepening as Will put a hand on her shoulder and gave her a playful squeeze.

'Wait?' Martin looked at Will's hand on Allie's shoulder

and then between the two of them in obvious puzzlement, which made Allie think that he should hold that look, because this situation was about to get a whole lot messier. 'You know Allie's name?'

Will looked down at Allie, his eyes seemed to be asking her what the correct response to this situation was, and, considering she had been about to do a runner thirty seconds ago, she really had no answer for him. She wasn't sure whether her red face and panicked look was adequately conveying this.

'Er?' Will scratched his head with his free hand and smiled bashfully. He was behaving exactly how you would want the man you were seeing to behave when he was startled into introducing you to his father. But right at that moment, Allie couldn't appreciate this. Luckily Martin either didn't see or didn't care about the awkwardness.

'Of course!' He put a hand to his forehead. 'Allie must have told you her name when you met at the party, right?'

'Right,' Will confirmed, and then Allie felt his arm stiffen as the penny dropped with him that there was something off with this whole scenario. 'Hang on. Dad, I thought you were meeting one of your writer friends?'

'I am!' Martin confirmed, presumably willfully ignoring the discomfiture in his son's voice. 'Allie *is* my writer friend.' If it had been under different circumstances Allie would have felt distinctly touched by the note of pride in Martin's voice.

'Oh!' Will was startled by this revelation. 'But … erm … OK. Wow.' He looked down at Allie and gave her a wide-eyed look that begged her to copy him, to laugh at this weird situation and then to explain in exacting detail just what he was missing and to reassure him that it really wasn't all that weird after all. Allie swallowed nervously. 'Lots to catch up on?' he said in a painfully reassuring voice.

'Yes!' Allie grasped at what she saw as an escape route of some kind. 'We should definitely do that.' She straightened abruptly, Will's hand falling from her shoulder as she did so. 'But I should get going. Don't want to interrupt your drink.'

She easily shirked off Martin's thanks for helping him with the latest murder scene, and less easily shirked off Will's attempts to kiss her goodbye, leaving him gracelessly hanging as she hurried away.

Chapter Nineteen

'**O**kaaay. That sounds all kinds of awks.' Jess looked at Allie, concern etched all over her face.

'You can say that again.' Allie picked up her drink and considered their surroundings. When Jess had told her where to meet her, Allie had merely tapped the address into her phone and followed the directions. So when she found Jess standing on the street in front of what looked like the entrance to an old-fashioned public toilet she had presumed that Jess would then lead her to some fabulous hidden away gem. And in fairness to Jess she had done just that, but this *gem* just happened to be hidden away underground, right down the steps of the old public toilet. In hindsight, Allie should probably have done more due diligence and asked Jess in advance what the dress code for tonight was as there was no mistaking the burlesque dancers doing their thing on a stage at one end of the room. And while earlier on in the evening, when trying to escape from Will and Martin, Allie might have regretted the cutesy ruffled rara-inspired skirt she was wearing, she was now regretting it for entirely different reasons; it really wasn't living up to the sexy decadent boudoir vibe of the bar.

Jess hadn't made the same mistake, presumably because she had suggested this place and knew exactly what to expect. Allie eyed her off-the-shoulder black top and her studded boots with jealousy and tried to keep her eyes off Jess's cleavage but was struggling. She wasn't sure what bra Jess had on but made a mental note to ask her at some point, because wherever it was from, whatever it cost, Allie needed one of those in her life.

'Jess, why are we here?'

'Work.' Which always seemed to be Jess's response but it never stopped Allie from asking.

'Okaaay ... are you thinking of a career change?' Allie smirked and gestured to the dancers.

'Yup.'

'Wait, what, seriously?' Allie put down her drink in surprise.

'Allie! I'm kidding. This is the hottest club that's opened this season in London. Didn't you see the queue of people waiting to get in? We're pitching to them next week,' Jess continued, 'to do all their marketing and PR. This,' Jess pointed to their two drinks, 'is research.'

'Nice.'

'You want another one by the way?'

'It's my round.' Allie made a move to stand, but Jess was faster.

'No,' she gestured to Allie to put her purse away. 'It's on me, I can expense these.'

'Well, thank you, I'll have the same again, please. What are you drinking by the way?'

Jess looked slightly furtive. 'Oh I can't remember what it

was called, it's a bit like a gimlet, I think, but all the drinks in here have burlesque dancer names. I'll have to ask the barman to remind me.'

'I'll have the same then if it's good.'

'Oh, no. You don't have to. You like the one you have.' And before Allie could protest further Jess had left and was already chatting to the barman, who, by the way he was looking at Jess's cleavage, seemed happy to make her up any drink of her choosing.

When Jess returned, Allie reached over and picked up Jess's drink. 'Can I try a sip?'

'No!' Jess grabbed her glass back, spilling some of the drink on the table as she did so.

'Everything OK?' A thought had begun formulating in Allie's mind, a small but insidious voice that was starting to shout louder and louder that Jess was being weird. She had been weird when Allie had phoned her the other day, evasive about where she and Tom were going. And now she was being downright odd about her drink, about its name, about Allie not choosing the same one, even about Allie trying a small sip of hers. Either Jess had become exceptionally territorial over her drinks, or she was...

'Everything's fine!' insisted Jess. 'Just Tom has a cold, and you know how it is. I probably have it too. Not that I have any symptoms yet, but you know they always say you're most contagious before you're symptomatic. So maybe best if we stick to our own drinks tonight. I don't want you catching anything.' She smiled slightly manically at Allie and then took a sip of her carefully guarded drink.

Allie narrowed her eyes. 'What about the olives?'

'I'm sorry?' Allie pointed to the plate of antipasto that was on the table in between them and which Jess and Allie had been happily sharing, right up until this revelation about Tom's 'cold'.

'We've been sharing those all evening. Are you worried about that too?' Allie tried to contain her smile, she was enjoying tormenting Jess.

'Gosh, you're right. I'm so sorry. I hadn't thought. Probably germs all over them now...'

Allie waited a beat, wondering if this was the moment that Jess would cave and confess her news that Allie was now convinced she was sitting on. It would be a challenge for either of them to spend the rest of the evening with an untouched plate of food between them, just to maintain the point that Tom had a 'cold'. But Jess said nothing and eventually Allie gave in. It was just too wrong to deprive a pregnant woman of food, if that was indeed what was going on. Let her keep her secret for a little while longer, surely she would tell Allie when she was ready. Jess shifted awkwardly in her seat and Allie was struck again by her boobs, which, now she came to think of it, could actually be entirely natural and nothing to do with the structured engineering of an excellent bra. Allie felt momentarily saddened by the fact that she was not about to be gifted the knowledge of a secret new bra that would transform her life.

'Don't worry,' Allie said, leaning forward and using one of the tiny cocktail sticks to divide the contents of the antipasto in half. 'There, you have that half and I'll have this.' Jess's reaction at being allowed back to her seat at the charcuterie board made Allie smile and decide she had definitely done the right thing, for now.

'So, what are you going to do about Will? How did you leave it?'

'Awkwardly, as we have already established.' Allie sighed.

'God I really don't know, Jess. He was so sweetly surprised to see me. Do you remember what it was like when we were teenagers and you were surprised into introducing your boyfriend to your parents? It was just like that.' Allie looked wistful.

'No idea what you're talking about,' Jess said through a mouthful of chorizo. 'Remember I went to a convent school. Didn't even talk to a boy who wasn't related to me till I hit freshers week.'

'And we all remember how that went down.'

'Hey!' protested Jess. 'You weren't even *there* during my fresher's week.'

'Yeah, but I've heard the stories, and seen the scars.' Allie grinned at Jess as she held up her hand where you could still see the faintly ghostlike trail of a line of stitches that Jess had earned after paying the student barman in kisses for all the tequila she had drunk that night, which resulted in her plunging her hand straight through a glass door. Jess still maintained that she hadn't seen the door there, but Allie had it on reliable information that prior to this incident Jess was proclaiming she had magic powers and could walk through walls.

'OK, but you can imagine what it must have been like. Proud you had a boyfriend, embarrassed that you were about to have to introduce them to your parents? Mortified that everyone in the room would know you were having sex?'

'Guess so,' Jess said noncommittally. 'Anyway, what happens next? Martin presumably now knows that you and Will are...' Allie interrupted with a strangled noise in protest at discussing precisely what Martin did or didn't know about the status of her relationship with Will. Jess ignored her. 'And Will now knows that you're Martin's secret writing partner?

And neither of them seem cross about it so that's good, right?'

'I don't actually think they *know* though...'

Jess cocked her head. 'Explain.'

'Well, yes, Will knows I'm working with Martin, but he doesn't *know* that we're discussing his parents' marriage or that I am using it as the basis for my next book. Nor does he *know* that I knew he was Martin's son before just now and that I didn't tell him.'

Jess frowned. 'I didn't actually realise that you were using their marriage in the book. That's a bit off, isn't it? Does Martin know?'

Allie reddened. 'Well, no, not exactly. I mean, he knows I was using some of his stories as inspiration but...' She tailed off. 'Christ, this is worse than I imagined, isn't it?'

Jess gave a big sigh and put the piece of crusty bread down that she was about to shovel into her mouth. 'I hate to say it, but yes, it's bad. I'm not sure how you're going to salvage this. Honestly, Al, what were you thinking? Did you not think that Martin and/or Will were eventually going to figure out that you were using both of them for your book?'

'I wasn't *using* them!' bristled Allie. 'I really like Will. I like Martin too. I'd started to think of him as a real friend.'

'But that's the thing, friends don't tell each other's stories without asking permission first. Imagine how I would feel if you'd used me or my relationship with Tom in one of your books?'

'I did! Remember book five? I used your meet cute at my book signing?'

'Yes,' replied Jess firmly, 'and you asked us beforehand if it was OK to do so.'

Allie was about to protest further and then she shut her

mouth. Because Jess was right, it wasn't OK for her to have used Martin's marriage for her book. She had justified it by telling herself that she had been frank with Martin about using some of the stories and situations he had shared with her. But she had never categorically pointed out that she was planning to use his and Angie's forty-year love affair, near catastrophic demise and the redemptive arc that Martin was currently climbing. Nor had she told Will. And how would she feel if she discovered that someone was using her parents' marriage without telling her or them? Once she had got over the shock she would have felt very betrayed. Especially if the betrayal had been conducted by someone she thought cared about her.

'Shit. I've messed up.'

'Can I ask you something? This whole thing with Martin? Do you, I mean have you … you don't think it's got something to do with your dad?'

'What?' Allie snapped. 'What do you mean?'

Jess paused, obviously wondering how to bring up the perennially sensitive subject. 'I just mean, I know how close you were to him, and I know how much you miss him…'

Allie squinted at her friend. 'Are you suggesting I'm *using* Martin as some kind of father figure?'

Jess sighed. 'I don't know, I just think you seem overly invested in making someone else's book work. And overly invested in his opinion?'

Allie started to go a little pink. 'That's because I *am* invested in his book working, because he's my friend. And I *am* invested in his opinion, *because he's my friend, and* a bestselling author.'

'But Allie, you're a bestselling author too. I'm just saying that maybe there's another reason this has all come about.'

'Daddy issues?' spat Allie.

'No,' Jess said resignedly, 'not like that. I'm just worried about you. I'm worried about your book, I'm worried that you're ruining a thing with a guy who you obviously really like. And I'm worried you're not thinking straight.'

'I am thinking straight and this has zero to do with my dad, OK?'

'OK.' Jess held her hands up in surrender. 'So what are you going to do next? Here, have an olive, you look like you're about to faint.'

Allie gingerly took the olive on a cocktail stick that Jess was holding out at her like a white flag.

'Well I need to come clean, don't I?'

'You do,' confirmed Jess.

'Do you think it will be OK?'

'In what sense? As in will Martin forgive you? Will Will still want to have sex with you? Will you still have a book to deliver? Which one?'

'All of the above?' Allie confirmed weakly, reaching for some salami and hoping the salt would revive her.

Jess considered this for a moment. 'Hard to tell, given I don't know either of them or much about the book publishing world.'

Allie groaned and put her head in her hands and not even the can-canning burlesque dancers could distract her from Jess's miserable suggestion that some of this mess could be put down to the fact that she still hankered after her dead dad's approval.

Chapter Twenty

I t was the sound of running water which woke Allie the next morning. For a moment she lay in bed and wondered what was happening. She couldn't normally hear the people in the flat above her but wondered if it was the sound of their shower that had woken her. She stretched and hit her hand on the smooth metal bed frame which gave her pause for thought; she didn't have a metal bed frame, hers was wood. Slowly she rolled onto her side and eyed the alarm clock that she kept by the side of her bed, except it wasn't there. Finally deciding that she really needed to accept the fact that she hadn't slept in her own bed last night, she sat up, pulled her hair into a messy bun and wrapped her arms around her knees.

She'd been here before, not metaphorically speaking, but actually, really, physically speaking. Here being Will's flat. And the sound she had been woken by was presumably Will doing something wonderfully domestic, like the washing up, hopefully while the kettle boiled. Allie knew that last night hadn't gone down in *entirely* the way that she had promised Jess it would, but she was hopeful, in the way that all Brits tend to jingoistically believe, that a good cup of tea would fix it all. She upped her wishfulness that the noise she could hear was in fact that kettle boiling.

A few minutes passed, during which Allie rehearsed both the conversation she ought to be having with Will, but also the arse-covering one she would inevitably have to have with Jess. She was just in the middle of an impassioned defence of her actions when the door creaked slowly open and Will's head appeared around it, his face immediately brightening when he saw that Allie was awake. Bringing two cups with him he nudged the door open further and came in. 'I hope I didn't wake you.' He put the cups down on the bedside table and looked down at her.

'I love your hair pulled up like that. You've got that sleepy hot girl look going on.' He groaned, leaning over her. 'You have no idea what you do to me.' He put his hand behind her neck, teasing the tendrils of hair that she had missed and pulled her gently towards him. He was going for a kiss but Allie ducked just at the last minute and he ended up kissing her hairline.

He laughed as she said, 'I'm not sure I smell so hot.'

'Here.' He picked up one of the cups and handed it to her, sitting down on the bed as he did so. 'I know you prefer tea but you need to try this coffee I picked up when I was away.'

Allie took the cup and watched him, chewing her lip as she did so, wanting to savour both the sensation of being handed a cup of coffee in bed, and the fact it had been handed to her by this excessively good-looking guy who really seemed to be into her. Because she was fairly sure he wouldn't be quite so into her when she finally confessed everything Jess told her that she needed to confess. She looked down at his hand, where it rested near her leg. Her eyes ran up his arm, seeing the tattoo, which she now knew the whole extent of. She blushed at the memories and cleared her throat.

'Will, why didn't you tell me you owned the company?' She nudged her own inevitable revelations a further five minutes down the line.

Will looked at her sharply. 'Does it matter?'

'Well no. But I feel like you let me believe you were waitstaff...' She trailed off not entirely clear on why she was pursuing this avenue of questioning right now.

'And that matters because?'

'It doesn't. I just, well I guess it feels a bit strange to me that you wouldn't tell me.'

Will leaned heavily back against the headboard. 'Don't tell me, this makes me seem pretty closed off, right?'

Allie gave him a good dose of side eye and then laughed. 'Sounds like you've heard that one before.'

'Yes, from my ex. Apparently I can come across as not very open. Which makes it kind of ironic that when I tried to be open with her and talk about how the relationship might not be working, she didn't want to hear it and dumped me before I could say anything substantial.'

Allie bit back a giggle.

'And before that...'

'Wait,' Allie put a hand on his arm, 'we're about to enjoy an extended trip through your relationship history? I need to get comfy for this.' She grinned at him.

'Enjoy?'

'Oh hell yeah. I'm going to fully enjoy this. Especially now I know that you find it hard to be open about things.'

'Well, that's because my ex...'

'The one we were just discussing?'

'No, the one before that one.'

'Am I going to need a paper and pen to keep tabs?'

'Very funny.' He leaned in and nipped her neck, which made her want to abandon all conversation and drag him horizontal again. 'My ex,' he began again, 'turned out to be not the nicest of people. I talked to her a lot about the business when we were setting up. Which she then turned round and used against me by sleeping with one of our key competitors.'

'No!' Allie exclaimed.

'Yup,' Will said grimly, 'and I didn't know for ages, then it all came out when she dumped me because she realised we weren't going to secure the next level of funding we needed and so therefore I wasn't going to be the rich boyfriend she was after.'

Allie dropped her smart-arse responses. 'I'm sorry, Will, that's really horrible.'

'Yeah, it wasn't great. And my business partner thought a lot of it was my fault for being so trusting, and he was probably right. And so after that I kept my cards close to my chest, which was what my last girlfriend didn't like. Oh, and the tattoo.'

'She didn't like your tattoo??' Allie asked in astonishment, running her fingers up the thing of beauty that was inked up Will's bicep.

'Said she wouldn't be able to take me home to meet her parents,' he began laughing, 'and she liked it even less when I said I wasn't sure I wanted to meet her parents, shirtless or at all. Sorry,' he said, grinning at Allie, 'I'm not sure why I'm telling you all my messed-up baggage.'

Allie squinted at him. 'I don't think it's messed up baggage. I guess we're all a product of everything that's happened to us up until this point in time. I'm kind of impressed that you have this level of self-awareness. Can't say that many men I've dated do.'

'Ah, so we're going to take a turn through your romantic history then?'

Allie shook her head firmly. 'Nope, you already know everything you need to know about Disappointing Dominic. So, it's back to you, I'm afraid.'

'OK.' Will put his head back on the headboard, 'well, if you really want to know why I don't like to talk about my company so much...' He turned his head and looked her straight in the eye. 'I'm not crazy about the fact that a lot of my work recently has been catering for publishing events.' He sighed. 'Given who my dad is, I didn't want anyone to think I was only getting the gigs because I'm some kind of nepo baby.'

Allie smothered a laugh. 'That's it? You really think people would think that?'

'Wouldn't you?' he asked.

'No! I'd just think it was amazing that you had set up a company and seemed to be making it a success. And doing something you loved too.' She bit her lip. 'I guess I was just confused as to why it wasn't a part of your life you wanted to share with me.'

Will looked distressed. 'That wasn't at all my intention. To be honest, I didn't tell you at the start, and then ... well, then it just became a thing and I was planning to tell you when I got back from York.' He paused, 'no more secrets?'

Allie nodded and crossed her fingers behind her back, and then listened as Will explained that his business partner, Matt, the one who ran the restaurant side of the business, was keen to leave London and had started putting plans in place to do so. Matt and his wife had been married five years, they had a two-year-old little boy and another one on the way and currently lived in what could generously be described as a one-and-a-half bed flat in Pimlico but was actually a one-bed with a large cupboard. Matt's wife was from York originally and with baby number two on the way was desperate to move back there and be closer to her family, and in a house where her children didn't have to sleep in a glorified cupboard.

'He's fixed on setting up a new restaurant there himself while he trains someone in the day-to-day running of our place here.'

'And you've found somewhere you think might work?' she asked.

'We saw one which would be amazing, if we can afford it. It's right on the river in the centre of York. It's already a restaurant so has some of the set-up we need, and the owners are keen to sell. But it needs investment so there's a lot to think about.'

'You think you'll go for it?'

'Looks like it. Loads of paperwork to sign and stuff to sort out but Matt seems happy with it all.' Will paused and raised his eyebrow. 'So, do you fancy a few weekends in York while we set up? I mean, now that you know all of my secrets.'

Allie squinted at Will, not being able to tell if he was joking or not. She had thought he was keeping things from her, keeping her at arm's length just as she had planned to do with him. But she was failing at that and she knew it; she really liked him, and it seemed he really liked her, not just because he was now suggesting city mini breaks together, but because of all the tiny things he did each and every time he saw her. The way he reached for her unselfconsciously, the way he wanted to be close to her wherever they were. He didn't play games. He asked to see her, he showed up, he made her feel wanted. Like, really wanted. She thought back to last night and felt a blush creep up her chest. But while Will didn't complicate their situationship, she did, and she wasn't sure how his feelings might change when she appraised him of that complication.

'So what do you think? Have you been to York before?'

Allie shook her head, and took a deep breath. 'Will?'

He looked up sharply, sensing the shift of tone in her voice.

'Erm, we need to talk.'

'About last night? About my dad?'

Allie nodded. She had meant to tell him last night, she really had. But when he had texted her and asked her if she was still out and could they meet up, she had diverted the cab to take her to Will's flat. And then one thing led to another and it seemed a bit rude to break the spell by suddenly revealing her secret to him and so instead of grasping the nettle and all that she had grasped something else entirely…

Will groaned and pushed his dark hair out of his eyes. 'I'm so sorry, it was really awkward, wasn't it?'

Allie blinked at him. 'What are *you* sorry for?'

Will shrugged. 'I'm not sure I handled it very well and I think I could have made it a less awkward experience for you, meeting my dad I mean, as *my* dad.'

Allie felt a rush of desire for this dreamy man who seemed so concerned to do the right thing by her, which was quickly followed by a sinking feeling when she realised that she really hadn't done the right thing by him at all.

'Is this going to be too weird for you?' Allie gave a small shake of her head, 'I know how important you've become to him, even though I didn't know it was *you*. But at the same time, I really, really don't want *this* to end.' He pointed at Allie and then back to himself again. Allie desperately wanted to reassure him that she didn't want it to end either.

'It's so funny,' he continued, 'I knew he was writing again

and I knew he had this writing mentor who he was meeting with regularly, but he refused to tell me much about them.' He laughed. 'To be honest, I pictured some grizzled old English professor, or at least someone more like his original editor, decked entirely in tweed.'

'You mean like your dad?'

'Hey!' he protested. 'Not fair. I've managed to whittle his tweed-wearing down to just the occasional jacket now.'

'Congratulations,' Allie quipped, 'I had noticed by the way.'

Will raised his eyebrow at her. 'Now if he had described you in the way I see you ... smart, funny, sexy as hell...' He leaned over her, putting his hands on her hips, pulling her towards him and beginning to kiss slowly up her neck. Allie thought this slightly unfair as they had already established that she became pretty much powerless when he pulled this move. She moaned slightly and put her hands in his thick dark hair. Morning breath be damned, she pulled him towards her and kissed him hard on the lips. And then just as suddenly she moaned again, for entirely different reasons this time, and pushed him away from her.

'Will, it's a bit more complicated than I think you believe it to be.'

He looked at her quizzically. 'Oh?'

'Yeah...' She sighed. 'So look, no more secrets right?'

Allie took a deep breath, this was it. Now she was here, he was here and she had started her confession, she needed to go for the ripping-the-plaster-off approach. If she hesitated, if she second-guessed herself, she wouldn't be able to do it, and so she said, as quickly as she could, 'I didn't know at first he was your dad. I mean when I met you both for the first time I definitely didn't know. And I honestly didn't know that he was your dad when all this started – between you and me. And between Martin and me. God no! Not like that, that sounds weird. I mean when Martin and I, I mean your dad and I, decided to start working together and helping each other with our writing. But then I saw your photo and realised, but by then it was too late and he had told me loads about your mum and about your sister…'

Will's face, which had been a picture of puzzled bewilderment as he listened to Allie vomit up her confession, suddenly twisted. 'Gigi?' he asked. 'He told you about Gigi?'

Allie nodded slowly.

'And about my mum?'

Allie nodded again.

There was a pause.

'What exactly did he tell you?' he said slowly.

'Pretty much everything.' Allie grimaced. 'I mean, not like really intimate stuff, don't worry. But about how he didn't think he'd been a good husband, how he and Angie, sorry, your mum, hadn't been getting along. About bailing out Gigi for years and how he needed to write this book because Gigi had already spent the advance…'

'Christ.' Will leaned back on his elbows on the bed. 'That really is pretty much everything.' He smiled grimly. 'And there I was thinking it might be a bit weird between us because you and my dad had been helping each other write. This takes it to a whole other level. I'm really sorry you had to deal with all that.'

Allie sat up straighter. 'Will,' she said earnestly, 'stop apologising. None of this is your fault.'

'I know, but I'm just sorry you've got dragged into it all. I can't imagine what gave Dad the idea that you would want to hear all about the sorry drama of our family.'

Allie swallowed nervously. 'For my book.'

Will looked at her sideways. 'What do you mean?' he asked sharply.

'It's for my book.'

'You're writing about my family *for your book?'*

'Well, yes, I mean no, I mean kind of,' Allie floundered. Finally, after looking up at the ceiling for inspiration she confessed, 'Not your family. Just your parents.'

There was a long pause. The kind of pause that made Allie wonder if she should just get up, get dressed and leave. She cast her eyes around Will's bedroom and wondered how long it would take her to gather up her clothes and how undignified she would look as she scrabbled about on the floor to get them. And whether this would make Will think she was more or less dignified than the revelation that she had been *using his parents to write her next novel.* She decided it was best to stay put and see what happened next. Because, after all, she did still have her knickers on, and was mainly covered by Will's duvet.

Eventually Will broke the silence and said in a tight voice that Allie had never heard him use before. 'Does my dad know?'

'Weeelll…' Allie almost asked him to define exactly what he meant by 'know', before deciding, on reflection, that the time to question semantics had long passed. 'No, not really. I mean, he knows I'm using some of his stories as inspiration, but I don't think he realises I'm using as much of their marriage as I actually am.' Allie thought sadly of the half a manuscript she had sitting on her laptop and about how much of her heart, along with Martin and Angie's love story, she had poured into it over the last few weeks. She knew it was different to any of the novels she had written before, more heartfelt, more heart-breaking in many ways. She had yet to reach the apex, the turnaround point, she was still in the darkness before the breaking of the dawn, and so Martin was still behaving like a jerk and misunderstanding the needs of Angie. And even though it was all rather sad at the moment, Allie already knew what was coming, she knew that Martin was about to embark on his grand redemptive journey, where he was going to turn things around, become the husband that Angie deserved. Allie almost started tearing up as she thought about it, crossing her fingers and hoping that her storytelling would do justice to Martin and Angie's love story.

'Will, tell me what you're thinking.' There was a note of desperation in her voice. 'I know this is weird, I know I should have told you.' She tugged at his hand, asking him to look at her.

'Yes,' he replied flatly, 'it's weird. I'm not sure how I feel about you … using *my* dad…' His voice petered out.

'Because of *my* dad?' Allie said suddenly, remembering Jess's accusation.

'No. What do you mean?'

'You think I'm using him as some kind of dad substitute because my dad is dead?' Allie couldn't help the defensive note that had crept into her voice.

'Christ, no, Allie. Of course not. I never said that. I never even *thought* that.'

'Sorry,' she said in a small voice. 'I shouldn't have said that.'

There was a long uncomfortable silence, which Will finally broke by saying, 'I'm not sure I can talk about this right now.' He was standing up from the bed and beginning to reorganise his bedroom, which mainly seemed to involve picking up Allie's discarded articles of clothing, folding them rather too aggressively and piling them in such a way as to suggest Allie would do well to get into them pretty quickly before the sentiment in the room deteriorated further.

'I'm really sorry, Will,' she said as she pulled her ruffled mini skirt towards her and wondered how many more times she could regret her decision to wear it. Having no other choice, other than to go home in just her knickers, she pulled it on underneath the duvet, making a very undignified hip wiggle as she struggled to straighten it.

'For what?' Will finally looked at her and she could see the hurt and confusion on his face. 'For using my dad? Or for not telling me?' Allie was stunned. She had known that this wasn't going to be an easy conversation to have and deep down she knew that there was a good chance that Will really wasn't going to be able to get past this. But she had so successfully buried her head in the sand that she really hadn't prepared herself for Will's reaction.

'I'm so sorry,' she stammered aware of how insufficient this now sounded. 'I didn't mean... I like your dad, Will, and I really like you...'

'Not just using us to write your book then?' A new hardened tone had entered Will's voice and it chilled Allie's heart to hear it, knowing she had caused it to be there.

'No!' she exclaimed. She stood up, thankful that she had managed to get her skirt and her bra on and as she wrestled with her T-shirt she said, 'I know how this looks, I really do. But I never meant it to get this far. I should have told you sooner, that I knew who your dad was and that we were working together. And I really should have told Martin that I was using his stories as more than just inspiration.'

'But you didn't?'

'No, I didn't,' she said quietly. 'And I am sorry.'

Will was staring at the floor. His look screamed dejection.

Eventually he sighed and looked at what he was holding in his hand. He thrust it at Allie. 'I think these are yours too.'

If there was a worse way of experiencing the morning-after effect Allie didn't want to know about it. Because right now she was sure that nothing beat standing in your *maybe* boyfriend's bedroom, who you really, really liked, knowing you had majorly fucked things up and that there was a good chance he might never talk to you again, and that you had a half written book which needed to go straight into the trash folder as soon as you got home, leaving you with nothing to show the next time Jake Matthews made his unwelcome present felt, *and* you were now clutching yesterday's sweaty socks that the aforementioned dejected *maybe* boyfriend had just handed you. Allie stood ungainly on one leg as she put her socks on.

'Should I go?' she eventually asked.

Will took a deep breath and just for a moment Allie thought he might be about to have a change of heart and that a reprieve could be on the cards. But then he said, 'I think that might be for the best. I feel there's a lot I need to think about.'

Allie nodded sadly. 'OK.' She walked towards his front door, bending to pick up her shoes and bag as she passed them. On the doorstep she turned. 'I'll talk to Martin, OK? I'll explain everything and I'll delete the manuscript.' She bit her lip and looked up at him. 'Will, I'm so sorry.'

He smiled weakly and said he knew she was, and then suddenly Allie was stood in her socks on the wrong side of Will's front door, not wondering how she had got here, because she knew exactly how it had happened, and that it was all her own fault.

Chapter Twenty-One

A llie stared at her laptop through teary eyes and read back over the words she had written so far. The tears weren't because it was bad, in fact, objectively, she could appreciate that it may well be the best thing she had ever written. It was warm and witty, she'd captured the original romance through a series of emotional flashbacks and the juxtaposition with the failing marriage of the present day was really quite moving to read. But neither were her tears the result of being moved by the emotional depth of the story; they were the hot, shameful tears of realisation that nothing could change the fact that it wasn't her story to tell, and she hadn't asked permission from Martin or Angie to tell it. And she hadn't told Will, either that she knew his dad or more to the point, was writing the story of his parents marriage. She bit her lip, viciously wiped under each eye and minimised the tab. She knew she should delete it, she knew she had told Will that she would, but she just needed a little more time to come to terms with the fact she was about to consign the best writing of her career to the oblivion of her MacBook trash can.

'Ugh,' she groaned and stretched and pushed her laptop away. Allie had been staring at it for hours, ever since coming back from Will's flat that morning. It hadn't gone well, but he hadn't actually ended things, he hadn't told her that he never wanted to see her again, so perhaps it wasn't completely stupid to hold out some hope that Will would take the time he needed to process the fact that while she had been economical with the truth, it didn't need to be that big a deal. Except it was, it really was, and she knew it. She groaned again and tried to ignore the sensation of nausea rising inside her. Not only had she screwed things up with Will, the only guy in a stream of many, many guys, who she actually liked. Not just liked, but really really liked. But she also now had absolutely no manuscript to share with Snake Eyes Jake, no word from Tessa that she might be about to save her skin, and no Martin to help her out with her writing. How had she let it all go so horribly wrong when just last night it had been going so wonderfully well? Images flashed through her brain, memories of the way Will had pulled her through his front door before she'd even finished ringing the doorbell. His hands all over her, his breath hot on her neck. The way she had pushed him backwards towards his bedroom, confident and insistent on what she wanted, what she *needed*. She could still feel him on her body, the sensation of her hands running through his hair, and she put her head down on her desk in despair at the realization of how badly she had messed up, and that no matter how angry Will was with her, it wasn't going to change the way *she* felt about him. She was still going to want him, still going to need him. Her phone beeped at her and she narrowed her eyes, wondering whether whoever was calling was about to heap misery on her predicament or assuage the pain. And the only person she knew who could do the latter would be Will, calling to tell her he had thought it all through and that he totally understood, he still fancied the pants off her and that he had talked things over with his parents and they were all totally chill about her using their story. She picked her phone up and read the name, 'Maybe: Verity Montagu-Forbes.'

'Verity?' Allie asked in surprise as she picked the phone up. 'Is that you?' Verity still hadn't used her new number to communicate with Allie since the whole Brinkman's debacle. For the most part she used Richard's phone, but once or twice she had used a completely different number, which led Allie to wonder whether Verity was using a string of burner phones and also whether she was taking this NDA a little too seriously.

'Allie, hi!' It sounded like Verity, and the call was indeed coming from a number that said it was 'maybe' her. But Allie hadn't heard Verity talk in a tone louder than a whisper, even when she was using someone else's phone, in weeks.

'Are you sure it's you?' Allie asked suspiciously.

'What? Yes of course it's me. Are you OK?'

'Am I OK? You're the one who should be answering that question!'

'Why?'

Allie grimaced. Obviously she was pleased that Verity seemed more like her usual self, but it was as if she had returned with a side order of amnesia, not recalling any part of the subterfuge she had engaged in over the last few weeks. Allie didn't have the strength to explain this. 'No reason, what's up?'

'Jake…' Verity left the name hanging there, leaving Allie wondering if she had imagined every event of recent times.

'Erm, OK. What about him?'

'I think we've got him.' Verity did a little squeal of nervous excitement which made Allie smile, it was so heartwarming to hear Verity's proper voice again.

'How?' Allie demanded. 'What's happened?'

'Tessa's going to do it!'

'She is?! Tell me *everything*.'

'There's this insta account, a publishing insider account? Like the *Gossip Girl* of the book world.' Allie had heard of it, had seen some of the posts before – calling out bad behaviour, suspect practices, evil corporate machines, the usual.

'Right. Oh god, don't tell me, the person behind it is actually Jake?'

'What? No! Allie, that would be insane. He's one of the prime targets of this account, not the instigator.'

'Yeah, course.' But Allie had already drifted off into a daydream where Jake was unmasked as the Dan Humphrey of the publishing world. Except without Serena Van Der Woodsen on his arm. In reality it wasn't a very satisfying daydream, Allie would prefer one in which Jake got his comeuppance, rather than being outed as the outsider trying to instigate change.

'Allie, are you listening to me?'

'Yes!' protested Allie. 'Instagram, *Gossip Girl*. I'm all over this Verity.'

'Hmm,' Verity didn't sound convinced. 'OK, well anyway, I know the person who runs this account, and before you ask, don't bother, I'm never going to disclose their true identity and I won't say any more other than to tell you that you would be VERY surprised to find out who they really are.'

Allie didn't think she actually would be. Other than Verity, her agent Mary Beth, who Allie could say with an absolute degree of certainty was not involved, and some of the sales and publicity people at Brinkman's, she didn't really know many people at all in publishing. So the only people she would be surprised to find out it was were Verity or Jake, which brought her back to her previous daydream.

'Allie!' It was as if Verity could read her thoughts. 'Concentrate, this is the exciting bit. So, Tessa gets in touch with this "*friend*" of mine and tells her everything she knows about Jake. And Allie, it's good, I mean obviously it's not good, it's completely horrific and he's a terrible terrible man, but it's exactly what we need to bring him down!'

'But now what? What can we do with it now?'

'She's going to go public! Or as public as naming and shaming a publishing executive can get. Let's be realistic, it's not like the tabloids are going to be clamouring for the story. But my "friend" has persuaded Tessa that she needs to speak out and that if she does, lots of people will support her. We've already heard rumours that other people are ready to speak too, if Tessa does.'

'Wow, that's great.'

'I know!' Verity's voice was breathless with excitement. 'Tessa has asked for a meeting with the CEO of Brinkman's, apparently it's going to happen tomorrow! Which means… Allie?' Verity's tone switched. 'Your wow, didn't sound very WOW! What's going on?'

'Nothing, it's great, I'm really thrilled for you.'

'Right, well you should be. Because I'm hoping they'll offer me my job back.'

'Oh wow! I mean proper wow this time! Honestly Verity this is great news. I'm so thrilled for both you and Tessa.'

'And what about you?'

'What about me?' Allie asked in confusion.

'Allie, if I get my job back, it will mean I'll be your editor again! We can work together on your new book!'

There was a long pause. 'About that…'

'About what?' Verity's voice tightened. 'Allie?' she said warningly. 'I thought you said you were writing again? I thought you said we had nothing to worry about on that front.'

'We don't! I mean, we didn't. I mean… I'm kind of back to square one,' Allie admitted.

'Explain to me, in publishing terms, what you mean by square one? Back at first draft stage? First read through? Needs more structural editing?' Verity's voice was now firmly on shrill mode.

'I mean…' Allie dropped her voice to shamefaced volume. 'Back to an empty screen.'

There was a muffled scream and a clatter from the other end of the line.

'Verity?' Allie asked in concern. 'Are you OK?' Images swept through Allie's mind of Jake Matthews having stumbled upon their clandestine, non-NDA-abiding conversation and wreaking his manic revenge.

'Allie!' screamed Verity, in a now very much not muffled tone. 'You promised me! You promised me you were writing again. Oh my god, I thought we'd fixed everything. Tessa agreeing to do one on Jake Matthews, me maybe getting my job back. And then you go and drop this shitshell.'

'Erm what's a shitshell?' Allie felt compelled to ask, knowing full well that she probably wouldn't like the answer.

'Like a bombshell,' shrieked Verity angrily, 'just stinkier and more messy. Exactly like this revelation you have just lobbed at me.'

'I'm sorry,' moaned Allie. 'I feel like I've ruined your celebratory moment.'

'Yeah well don't expect me to disavow you of that opinion. But what the hell happened or were you just lying to me?'

'I wasn't lying! I had been writing. I *have* been writing. Oh and Verity,' Allie moaned again, 'it's really good. I mean, it needs your expertise of course, but I feel like it's one of the best books I've ever written.'

Verity interrupted. 'I don't understand, what part of this explains the fact you now have no manuscript? Oh god, you didn't back up, did you? Allie! For god's sake, how many times do I have to tell you? I thought you'd learned your lesson after losing those six chapters?'

'I haven't lost it! It's right here in front of me.'

'So why is your screen blank!' Verity blurted.

'Metaphorically.'

'I'm sorry, what?' Verity sounded as if she was about to completely lose her grasp on reality.

'I've written it. But you can't publish it.'

There was a pause and then Verity sighed the sigh of an editor who had been here many times before with nervous, overwrought writers and was used to knowing how to grapple with the sensitive creative types. 'Of course we can. Allie we've been here before. I know it feels like it's not publishable right now. But you just said, it's your best work to date. We can do the edit together. I promise we'll get it to just where you want it to be before we publish it.'

'No, I mean, you can *never* publish it. It's not my story to tell. I stole it.'

'Freaking what now?! Allie! You know that's illegal right? You know plagiarism is like, really, really bad? But you said it was good?' There was a pause. 'So, whose is it? And do they have an agent I can speak to?'

Despite everything, Allie smiled, Verity was always on the lookout for the next big thing. 'It's Martin Clark's story. Well, his and his wife's.'

There was a long pause before Verity exhaled in relief. 'Oh, I get it! Look, I know you feel he helped you write it. But you helped him with his right? It's just part of your deal. It's all your own words. It *is* all your own words, right?'

'Yeah, it is. But it's Martin and Angie's marriage, as in *their* story. And he doesn't know I've written it like that.'

There was a sharp intake of breath from Verity. 'You didn't tell him? You didn't ask?' Allie didn't need to respond to these questions, Verity was just busy confirming things in her own mind before launching into damage control mode. 'OK OK. Well look, maybe he wouldn't mind? I mean you did say it was the best writing you'd ever done. Maybe he and his wife would like their love story immortalised?'

'Would you like me to write about you and Richard, without telling you I was doing it first?' Allie asked incredulously.

'Well no. I mean, I guess not. It's quite the deception, isn't it?'

'Alright, don't rub it in. It gets worse.'

It was Verity's turn to sound incredulous. 'You've stolen someone else's love story and you no longer have a manuscript for me to edit. Please explain how this can get any worse?'

'Will is Martin's son.'

'What?! Will as in hot waiter is Martin's son? Do they know?'

'Well yes, Verity, I should imagine they do know that they're related.' Allie couldn't resist with the sarcasm.

'You know very well what I mean.'

'They do now. I came clean to Will this morning.'

'And? How did he take it?'

'The overriding sense I got from him was one of confusion.'

'OK, confusion's not bad. We can live with confusion.'

'But then I told him I had written about his parents' marriage…'

'Go on…'

'And then it went from confusion to … well, if I was going to put a sentiment on it I'd go for sadness. And if I was allowed a second sentiment, I'd pick betrayal.'

'Oh god, sad betrayal. The worst.'

'I know, right?'

'Couldn't he at least be angry at you?'

'Well, he may well be at the angry stage by now. It was a few hours ago.' Allie shook her head sadly. 'Although, to be honest, I was hoping he'd skip the angry stage and just decide he liked me enough to overlook my massive error of judgement.'

'Oh Allie. You really like him, don't you?'

'Yup.' Allie bit back a sob which had been slowly creeping its way up inside her ever since she had left Will's flat that morning, and which she had, with ever decreasing success, been trying to suppress by telling herself that everything was fine and of course Will would understand.

'He's not going to skip over it, is he?'

Verity sighed. 'Babe, I honestly don't know. You'll have a better read on it than I will. But if I were you, I'd go apologise again. Or, I don't know, make one of those grand romantic gestures you put in all your novels.'

Allie smiled wanly. 'Not sure that's going to cut it this time. Didn't I tell you I've stopped believing in happy-ever-afters? I so should have seen this coming.'

'Hey, you don't know it's over till he tells you. Come on, you've got to fight for this. And by the way, while you're busy planning whatever grand romantic gesture is going to win him over, maybe you could also write a novel about it? If I do get my job back we're going to be on a serious deadline to get your next one published on time. But if you're going to do that, *ask him first*,' she said firmly.

Allie wiped her eyes with one hand. 'Didn't you hear me? I've stopped believing in romance. Can't I go and write that serial killer thriller?'

'No,' Verity steadfastly replied.

'Why not?' whined Allie.

'Because in case you've forgotten, you gave that idea to Martin. So, unless you want to go explain to him that you want your idea back and in return you can swap him the story of his marriage, which you stealth wrote, you're going to need to go back to the romance drawing board.'

'But I can't!' protested Allie.

'You can. Just write what you know.'

Allie stared daggers at her phone, feeling unheard and dismissed.

'Right. Well look, let's look on the bright side.' This positivity was what made Verity such a good editor and such a good person, but right now it was also about to get her slapped by Allie who was just grateful that they were not having this conversation in person and so she didn't have to add 'buy editor some flowers to apologise for the slapping' to her crowded schedule.

'This is a kind of good news/bad news situation here. So, I need to go work on the good news part, and you need to go fix the bad news. Oh, and by the way, something else you should know … Tessa said you're the person who inspired her to go public.'

'She did?'

'Yes. Apparently your speech about doing the right thing hit a nerve with her. So, Allie? Don't let me down, and don't let

Tessa down. Just write the damn book, and do the right thing. I believe in you.'

The line went dead and Allie wrinkled her nose in frustration. Verity was right, she needed to do the right thing and write this damn book and it was always best to write what you knew. But Allie wasn't sure what she knew anymore, other than that writing Martin and Angie's story without prior permission was definitely not the right thing. She stared morosely out into her garden and caught the eye of a judgemental robin which was out there terrorising the worms. He cocked his head at her and she tried to look away. It was bad enough being called out by Verity, she didn't need half the wildlife of west London jumping on the bandwagon. She leaned forward and banged on the window repeatedly. The robin startled and flew off, which, surprisingly, didn't make Allie feel any better about the situation she found herself in. Grand romantic gestures … write what you know. She stood and paced the kitchen, stopping to put the kettle back onto boil and dumping yet another tea bag in her mug. She ran through her conversation with Will once again, the look in his eyes when he had realised what she had done, the feelings she got when she understood she might have ruined it all. The empty space she felt yawning open when she thought about not seeing him again. By the time the kettle had boiled, the tea had brewed and Allie was sat back at her laptop, she felt the beginnings of an idea starting to percolate through her brain.

Chapter Twenty-Two

The last time Allie had written like this was the infamous time of her writer's block on book two, when she had spent two months staring at a blank computer screen trying to make the plot work, gone for an afternoon nap and woken up with it entirely mapped out in her head. It had been pretty epic and she had managed to lose ten pounds at the same time, having been so engrossed in getting her story onto the page she had almost completely forgotten to stop for food. Sadly, by the time publication came around she had put all the weight back on and had to return the dress she'd optimistically bought the afternoon she finally delivered her manuscript. But this time it was different – although she was focused on her writing, she still had half an eye on her phone, and every time it lit up and it wasn't Will, she tamped down her sadness with a few squares of Dairy Milk. By day three, Allie had written a third of her new draft and was, by her estimation, at least sixty percent chocolate.

And she was feeling better than she really had any right to. Despite the fact she missed Will, in every humanly horny way possible, and despite the fact she kept wanting to ask Martin what he thought of a paragraph she had drafted, and despite the fact she knew she had completely and royally fucked everything up, she was beginning to see the woods for the trees. Ever since she had realised who Will was, she had been treading on eggshells, so afraid of him discovering her secret that she hadn't really been enjoying the excitement of the early days of a new relationship. All the time she had been wondering how long it might last and knowing she should tell him the truth. Now, with the idea for her new book unfolding on her laptop in front of her she took a deep breath and clicked minimise. Right behind her new draft document was the original one. The one she now knew she had essentially stolen from Martin and Angie. She swallowed and began to read.

Allie didn't stop reading till she had read the whole thing, and when she stopped she once again had tears in her eyes, partly because it was, without blowing her own trumpet, really rather moving, but mainly, and she wouldn't want to admit this to anyone but herself, because she knew that she could never publish it. She pushed her laptop away from her and stared out into the garden, wondering where the robin was and whether he would ever forgive her or whether he was destined for the same fate as Will and Martin – someone she once knew who, because of her bad choices would never feel comfortable in allowing her back into their lives. She brushed her hands fiercely under her eyes and swore to herself she was moved by her predicament, not by the departure of some bird she had anthropomorphised because she seemed to be suffering from a distinct lack of actual real-life people in her world right now.

Allie pulled her laptop back towards her, hands hovering over the keyboard, focused on the final words she had written of Martin's story. She tipped her head to one side, flexed her fingers, made a decision and began to type. Because while she knew she couldn't publish this thing, she did think there might be one way she might atone for her mistakes, and if she was to embark on that journey, she would need to finish not one, but two books in the next couple of weeks.

'Have you seen this?' Jess's voice barked down the line.

Blearily Allie dragged her mind away from the computer screen and tried to focus on what Jess was asking her. 'I haven't seen anything except Microsoft Word for the last eight hours,' she admitted wearily.

'OK, well pull up your socials, you're a writer, this is going to be everywhere.'

For a brief moment, Allie's stomach plummeted. She imagined Will, or more likely Martin, had written an exposé on the latest literary scandal and their brush with a plagiarising romance author. She wondered how quickly her name would become mud, how quickly Brinkman's would drop her. She imagined Verity putting out a carefully worded statement, distancing herself from Allie. Her mum being inundated with reporters outside Nigel's condo in Marbella, all desperate to understand the psyche of the thieving daughter she had raised. Allie wondered if it was too late to shut down her socials, change her name and retrain as a … as a what though? Really, what else was there for Allie to do but write novels? This was a well-trodden thought pattern over the last few months and at the end of it, each and every time, Allie came up empty handed.

'Allie?' Allie pulled herself back from her spiral, it was amazing how dark and how fast her thoughts could turn.

Something she really ought to put to work more, maybe a change of name would be enough for her to turn to crime writing, as it seemed she was developing a natural leaning towards the macabre.

'Allie! Are you still there?'

'Yes, sorry, I just don't know what to say.'

'Well, aren't you pleased?'

Allie wondered on what planet she would possibly be pleased that her entire career was swirling down the drain because of a stupid decision she had made, a reality glossed over, a kiss with Will gone too far. She held back a moan which almost escaped her at the thought of his lips on hers, and how much she missed them (and him, of course.) And then she noticed something, Jess's tone wasn't tinged with panic and concern, or even incredulous anger as it might be had Allie's literary purloining been exposed. Instead, she was excited, gleeful even. Which made Allie wonder if she hadn't entirely got the wrong end of the stick, and perhaps Will (and/or Martin) hadn't yet gotten around to writing their exposé, and that maybe Jess was ringing for entirely different reasons altogether, to draw Allie's attention to something rather more happy-making than career ending.

'For god's sake Allie, just get on insta and look for #publishinginsider. It's going to be everywhere on your feed.'

Immediately, Allie's brain sharpened into focus, all thoughts of Will and literary theft swept away in the pure knowledge that Tessa's story, her exposé on Jake Matthews had gone viral. Allie's stomach clenched in sympathy for what she could only imagine Tessa was feeling right now. She thumbed her way on her phone, praying that the narrative was playing out the way Verity and her 'friend' had been confident it would.

'It says industry figures are seeking to distance themselves from Jake Matthews and his deplorable actions. That they had no idea of the extent of his undue influence,' Jess read breathlessly.

Allie scoffed at what she was hearing. As if no one else had known about what Jake Matthews was up to. But this was always the way, 'hiding in plain sight' was a well-worn defence.

'I can't believe he had so many office affairs. And the drugs?! Good grief, where did he find the time and energy?'

'Amazing how much free time a publishing executive can find when they have zero interest in books.'

'Did you know about all of it?' Jess asked. 'One account is suggesting he might be responsible for several relationship break-ups.'

'Allegedly,' Allie said ironically. 'Verity told me about some of it, and of course I knew Tessa's story, but I didn't know how much they were going to get on the record.'

Allie scrolled through posts and posts of supportive comments, vitriolic attacks on male privilege in publishing. Of course, there were one or two trolls, there always were, people questioning Tessa's timeline, her account of Jake's behaviour and her motivations in coming forward. But they were completely drowned out by Tessa's supporters, and by other women, calling out similar behaviour at the hands of other men in positions of power. Allie's face scrunched into a semi-smile. She was thrilled at how this seemed to be going down so far. Proud of Tessa for having the guts to tell her story. But just reading the comments, she couldn't help but feel depressed at how universal Tessa's story was. It wasn't a one-off, it wasn't something that people were shocked by, it seemed most women, from all walks of life, had their own similar story to tell.

'It's pretty amazing right?'

'Yeah,' Allie agreed, 'but depressing too.'

'God yeah. Sometimes I think that the world has moved on, that this kind of stuff can't be swept under the carpet anymore. And then I don't know why I'm always so blindsided every time one of these stories comes out. It's not like it's unusual.'

They both paused, considering the patriarchy, the systemic structures in place which kept seemingly everyone except heterosexual white males from reaching the apex in most industries. And at the same time Allie was quietly contemplating her word count and whether she had got enough done today to justify asking her next question.

'Fancy meeting for a drink?' she blurted out.

'Hell yes!' Jess practically gasped. 'Thought you'd never ask. I know you're on deadline so I didn't want to distract you by asking you myself. Elliot's?'

'Elliot's?' Allie asked in surprise. Elliot's was the wine bar that they used to go to when they had something to celebrate, although using the description of wine bar was pushing the boundaries of accuracy somewhat. They thought it was fancy in their early twenties, because you could sit at the bar and they would bring you your bottle of white wine in a champagne bucket. Although you couldn't be picky in what you drank, there was red, white and, sometimes in the summer, pink. Very occasionally they'd splash out and get a bottle of prosecco, which Allie would always regret the next morning when she woke up feeling as if she'd eaten a bunch of rotten flowers. But if you got the prosecco, not only were you guaranteed the champagne bucket but they would also dig out the champagne coupes, which made them feel extra specially fancy, and if you got the right bartender, he'd throw in some salted almonds with their order. They hadn't been there in years, Allie wasn't even sure it was open anymore.

'For old times' sake?' pleaded Jess. 'What time can you be there?'

Allie looked at her watch, calculating how long it would take her to make herself presentable and then get down to Elliot's. It was an easy bus ride from her flat and Allie was fairly sure she could get away with what she was wearing but given she was meeting Jess she ought to make the effort and at least change out of her ancient hoody, which she had been haunting on and off for days.

'An hour?'

'Done. See you there.'

Jess was already at the bar when Allie walked in. Allie had spent the bus journey bleakly fantasising about the way Will kissed her and checking that Elliot's still actually existed. Which it not only did, but it even had a website. Allie marvelled at the fact that they seemed to have branched out and currently served at least four different kinds of wine of each colour. Seeing Jess sat on her bar stool made Allie pleased she had made the effort to change. She might still be wearing trainers, but they were expensive trainers, and she'd paired them with her black wide-legged trousers and a stripy T-shirt she had forgotten she had, discovered at the back of her wardrobe as she rummaged for something to wear. Jess exuded sophistication as she always did, so Allie hoped she was at least stumbling in the direction of Parisian chic, even if she had yet to reach the Champs-Élysées.

'Feeling nostalgic, hey?' Allie gave her friend a kiss on the cheek and gestured to their surroundings. 'To be honest I wasn't sure this place still existed.'

Jess laughed. 'I actually came here with Tom the other day. Do you know, I don't think he'd ever been here before?'

Allie looked at her incredulously. 'Really?'

'Uh-huh. I mean think about it. By the time I'd met Tom we both had proper jobs and could afford to go to places that had more than one type of wine. But look…' Jess held up a wine list, which despite the fact it was printed on cheap paper, was an actual list, which was more than Elliot's had when they used to meet there.

'I know!' Allie laughed. 'I was looking at their website on the way here. What did you go for in the end?' she asked, pointing at the champagne bucket, which looked identical to the ones they had drunk from a decade earlier.

'Pinot grigio, thought it was the safest option. Probably best not to get ahead of ourselves don't you think?'

Allie pulled herself on to a bar stool while Jess poured her a glass of wine, Allie noted that Jess's glass was, as yet, untouched. 'What did Tom make of the old place and what on earth made you want to bring him here?'

Jess shrugged, her eyes glazing over slightly and slipping off into the middle distance behind Allie. 'I don't know. Just thinking about the past, no real reason,' she answered vaguely.

Allie narrowed her eyes, Jess was being weird again.

'So, what's going down in the world of publishing? Is it all over for Jake Matthews and has Verity finally got her job back?'

'Still up in the air, at the moment. I called Verity while I was on my way, but she was too excited to get much sense out of.' Allie chugged a large part of her wine, delighted to have smashed her word count that day AND be out of the flat. 'As far as I can make out, Brinkman's are in crisis mode, lots of closed doors, lots of high-level meetings. Verity seems to think something will happen overnight and Jake will be summoned to a meeting tomorrow.'

'Well, that's exciting!'

Allie shrugged. 'I'll believe it when it happens. Let's be honest, we've seen men get away with far more serious things. I'm just really glad that other people came forward to support Tessa's allegations, so she didn't have to do it alone, but I hope she's OK. I can't imagine how brave she must be to have put herself out there like that. Makes me feel a bit guilty about thinking so little of her before.' She pulled a face and Jess reached over and squeezed her hand in sympathy.

'Hey. You were doing your best with the information you had at the time. And just remember, she was pretty dismissive of you, and it's not like you were awful to her.'

'No, but I do feel bad for presuming she was just one of Jake's lackeys though.'

'Huh. I don't think there was much else you could think at the time. It's OK Al, I don't think you've done anything wrong and you're supporting her now, aren't you?'

'I guess. I mean it all feels a bit like virtue signaling, doesn't it? Liking tweets and hashtagging I stand with women?'

'Al, seriously, what else are you supposed to be doing right now? It's not like you can pull your contract from Brinkman's? And by the way, I thought your statement was exactly spot on.'

'Thanks, that means a lot. I'd been drafting it in my head ever since Verity told me they were going to go public.' In the short space of time between talking to Jess and arriving at Elliot's, when she wasn't hunting for clothes at the back of her wardrobe and googling the wine bar, Allie had issued a brief statement on her socials. It hadn't badmouthed Brinkman's and she had just about managed to steer clear of libelling Jake Matthews, but she had managed to say that she welcomed a swift investigation into these troubling allegations and made it clear that her sympathies and loyalties lay with the women coming forward.

'Ugh, I just hope some good comes of it and it doesn't all get brushed under the carpet.'

'Let's drink to that.' Jess tipped her wine glass towards Allie, but didn't actually drink. 'And also to the fact you're writing again.'

Allie scrunched her nose, wondering whether now was the time to come clean. 'Yup, good news. Especially as it's not the book I was writing before.'

'Okaay…'

'I told Will.' Allie paused. 'I told him everything.'

'Aaand?' Jess watched her friend with concern.

'Haven't heard from him since. Which isn't really surprising, is it? There's a lot for him to process.'

'OK. Well, I'm proud of you for telling him. It was the right thing to do. But now what? Why the new story?'

'Because I want him to realise how sorry I am about the whole thing. And that, to me, his feelings are more important than delivering a manuscript.' Allie left her confession and the implication of it hanging. Jess's eyes went wide.

'More important than reneging on a contract?'

Allie nodded.

'More important than your writing career?'

Allie nodded again.

Jess exhaled heavily. 'So it's serious then?'

'I think so.' Allie felt dejected. 'But I also think I've messed it up completely.' She wanted her friend to disavow her of this uncomfortable thought but Jess said nothing, and, for that

Allie was actually grateful. It meant Jess wasn't just filling her mind with platitudes.

'So, what do you have planned?' Jess asked eventually.

Allie took a deep breath. 'I'm going for the grand romantic gesture. Hoping that might get his attention. Make him realise I'm serious, about him.'

'And that entails writing an entirely new story?'

'Yup,' Allie said much more confidently than she actually felt. 'But I'm also going to finish writing Martin and Angie's story, and then I'm going to give it to them. As a gift. A tribute, if you like.'

'What if they end up splitting up?'

Allie felt tears forming in her eyes at the thought. 'God, Jess, seriously? It's bad enough that I've messed things up with Will. I think my belief in true love would be terminal if that happened. Ugh. Who am I kidding? I think my belief in true love died a long time ago.' Allie slugged back the rest of her glass of wine and reached over to grab the bottle. 'I mean, maybe I should have just sucked things up with Dominic and realised that was the best I could hope for.'

'Don't say that!' A look of abject horror was now on Jess' face. 'He cheated on you!'

'We don't actually know that.'

'How else do you explain the "Uber driver"?' asked Jess.

Allie considered this, putting her creative mind to work. In a book there were loads of ways she could have explained it away, a trick of the light, an overfamiliar Uber driver that Allie then missed being reprimanded by a horrified Dominic. But in the light of real life, she had to admit it was hard to place a positive spin on seeing your ex-boyfriend kiss another woman in a car right outside your flat.

'Yeah, but maybe we could have worked through it. Maybe

we *should* have worked through it? I could have put more effort in. Not have expected so much.'

'I don't think we should even be discussing this,' Jess said tartly.

And so, Allie shut up. Because she didn't want Jess judging that small part of her brain, which had a very loud voice in vulnerable moments, which was now suggesting that maybe what she and Dominic had was *good enough*, and that if she'd made an effort to talk things through with him, work things out, then she wouldn't feel so alone right now.

'So, if we're in the mood for confessions…'

Allie turned her head sharply at Jess's words. 'You're pregnant?' she blurted out.

'No!' protested Jess. 'Look?' she said, pointing at her glass, then the bottle of wine, and finally chugging half of it back. 'Also, why is that the first thing people suspect when a woman in her thirties says she has news? It's such a product of the patriarchy. Men NEVER get asked that question,' she grumbled.

Allie felt her feminist credentials suitably questioned and went slightly red.

'But what was with the whole 'Tom has a cold' business the other night?'

'What? Oh that,' replied Jess. 'I just felt like I should cut down on drinking, and I didn't want to make a big thing out of it, so I just pretended my drink *was* alcoholic.'

'You could have told me,' Allie complained, 'I'd have been supportive.'

'No, you'd have made a big deal out of it and then thought I was pregnant anyway. Exactly like you're doing now,' retorted Jess.

'Sorry,' Allie mumbled.

'No, it's OK,' Jess sighed. 'I guess I need to find a better way of imparting big news.'

'Well, go on then...'

'Tom and I are moving out of London.'

If Allie's jaw had been physically capable of dislocating and hitting the floor it would have done so. Allie couldn't think of anyone in her social circle who was more *London* than Jess. She'd grown up in the city, hated being out of it for university, and had made it abundantly clear that if Allie wanted to stay best friends, Allie would have to move to London with her. Not that Allie minded, she was pretty clear herself that London was where her heart lay. So, she couldn't help but feel a small niggle of betrayal inside her at Jess's confession.

'Oh,' she managed. Not wanting Jess to bear the weight of her confusion and impending sense of loneliness, which she was undoubtedly going to experience in the weeks, months, *years* ahead, when Allie would be in London and Jess would be... *gone*...

Jess's face scrunched up, her eyes going a little bit watery. 'That's all you've got?'

'Well, erm, I guess I'm a bit surprised?'

'You won't forget me?!' Jess lunged forward and grabbed both of Allie's hands dramatically.

'What? No! Of course not.' Allie said, startled by Jess's announcement and her behaviour. 'But erm, can you catch me up on this ... news?'

And so Jess told Allie that this was something she and Tom had been thinking about for a while. Tom had never been as keen on London as Jess had, viewing it as a necessary evil to being close to the office, although a necessary evil with the benefits of pubs and bars and cab rides and Tube trains attached. But now that things were more flexible in terms of office location, he had been pushing to move back closer to where he (and Allie) had grown up. Allie had to shake off her shudder at certain childhood memories when Jess had told her this. And Jess had said she was feeling restless, ready for something new, maybe a different pace of life. Maybe a dog?

'Not kids then?' Allie had asked.

'No. I mean, I feel less adverse to the concept than I did previously, but not so much in favour that I'm ready to just whip out my IUD.' Allie had winced at the thought and wondered whether she would ever need to worry about contraception ever again before pulling herself back into the present where Jess now had her phone out and was showing her pictures of houses she and Tom had been looking at.

'So you're pretty far down the line then?' Allie had asked, trying not to sound too hurt and judgemental that Jess had been going behind her back with property websites.

'Yes and no,' Jess admitted. 'We've decided on location, but haven't found anything quite right yet.'

Allie's mind went back to the phone call she'd had with Jess the other day, the midweek one where she and Tom had been in a car, going somewhere mysterious. 'That's where you were going the other day when I called you?'

'Uh-huh, you know the good thing is that if we find somewhere close to that, we won't be far from your mum! So, it'll be easier to visit?!' Jess said, sounding somewhat desperate for Allie's approval.

'Except when she's in Spain,' Allie couldn't help shooting back.

'Well, yes, I guess,' admitted Jess reluctantly. 'But it does mean you could stay with us rather than at her house every time!'

Allie brightened at that prospect although she wasn't quite

ready to allow Jess to revel in the realisation that actually it would be pretty nice to be able to stay with Jess and Tom and not have to sleep in a box room for a week every Christmas.

'Promise me you'll find somewhere close enough?' she said reluctantly.

'Yes! Promise!' Jess grabbed on to the idea enthusiastically.

'And you promise you're not going to become smug and lazy?' Jess frowned at Allie. 'I mean,' she explained, 'not always going on about how *the country is so much better than London*, because let's be clear, it's not.' Jess bit back a smile at Allie's tone. 'Or too lazy to ever come into London again?'

'I promise,' Jess said solemnly. 'Never too smug or lazy.'

'Even when it's winter and dark and cold?' Allie said challengingly.

'Even when it's winter and dark and cold,' Jess agreed.

'Even when there are train strikes?'

'I promise not to turn my nose up at rail replacement bus services.'

'Even when London is sweltering in forty-degree heat, the Tube is like a furnace and the tracks are melting?'

Jess fixed Allie with a look. 'Allie? Be reasonable.'

'OK, fine,' she grumbled. 'I'll come to you then.'

Jess clapped her hands in delight. 'And guess what?'

'What?' Allie asked reluctantly.

'The place we're looking at this weekend has a sex shed.'

'A what?!'

'You know, one of those home offices that people went crazy about and built in their gardens?'

'Yeees, but why would you call it a sex shed?' Allie didn't want to know what Tom and Jess were planning with the shed, but she couldn't help but ask.

'Don't you think that's what most people built them for?'

'No,' said Allie incredulously, thinking about their friends who had them in their back gardens and then shuddering slightly at the thought that all this time she had been presuming they had been using them as a home office, and all this time maybe 'working from home' had a totally different meaning for the vast majority of the population, who, unlike Allie, worked in an office for most of the week.

'Well, I think it is.'

Allie stared at her friend, momentarily jealous about the sex life that she and Tom evidently still planned to have even when they had left behind their London youth and moved out to the provinces. 'Anyway,' she said, shaking unwanted images from her mind, 'why on earth are you excited to tell me about this sex shed?'

'Because I thought you could use it!' Jess said excitedly.

'What? We've just established that my relationship with Will is over and that my ex is too disappointing to be considering getting back together with.'

'You're not seriously thinking about getting back together with him, are you?' Jess asked in concern.

'No.' Allie batted Jess's question away, not willing to delve into the depths of her concerns about loneliness right now. 'So, who do you think I'm going to be using your shed with?' Allie harboured some vague hope that Jess might have her romantic future all mapped out and that the property details she had been looking at had listed 'hot single neighbour' in the particulars. It was Jess's turn to look confused.

'Oh, no, not for sex! God no.' Allie couldn't keep the look of disappointment off her face that Jess had seemingly quickly dismissed the idea of Allie having any kind of sex, with anyone, anytime soon. 'I meant for writing!'

'Oh, OK.'

'You could come down and write in there, whenever you wanted to! It would be great.' Jess's face was a picture of nervous expectation. 'A break from London, a change of scenery could really help with the writer's block! Tom could cook dinner every night.' Allie felt grateful that at least Jess hadn't suggested *she* cook dinner every night, knowing that this would result in smouldering ashes and fire blankets, which was recoverable when there were a billion different options on Deliveroo, but not so much when the local chippy was, from Allie's recollection, a twenty-minute drive away, and closed at 7.30pm each night. And Allie didn't have the heart to tell Jess that her writer's block was never a result of her environment, and that actually she loved writing in her flat, and was even starting to feel guilty about scaring her friend the robin away.

'Sure, that sounds lovely.' Allie couldn't help smiling at the look of relief and pleasure that spread across Jess's face as she agreed with her. And who knew, maybe it would be nice to have that escape. Maybe she wouldn't have quite so many ties to London in the future… Allie's heart clenched at the thought of leaving London and all those in it, and one person in particular, behind…

The beep of her phone dislodged the uncomfortable lump in her throat and she was grateful for the distraction. 'Sorry, I just should check this…' she said fumbling in her bag. 'It's Verity,' she said, looking up at Jess. 'She says she's heard on the publishing grapevine that Jake is definitely being summoned to a meeting tomorrow morning at Brinkman's. Rumour has it he'll be leaving the office with his belongings in a box!' Allie grinned.

'Result! This is great, just what you wanted, right? And what about Verity? Any news on her job?'

Allie's smile widened. 'She's being invited back in for a meeting straight afterwards. I can't imagine it means anything other than a grovelling apology and her job back, can you?'

'Brilliant. You should go.'

'What?'

'You should be there. Watch it all unfurl. It will be cathartic.'

'I can't just march into Brinkman's and insist I attend the meetings.'

'No, but you can watch from outside.'

Allie contemplated Jess's suggestion for a moment.

'Wouldn't it be something though? To watch Jake leave, carrying a box?' Jess prompted.

'I guess I could… I mean, there's a cafe over the road, I could watch it from there I suppose … it would be fun to actually witness his downfall.'

'And Verity's redemption,' reminded Jess.

'Yes, yes of course. Maybe I could deliver her some flowers straight to the office as soon as it's confirmed?'

'One hundred percent, and then you can ask her for a small extension seeing as you now apparently have two books to write.'

'Don't remind me!' Allie sighed and glugged back the rest of her wine as Jess's phone took its turn to interrupt them. 'Tom?' she asked.

'Of course,' replied Jess. 'Honestly it's depressing how little anyone but you and Tom ever contact me.'

'Yeah, well, it will only get worse when you leave London.' Allie couldn't resist the dig. 'Bet they don't even have a proper phone signal down there yet.'

Jess fixed her a stare over the top of her phone. 'First thing I checked actually,' she said primly. 'Anyway, I better go. Tom wants to discuss house-buying strategies for our trip down there this weekend and if I drink any more, that sex shed you'll be writing in will end up being a swimming pool.'

'I'd quite like a swimming pool.'

'Tough, can't afford it. You can make do with the sex shed.'

Allie shrugged and picked up her bag. 'I should go too. Maybe half a bottle of wine is just the right amount to consume before writing. Don't want to tip over the edge into maudlin and depressed.'

Jess put her phone away and looked at Allie seriously. 'I am sorry, Allie, about Will. Don't give up. Please? Give him some time. And that grand romantic gesture? Just remember you're amazing at writing them, I believe you can pull one off in real life.'

Allie hugged Jess and said a muffled 'thanks' into her shiny hair, hoping that even just a smidgeon of her friend's belief in her might transfer through hair to skin contact.

'Keep me posted on those houses?'

'Of course.' Jess turned to leave.

'And Jess? Don't forget me, will you?' Allie was half joking, but there was a note of sentimentality in her voice that she knew Jess could hear.

'Never!' Jess insisted adamantly. 'This won't change a thing.'

Allie followed her friend out onto the street, where Jess turned to go one way and Allie turned to go the other, leaving her realising that this might just be the metaphor for the turning point in their lives. Jess was adamant nothing would change, whereas Allie saw, quite clearly and with acceptance, that no matter how much Jess insisted, it *would* change, *they* would change, and surprisingly, Allie didn't feel abject despair at the idea. It would hurt, and she would be lonely at times, but life was about change, and you couldn't sit still for too long or it would pass you by. Her phone buzzed with a message from Martin, interrupting her philosophical deep dive.

We should talk.

Allie tipped her head back and stared up at the cloudy London sky. She took a deep breath. She was OK. She would be OK.

Chapter Twenty-Three

For once, Allie was glad that the London weather was doing what it did best: raining. Not pouring rain, that would be too dramatic, just the usual, run-of-the-mill grey drizzle which messed with your hair and your mood and mysteriously managed to creep into the most waterproof of footwear. Allie's plan to hide in the cafe over the road from Brinkman's and observe the unfolding of events from there had been thwarted by the CLOSED sign she had found on the door when she had arrived about twenty minutes earlier.

'For fuck's sake,' she had growled to herself and mentally blamed Jess for putting this stupid idea into her head in the first place. What did she really expect to see? Of course, she was hoping for something theatrical: Jake being physically ejected from the building by two burly security guards, the police leading him out in handcuffs or a group of Brinkman's employees hurling rotten vegetables at him as he scurried out of the office, seeking shelter from their wrath. Instead, right now, she was staring at the nondescript red brick building from the doorway of the closed cafe, the rain giving her a measure of anonymity as she huddled under her umbrella. The worst thing would be to be spotted here, embarrassingly stalking her editorial nemesis.

'Morning, I see you had the same idea.'

Allie winced at the sound of the familiar voice and came face to face with a black umbrella. It tipped back slightly, revealing Martin who at least was smiling at her, which she hadn't expected, given the manner in which she had left things with Will after she had dropped her revelation. And the fact she hadn't yet had the guts to reply to Martin's message.

'Oh, hi,' Allie said somewhat warily. 'Yeah, guessing you're here to see if Jake gets kicked out?'

'I am. I'm hoping it won't take too long, given this...' Martin indicated towards the sky.

'How did you hear about it?' Allie asked, hoping to delay the inevitable conversation about books and writing, and writing of said books and where the inspiration for certain plot lines came from.

'Production director gave me the nod, said there had been a lot of closed doors and it wasn't looking good for Mr Matthews. Thought I'd come down here and see if it was worth watching. Great minds, hey?' He gave Allie a sideways look, which she met, smiled again somewhat sheepishly and looked down at her feet. 'Did you get my message?' he asked.

She nodded and decided to bite the bullet. 'I'm guessing you've spoken to Will?'

'I have, we had an interesting conversation.'

Allie grimaced and waited to see what he would say next.

'Look, Allie, I can imagine how awkward that whole meeting must have been for you, and what a surprise it must have been to have realised that myself and Will are related.'

Allie opened her mouth to put Martin straight and tell him

that she had known, before that awkward meeting, that he and Will were related, but then she paused as she realised something. Will hadn't told Martin that Allie knew beforehand that Will was his son. He hadn't told him that she had done nothing about the situation, or confessed to either of them that she knew. Which must count for something? Surely if Will was irreparably angry with her, then he wouldn't have bothered keeping something like this from his dad? She felt a surge of hope inside her and then realised that it was her job, not Will's, to set Martin straight. Because if there was a chance that she might be able to put things right with Will, it was going to start with being as honest with Martin as she could be.

'I knew,' she said plainly, 'before the other night. I knew Will was your son, I realised when I saw the photo at your house. And I didn't admit it to either of you.' She allowed the silence to hang in the damp air between them, giving Martin the time to realise what she was admitting to.

'Oh. Well, I see.'

Allie looked hard at him. He didn't look cross or especially surprised or concerned. 'I'm not sure you do,' she pressed. 'Did he tell you about my story?'

'You mean mine and Angie's story?' Martin chuckled.

'Look, Martin, I'm so so sorry, I never meant to…'

Martin continued to laugh, and then waved his hand at her. 'Allie, I'm teasing you. I know Will seems to have taken this badly, but I honestly don't know why, and I think that says more about his relationship with us than it does about your creative process. We agreed to switch plots, remember? Why do you feel telling our story is so bad?'

'Because it's yours and Angie's story, Martin,' Allie protested, 'and I wrote it without telling you.'

Martin looked puzzled. 'No, you didn't. We agreed from

the outset, you gave me that brilliant serial killer plot line and I swapped it for mine and Angie's marriage story. Or at least the happy version where we don't end up almost divorced.'

'You're getting a divorce?' Allie eked out in a hoarse and horrified voice. 'I thought things were getting better?'

'No! I mean, I can't speak for how Angie felt in the past, but things are OK now, better than OK. And really that's down to you.'

'It is?' Allie was struggling to follow this conversation.

'Well, you're the one who showed me what an idiot I was being. And you're the one who told me I needed to fight for my marriage, not take it for granted. What was it you were always going on about? Grand romantic gestures? Not sure Angie would agree that I'm any good at those, but I'm getting better at not taking her for granted, making the effort and all that. She even said so herself last night.'

'She did?'

'Yes. I took her for a romantic stroll in Richmond Park at sunset. It was lovely. Not sure why we don't do it more often.'

'Because you live in south-east London?' said Allie, not liking to think back to the walk she had taken in Richmond Park with Will. What on earth had made her suggest it as a date night for his father? She groaned internally and promised herself that no matter what happened with Will, she would never, ever share suggested date locations with a romantic interest's parents again.

'Well, that's, erm, great, Martin. I'm really pleased for you. But are you sure you're OK about my book?'

'I think it's rather sweet, actually. Angie does too. I told her. Well, actually, Will told her and then I filled her in on it all after he left.'

'She doesn't think I'm awful?' Allie had a horrible feeling in the pit of her stomach that even if she did manage to get Will to talk to her again, his mother would always think badly of her.

'Not at all. You know what a fan she is of yours from the other night; I think she's excited to be immortalised by you. By the way, I still want to get her books signed by you, as a surprise. What do you think of that as a grand romantic gesture?' Martin looked expectant. 'Would you be OK to do that?'

'Erm, sure.'

'We'll have to keep it a secret from Angie of course, which I'm not so comfortable doing.'

Allie would have thought this quite a sweet statement if she didn't know that Martin had already kept many, many other things from Angie over the course of their marriage. Allie mulled over these revelations. Angie knew about her story, Angie was excited to be written about, Angie still liked her. She knew she should have felt more relief than she did, but actually she really wanted Will to be OK with it all, Will to still like her.

'Do you think it was worth coming?' Martin said after a while, nodding over the road where the front of the Brinkman's building was still just as lifeless as before.

Allie shrugged. 'Depends. If we get to see Jake slink out with his tail between his legs and order restored, then yes. But I have a horrible feeling he'll just wriggle his way out of the whole thing and get away with it.'

'Do you really think so?' Martin looked at her in surprise. 'But there's so much evidence against him.'

Allie raised her eyebrow. 'Seriously, Martin? You're going to question whether it's possible that a straight white man gets away with years of abuse despite overwhelming evidence against him?'

'OK, fair point.' Martin had the good grace to look a little ashamed. 'Look, something's happening...' Martin pointed over the road where the revolving doors of Brinkman's had just started turning. 'Is it ... do you think it might be?' He squinted.

'Yes! Yes, look!' Allie grabbed Martin's arm with her hand and squeezed it. 'It's him! It's Jake, look he's coming out.'

Sure enough, a figure that seemed to match the description of Jake Matthews was slowly emerging through the revolving doors, there was a flash of movement and suddenly there he was deposited on the pavement. And it definitely looked like Jake, or at least a version of him. Allie couldn't quite put her finger on it, but there was something changed about him, he seemed diminished somehow.

'Does he look...?' she started.

'Different?' Martin finished for her. 'Yes. He looks ... *less* somehow.' They both turned to look at each other, for a moment neither of them knowing how to feel about witnessing what was surely the downfall of Jake Matthews.

'What's he holding?' Allie asked.

'A box. Goodness, he's been given the cardboard box treatment!'

Jake was indeed clutching a small brown box to his chest, trying to shelter it against him and out of the rain, but with little success. Even from this distance they could sense the anger in his body language. He stepped closer to the curb, transferring the weight of the box (which seemed quite slight, if it really did contain all his personal office possessions) to one hand and raised the other one into the air, attempting to hail a cab. But it was

London and it was raining, so for once, the odds were stacked against him. Two cabs went by, their lights out, not taking any fares. Martin and Allie stood and watched, both wondering how long it might be before Jake gave up the hope of hailing one and headed for the Tube. But just then, a black cab with its light on came down the road towards Jake. He stuck his hand up once again and for a moment it looked like the cab was slowing down, before it sped up again and raced past him, splashing him with water and screeching to a halt further down the road to pick up someone else. In his rage, Jake misstepped, one foot went off the pavement, his cardboard box tilted and then upended and the contents spilled out across the wet pavement.

Allie couldn't help but cry out in astonishment at how the luck of Jake had turned. He couldn't have heard her above the sound of the traffic, but something made him look up at that moment to see her and Martin standing across the road, watching his demise. His face was a picture of surprise for a moment, before his eyes narrowed and he scowled at them as he scrabbled to pick up his now soggy belongings and stuff them back into the box. He gave them one last foul look over his shoulder before he stalked off in the direction of the Tube.

'Wow,' Allie said eventually. 'That was quite cinematic, wasn't it?'

Martin gave a low whistle in agreement. 'Reckon you can put that in your book?' he asked.

Allie considered this for a moment before shaking her head. 'My book doesn't really have a villain, unless you count yourself before your redemption,' she joked.

Martin grinned at her broadly. 'You mean before *your* intervention.'

Allie gave a little curtsey, in acknowledgement.

'So,' he continued, 'if you're not going to use it, can I?'

Allie nodded. 'Be my guest. I think I owe you. I should have told you and Will as soon as I knew about the two of you.'

Martin put his hand out from under the umbrella and held it there for a moment. 'It's stopped raining,' he said, before turning to look at her. 'Yes, you probably should have. But I know why you didn't. And I understand. I'm sure I would have done the same.'

Allie gave a small, tight smile in response. 'Thanks, Martin, I appreciate that. But I don't think Will sees it that way. And look, I know he's your son and you probably don't want to know any of this. But I really liked him. I mean,' she corrected herself, 'I really like him. He makes me feel...' She paused, wanting to make sure she got this right. 'He makes me believe in happy-ever-afters again.'

Martin took her hand and gave it a squeeze. 'I don't know if this will help, but before this all happened, Angie and I hadn't seen Will that happy in years. I wish I'd known you were the reason.'

Allie bit back the tears at Martin's bittersweet revelation. 'Phew,' she breathed out heavily. 'Getting a bit deep here, Martin!' She gave his hand a squeeze and then dropped it firmly, wanting to grasp back some dignity and control in this awkward situation. She felt her phone vibrate in her pocket and, grateful for the distraction, pulled it out to look at it. 'It's a message from Verity,' she said. 'She says it's done – well, we knew that! – and that she's on her way into Brinkman's for her meeting. She's arranging drinks on Friday at a pub, for her authors, to celebrate.' Allie looked up from her phone. 'You should come,' she said to Martin. 'It's not like you have another editor at Brinkman's now.'

'Don't remind me,' groaned Martin. 'Anyway, I can't. Angie and I are going to the cinema on Friday.'

'So sweet, popcorn and back-row seats?' Allie couldn't resist the tease.

Martin ignored her. 'You should keep writing,' he said, '*your* book.' Allie couldn't help but notice the emphasis he placed in that sentence and was grateful for it. 'Angie and I are really touched that you would think us worthy of writing about. You should finish it.'

Allie nodded and they said their goodbyes, both of them relieved to have had this conversation and to have had it against the backdrop of Jake's unceremonious firing. It started raining again as Allie made her way to the Tube station and she hoped there hadn't been any delays and that she wouldn't bump into Jake on the platform, which would be beyond awkward. But the Tube was running a good service and the platform was empty, leaving Allie alone with her thoughts. Martin was right, she should keep writing, and she would keep writing. But she wasn't going to do what he thought she ought to do with the finished result.

Chapter Twenty-Four

I t was a knock at the door that pulled Allie from her four-hour writing spree. She groaned, less at the interruption and more at the manner in which her legs protested at this sudden movement.

'Coming,' she shouted, more in hope than expectation; the walls of her Victorian conversion were too thick for her shouting to have any real effect, which was great for drowning out the neighbours, not so great for making the Evri delivery person wait. Because that's who she was expecting it to be, or perhaps some Jehovah's witnesses. It wasn't like normal people just called round to friends' houses without prearranging via text, and double checking several times beforehand that you really weren't inconveniencing them, before sending a final confirmation as you walked the last 500 yards towards their home.

Allie jerked open the front door, only expecting to have to apologise for keeping the person waiting and then realising very quickly that the homeless chic look she had been sporting was not what she would have chosen for an unplanned encounter with an ex boyfriend. Her wavy hair was piled on her head, her glasses shoved up there too, her leggings had definitely had stretch in them at some point but probably not in the last decade, and her sweatshirt bore the distinct marks of the tea she had poured down it three days ago as her writing had temporarily (she hoped) caused her to lose the ability to transport a cup of tea safely from her desk to her mouth.

'I'm on a deadline,' she spluttered, 'hence the…' She gesticulated at her get-up.

'I'm sorry, should I go?' Asked Dominic.

Allie sighed, she wanted to say yes. She wanted to go back to her writing and not have to explain her clothing and the state of her flat. She wanted to point out that when boyfriends left in red sports cars, kissing the driver on the lips before they pulled away, then really they couldn't expect to be invited back in. She stared hard at the intruder before sighing again and allowing the front door to swing open.

'Oh, come on then,' she said, adding, 'but take your shoes off,' knowing how much it irked Dominic to be asked to remove his shoes before entering someone's house. She grinned to herself as she walked back inside, pleased to have regained the upper hand.

'So, what do you want, Dominic? Why are you here?'

Dominic shuffled in his socked feet. She knew she wasn't making this easy on him, offering him neither the chance to sit down nor a drink but she felt she owed him nothing really, and had been rather enjoying forgetting he had even existed.

'I brought your things,' he held up the box he was carrying, 'and I read about Brinkman's.'

Allie looked at him in surprise. 'You did?' She wondered what kind of messed-up intersection had brought her world into his.

'There was an article about it in *The Telegraph*.'

Allie rolled her eyes. 'Of course there was.'

'Hey, don't be so dismissive. I came to check you were OK.'

Allie arched her eyebrow at him. 'Really? You came to check I was OK?' Dominic nodded, but in a rather hesitant fashion. 'Now why would you want to come and check I was OK after an article you read? When you couldn't be bothered to check I was OK after you left here in your new girlfriend's car?'

Dominic flushed immediately. He opened his mouth a few times as if searching for an explanation, before realising that Allie was not in the mood. 'She's not my girlfriend,' he said mutedly.

'Not now? Or never was?' Allie put her hand on her hip. She was enjoying making Dominic squirm but was also discomfited by the fact that it was causing her pain to relive that night. She thought she had buried it all, thought she was over Dominic, had proudly declared herself over him before the relationship had even formally ended. And now she realised, with a pang that that wasn't quite true, and it wasn't just her pride which was hurting, she genuinely missed having someone, even Dominic, sharing her life. She swallowed down the lump in her throat and tried to stare him down.

'Never was,' he said softly. 'Allie, I'm sorry. I've behaved like an idiot.'

Allie was probably supposed to jump in here and make him feel better, but she remained tight lipped.

'She's a colleague, an ex-colleague now, anyway. She had been flirting with me for ages.'

'And you couldn't help yourself?'

'No! Honestly, nothing really happened.'

Allie narrowed her eyes at this statement. 'Just be honest with me, Dominic.'

'OK, I had told her we had been having issues. What?' he said, seeing the look on Allie's face. 'Come on, be honest, we hadn't been happy for ages. I said I was going to come and talk to you, she offered me a lift, and stupidly I said yes. I didn't actually think she was going to wait outside for me. And yes, when I got in the car she leaned over and kissed me. But that's as far as it went. And I haven't seen her since, not outside work, and she's left now anyway.' He paused. 'Allie, I'm sorry. I really wish it hadn't happened. It was really disrespectful.'

Allie grunted slightly in recognition of both the apology and – begrudgingly – the explanation, which did seem to get Dominic off the hook for being a complete swine. Just half pig then. It was Allie's turn to shuffle awkwardly. Just because he'd apologised it didn't mean she wanted him in her flat, but now that he had apologised, and being so terribly British, she really felt she ought to offer him a drink.

'Do you want a cup of tea?' she said, in a tone that suggested Dominic would be stupid to say yes. Dominic's eyes lit up, evidently he hadn't put on his listening ears that day.

'That would be great.' He plonked himself down in one of Allie's kitchen chairs which seemed to suggest he would be staying for a while. Allie watched him for a moment, wishing she hadn't offered, before turning to fill the kettle and reminding herself that this was her house, and if she wanted him to leave, she just had to tell him that.

'So are you OK about the Brinkman's thing then?' Dominic asked as he sat, rather too at home in her kitchen, nursing his cup of tea.

'Yes, it's good news.'

'Right, yes, of course.'

Allie rolled her eyes. 'Oh god, do I want to know what *The Telegraph*'s take on it all is?'

Dominic looked at her over his tea. 'Want to take a guess?'

'Has #metoo gone too far? Are innocent publishing executives being taken down by militant feminazis?'

Dominic laughed loudly. 'That's about spot on.'

'Seriously? Why do you read that rubbish?'

'That was always a problem, wasn't it?'

'What do you mean?' Allie suddenly felt defensive.

'With us. You hated that I was different to you. Hated the fact I wasn't creative, had a boring office job.' Allie bristled, ready to defend herself but Dominic continued. 'It's OK, I know. I do have a boring office job. I am essentially boring. Far too boring for you.'

'Dom, it's not… I don't… It wasn't like that.'

'No? You know, I never felt good enough for you. I knew you could do so much better. Find someone so much more interesting.'

Allie felt her heart constrict. Dominic was right, she *had* always thought he had a boring job, that he could never understand the creative industries, didn't care enough about her work. But she hated the fact he'd realised that, hated the fact she had been 'found out'.

'I never thought you weren't good enough for me,' she said quietly, 'but yes, we were, *are*, so different. I don't think we ever really got each other, did we?'

Dominic shook his head a little sadly. 'But things are OK, are they? At Brinkman's? You're going to be OK, aren't you?'

'Yeah, I am. I mean, I need to finish this book, but they've brought Verity back in…' She saw the look on his face. 'Oh right, yes, you wouldn't have known. That guy, Jake, the one in the article, he got rid of Verity. But it's OK,' she said quickly, seeing panic etched on Dominic's face. 'They fired him and gave Verity her job back. So, I've got my editor again.'

'Well, that's good. I know how much she means to you.'

Allie bit back a smile remembering the time she had introduced Verity and Dominic at one of her book launches. It had been like introducing people from different planets, with each of them falling over themselves to be nice to the other alien because they knew how important they were to Allie.

'Yup. She really does mean a lot. This whole thing has made me realise how important some people are to me.' Allie was talking into her cup of tea and so didn't see the look of hope that had sprung up on Dominic's face. Because if she had, she might have thought twice about mentioning Verity's drinks celebration, or indeed where and when that celebration was happening.

Chapter Twenty-Five

'Let me get this straight.'

Allie braced herself for whatever Jess was about to throw at her; she knew this tone, she had previous experience of being on the end of it.

'You told your ex, Dominic – Disappointing Dominic – the man who, after breaking up with you, left your flat in the car of his new girlfriend, the exact time and place of a party you are going to?'

'Yes and?' Allie was failing to grasp what Jess was getting at.

'Don't you think he'll have taken that as an invitation to turn up?'

'No!' exclaimed Allie in absolute disbelief. 'Of course not, why would he?'

'Because,' sighed Jess, 'he came round to your flat because he wanted to see you, because he's hoping you'll take him back.'

'No!' interjected Allie again.

'And then you tell him exactly where he can find you on

Friday night?' Jess continued, ignoring Allie's protestations. 'What were you thinking, Allie? He just told you he'd split up with his new girlfriend, an open invite to see if you were still interested!'

'Not his girlfriend,' interjected Allie.

'Not the point,' sing songed Jess in return. She was really not impressed with Allie, and given the circumstances, and the way in which Jess had just presented her with the evidence, Allie was beginning to understand why.

'I have one question … why?' There was a muffled exchange on the end of the phone while Jess pointed out one or more flaws in the house that she and Tom were viewing that day. 'No, not there.' Jess sounded exasperated and Allie kind of hoped that, much as she loved Tom, it was him testing Jess's patience that day and not her. 'It's not going to fit there, is it?' There was a pause. 'Over there, yes, it could definitely fit in that space.'

'Going well, is it?' Allie asked.

Jess harrumphed in response. 'It's a nice house, good location. Just trying to work out if we'll fit my wardrobe in any of the bedrooms.'

Allie said nothing. The size of Jess's wardrobe had been the sticking point to every single flat and house move of the last decade. Sometimes it was nice that nothing changed, and sometimes Allie wished that Tom had the guts just to tell Jess that her antique wardrobe would have to find a new home.

'Anyway, beside the point. *Please* tell me why you told Dominic about this party?'

'Oh, I don't know. He turned up all contrite, and I was feeling vulnerable and didn't think it through. You don't actually think he's going to turn up, do you?'

'I think there's a good chance…'

Allie thought this over. 'I guess it would be nice not to go to the party on my own.'

'No!' It was Jess's turn to protest. 'Do not even go there. If you want a date, you could ask me.'

'No, I can't. You're leaving me, remember? Moving out of London,' Allie said sulkily.

'Al,' Jess said in a warning tone, 'not fair. I haven't moved yet and anyway I'm not leaving you.'

'Whatever,' Allie muttered.

'Don't whatever me. You should make sure Dominic hasn't got the wrong idea.'

'He has *not* got the wrong idea. I made it quite plain that I was not interested in getting back together with him.'

'Oh, you did, did you? And how did you go about doing that?'

Allie thought back to her conversation with Dominic and struggled to work out exactly where she had made it crystal clear that she was not interested in having him back in her life. It was glaringly obvious to her but perhaps not so glaringly obvious to Dominic and perhaps, god forbid, Jess had a point and that she had made a terrible terrible mistake just by allowing Dominic back through her front door.

'Just don't blame me if this all comes back to bite you...'

Allie stuck two fingers up at her phone and silently wished for Tom to finally win the battle of the antique wardrobe.

'I'm so glad you came!' Verity engulfed Allie in a hug, wrapping her in a floaty delight of orchid patterned silk and her signature scent of verbena and lemon, which Verity seemingly now knew to spritz rather than douse and was all the more appealing and less suffocating for.

'Of course I came,' came Allie's muffled reply, ensconced as she was somewhere close to Verity's boobs. She extracted herself as tactfully as she dared. 'It's a celebration, right?'

'It *is* a celebration, isn't it?' Verity's eyes flashed with excitement. 'We did it, Allie, we really did it.'

Allie shook her head. 'Oh no, I take no credit for this. *You* did this Verity, you and Tessa. Is she coming tonight?' Allie looked around the crowded room wondering just how many authors Verity was responsible for now and suppressing a moment of panic that maybe Verity really didn't have time for her and all her nonsense.

'She said she might. I think it's been a lot for her the past few days. She's been so brave, but she's had to do a lot of talking to a lot of people, and I think another round of that, albeit in a party situation, might just be too much.'

'Yeah, of course. The poor kid. I still feel bad about dismissing her and thinking of her as just one of Jake's lackeys.'

'Don't.' Verity took Allie's hand. 'Remember, she said it was partly you who inspired her to tell the truth about Jake.'

Allie looked at Verity sceptically.

'This comes direct from Tessa herself,' Verity continued, 'she said you gave off an air of not giving a shit, about not believing in Jake's special brand of coercive control, and it gave her the courage to do the same.'

Allie raised her eyebrows. 'Wow, well, I'm glad that my total bafflement in the face of insidious evil worked out this time. Will you say hi from me next time you see her? Will she come back and work for you at Brinkman's? Now that you practically run the place!'

Verity wafted her hand in dismissal. 'Oh, don't be silly, I don't run the place.'

'You don't?' Allie questioned teasingly. 'Remind me of your new job title?'

'Publisher.' Verity coughed and looked slightly embarrassed.

'Sounds like you run the place to me.'

'Well, I *am* the boss of *you*, so don't go forgetting that, will you?'

'Absolutely not.'

'Good. Now about this plan of yours, for your book. How's that coming along? Of course, I *am* one hundred per cent in charge now,' Verity grinned at Allie, 'but I still don't think I can swing you any more extensions.'

'I've got it all under control,' Allie confirmed. The butterflies in her tummy were trying to persuade her otherwise, but she felt more and more confident with each chapter that she wrote.

'Good. By the way, you should try some of the canapés here, they're really good.' Verity winked at Allie and then saw someone over her shoulder, and with a 'Darling!' she raced off to greet the newcomer, leaving Allie confused by that wink.

Allie made her way to the bar and picked up what looked like a margarita from a silver tray. She took a sip and turned round to face the room, wondering who she might know that she could talk to and wishing that Martin would have a change of heart and would turn up, bringing Angie with him. But on second thoughts, Allie decided maybe she wasn't quite ready to face Angie yet. Soon, yes, but she needed a little more time to work on something first.

She raised her glass to a couple of authors she recognised, and was just about to make her way over to say hello when she felt a hand on her elbow and a platter of canapés came into view under her nose. She took a sharp intake of breath, immediately realising why Verity had winked at her when she mentioned the food and cursing herself for not thinking this could happen.

'Hi,' she said and turned to look up at Will, who was, of course, the person holding the tray.

'Hi,' he said gently, the corner of his mouth turning up in a slight smile. She bit her lip, not daring to hope what that faint smile might suggest.

'You'll be pleased to see that management took your feedback seriously and implemented some changes...' Will held the platter a little higher, his grin spreading across his face.

'What? Oh, I see!' Allie looked down at the platter, seeing row upon row of tiny, perfectly formed vol au vents, filled to just the right level with no risk of spillage and no need for more than one hand.

'You want to try?'

Allie took one and lifted it to her mouth, flushing slightly as Will watched her carefully.

'Perfectly bite-sized?' he asked.

Allie flushed a deeper red. 'Are we still talking about the canapés?'

'Do you want us to be?' Will held her gaze.

'Not really, no.' She bit her lip again, and then a grin broke out on her face. 'It's nice to see you. I probably should have guessed you'd be catering for this.'

'Because I'm a spoilt nepo baby?'

'Yes, precisely for that reason.'

'Well, I thought about turning it down, just to prove a

point. But then Verity showed me the guest list and suddenly it seemed hard to say no…'

'I'm glad you said yes,' she exhaled breathily. 'Look, Will, I'm not sure here is the right place to talk properly, but I want you to know how sorry I am for what I did and how it all went down.' Will waved away her attempt at an apology. 'No,' Allie insisted, 'I should have told you as soon as I realised, and I definitely should have told you, and your dad, exactly how much of the book was based on his story.'

'Allie, stop.' Will put his hand on her arm, which made her not want to stop anything at all. 'I owe you an explanation. I shouldn't have shut down like I did that morning. I shouldn't have let you leave.'

'Not sure you actually *let* me do anything,' Allie half-muttered and it was Will's turn to flush.

'You're right. I behaved really badly. I shouldn't have *made* you leave.'

Allie looked up at him. 'So, what changed?'

'I did. I did a lot of soul searching. Been doing a lot of work on myself.' He said this with such a po-face that Allie couldn't help but laugh.

'So, what did you find on that soul searching mission?' she questioned, raising an eyebrow in such a way that her nine-year-old self would have been immensely proud of, justifying as it did all that time and effort practising in the mirror.

'I found that I was a pompous ass and that I shouldn't shut down just because a situation overwhelms me emotionally.'

At this Allie really did laugh. 'Therapy?'

Will nodded. 'I'm a work in progress. And the other thing I found on my soul search was that I really, really didn't like my life without you in it. And that if my parents were fine about you using their story as inspiration then I really didn't have an issue with it either.'

'I am sorry Will. I should have—'

Will interrupted her. 'Allie, it's OK. I actually don't think you need my forgiveness, but knowing you, I expect you'll be worrying about this until you have it. So, you have it, OK?' He took her hand in his and then pulled her closer to him, his head resting on hers, his lips in her hairline as he whispered, 'You have my heart, too.'

Allie went wobbly. She reached to the side, putting her cocktail glass down on the bar, grateful it was still in close proximity. It all seemed so easy … too easy? She'd never been so swept off her feet before, she'd never felt so clear on how she felt about a guy before. With Dominic, they had danced around their feelings for each other; every so often, when he had one too many beers and his face was a little shiny and red, he would call her 'his girl', and tell her she was the one for him. But it never felt as certain and stomach swoopingly delicious as hearing Will whisper these words into her ear. She pulled back and looked up at him. 'I think you have mine, too.'

Will laughed. 'You think?'

'Well, let's not jump the gun. You can't sweep in here expecting me to declare my intentions when I have only seen one of your trays of improved canapés so far.'

'We're definitely not talking about the food, are we?'

Allie stood on her tiptoes and reached up, pulling Will's head towards her, finding his lips with hers. 'No, we're not.'

'Okaaay,' Will exhaled deeply. 'I should go check on the rest of the food and, erm, I guess we should save this for later? I don't want everyone here thinking this is what they get as a side order tonight.'

'I'm the only one who gets you as a side order tonight…'

Allie picked up her margarita and put it to her lips before saying, 'I think we're done with the food-related double entendres tonight. Should we agree on that?'

'I agree with anything you say.' Will squeezed her waist. 'How long are you staying?'

'How long do *you* have to stay?'

Will looked around the room. 'Think you can entertain yourself for half an hour while I check everything is OK? My van is parked round the corner, I could meet you there?'

Allie's smile couldn't get any bigger. 'Absolutely,' she said.

For Allie, the next half an hour was one of the longest of her life. She caught a glimpse of Will a couple of times and each time she did her heart did the sort of thump that would have made her worry she was having a heart attack if she didn't know with complete certainty that it was the promise of meeting up with Will later that was having that effect. She didn't want to be the annoying party guest who constantly checked her watch and as she knew she was on thin ice with Verity she wanted to be seen to be politely chatting to fellow authors, enquiring about the lives of the publicity team, who never seemed to ever get asked those sorts of questions and always seemed so surprised to even be thought of, which made Allie feel uncomfortable, given these were the people who consistently anticipated every author's need. But she was all out of oohs and aahs, having been subjected to dozens of baby photos from a publicity manager who appeared to be fresh back from maternity leave and wasn't yet comfortable with being more than arm's length from her child. Happily, the death of the publicist's phone battery coincided with the half hour being up and so Allie left the poor woman to frantically go searching for a charger so that she could check in one more time with her presumably long-suffering partner at home. Allie secretly thought that the partner might be quite relieved not to be subjected to constant demands for updates on the sleeping/feeding/pooping of their baby.

Allie was halfway down the stairs that led from the private function room down to the street-level public drinking area when she came face to face with Dominic, and so surprised was she that she put out a hand to stabilise herself and found it resting on his chest. She quickly moved it, but not before she noticed a rather smug, pleased-with-himself expression cross Dominic's already shiny face.

'Dom!' she exclaimed. 'What are you doing here?' She quickly thought back to Jess's words of warning and not for the first time wondered whether the universe was conspiring against her.

'I thought it would be a nice surprise.'

Allie wondered how best to phrase the proper response, which should have been. 'Well it's not, please leave,' and, because she really couldn't help herself she politely settled for an ambiguous, 'Erm, OK, it's a surprise certainly.'

'And I brought you this.'

Allie peered at the item that Dominic was now brandishing towards her.

'What *is* that?'

'Tweezers.'

'Tweezers? Why did you bring tweezers to a party to surprise me with?'

'They're yours.'

'They are?'

'Yes, I forgot to put them in that box I brought round the

other day, so I thought I ought to bring them to you. And as I knew you were going to be here...' Dominic tailed off, and he looked from Allie to the pair of tweezers he was now holding limply in one hand. If he had more self-awareness, Allie might even begin to think he was realising how ridiculous his excuse sounded.

'I also thought you might want some support. I thought if I came along about now you might be ready to leave and I could give you a good excuse to do so.' He paused. 'You are leaving, aren't you?' His face brightened. 'See? Perfect timing. I can get us an Uber.' He reached in his pocket for his phone.

'Will they be driving a red sports car?'

'Allie, I said I'm sorry.'

'Yes, and I hadn't said I'd forgiven you.' She thought back to her conversation with Will earlier that evening. How loaded it had been with attraction, how easy it had been and how far it was from this awkward exchange with Dominic, which was loaded only with recriminations and an eye on the closest available emergency exit.

'Well look, Dom, I wish you'd told me you were thinking of coming, because I would have told you not to.' She watched him try to digest this news and then compose his features accordingly. Dominic had never been the sort of man to not have the world arrange itself in ways solely to please him. 'And if it was about the tweezers I could have just told you that I bought another pair.'

'I thought we could go get dinner, you and me?' He raised an eyebrow as he suggested this and once again Allie couldn't help but compare this to the effect that Will had on her when he raised his eyebrow.

'Dominic. No. I think you got the wrong end of the stick when I invited you in the other day. I don't want to go for dinner with you, I don't want to get back together with you and I really don't need rescuing tonight.' She started down the stairs past him, keen to put as much distance between her and Dominic as possible and wishing that Georgian-era builders had the foresight to build slightly wider staircases, so that one wasn't forced to make bodily contact with ex-boyfriends when trying to leave parties. 'Sorry, excuse me,' she said as she awkwardly navigated Dominic's body, which could have been a metaphor for the entirety of their sex life.

'Come on, let's just go get a drink?' Dominic's tone was switching from authoritative to plaintive.

'No, Dom. I'm sorry. You shouldn't have just turned up here for many, many reasons. Firstly because I didn't invite you, and second because ... to be honest, this is going to be awkward.' By now Allie was stood on the pavement outside the pub, Dominic hot on her heels. She looked around for Will's van, wondering where exactly he had parked and whether she could shake Dominic off before she had to make incredibly uncomfortable introductions. Or whether it might be possible just to jump in the front seat of the van and shout 'drive' at Will, leaving Dominic spluttering in a cloud of exhaust fumes. But even that would require an explanation, and given she still felt she was on shaky grounds with Will in regards to being upfront and honest, she didn't feel keen to pretend that Dominic was an overzealous marketing manager, who was desperate to try and get her to record bonus material for the audio book.

On all these points she needn't have worried, because she quickly spotted Will's van, parked as he had said it was on the corner of the side street. Except it wasn't really parked, it already had its lights on and the engine running and was now beginning to pull away from the curb. Allie put up a hand to attract Will's attention, he must be going round the back of the pub to collect more things, or perhaps he was looking for a better parking space. Because, yes, that space that the van was now rapidly exiting did look like it might be too small. But now the van was speeding up, and now it was pulling into the main road and going just a little too fast to beat those lights and to get as far away from the pub outside which Allie was standing and outside which she had arranged to meet Will.

'Oh!' she exclaimed, wondering what to make of this new development.

'That's the caterer's van. Looks like he's finished for the night.'

'Yes,' agreed Allie sadly, it really did look like he had. 'Wait...' She turned towards Dominic and held up an accusatory finger. 'How do you know that's Will's van?'

'Who's Will?' Dominic looked confused. 'Oh right, the catering guy. I didn't know his name.'

'OK, but how do you know he was the catering guy?'

'We were chatting.'

Allie's eyes narrowed and she advanced menacingly towards Dominic who seemed aware of the shift in temperature of this exchange, which had gone from testy to properly threatening in the space of time it had taken them to walk down the stairs and out into the street.

'And what,' Allie's eyes were now boring a hole into Dominic, 'exactly were you "chatting" about?' Allie said the word 'chatting' in the tone of voice more commonly associated with gangsters.

'Just ... just...' Dominic looked suddenly very aware that Will wasn't 'just' that catering guy; the penny was dropping. 'Well,' he floundered, 'I helped him carry some of those trays out to his car, held the door open and such...' His voice petered out.

'And what did you discuss while you were being ever so helpful?' asked Allie in an icy tone.

'He asked me why I was here, and I told him I was here to meet you,' Dominic blurted out.

Allie knew what was coming next, it was so obvious, and she cursed herself for ever letting Dominic back through her front door and then having the stupidity to mention tonight to him. She took a deep breath, deciding to rip the plaster off. 'Dominic, think very carefully.' She hoped her measured tone struck fear into Dominic. 'Did you, or did you not, suggest that there might be something going on between the two of us?'

The chatter of the people drinking in the pub reverberated around the question she posed. The door swung open behind them, two men making their way to the designated outside smoking zone, cigarettes already between their lips. The lights up the road, the ones Will's van had so recently sped through, changed once again and still Dominic said nothing, he stared down at his feet.

'Dominic!' Allie shouted, making both Dominic and the smokers jump. 'Just answer me.'

'I might have done,' he admitted in a quiet voice.

'Oh, for fuck's sake, what were you thinking?'

'I was hoping... Are you and he...' He pointed up the road in the direction Will's van had travelled. 'Are you two seeing each other?'

Despite her rage Allie could see how much this question pained Dominic, and she didn't really have a good answer. Was she seeing Will? She certainly had been at one point, and then she hadn't. But she had hoped earlier on this evening that she might be again, and now... given what Dominic had said, and the way Will had left, she very much felt that all the signs were pointing towards not – they were *not* seeing each other. Allie felt tired and dizzy at all the comings and goings, the changes, about Dominic showing up here, about Will leaving so quickly, and at all the very many words she still had to write to keep Verity and the Brinkman lawyers happy. One thing she did know for certain, was that it really was none of Dominic's business who Will was or was not to her.

'Oh, go home, Dominic,' she said wearily, 'and let's agree not to contact each other again. You can keep the tweezers.' She turned on her heel and walked off towards home.

Chapter Twenty-Six

It was like Groundhog Day. Allie was back at her computer, crashing out the words, Will had gone AWOL, presumably trying to make sense of what on earth was going on and whether he could ever trust her again and Jess was repeatedly calling her asking her to go to an exhibition opening later on that week.

'Absolutely not,' Allie had said upon hearing where the exhibition was being held.

'Why not?' whined Jess in her annoying but ultimately effective tone that almost always resulted in Allie doing whatever she was demanding she do.

'I don't ever want to go back there.'

'To the V&A?' Jess sounded bemused by Allie's vehemence.

'Yes. Never going there again.'

'Okay, care to elaborate?'

'It's where I met Will. Don't want to be reminded.' Allie was only half listening to Jess as she was busy re-reading through what she hoped might be the final draft of her novel. But her ears had pricked up when she had heard Jess say

'V&A' and immediately she was back there, where all of this had begun, ogling Will's forearms, trying to negotiate his unwieldy canapés and wishing they were on speaking terms so that she could see if she could make him laugh with that euphemism.

'Strictly speaking, didn't you meet him *outside* the V&A?'

'Semantics.' Allie was keen to get Jess off the line and rewrite an especially clunky sentence she had just spotted.

'Well, you would be accompanying me *inside* the V&A, so technically you'd be OK.'

'And how would you expect me to get *inside* the V&A, without first being *outside* the V&A?' Allie could feel her resolve wavering. 'Why can't Tom go with you?'

'He's away. LA, work, again,' Jess said morosely. 'Please?' She paused. 'And anyway, soon enough we'll move and I won't be in London to go to these events.'

Allie started. 'Hang on, you promised things wouldn't change? Jess? Jess, you promised we'd still do things together?'

'Well, it will be hard to say yes to tickets to these sorts of things if I don't know that you'll agree to go with me.' And there it was – game, set and match to Jess.

Allie seethed 'Fine. OK. On one condition though.'

'Anything,' Jess replied in a sickeningly saccharine tone.

'That I've finished my first drafts before then.'

'Suppose so. How close to finishing are you, honestly?'

'Pretty close.' Allie couldn't keep the note of excitement out of her voice. Because despite everything, she knew what she was going to do and she still had a smidgeon of hope that it might just be enough for her redemptive arc, to stand as a grand romantic gesture and so that everyone (Will in particular) would forgive her. 'Close enough that it should all be done by Friday.'

'OK,' Jess replied somewhat sulkily. 'Write faster though, OK? I've got a fabulous dress and it has been making "take me out" eyes at me ever since it came into my life.'

Allie snorted with laughter. 'Got it. Can I go now?'

Jess agreed that yes, Allie could indeed go. Allie put her phone face down and silenced it so she wouldn't be interrupted again. She looked up into the garden where just that morning her friend the robin had returned. It was the first morning Allie had seen him since she had banged on the glass and frightened him away. Allie had spent an inordinate amount of time researching the best seed for robins and an obscene amount of money on purchasing said seed. And then finally, this morning, it had paid off. She raised a hand in greeting. The robin startled, as if expecting the crazy woman to pound on the glass again, but then he fixed her with his beady eye and if Allie could speak bird she was sure he would be saying, 'What are you waiting for? Get on with it then.' So she did as she was told and went back to her writing.

Chapter Twenty-Seven

'Allie! This is a surprise. Is Martin expecting you?'

'No, erm, actually it was you I came to see. Well, both of you really. But mainly you.'

Allie squirmed as she stood on the steps of Martin and Angie's beautiful home. She had been preparing for this moment for ages. But her preparation had been the frantic typing variety and not the planning what to say when you got there kind. And now that she was here, she didn't really know how to express all the feelings she was experiencing.

'Here, these are for you.' She thrust one of the bags she was carrying into Angie's hand and took a step back, momentarily teetering on the edge of one of the steps before righting herself.

'What's this?' Angie asked in surprise and glanced into the bag. 'Are these my books?' She picked one out and flicked to the front page. 'You signed them all?' She looked up at Allie. 'To me?'

'Well yes. I did suggest we go for a bit of variety and swap in some different names. But Martin told me I was being weird and to get on with it because he wanted to surprise you this side of Christmas.'

Angie put the bag down on the steps and picked another book out, flicking again to the front page. 'They're all different?'

'Yes. I mean, they're all signed to you. But Martin wanted me to add in something about what was happening in your lives, or where you were when you bought the copy.'

With painstaking accuracy, Martin had gone through all the copies of Allie's books that he had discovered Angie had, and worked out what they would have been doing when Angie had bought each one.

'Oh goodness. This one I bought in the WHSmith at St Pancras when we were going to Paris for a long weekend. He remembered?' Her eyes filled with tears as she looked at Allie and for a horrible moment Allie wondered if she and Martin had completely misjudged this and that maybe some of these weren't happy memories for Angie. But Angie's face broke into a smile. 'He remembered,' she said again softly. 'That was such a fun weekend. We hadn't been to Paris in years. We had all these plans to do all the touristy things but instead we spent the weekend drinking red wine, eating delicious food, people watching...' Her voice drifted off and a different smile spread on her face, a secret smile this time.

'I remembered,' confirmed Martin who had come up behind Angie and now put his arms around her and softly kissed her neck, 'or at least I worked it out.' Allie didn't know whether to look away or just leave. But this was actually sweet, not voyeuristic. She could sense their shared history, their happy memories.

'Thank you, my love.' Angie turned and cupped Martin's face in her hands and kissed him. 'And thank you!' She turned back to Allie. 'I love these. I love that you both did this for me. Will you come in?' she asked.

Allie shook her head. 'No, I've got somewhere I need to be. But I have something else for you, too.' She put down her rucksack and carefully lifted out a bound manuscript. 'No, wrong one.' She slotted it back into her bag and took out a second similarly sized manuscript. 'This is for you both.' She held it out.

'What's this?' Martin asked, reaching around Angie to take it.

'It's yours, it's your story.'

'You finished?!' Martin stared at Allie with wide eyes. 'Good god, Allie, that's amazing. Need to get cracking with mine now; you're putting me to shame. I can't wait to read it.'

Angie looked piercingly at Allie. 'Sweetheart, why are you giving this to us?'

'As I said, it's your story.'

'Yes, but it's *your* story too,' Angie said gently, 'you're the one who's telling it.'

'And I will,' said Allie more decisively than she felt. 'But I need to know you're OK with me doing so. So, this is it.' She pointed at the parcel of paper that Martin held. 'I know I could have emailed it, but it felt more symbolic bringing it to you like this. And no one else is going to read it until both you and Martin have, and are happy for me to share.'

'You haven't sent this to Verity yet?' Martin sounded incredulous.

Allie shook her head. 'No. I'm not going to. Not unless and until you're OK for me to do so.'

Angie stepped down towards Allie and gave her a big hug. 'You sweet, sweet girl. I cannot wait to read it, and thank you for doing this.'

Allie could have stayed in Angie's embrace for hours, but she had places to be, or more specifically, one place to be. Reluctantly she disentangled herself. 'Complete honesty?' she said, fixing both Angie and Martin with a stare.

'Complete honesty,' Angie agreed, while Martin held up his hand in something which probably approximated the Boy Scout salute back in 1955.

'OK, well, let me know...' Allie turned and walked back down the steps, down the path.

She was at the gate when Angie called, 'Allie? What's the other one for? The other manuscript you've got in your bag?'

Allie bit her lip and turned back. 'That's a different story. And it's something I needed to do, to make amends. And, also, to remind myself that I still should have faith in happy-ever-afters.' Angie looked at her and Allie felt that she knew exactly what that story was and where Allie was heading next. Martin simply looked bemused by this exchange and ushered Angie back inside muttering something about the bar opening and it being G&T time. Allie smiled to herself as she headed back out into the London street. One grand romantic gesture down, one to go.

Allie wasn't feeling so romantic as she stood on the street outside Will's flat, clutching the rucksack containing her hopes and dreams to her chest, waiting for him to answer the doorbell. She stood and waited, and waited some more. This one she had all worked out. She knew exactly what she wanted to say, she knew exactly what she *needed* to say. And in the rucksack she was clutching, she had what she wanted to give to Will. It was all part of her grand romantic gesture, her plan for catching and keeping that happy-ever-after that had eluded her for so many years.

But because fate was a fickle thing and because the universe definitely was conspiring against her, it looked very much like Will wasn't at home. Allie thought about waiting it out. Perhaps he had nipped to the shops? He might not be long. Wouldn't it be romantic for him to come back and find her on his doorstep, not quite having run through the rain, but certainly having braved the weather for him? But as the minutes ticked past, Allie had to concede that expiring on Will's doorstep might not be quite the romantic gesture she had been aiming for. Admitting defeat, she sighed and opened up her rucksack, carefully taking out the bound manuscript and placing it on the doorstep, arranging it in such a way as to be tucked under the lintel but still visible so that Will wouldn't miss it when he finally got back from wherever he was. Allie took a deep inhale and stepped back, put her rucksack on and started to walk away before changing her mind. She should leave a note. She should definitely leave a note. She patted down her pockets looking for something to write on and came up with half a crumpled tissue. She scrunched her nose up. No matter how important she felt it was to leave a note, she couldn't face Will thinking she'd left it on a used tissue. Searching through her bag she found a chewed biro, but no paper. Looking back down at the manuscript, she sighed and picked it up. Ideally she wouldn't deface the cover of her carefully bound love letter to Will but realising that it was probably fitting to dedicate it to him and before she could overthink yet one more thing in her life she leaned against the brick wall and wrote:

Will, this is for you. I no longer think you have my heart, I know you do. A xx

If someone had been watching, Allie would have held the manuscript to her lips and kissed it dramatically, just to add to the romantic gesture. But no one was about, certainly not anyone who gave half a hoot what she had just written. So instead, she carefully placed the manuscript back down and turned and left, hoping that Will would make it home before the arrival of the inevitable London rain.

Chapter Twenty-Eight

'What do you think?' Jess was twirling away in front of the mirror, making enough noise that it would be seemingly impossible to ignore her, but Allie was doing her best to try. She was staring out of Jess's window, seeing nothing but the manuscript she had left on Will's doorstep a few days before.

'Allie? Are you listening to me?'

Allie snapped to attention. 'Yes, absolutely. I definitely think we should.'

'Should what?' There was an icy pause.

'Oh alright. I've no idea. I wasn't listening.'

Jess flopped down onto the bed almost causing Allie to fall off. 'Thinking about Will?'

'Uh-huh.'

'No news then?'

'Jess. You know I'd have told you if I'd heard from him.'

Jess lay back on the pillows and arranged the elaborate feathering of her black dress around her. If Allie had been thinking of anything other than the fact she had not heard a peep from Will since she had left her manuscript and her heart on his doorstep, she would have teased Jess about how many black swans had died to make her dress. But Allie barely noticed, her heart felt too heavy to make any well observed quips.

'So, what do you think?'

'About what?'

'Will, of course. What do you think it means that he hasn't contacted you?'

Allie lay back next to Jess, moving some of the feathers to avoid crushing them as she did so. 'I want it to mean that he's away. Or that the manuscript got stolen. Or that he picked it up and put it on his TBR pile and hasn't quite got round to it yet but that sometime over the next few months he might just have the time to put his feet up and read my love letter to him.'

'Al?'

'Yes?'

'I'm sorry about what I suggested about Martin. Before. That he was some kind of daddy substitute for you.'

'S'OK.'

'No, it's not. I know how much your dad meant to you, and how important his memory is. I shouldn't have said it.'

Allie exhaled. 'Maybe you had a point. I guess I'm always thinking about what Dad would have thought about my life. Whether he would have been proud of me. I've never told anyone this before…' She paused and then took a deep breath in. 'The last thing he ever said to me was that he hoped me and Martha would find a love like he and my mum had.' Allie paused, her throat thick with tears. 'For a long time, I didn't think I'd have that kind of luck, that I should just settle for someone like Dominic. And then I met Will. And he was everything I think my dad was talking about. I feel like he brought me back to life. That sounds so silly.' She felt Jess shake her head next to her on the bed. 'But he made me believe that happy-ever-afters could really happen and that maybe I had found mine. And now he won't talk to me, not even after everything I wrote. So yeah, I guess I'm hoping that maybe he just hasn't got around to reading it yet.'

Jess took Allie's hand in hers and squeezed it tight.

Allie stood in front of the huge doors to the V&A and bit her lip. She shivered, more from the memories of how she felt when she left here last time than from the cold air, which was nipping at her exposed legs. If she had the energy to care, she would have been regretting the short dress that Jess had persuaded her into, but all her energy was focused on putting one foot in front of the other and pushing all thoughts of Will from her head. She had put her plan into action, she had almost killed herself writing two books: Martin and Angie's love story, which she had delivered to them, and a second romance, a twist on her and Will's meet cute. But she had made up the ending of that one before she had discovered how it truly ended. And now here she was, rethinking the whole thing, thinking she should have trusted her gut, realised that happy-ever-afters really only did happen in books, and she should have been honest with her readers and told them that actually the girl doesn't always get the one she wants, that true love doesn't always win out, and that sometimes it would be easiest just to write a murder mystery and be done with it.

'Come on.' Jess took her hand, simultaneously pinning a name badge on Allie's front as she did so and pulling her in through the front doors. It was a Chanel retrospective that Jess had cadged preview tickets for and as such it was quieter than it would be when it finally opened to the general public next week. Jess grabbed a couple of glasses of champagne and thrust one into Allie's hand, ushering her through into one of the darker galleries, where the iconic Chanel dresses were encased in glass domes.

'Where are we going?'

'They've got the first little black dress here that she ever designed. It's not shown very often. I want to get a glimpse before everyone else gets here.'

Allie allowed herself to be pulled by Jess, eventually coming to stop in front of a glass case, standing in isolated splendour in the darkest of all the galleries. Allie could barely see anything past the case itself and as it was, she was mesmerized by the dress inside. So simplistic in design, yet so chic. Allie tugged at her own hem, wishing she had the effortless style that Chanel embodied.

'Tell me about your book,' Jess said into the semi-darkness.

'What?'

'You normally tell me about your books. But you haven't told me anything about this one. The one you left with Will.'

Allie sighed. Truth was, she wanted to tell everyone this story, she wanted to shout it from the rooftops, but she wanted it to end how she had written it, not how it seemed to be ending, with her stood alone rather than wrapped in Will's arms. 'It was supposed to be a twist on our story, on mine and Will's,' she started. 'The meet cute is two waitstaff, at an event like this,' she gestured to their surroundings. 'She's the stuck-up little know-it-all, who has a hot take on everything, who doesn't believe in true love, who thinks romance is for losers. He's the sweet sensitive one who does believe, who ends up listening to all her complaints about the company they both work for, about the size of the vol au vents they serve...' Her breath caught as she said this. 'About anything and everything she could complain about. And he listens, patiently, and some of the things she complains about are right – like the vol au vents.' Allie gave a rueful smile. 'And some of them she's wrong about, but he listens nonetheless. Because it turns out that he's not just the lowly waitstaff that she had him down as, but he runs the company, and just happened to be helping out that night, and was so mesmerized by this bossy, opinionated girl that he met – who was sometimes right and sometimes wrong – that he put himself down to work every other shift that she was working. But she gets scared, because she had stopped believing in true love, stopped thinking that a happy-ever-after would ever come her way and really didn't believe she deserved one anyway. She thought that love died when the butterflies disappeared and hadn't realised that her best friend was right, and that the butterflies couldn't last forever but that if you were lucky, what you were left with was even more special. And so she keeps messing up, and keeps doing stupid things, things that any other normal boy would run a mile from. But he never gives up on her and he keeps believing in her and keeps showing her that love is real. Until little by little, very gradually, she starts to see him for what he really is, and she stops being so opinionated, and stops being so dismissive, stops trying to see him as just a means to an end, and just as he fell in love with her from the start, she falls back in love with him, and gives him her heart.'

There was a long silence. Jess reached for Allie's hand in the semi-darkness and squeezed it and in a voice thick with tears said, 'Thank you for telling me your story.'

Allie shrugged. 'I just wish my real one ended the same way.'

'It still could.' Allie spun round at the sound of the low familiar voice.

'Will?'

'Hi,' he said shyly. 'Hey Jess.'

'Wait, you two know each other?' Allie stared between them trying to figure out just what was going on.

'I should go,' Jess said, picking Allie's hand up and kissing it before walking quickly away.

'Jess!' Allie called after her retreating form.

'Talk, Allie,' Jess shouted back, 'don't just write it in a book.'

'Will?' Allie looked up into those beautiful grey eyes questioningly.

'Allie?'

'What are you doing here?'

'Finishing our story.'

'Oh.' Allie's stomach dropped.

'Sorry, no, I didn't mean... I guess I meant to say continuing our story. I should leave the words to you, you're the writer after all, not me.'

'But you never called, after I left you our story, you never came to find me.'

'I was in York when you left it on my doorstep. It sat there for two days. And then when I got back I read it from cover to cover and Allie? It was weird. Good weird, but weird to see us written down like that. And weird to see the ending that I didn't think we had a chance of finding after having met Dominic at that party.'

Allie groaned. 'I'm so sorry about that. He's *definitely* an ex. He got the wrong end of the stick and came to that party thinking we were getting back together. We're *not* getting back together by the way, we never were, I want to make that completely clear.'

'Yeah, I understand that now. But it was a confusing message to receive, and something that messed with my head a bit, especially coming after everything else.'

'And what did you think to the ending of our story?' Allie asked softly. 'Because I left it there five days ago, so what's been going through your mind since then?' She held her breath waiting for his response.

'Well, you can blame my delayed response on Jess.'

'What do you mean?' she asked sharply. 'Why is it Jess's fault?'

'Because, and I'm going to quote her here, remember these are her words not mine,' he said warningly, catching Allie's eye and smiling, '"she might be a great writer, but she's a terrible communicator".'

'What?! What does that mean?'

'So, after you left your manuscript at my door, and after I hadn't been in touch for a day, because I was in York.' He arched his eyebrow at her. 'Jess tracked me down and demanded a response. And of course, because I wasn't at home, I didn't have a clue what she was talking about. So, I booked the first train back, took a cab from Euston and sat up all night reading.'

'And then what?' Allie felt herself trembling under his gaze.

'Then Jess got to me before I could come and tell you how reading your words made me feel. And she explained to me that you'd lost your faith in true love, and didn't think that happy-ever-afters were real. But then you met me and changed your mind but were too pigheaded and messed up to act appropriately – again, her words not mine.' By now he was grinning at her outraged expression. 'So that by the time you'd finally realised how you felt about me, everything had gone so wrong that you felt you could only fix it with a grand romantic gesture. And that as a writer this meant writing not one, but two novels – one of which turned into our story – and then leaving that copy on my doorstep to read.' He paused. 'Allie…' The way he said her name made her stomach swoop. 'Look at me.' She hesitated before she looked up into his eyes, his hand caught her waist and she could feel her heart racing.

'Allie,' he said again, 'this is how you make me feel, this is how reading your words made me feel. This,' he waved to their surroundings and then placed his hand softly around her back, 'this is *my* grand romantic gesture. When I'd read your words, when I'd spoken to Jess, I realised I wanted to show you how I felt. Not by calling you or sending you a badly written text. Not by turning up at your flat uninvited. But by bringing you back to where it all started and telling you that I love your way with words, I love the start of our story, I can't wait to read more, and I love you.'

Allie's throat constricted, his words taking her breath away. 'Shouldn't we be outside? In the alley round the back if we're really going back to where this all started?'

'Allie,' he growled her name and pulled her towards him. 'Surely this is better?'

And as she felt his lips on her neck, his hands on her body and in front of a priceless, original, one-off Chanel black dress, she agreed that yes, this was immeasurably better than how it had started.

Epilogue

Ten months later

'So, how does it feel?'

Allie was taking a moment to herself in the backroom of Daunt's. It was almost two years since she had launched *The Wishlist* here and some things, like the fact it was still Simon checking in on her, arranging the books, and generally organising the whole thing, never changed. And in other ways, it felt as if her whole life had turned around in that time.

She smiled at Simon as he busied himself about, tidying book boxes to the side and shutting down his computer for the evening, ready to head out into the shop to celebrate.

'Sometimes I can't believe I managed to write another book. There were definitely times when it felt like I never would.'

Simon chortled amiably. 'They all say that. I think it's nice that Brinkman's gave you that time off. They should do it for more authors, look what it's done for you! I heard your new sales manager saying your pre-sales were your biggest yet!'

'Shh!' Allie laughed. 'Don't jinx it.'

'Right, I'd best be getting back out there. Sure you're alright? You don't need anything?'

Allie peered round the door into the shop and confirmed to Simon that she was absolutely alright and that everything she needed was right there, she just needed a few more minutes to take it all in.

She stood just out of sight of her guests in the shop, able to watch but not *be* watched. It was the first launch in a while that her mum had been at. Allie had a feeling that Martha might have had a word, pointing out that perhaps it would be nice if she showed up and so their mum and Nigel had flown in from Spain especially. Nigel seemed to be quizzing some of the sales team on selling techniques while her mother was making the head of design blush to the roots of his carefully styled hair. Allie shook her head, not wanting to know what her mother was talking about.

Martha was there, hovering awkwardly about. Obviously close enough to witness their mother's antics but not close enough to stop whatever it was that was going down. Allie felt a rush of affection for Martha who was doing her best to be here for her, when she would probably much rather have been somewhere else and surrounded by more sciencey people. But she had shown up for Allie and had been doing a lot of that recently. After Allie had introduced Will to Martha a few months back, Martha had pulled Allie aside and told her that she knew their dad would have approved, that she could tell Will was the one he had been talking about. Which made Allie wonder whether she wasn't quite as good at hiding her emotional scars as she had thought she was, and that perhaps Martha had realised all along. Or perhaps Martha had just had one too many drinks that night, because she really wasn't used to having more than one glass of anything.

Incidentally, Jess and Tom seemed to be in fine spirits, downing as much of the free wine as was possible. Allie's fears about their move hadn't materialised; after several months of looking, Jess had declared that she didn't want to leave London actually anyway and Tom said that as long as they could afford a second bedroom he was happy to remain within walking distance of a Tube. And so that's what they had ended up doing, the only casualty being Jess's huge antique wardrobe, which wouldn't fit into either of the bedrooms in their two-bedroom semi in Ruislip. And so Jess had bid it a teary farewell and only brought it up when she had a few too many drinks and was feeling maudlin. Allie tried hard not to believe it was her fault that the wardrobe had met its demise, caused by that wish she had made all those months ago when Jess had quite rightly pointed out that Allie was being ridiculous.

Speaking of, Mary Beth was here, back from maternity leave and always telling Allie that none of what had gone down would have happened on her watch. And perhaps she was right, but Allie actually felt OK about how everything had turned out. And despite all the long dark nights of the soul and all that damned writing, she really wouldn't have changed a thing. Mary Beth was also kept busy, and off Allie's back, with her new client, Martin, who had happily signed up to Mary Beth's agency and was only too glad not to be handling any of the business end of his writing. He was here tonight, along with Angie. It would be his turn soon. His book was due to be published the following month and Allie had promised that she would be at his launch, just as he was at hers. And she sort of had to be, because Netflix had optioned the screen rights to his book and when they brought Martin on board as a screenwriter and consultant he had insisted they do the same with Allie. So, it ended up being that they hadn't really switched plots after all and they both had really quite a lot invested in *all* of the stories. Allie thought back to that conversation she'd had with Jess, about her dad and about Martin and how defensive she had been. And now she could tell that there was probably an element of truth in the whole thing and that wasn't such a bad thing after all. Had her dad still been alive, Allie was sure she would have been able to talk to him about her writing, bounce ideas off him and rely on him to be one of her greatest cheerleaders, which was exactly what Martin had turned out to be. He was deep in conversation with one of the young editors at Brinkman's and Allie could just tell from the angle of his head and the flash of his eyes that he was pitching an idea. She smiled to herself. He had said this was his final book, his swan song, but it was obvious that Martin was far from being done, and the only person happier to see this than Allie was Mary Beth.

Allie had spoken to Angie earlier on. Allie still worried that Angie was upset that Brinkman's had decided to publish *Waiting For You* first and that Martin and Angie's story would have to wait. But Angie was just delighted to see Allie so happy and successful and Allie had reassured her that the fact that the sales team were still arguing over just the right title for the next book, meant that they cared an awful lot about publishing it right. So, Allie had two books under her belt and some free time to look forward to in the future. She had a few ideas about how she would be filling it...

There was one person missing and Allie felt her absence keenly. Verity wasn't there. It was the first of Allie's books that she would launch without her beloved Verity by her side. Allie had worried that when it came to it she would feel very wobbly about the whole thing but she felt surprisingly OK.

Now that Verity was in charge of the whole UK arm of Brinkman's, and busy planning her *engagement* to Richard (an event that Allie wasn't quite sure whether Richard was even aware of yet), she often found herself pulled away from her first love, the books. Right now, she was at an investor meeting in New York but she had FaceTimed Allie earlier on and given her a pep talk, reminding her of how far she had come, and how much she deserved her success. And anyway, Allie was really starting to get to like her new editor. She could see her now, over in the corner of the room, pacing up and down, working on her speech. This would be the first major launch of Tessa's career and she was taking the whole thing very seriously. She smiled as she saw the girl frown and cross something off the piece of paper she was holding and begin pacing once again. Allie knew she was in good hands; Tessa had come into her own and really flourished since Jake's demise.

And then her gaze caught on someone else and she knew she had been spotted. And even though she was now used to seeing him every day, used to seeing his smile, feeling his eyes on her, the touch of his hands, the feel of his lips, she still felt her breath catch as it had the very first time she had met him, across vastly oversized canapés in the courtyard of the V&A.

'There you are,' Will said, his eyes sparkling with amusement at having found her hideout.

'Here I am,' she confirmed, smiling back and biting her lip.

'You OK?' he asked.

'Yes, just, y'know, taking it all in.'

Will took her hand in his. 'Ready to go out? I think Tessa might explode if you don't get her up there doing her speech soon.'

Allie laughed. 'Just one thing before then. Will? Thank you.'

'For what?' He smiled in confusion.

'For all of this. I wrote it for you, it's all for you. It has been ever since we met. *You* are my happy-ever-after.'

Will caught her chin in his hand and tilted her head up towards him. 'Just promise me something?'

She tipped her head questioningly.

'That you'll always feel you can use me, any time you need some inspiration.'

Allie smiled and felt his lips on hers. Truly, she couldn't imagine ever feeling any other way.

Acknowledgments

Thank you to Becky Thomas and Charlotte Ledger who remain my publishing heroes. And thank you to everyone at One More Chapter and HarperCollins who make all of this possible; in particular to Jennie Rothwell, Chloe Cummings, Emma Petfield, Aje Roberts and Kara Daniel. Chloe Quinn, I love this cover, thank you!!

Lucy Vanderbilt and Lauren Fortune – you were two of the first to read *The Plot Twist* and you both gave me amazing feedback and perfect encouragement just when I needed it most. Thank you. I hope you realise you were signing up to do this every time?!

Thank you to my found family in Chapel Hill, to all of the people who have made me feel so at home here. Particular shout out to Jenna Fitch, who has gone above and beyond in making sure I understand all of the local customs; I wish all of our meet ups involved donuts and fairground rides!

I want to thank everyone who bought, read, reviewed or even just delivered words of encouragement when *The Fallback* was published. To all the readers, influencers, bloggers and other authors – THANK YOU.

Charlie, I love you for many reasons, but in this instance it's for patiently listening to every storyline idea and each plot development and never once complaining when I just went ahead and wrote what I was going to write anyway.

To Nancy and Edie – my loves – this one is for you xxxx

ONE MORE CHAPTER

The author and One More Chapter would like to thank everyone
who contributed to the publication of this story...

Analytics
James Brackin
Abigail Fryer

Audio
Fionnuala Barrett
Ciara Briggs

Contracts
Laura Amos
Laura Evans

Design
Lucy Bennett
Fiona Greenway
Liane Payne
Dean Russell

Digital Sales
Lydia Grainge
Hannah Lismore
Emily Scorer

Editorial
Kara Daniel
Charlotte Ledger
Ajebowale Roberts
Jennie Rothwell
Caroline Scott-
Bowden

Harper360
Emily Gerbner
Jean Marie Kelly
emma sullivan
Sophia Wilhelm

International Sales
Peter Borcsok
Ruth Burrow
Colleen Simpson

Marketing & Publicity
Chloe Cummings
Emma Petfield

Operations
Melissa Okusanya
Hannah Stamp

Production
Denis Manson
Simon Moore
Francesca Tuzzeo

Rights
Helena Font Brillas
Ashton Mucha
Zoe Shine
Aisling Smythe

Trade Marketing
Ben Hurd
Eleanor Slater

**The HarperCollins
Distribution Team**

**The HarperCollins
Finance & Royalties
Team**

**The HarperCollins
Legal Team**

**The HarperCollins
Technology Team**

UK Sales
Isabel Coburn
Jay Cochrane
Sabina Lewis
Holly Martin
Harriet Williams
Leah Woods

eCommerce
Laura Carpenter
Madeline ODonovan
Charlotte Stevens
Christina Storey
Jo Surman
Rachel Ward

**And every other
essential link in the
chain from delivery
drivers to booksellers
to librarians and
beyond!**

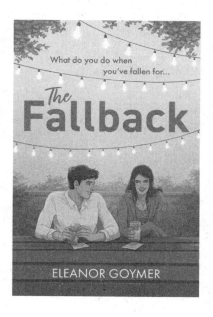

ONE MORE CHAPTER

**One More Chapter is an
award-winning global
division of HarperCollins.**

Subscribe to our newsletter to get our
latest eBook deals and stay up to date
with all our new releases!

[signup.harpercollins.co.uk/
join/signup-omc](signup.harpercollins.co.uk/join/signup-omc)

Meet the team at
www.onemorechapter.com

Follow us!
 @OneMoreChapter_
 @OneMoreChapter
 @onemorechapterhc
 @onemorechapterhc

Do you write unputdownable fiction?
We love to hear from new voices.
Find out how to submit your novel at
www.onemorechapter.com/submissions